BEACON BEACH

BE SWEPT BACK IN TIME, TO WHERE LOVE IS AN ADVENTURE...

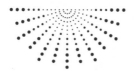

MAGGIE FITZROY

ISBN: 978-1-7330262-0-8 (print)

ISBN: 978-1-7330262-1-5 (ebook)

❀ Created with Vellum

A huge thank you to Cape May N.J.'s Mid-Atlantic Center for the Arts &
Humanities, which helped me with the research for this book.

PART I

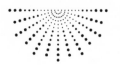

CAPE MAY N.J

EARLY JUNE, 1886

Jacy James floated atop the sun-splashed sea, amazed her bothersome bathing costume was actually proving to be a blessing. She drifted lazily with her arms and legs spread out like a giant letter X, gently bobbing up and down with the swells as the air trapped in her billowing wool skirt puffed up like a fat balloon. To stay afloat, she gently flapped her arms and kicked her slippered feet.

At the shore, Aunt Helen stood watching in horrified disapproval, her hands planted on her hips. Even from a distance, Jacy could see the pinched expression around her mouth.

Jacy closed her eyes and tried to relax. Her aunt would not dare call out her name or try to wave her in with wild arm gestures. That would bring unwanted attention to the situation, a fate worse than drowning.

Jacy smiled as the sun warmed her face. *I'm fine. She'll see,* she thought.

Aunt Helen knew Jacy could swim well. She just did not approve of her bathing alone. The water was far too cold for sensible people. She also fretted about Jacy's appearance when she stepped out of the water. Might her costume cling to her figure and—horrors of all horrors—reveal all her curves?

Jacy giggled. Respectable women were not supposed to go swimming, out beyond the breakers, no less. At most, they were expected to wade up to their knees and fanny-dip with a pretty squeal while reaching for the hand of a helpful gentleman.

Most members of the fair sex would not even consider braving the cold ocean until after Independence Day. Many would wait until August, when the water was as warm as it would get. Her behavior was already outrageous, attracting spectators was the last thing her dear aunt wanted. Summer was just beginning, and the guests at the White Caps Hotel, and all of Cape May, would think Jacy a common woman. That would not do.

Wiggling her fingers, Jacy scrunched her nose after a wave showered her with icy droplets. Aunt Helen would just have to get used to her enjoying Neptune's realm whenever she liked. She could swim better than most people, even most men. She sure was not going to spend the next three months sitting on a chair on the sand.

Anyway, it took her mind off Edmund. That is what everyone wanted. Her father, her aunt, her cousin, Poppy—they all wanted her to forget about Edmund.

"Jacy, Jacy!"

Startled, Jacy lifted her head. Wiping stinging salt water from her eyes, she looked toward shore. Poppy was screaming her name and waving her arms and Aunt Helen was not trying to stop her. The older woman seemed frozen in place, her mouth agape.

That was the last thing Jacy heard before a huge wave crashed over her, shoving her to the sandy bottom. The ocean sucked her back up just as another wave engulfed her and propelled her in the direction of Europe.

Struggling to put her feet down, she was in over her head.

Drat. The bubble in her bathing costume had collapsed, and now the heavy material was dragging her down.

Clawing her way to the surface, she shouted for help. She swam a few strokes, but her stockings and shoes weighed too much. *This is not*

4

fair. She gritted her teeth and took another stroke, and another. *It is not fair at all. Men don't have to wear so many clothes when they swim.*

The ocean closed over her again. Struggling, she surfaced and sucked in a mouthful of air before another wave smashed into her face.

Just as she tried to right herself, a pair of strong hands grabbed her under her armpits.

Someone yanked her up. Whoever it was, they were guiding her to shore.

She gulped air like a dying fish as her rescuer carried her to the beach and deposited her, rather ceremoniously, onto the sand, flat on her back.

"Glad I could be of service, ma'am," her tall savior said as a crowd of people rushed over. Gathering around, they peered down at her, gaping. She felt like a museum curiosity.

"What was she doing out there by herself?" one woman muttered. "I've never in my life…"

"Jacy," Poppy said, hurrying over. She squatted down next to the man who had plucked Jacy from the briny sea.

Jacy blinked several times. For some reason, her rescuer was regarding her with an expression of admiration. She looked at the faces of everyone around him. They seemed relieved she was alive, including Poppy and a pale, hand-wringing Aunt Helen.

Her rescuer brushed his wet, dark brown hair out of his eyes and let out a triumphant laugh. "I can see she is going to be just fine, folks," he said. "I have never seen a woman take to the sea like this brave lady here, and so early in the season. She obviously knows how to swim and isn't afraid to do so."

He let out another bark of laugher. "Although it was a good thing I was on duty, as it turned out." He stood and put his hands on his hips, his muscular arms and legs visible through his black sleeveless shirt and calf length, tight-fitting black pants.

He was clearly fit, strong, and proud of it. "For those of you who don't know me, I am Frank Lynch, volunteer captain of the White Caps lifeguard crew," he announced. He knelt back down next to Jacy.

"I'm sorry I didn't get to you sooner, before you went under," he told her. "It's just that I wasn't expecting anyone to go swimming on the very afternoon they checked into the hotel. It's only opening day."

"Thank you, sir." Jacy hoped she sounded appropriately sincere. It had been good of him to rescue her, but she probably could have made it without his help.

He offered his hand to help her sit up, and she graciously accepted it.

Taking a deep breath, she released his hand and pushed her straggly, dark-brown hair out of her eyes. Glancing down at her palm, she winced. It was coated with sand. So was her forehead, and her mouth when she ran her tongue around inside it.

Grimacing, she did not yet trust herself to stand. "You are right, sir," she said. "I can swim, and I am not usually in need of the services of a lifeguard."

Jacy looked at Poppy, whose curly, copper-colored hair was tucked under a fashionable pale-blue beach bonnet. Jacy smiled at her, then at her rescuer. "It's just that…as a woman…I am forced to wear a ridiculous amount of clothing on the beach and while ocean bathing." She ran her hand over her sopping wet dress and frowned. "Clothing that doubles in weight when wet." She patted the top of her head. "By the way, where is my bathing bonnet?"

"I think you lost it," Poppy said. "It must have come off in the surf."

"I warned you," Aunt Helen said in a barely audible voice. "But you wouldn't listen to me."

"I suppose I shall have to buy another one," Jacy said. "As it won't be proper for me to bathe without one. And I do want to be proper, Aunt Helen. I really do."

Aunt Helen twisted her hands together and cast a humiliated expression at the men and women surrounding her. Most of the people were as stylishly dressed as she, looking their finest on the celebratory first day of the summer season. Aunt Helen's elegantly coiffed silver hair was pinned up and framed by a huge black hat adorned with ostrich feathers. Her ankle-length, long-sleeved dress kept the sun off her fair skin, as did her matching gloves and boots.

"Jacy, we shall discuss this later," Aunt Helen said, suddenly regaining her composure. She lifted her head in the proud, self-confident way Jacy knew well and arranged her lips in a thin smile that all but concealed her embarrassment. "The most important thing is that you are alright. You really should introduce yourself to Mr. Lynch here. We all should." She turned to him. "Sir, I am Helen Bainbridge, of Philadelphia. This is my daughter, Poppy. And this...this is my niece, Jacyntha James. Or, as everyone calls her, Jacy."

"Pleased to make your acquaintance, ma'am," Frank Lynch said. "I too have a room at White Caps, on the third floor. I expect we shall all be friends before long. At least I hope so." He raised his eyebrows and looked hopefully at Jacy.

Aunt Helen stiffened, clearly confused. "So, Mr. Lynch, you aren't hired staff?"

"Do you mean am I one of the working stiffs?" He chuckled, obviously finding that amusing. "No, no. I assure you, Mrs. Bainbridge, that if I wished, I could easily summer here and do nothing but partake in the whirl of social activities, just like all the other White Caps guests." He gave her a polite smile. "But that's not who I am. No, no. I'm far too restless for that."

He turned to Jacy. "Fortunately for you, I save lives in my spare time. Volunteer lifeguards rescue many people every summer. And I have been doing this for the past four years at Cape May's finest establishment."

Jacy stared at him. His community service was admirable and certainly important. Must he display such bravado, however? He was a fine-looking man, with a square chin and chiseled cheekbones. A touch of humility would make him even more attractive in her eyes. *Handsome is as handsome does.*

It was time to try to stand up, without his help. She flipped onto her knees and struggled to her feet. Now at eye level with the spectators, she smiled and thanked them all for their concern.

Her legs felt too shaky to walk. To stall for time, she looked around, nodding at the people staring at her. She glanced beyond the crowd and noticed a young man in a wheelchair. Behind him stood a black man all dressed in white, his hands firm on the wheelchair handles.

Jacy met the convalescent's gaze and gave him a smile. She saw sadness in his eyes as he responded with a weak smile of his own. She looked away. Had the spectacle of her dramatic rescue drawn *every* White Caps guest down to the beach? Even those who required the assistance of an orderly to get there?

Jacy felt a bit dizzy. Her cousin scurried over to take her arm. "Thank you, Poppy," she whispered. "I'm sorry," she said as the two of them slowly navigated the walkway to the hotel. "I didn't mean to draw attention to myself. I promise I will try harder to be proper."

Poppy patted her hand and gave her a reassuring smile. "I know."

Jacy turned and glanced over her shoulder. The crowd was trailing them, with Aunt Helen leading the way.

Jacy sighed. She meant what she had told Poppy. But she was not entirely sure she could be the woman everyone expected her to be.

She had already failed at that.

And only Edmund knew.

CHAPTER TWO

The White Caps dining room hummed with animated conversation as Jacy, Aunt Helen, and Poppy walked in.

Jacy was cheered by the sight of elegantly clad guests and the sweet strains of the hotel orchestra, planted by the floor-to-ceiling windows overlooking the lawn and the sea.

Most seats at the round tables, covered in starched white table-cloths set with gleaming silverware and flickering candles, were taken. It was still early in the season. Jacy doubted everyone in the room was staying at the hotel, as the dining room was open to the public. White Caps was obviously a place to see and be seen.

"Everybody who is anybody comes to Cape May," Aunt Helen was fond of saying. People had been saying that for years.

Growing up, Jacy had visited the seaside resort at the southern tip of New Jersey every summer with her family. This was her first stay at White Caps. Several couples were waltzing on the wide, wooden dance floor. Stifling a sigh, she thought about Edmund. If only he were here to dance with her.

Frank Lynch hurried over and planted himself before Jacy and her family. "Mrs. Bainbridge, Miss Bainbridge, Miss James." He bowed. Dressed in black tails and a carefully arranged red silk tie, he looked far different than he had a few hours earlier. Appearing just as self-assured, he looked even more handsome.

"Mr. Lynch," Aunt Helen said in her polite, prim social voice. "Nice to see you again."

"It is so good to see all of you again," he said. He grinned and faced Jacy. "Especially you, my dear. I see you have recovered fully from your ordeal." He stepped back and looked her up and down. "In fact, you look more than recovered. You are a vision of loveliness."

Jacy felt her cheeks grow hot. After her embarrassing ocean rescue, she had felt the need to shore up her confidence, so she donned her favorite gown, a soft, green taffeta trimmed with white lace around the waist.

It was rather low cut, but that was the style, and the V-shaped neckline showed off her favorite necklace to advantage. It featured three glistening rows of intertwined emeralds and diamonds. Her father had given it to her for her twenty-first birthday, the previous October. "It was your mother's," he told her. "I have been saving it for you all these years. Your eyes are the same color as hers, jade green. So, it will look as magnificent on you as it did on her."

At the time, she was glad he had not given the stunning heirloom to her stepmother, Ethel. Jacy was only three when her mother died. After five glorious years of having her father all to herself, he had married again.

Her father's international shipping business had consumed much of his time. Ethel proved to be an extremely fertile woman, bearing him three sons and two daughters in less than ten years, so Jacy soon learned to fend for herself.

She fingered the necklace. Her father loved her. Remembering that gave her the courage she needed to face the stares of many people in the room. She recognized some of them who had been down on the beach. They were now whispering to others while looking in her direction.

"Perhaps, Mr. Lynch, you will have the opportunity to pluck someone else from the sea sometime soon," Jacy told him. She surveyed the room, then looked back at him with a bemused smile. "If and when you do, I will no longer have to endure being the topic of everyone's conversation. I will be old news."

He chuckled. "Don't worry. My heroic rescues will be the topic of conversations all summer. They always are." He narrowed his eyes and looked at her. "I would very much like it if you would call me Frank. And may I call you Jacy?"

She was taken aback, but nodded. "Of course." She turned to her cousin. "Poppy, do you mind if Frank calls you by your first name as well? He wants to be our friend."

Poppy looked shyly down at the floor, then briefly into Frank's eyes before looking away. "Of course."

"You look lovely, too, Poppy," Frank said. "Creamy beige is quite becoming to your red hair."

"Thank you," Poppy said. "Mother always tells me that."

Frank pivoted back to Jacy. He made it obvious she was the woman who interested him. Jacy found that most unfortunate, because she was not the slightest bit interested in him. She was not there to meet men.

There is no room in my heart for any man but Edmund.

Frank leaned over and whispered in her ear. "Surely you know how beautiful you are. Even lying on the sand, with seaweed in your dark-brown hair."

She gasped and stepped back. "There was no seaweed."

He laughed. "I know."

Aunt Helen cleared her throat. "Mr. Lynch."

"Frank to you as well, please."

"Alright, Frank." Aunt Helen said with a stiff nod. "We need to find a table. It looks like we might be too late to find seats."

"You are in luck," he said. Gesturing for them to follow, he turned when he reached a table with several empty chairs. A sly smile slid across his face. "I purposely saved these for you fair ladies. And as you can see, my table just so happens to be next to the dance floor."

"Of course," Jacy said under her breath. Poppy caught her eye and giggled.

With a regal air, Frank took turns seating Aunt Helen, Jacy, and

Poppy and then introduced them to the others at the table. He was sitting with several dashing young men, all volunteer lifeguards, and their beautiful, fashionably dressed dates.

Frank sat down between Jacy and Poppy and slowly slid his chair slightly closer to Jacy. He leaned toward her. "Would you care to dance?"

"Dance?" Flustered, Jacy stared at him. "Now?" She shook her head and blurted out before she could think, "But I'm famished."

"Oh." Frank threw his head back and laughed so loudly that people at nearby tables turned to look. Jacy wished they could sit elsewhere, but it was too late. Moving would be rude, and the dining room was packed.

Frank gave her a half smirk, and she had the ominous feeling she had insulted him. "Forgive me, my dear. I should have realized that you would be hungry," he declared. "I bet you have not eaten anything since your swim. You must be weak with hunger."

He raised his hand and signaled a waiter nearby. The young man, wearing a freshly pressed navy blue jacket with white pants uniform, hurried over.

"I am wondering, what is the holdup with dinner, my good chap?" Frank asked, his voice haughty and impatient. "Will you be serving soon?"

The server's face turned red. "Yes sir, of course, sir. Normally we would be serving by now, but this is opening night. We wanted to give people a chance to socialize first, enjoy the music."

Frank stared at him. "I see." He was silent a moment. "When you do serve, good chap, might you serve our table first?" He placed his hand on Jacy's. "This poor young lady is very hungry."

The waiter blinked at Jacy. She pulled her hand away and stopped herself from ducking under the table. Frank's voice was so loud that people at surrounding tables seemed to hear him, even over the orchestra. Smiling apologetically, she looked down at her lap, hoping he would not say anything else.

"This lady here is famished," he said, raising his voice even louder. Conversations halted. People looked their way. Aunt Helen glared at

Jacy, as if the situation was all her fault. Jacy wished she had just accepted Frank's offer to dance.

"She almost drowned this afternoon," Frank told the waiter, who seemed too humiliated to move. He tightened his grip on the tray and just stood and stared at Jacy, nodding wordlessly.

"But here she is, alive and well," Frank continued. "And now she needs something to eat, to regain her strength."

"Oh…" The waiter cleared his throat. "Yes, of course, sir. Right away, sir. I didn't know, sir."

Frank stood up and bowed. "Now you do." He glared at him with a half-smile. "Now you *do*."

Jacy had never felt so humiliated. Pushing her chair away from the table, she bounded to her feet after the waiter hurried off. "I need to get some fresh air," she said, addressing everyone at the table. "Alone."

"Jacy…" Aunt Helen said.

But Jacy pretended not to hear.

Fixing a cheerful smile on her face, while on the verge of tears, she lifted her skirts and dashed toward the door at the back of the room. How on earth was she going to get through the summer?

As she weaved around tables, she noticed a young man, who looked to be in his twenties, in a wheelchair. He was the man she had seen on the beach.

As she passed him, he lifted his hand and waved. She slowed down and turned.

Most people were regarding her with shocked curiosity.

His eyes communicated sympathy.

She met his gaze.

"Be careful out there in the dark," he said with a smile that seemed to require all his energy.

He was obviously quite ill. His face was thin, pale and wan under a shock of thick, light-brown hair. But his eyes held a spark. For a brief moment, Jacy caught a glimpse of the man behind the illness: boyishly handsome, kind, and brave.

"I don't think the lifeguards are on duty at night," he said. "So, don't go too close to the water."

13

"Ha," Jacy said. "I know they're not on duty because they're all sitting at my table. But don't worry, I'll be careful."

He nodded. "When you come back, feel free to sit with us at our table, if you'd like. My brother and his wife won't mind. You can have my chair." He grinned. "As you can see, I don't need it. I have my own."

Jacy sighed. "Thank you." She was truly touched. "That is very kind of you." She looked past a sea of faces and saw Aunt Helen staring at her. She did not look happy. "But I think I dare not take you up on your offer," she whispered. "My aunt and cousin expect me to sit with them."

"I understand," the man said. "The summer has only just begun, so I am sure we will meet again." He weakly lifted his hand and held it out to her. "My name is Cole Stratton, by the way. Everyone calls me Cole."

She took his hand and shook it. It felt warm, feverish. "Jacy James," she said. "My real name is Jacyntha, but please don't ever call me that. Just Jacy."

An awkward silence rose between them. She rushed to fill it. "Are you staying at White Caps, Cole?"

"Yes," he said. "We have rooms on the first floor for the season."

"Wonderful," she said. "We have rooms on the second floor through August. So, I am certain I'll see you around."

CHAPTER THREE

*J*acy dreamed about Edmund that night. He was sitting in a wheelchair…a wicker one…at the end of a long hall… attended by three nurses wearing pointy white hats.

For some reason, bandages covered his arms and legs. He stared at her with sad eyes, mouthing her name.

She wanted to run to him, but the hospital's head nurse held her back. She said Jacy did not have permission to visit him because she was not "family."

"But I am," Jacy insisted. "I am his fiancée."

She could not prove it, though, as no one knew they had become engaged.

She awoke with a start. It was still dark outside. That was a relief. The sun would soon slip above the horizon, and she needed to set out for the lighthouse long before it did.

Her dream had been odd and disturbing, but at least it woke her up.

The Cape May Lighthouse was about a mile away, in the adjacent town of Cape May Point. She could get there by walking along the beach. The sand, even at high tide, was wide and hard packed. The beach, which rounded the tip of New Jersey, was mostly uninhabited

—just sand and dunes framed by woody scrub. Jacy assured herself that, as a woman walking alone, she would be perfectly safe.

She must get going before Aunt Helen woke up, or her aunt would try to stop her. She would tie herself in knots if she knew where Jacy was going at such an ungodly hour. Aunt Helen was Jacy's only aunt, the younger sister of her father, Tobias James. After Jacy's mother died, the sweet woman saw that little Jacy desperately needed a mother's love. She had tried to give her as much maternal attention as she could. But Aunt Helen had three daughters of her own, including her youngest, Poppy, and Jacy understood she could only do so much.

Jacy threw off her covers and sat up. With any luck, she would get back before her aunt had dressed and was ready for breakfast. If not… well…she would deal with the woman's scolding when the time came.

As for Poppy, she would just have to understand. Six months younger than Jacy, she had always been Jacy's best friend. Poppy was timid, however, while Jacy was bold. Poppy was shy, while Jacy was outgoing. They got along fabulously, despite their different personalities, but she had not confided in Poppy about the lighthouse. Her cousin had no idea she planned to go there every morning that summer to look for Edmund's ship.

Climbing the lighthouse would calm her nerves; give her something constructive to do. That is what she kept telling herself.

The lighthouse was the sole reason she had agreed to summer in Cape May in the first place.

Aunt Helen did not know that. When she eventually found out, she would just have to accept it.

Jacy slid out of bed. She peered at Poppy, asleep in her own bed on the other side of the room, and prayed she didn't wake up.

Tiptoeing over to the armoire near her bed, Jacy eased the door open slowly so it did not squeak. She pulled out one of her day dresses, a blue-and-green-checked muslin. It was easy to slip on without a maid's assistance, which was why she had asked her father to buy it when he took her shopping for clothes. He was so relieved she had agreed to spend the summer in Cape May, he had bought her five dresses just like it in a variety of colors. That suited Jacy just fine.

Florence, the year-round Cape May resident Aunt Helen had hired as their maid, was scheduled to arrive at the hotel at 7:30 every morning. Since Jacy planned to set out for the lighthouse well before then, she had to dress herself quickly and quietly.

Jacy's father had assumed she was looking forward to an active, carefree summer where looking pretty was all she had to worry about. If only that were true, she thought as she stepped out of her nightgown and eased the dress over her head.

"Where are you going?"

She jumped. Poppy was a light sleeper. *Drat.* She had not been quiet enough. "What do you mean?" Jacy whispered. "Go back to sleep."

"Are you getting dressed?" Poppy sat up and rubbed her face. "What time is it?"

"Not time to get up yet. Go back to sleep."

Poppy shoved off her covers and swung her bare feet onto the floor. She stood up and padded over to Jacy, peering at her in the dim light. "You're wearing one of your new frocks. Where are you going?"

No time to explain. She walked over to her dresser, found a candle, lit it, and peered at herself in the mirror. Snatching some pins from a bowl, she arranged her long, wavy locks into a bun and grabbed her blue bonnet off the top of the armoire. Shoving it onto her head, she hastily tied the ribbons under her chin.

"Jacy..."

"Shhh. If you must know, I'm going for a walk."

"Now? It's still night."

"Shhhh. It's almost dawn. That's good enough." Jacy sat on a chair, fished for her boots underneath the bed, and yanked them on. "I'll be fine. Just need some exercise."

"What? Now?"

"Yes, there is no better time." Jacy glanced at the door that separated their room from Aunt Helen's suite. It was thick and latched. Fortunately, unlike her daughter, Aunt Helen was a sound sleeper. Even so, Jacy's plans would be dashed if she woke up. She held the flickering candle close to her face and put a finger to her lips.

17

Poppy got the message. She lowered her voice to a whisper. "But where are you going?"

"If you insist on knowing, to the lighthouse."

"*What?*"

Jacy put her finger to her lips again. "I'll tell you later, when I get back. I won't be long."

Poppy's hair was askew, with curls sticking out in all directions. She shook her head and scurried over to the door. Leaning against it, she crossed her arms in front of her chest. "I won't let you leave until you tell me why you're doing this. Mother will be aghast."

Jacy pursed her lips. "I just want to go for a walk."

Poppy narrowed her eyes. "Alone?"

"Yes. I don't know anyone here yet, so yes."

"What about that man in the wheelchair you were talking to last night? Are you going with him?"

"What? Why would you think that? Don't be silly. I just met him briefly, and besides, he can't *walk*."

"Frank Lynch? Are you going with Frank?"

Jacy groaned. "No. Of course not. I am going alone. Why don't you believe me?" She needed to get going, so she would just have to tell Poppy the truth. Poppy would find out soon enough anyway. "I am going to climb the lighthouse to look for signs of Edmund's ship. There, I said it. Now, let me go."

Poppy put her hands over her mouth. Dropping them to her hips, she stared at Jacy wide-eyed. "We brought you here so you could forget about him. And you came here to look for him?"

"Yes."

"But he's dead." Poppy's eyes glowed like big white moons in the dim light. "His ship was lost at sea."

"I believe he's still alive." Jacy stared at her. "I know he's alive. And since his ship was sailing down the Atlantic Coast toward Delaware Bay when it was last seen, I believe it still might show up around here."

Poppy gasped. "But that was months ago, Jacy. Accept it. He's gone." Poppy glared at her. "And everyone is glad he is gone. Except you."

Poppy's reaction was predictable. But that did not make it hurt any less. Jacy's entire family disliked Edmund Overton. Hated him. The problem was, they did not know or understand the distinguished sea captain. He had loved her as no one else ever had.

"Everyone is wrong about him," she told Poppy. "And he is alive. And I mean to find him." She reached around Poppy for the doorknob, and her cousin sighed and stepped out of her way.

"Don't do this," Poppy said. "I implore you."

"I expect to be back before breakfast is finished being served," Jacy said as she opened the door and stepped out into the hall.

She put her finger to her lips again. "But if I am not, tell your mother not to worry."

* * *

THE WALK to the lighthouse took longer than Jacy expected. Even so, it was a pleasant and invigorating jaunt. For the first time since Edmund disappeared, she felt a sense of purpose.

The moonless sky was inky black when she walked across the White Caps lawn and scurried down onto the beach. Inhaling deeply, she smiled, finding calmness in the soft, repetitive swooshing sound of the surf. The ocean that morning perfectly matched the hotel's name: dark waves peaking, rolling, capping and crashing into whiteness.

Swinging her arms as she walked, she looked back at the White Caps, now illuminated by gas lamps. One of Cape May's grandest hotels, it was L-shaped, with three stories—one hundred rooms on each floor—all overlooking the Atlantic Ocean. Its wide front porch faced a vast green lawn and a walkway down to the boardwalk. Just beyond that, the strand and the sea.

Jacy hiked past the look-alike hotel next door, Congress Hall, and its long line of bathhouses. After passing a few oceanfront homes, she left civilization behind.

A half hour later, she reached The Light of Asia, a huge, whimsical elephant-shaped building that sat, like a misplaced circus attraction, at the edge of the beach.

She gazed up at the pachyderm landmark and grinned. She had visited the popular advertisement-turned-tourist-attraction in summers past. It would not be far to the lighthouse, just over the dunes.

The rising sun had painted the sky pink, with a swirl of orange and blue, by the time she had approached the lighthouse grounds.

By the time Jacy reached the keeper's modest clapboard cottage, next to the soaring beige-brick tower, the sun had fully breeched the horizon. She crossed her fingers as she stepped onto the porch and knocked on the door.

No one answered, so she knocked harder and then pounded.

"Hello?" The man opening the door wore a puzzled expression on his face. "Can I help you?"

He was tall and wiry, and Jacy was relieved to see that at least she had not woken him up. Middle-aged, he was neatly outfitted in his keeper's uniform: a navy blazer with a gold braided lighthouse logo patch on the pocket and a matching brimmed cap.

He squinted at her in the sunlight, shifted his weight to peer behind her, then looked back at her and blinked. "Yes, miss… is there something I can do for you?"

She nodded. "Sir," she said, clearing her throat. "I would like to climb the lighthouse if you don't mind." She smiled sweetly, hoping to convey she was perfectly sane; just an extremely early visitor, eccentric, but harmless.

"Climb the lighthouse. *Now?* It's…" He glanced behind her again, frowned, and stared at her. "Are you alone?"

"Yes, sir." Her words came out in a rush. "I'm an early riser and I know you allow visitors and I climbed the tower last summer when I was here. In fact, for the past few summers…"

"You did, did you?"

"Yes, sir, I—"

"Many people climb the lighthouse, miss."

"Right, sir, I know, sir, and that's why—"

"Just not at dawn."

Jacy smiled sweetly again and nodded. "Yes, sir, I realize that, sir. But—"

"And I suspect when you visited in the past, you were not alone. This is a very popular attraction, especially with the Cape May summer set. But women don't usually visit by themselves."

"No, that's true. I always came with a group. Family and friends."

"So why are you here so early, and unaccompanied? I suggest you come back later, around ten o'clock or so, and bring someone with you." He chuckled. "A woman as pretty as you must have a great many friends who would like to share the adventure of climbing a lighthouse. As you know, the view from the top is spectacular."

A knot of frustration rose in Jacy's throat. "Yes, it is, but I am not here to enjoy the view. And I purposely came alone. I came early, so I could be alone."

"Excuse me." He stepped outside onto the front step, scooted around her, then bounded down the steps and motioned for her to follow him onto the lawn between his house and the tower. "Let's continue this conversation over here," he said. "I don't want to wake my wife."

A crease appeared between his brows. "Now tell me. Why do you want to be alone? And if you're not here for the view, why are you here?" He put his hands on his hips. "You are not here to jump, are you?"

She shook her head. "No, no, no... No. I am here to look for a ship."

"Pardon me?"

"A missing ship." She took a deep breath. "One I believe might have disappeared on its way here...sometime in the spring. Perhaps you've heard of it? It was a merchant vessel, *The Largo*."

"Hmmm." He ran a hand over his closely cropped brown beard. "That does sound familiar." He squinted at her. "But what makes you think you could spot said ship from this lighthouse? If it's missing, it's very unlikely to just show up one day, like a ghost."

Jacy sighed. "That is exactly what I am expecting. Hoping for. Praying for. You see, a dear friend of mine was the ship's captain. Edmund Overton. Have you heard of him?"

He shook his head. "No. I'm sorry, I can't say I've ever heard that name." He looked up at the sky, then back at her. "But, my dear..." He seemed to be searching for the right words and she saw a flash of pity in his eyes. "If this Edmund Overton was the ill-fated vessel's captain... I assume he is missing as well? And likely presumed dead?"

She shook her head. "No. Yes. Well...that is what everyone says. But I refuse to believe it. We were close, you see. I know he is alive, somewhere. Don't ask me how I know, but I know. And I believe he is on his way back—back to me."

"But how could you possibly know such a thing?"

"Because he was not on a fixed schedule. *The Largo* was a large steamship that changed course whenever necessary to pick up last-minute loads. It sailed up and down the Eastern Seaboard to the Caribbean. The crew signed up for that type of life, that kind of work. They never knew what port they might be heading to next. It's possible they went to a city that wasn't part of their original destination and broke down on their return route."

Jacy met his gaze and tried to ignore the doubt in his eyes. "Look, maybe they got the ship repaired, and maybe, just maybe, they are now on their way back to Philadelphia, where they had departed. If that is so, they will sail by here."

"Miss..."

"Yes..."

"What is your name?"

"Jacy...Jacy James."

"Pleased to make your acquaintance, Miss James. I am Joseph Carver, head keeper here for the past twenty years." He looked at her as a father might regard an emotionally distraught child, one who desires something not in a father's power to give.

"Look, Miss James, I would like to help you. I really would. But you must realize that the chance of Captain Overton's ship reappearing one day, just showing up here, is almost nil."

Jacy lifted her chin. "Yes. But it is not entirely outside the realm of possibility."

"No." He shrugged. "Perhaps not entirely."

"So, all you have to do, if you really want to help me, is let me climb to the top of the lighthouse. I promise to come right back down. You have my word."

"Well…" He craned his neck and looked up at the narrow observation deck at the top. "I suppose that would be alright." He stepped back and regarded her clothing. "I can see you dressed well for the excursion, not too fancy, short heeled boots."

She nodded eagerly.

"Alright, then, go ahead up. You've done this before, you say, so you know it's not an easy climb. Strenuous for a lot of people."

Jacy beamed. "Thank you, sir. Thank you so very much. I am under no illusions about the number of steps and steepness of the climb. But don't worry, I'll stop to catch my breath when I need to. I promise, after I look around, I will come right back down."

"Be careful and good luck." He put his hand up. "Wait. You are a summer visitor, I take it. Where are you staying?"

"In Cape May."

"How did you get here?"

"I walked. Along the beach, from the White Caps Hotel. And I plan to walk back."

"What are your plans, if a miracle doesn't happen, and you don't see the ship today?"

"To come back tomorrow… and the next day… and the day after that. Please, Mr. Carver, I won't cause you any trouble."

He nodded. "I expected you would say that. You are an unusual woman. I grant you that. And I suspect your Captain Overton is much more than a friend."

Jacy did not know what to say, so she said nothing.

"Okay," he said, walking over to the lighthouse door. He held it open for her and waved her in. "It is unlocked, so feel free to go up every morning. Will you always come alone?"

"I expect so." She placed a foot on the first step and turned to face him. "Thank you again."

She heard him quietly close the door as she grabbed the handrail and raced up the circular, iron latticework steps.

Up and around and up she went. She stopped to rest when she got winded, then forged on until she finally reached the top. Easing the observation deck door open, she stepped out and caught her breath as the cool ocean wind whipped across her face.

Pressing down on her bonnet to keep it from blowing off, she grabbed the deck rail with her other hand and took in the view.

"Ahhh," she murmured. It was as delightful as she remembered. Directly below sat charming Cape May Point, with its summer cottages, beachfront mansions, and hotels.

Beyond was the beach, and beyond that, in every direction all the way to the horizon, lay the great, glimmering Atlantic Ocean.

Jacy frowned. *No ships. No Largo. No Edmund.*

Tightening her grip on the rail, a powerful feeling of futility and emptiness overwhelmed her. Was she surprised? No. She had expected it, but she felt like a fool.

In despair, she wiped a tear from her cheek, returned to the stairs, then headed down.

Her descent was much slower than her ascent. But she kept her head up.

She would be back.

CHAPTER FOUR

ole Stratton sat in his wheelchair on the White Caps front porch, contemplating his view of the beach just beyond the hotel's sweeping green lawn.

The sun had just risen, and he suddenly longed to be down on the sand, as close to the glistening waves as he could get. He looked at his orderly, Samuel Pershing, who was relaxing with his eyes closed in a wicker rattan chair nearby.

"Samuel." Cole realized his voice sounded hoarse and weak. He tried again. "Samuel."

Samuel opened his eyes and looked at him. His dark face creased with concern. "Yes, Mister Cole?"

"Could you please wheel me down onto the strand? I would like to get closer to the ocean."

Samuel stood up and regarded him with his usual kind and patient smile. "Now, Mister Cole? But you ain't even been to breakfast yet."

Cole grinned. "They tell me I'm here for the sea-air cure. So, let's get me on down to the sea."

Samuel put his hands on his hips and shook his head, returning Cole's grin with an even larger one. "You breathin plenty of sea air from up here. And you know what the doctor say. You need to eat. Get your strength up. Breakfast be served soon."

Cole looked at all the empty rattan chairs lining the veranda. By noon, happy, chatty people would occupy them. At the moment, he and his orderly had the place to themselves, so they might as well go down to the beach.

"They say breathing the sea air is my last hope," he said, coughing just a little. A month earlier, once he started hacking, he could barely stop. "If what they say is true, then I imagine getting as close to the water as possible is the best medicine."

"I suppose you're right," Samuel said. "But—"

"No, I don't want to go eat first. I'm not hungry."

"But you know what the doctor—"

Cole raised his hand, slowly and with more effort than he would have liked. He hardly had the energy to move it at all. "I know what Doctor Morris said and I don't care. If I don't have an appetite, I am not going to force food down my throat." He nodded toward the beach. "I will work up an appetite down there."

Samuel shrugged and winked. "Okay, Mister Cole. Already, I can see what is happening. This summer I'm gonna be your partner in medical crime."

Cole laughed. He had not laughed in a long time. Samuel's cheerful personality and sense of humor did more for him than any medicine his physicians had prescribed. "You have it right, my man," he said. "I will follow doctor's orders when I feel like it, and I will follow my instincts when they make better sense. Thank you for understanding."

"Just happy to do my job," Samuel said as he bent over Cole and adjusted the blue wool blanket over his legs. "Just hope Mister Henry and Mistress Lydia don't get upset."

Cole met his eyes and smiled. "My brother always worries too much. You know that. And when he married Lydia, he found his perfect mate. An amazing woman—capable of matching him fret for fret." He shrugged. "But don't worry; Henry and Lydia are my problem. Henry went back to bed after helping me dress, so he has no idea what I am up to."

"Okay, then," Samuel said, whistling cheerfully as he grabbed the handlebars of Cole's chair and pushed him onto a ramp down to a pathway to the beach.

Cole looked around as they passed the hotel's line of bathhouses. Samuel maneuvered the wheelchair over the hard-packed sand to the strand, the wide stretch of softer sand that met the sea.

"Thanks for getting here so early," Cole told Samuel as he parked him at the shoreline. "I wish you could stay at the hotel with us, but I hope your room is to your liking."

"You know there ain't no room at the inn for servants, black or white," Samuel said with a shrug as they stared at the water. He shaded his eyes with his hand. "I like my accommodations in the boarding house just fine, Mister Cole. Don't worry 'bout that. Mighty nice. Maybe a five-minute walk to White Caps. If I walk fast."

He looked down at Cole. "You just try to get better. Don't go worrying yourself over stuff and silly rules you can't do nothing about. Between Mister Henry and Mistress Lydia and me, you be well cared for. What I can't do for you, Mister Henry can. And Mistress Lydia worries 'bout you like she your mother."

"I know," Cole said. "It's just so frustrating being sick. I hate it."

"Least you getting better. I can tell."

"Thanks. I hope you're right." He stared out at the water. A flock of seabirds flew past. He felt a tickle in his throat and tried to ignore the familiar ache in his chest. "Samuel," he said. "I hate to ask you this, but could you please go back to the hotel and get me a big glass of water? Make it two. I don't want to start coughing out here and not be able to stop."

Samuel nodded. "Sure thing, Mister Cole." He pressed his lips together, regarded him with mock sternness and shook his index finger. "Now you stay right here, don't go off nowhere, promise me."

"Very funny," Cole said, trying not to laugh. He didn't dare, lest it trigger uncontrolled hacking. "I promise."

"Okay," Samuel said as he turned to go back to the hotel. "I be right back. I hope you be okay by yourself. This beach empty except for the birds."

Cole closed his eyes and waved him off. "I'm sure I will be fine. And I promise not to go in the water."

The sound of Samuel's footsteps faded away. Cole rested his head on the back of the wheelchair. It was easier to breathe that way. He relished the salty tang in the air and the tingly mist on his face that wafted over from the breaking waves.

His thoughts drifted back to past summers, when he was well and came to the beach to enjoy his life, not to try to save it. He had suffered asthma on and off as a young child, but outgrew it. He had enjoyed good health until last winter, when he came down with a serious case of bronchitis on a European tour.

He and his younger brother, Henry, were both attorneys in their father's Philadelphia firm, Stratton, Stratton & Stratton. Feeling over-worked, Cole had taken time off, at his father's urging, to explore a different part of the world with friends.

He had hoped to come back refreshed and with clearer insight about his future. Everyone expected him to propose to his sweetheart, Priscilla Day. His parents certainly expected it, as did Priscilla. He wasn't sure, however, and hoped being away from her would give him clarity about their relationship.

His sudden illness had forced him to cut short his trip. His father, William, hired a British doctor to accompany him on an ocean liner that set sail in Southampton. After spending the month of January in a hospital in New York City, he was discharged home to Philadelphia.

Still bedridden, and seriously ill, his family hired Samuel to be his personal orderly. Samuel's assistance was a blessing to everyone, including Cole's mother, Rose, who hovered over her son, but was physically incapable of doing more.

Twenty-year old Samuel was the son of freed slaves, Nate and Belle, who had moved north from Virginia after the Civil War. Belle was a midwife, and when he was twelve, Samuel began working as her assistant. With his medical experience, Samuel came highly recommended and proved to be a strong and compassionate caregiver.

He soon became more than that. Other than Henry, no one knew

Cole better. Samuel became more than an employee, he became a good friend.

At first, American doctors suspected Cole might have tuberculosis, which could have been a death sentence. Dr. Morris, however, insisted he only had a stubborn case of bronchitis. Other physicians concurred and it turned out they were correct. Unfortunately, the bronchitis turned into pneumonia.

Cole was determined to live and fully recover. Miraculously, he did get over the pneumonia by April, and the bronchitis finally started to clear up by May.

Unfortunately, months of being seriously ill, at times near death, left him too weak to stand. If he could not stand up, he could not walk, and if he could not walk, how could he ever regain his health?

That was what brought him to Cape May in June.

For years, invalids and convalescents had flocked to the seaside resort for its clean, refreshing sea air. They came to escape grimy city environments, following doctors' orders to "recreate" themselves. Some succeeded; some did not.

Cole was determined to regain his health completely by August.

He heard soft footsteps and assumed Samuel had returned with his water.

Opening his eyes, he was surprised to see it was not Samuel. It was the pretty, young woman he had met the previous evening.

What was her name? Jacyntha...Jacy. A lovely name that suited her.

"Jacy James," he said, smiling up at her.

"Right," she said, returning his smile. "You remembered. I'm flattered. And you are Cole Stratton, right?"

He nodded, surprised but pleased. She was flattering him.

She pursed her lips and looked around in confusion. "But what are you doing out here? So early and...alone?"

He grinned. "I could ask you the same thing. Where did you come from just now?"

"A walk. Along the beach."

"But from where? I didn't see you. I didn't see anyone out here."

"That's because you had your eyes closed, silly." She tilted her head.

She was wearing a blue bonnet. Tendrils of her wavy, dark-brown hair escaped from it, framing her fine-boned face.

He stared into her eyes. They were a striking shade of green.

She smiled. "I'm sorry. I didn't mean to embarrass you by calling you..." She nibbled the side of her lip. "Of course, you had your eyes closed. You look like you might be here for the sea-air cure." She winced. "I apologize if I sounded insensitive."

"You didn't. Don't worry, you didn't." He shook his head and struggled to sit up straighter. It was an effort, but he managed a few inches.

"I am actually feeling better being down here close to the ocean," he said, eager to put her at ease. "My orderly just went to fetch me some water." He looked down at his hands in his lap and back up at her face. She had a kind smile, high cheekbones slightly pinked by the sun, and mesmerizing sea-green eyes.

Placing his hands on the seat of his chair, he pushed up with all his strength to lift himself a little higher. "And yes, you're correct. My doctor sent me here for the sea air, hoping it will restore me to health. I believe they're out of other solutions."

"Oh," Jacy said. "I do hope it helps. I'm sure it will." She tilted her head and smiled sweetly. "Do you mind if I sit with you and keep you company until your orderly returns?"

"I would be delighted. Glad for the company."

To his surprise, she plopped down next to him, directly on the sand. Adjusting her skirt around her legs, she left a thin slice of ankle peeking out over her boot. She looked at the sun-sparkled sea, sighed, and slid him a sideways glance.

"So..." she said. "Forgive me if I am being rude for asking...but what..."

"Is wrong with me?" Cole lifted a corner of his mouth, met her sympathetic gaze, and told her about Europe and his slow recovery.

He stared at a flock of gulls flying by. "I'm twenty-eight years old and too young to die. So, I'm determined to live. I mean to be healthy again by summer's end, or hopefully sooner. I would like to have some fun while I'm here."

"Yes, of course."

The pity in her voice caused him to wince.

Already self-conscious about his condition, he nearly hadn't recognized himself when he looked at a full-length mirror that morning. That man with the hollowed-out cheekbones, pasty skin, and dark smudges under his eyes was not him.

He hated for the world to see him that way.

"I believe you will get well," Jacy said quietly. "In fact, I know you will." She scooped up sand with her hand and let it sift through her fingers. "You said last night you are here with your brother?"

"Yes. My younger brother, Henry. And his wife, Lydia."

"I see."

He gave her an embarrassed smile. "Henry and Lyida were married a few weeks ago. Believe it or not, they are on their honeymoon. Three months in Cape May, and they brought me along. Can you believe it? They are that concerned about me." He stared out at the ocean. "I have a very supportive family. In that regard, I am very lucky."

Her eyes widened. "Yes, you are."

In that brief instant, he caught something in her gaze. A flash of envy, perhaps, followed by a flicker of sorrow. Then it was gone. He told himself he must have imagined it. But he had seen much sorrow during his stay in the hospital, and this woman was trying to hide sadness.

He studied her face, hoping he was wrong.

Suddenly, with a cheerful grin, she turned and waved to someone coming up behind them from the direction of the hotel.

"I think this is your orderly coming back," she said. "He's carrying two big glasses of water."

Cole felt a stab of disappointment. Why did Samuel have to return so soon? He was enjoying his time with Jacy.

"Hello," Jacy said, springing to her feet. She brushed the sand off her palms.

"Jacy James, meet Samuel Pershing."

"I was just keeping Cole company until you returned," she said. "We met last night at dinner."

"Mighty nice of you," Samuel said. He had a twinkle in his eye. He handed Cole one of the glasses of water and bent down to wedge the other one in the sand.

"Well, I should take my leave," Jacy said. "I've been gone quite a while. I fear my aunt will be furious with me."

Cole nodded. "Thank you for brightening my morning."

"Thank you for brightening mine." Jacy sounded as if she truly meant it. With a happy wave, she hurried off toward the hotel.

Samuel stared at Cole. The expression on the orderly's face was a mix of amazement and confusion.

Coe laughed, which was not a good idea because he started coughing. He bent forward, took a sip of water, and leaned back in his chair.

"Where did that woman come from?" Samuel asked.

"I don't know," Cole answered, shaking his head. "She said she was coming back from a walk. But come to think of it, she never did say from where."

* * *

FRANK LYNCH idly tapped his fork on the table as he kept a close watch on the dining room door.

"Can I get you anything else, sir?"

He glanced up at the waiter, the same annoying guy who had waited on his table at dinner the night before. Looking back to the door, he impatiently shook his head. "No, I told you. I am fine with coffee for now. I am waiting for someone to join me before I place my order."

"Yes, sir. Just let me know."

Frank glared at the man as he wandered off to serve the next table. Then he looked back at the door and wondered—for what felt like the hundredth time that morning—where in the dickens was Jacy James?

All around him, he had endured the chatter of merry hotel guests and the savory aroma of omelets topped with bacon and his favorite, creamy chipped beef on toast.

He was hungry, and he needed to go soon to guard the beach. But he was waiting, hoping Jacy would join him for breakfast.

His heart leapt as a woman walked in the door. It was Jacy's aunt. He held his breath as she turned and motioned for someone behind her to hurry up. His heart fell. It was Jacy's cousin. He kept watching. The aunt looked angry, the cousin contrite. Where was Jacy?

When they saw him, they hurried over.

"Mrs. Bainbridge, Miss Bainbridge," Frank said, standing and bowing. "Do please join me for breakfast." This was lucky, he thought, because Jacy would likely soon join them.

Pointing to the empty chairs around his table, he said, "I have been hoping for good company this morning, and have not yet had time to order."

Helen Bainbridge frowned. She appeared agitated, not in the mood to eat. She glared at her daughter, who was staring at the floor.

"Thank you, Mr. Lynch," she said in her haughty, high-pitched voice. "But we are looking for Jacy. Have you seen her?"

"Seen her?" He was startled. "Why, no. I'm afraid not." He tried to appear casually concerned. "Why, is she missing?"

Helen Bainbridge nodded primly, her lips drawn into a straight, thin line. She glanced at her daughter, who was staring out the window. "She told Poppy hours ago she was going for a walk. And she has not returned."

"It wasn't hours ago, Mother," Poppy muttered. "It was—"

"She should not have gone off by herself," Helen Bainbridge hissed. "Certainly not at dawn."

"Dawn?" Frank raised his eyebrows and looked at Poppy. What was that intriguing chit, Jacy, up to now? "Poppy, where did she say she was going?"

Poppy's face reddened. Then, as she opened her mouth to reply, Jacy appeared in the doorway.

Cheeks flushed and her hair a tangle of curls, Jacy did indeed look as if she had been out for a walk, perhaps a long one.

Clutching her bonnet by the ribbons, she hurried over to their table.

"Good morning, Jacy," Frank said cheerfully, before her aunt could berate her. "You are looking very fine this morning. Please join us for breakfast." He stood, and pulled out a chair for her, winking at Helen Bainbridge as she glared at him. What did it matter where Jacy had been? The way he saw it, she was here now, and that was what was important.

Jacy glanced at her aunt out of the corner of her eye and then flashed Frank a grateful smile. Women smiled at him all the time, but not like that. This woman was different from most. She was special, unique. When he had plucked her from Neptune's embrace, on her first day at White Caps, she had piqued his interest like no woman ever had—and many women had piqued his interest.

"Why, thank you, Frank," Jacy said. "I can see I am just in time to join all of you. How fortunate."

"Fortunate, indeed." Helen Bainbridge sniffed. "We will discuss this later." She nodded at Poppy, who almost jumped into the chair Frank held for her. Plopping herself down, she unfolded her napkin and placed it in her lap.

Frank signaled for the waiter and informed him they were ready to order.

He turned to Jacy and smiled. The morning had not exactly gotten off to the start he had expected, but she was finally sitting next to him at breakfast.

He promised himself he would find out where she had gone off to, alone, before sunrise.

She fascinated him. He longed to get to know her better and he *would*. He had a way with women. Women loved him. She *would* love him.

It was going to be his best summer yet.

He leaned over to remark about the beautiful weather, but his words trailed off. Jacy was not listening. She was waving to someone across the room, giving them a bright smile, as if greeting a long-lost friend.

He followed her gaze. She was waving to an invalid in a wheel-chair. A man in his late twenties, wearing a silly grin on his face.

Who might he be? Frank didn't recall seeing him around the hotel.

He looked closer. The sickly man was being pushed across the room by another young man who resembled him, only healthier. Sandy brown hair, with the kind of open, boyish handsomeness women seemed to like.

Accompanying them was an attractive, pleasantly plump young woman with dark-blond hair, wearing a lacy pink dress and carrying a matching parasol. She had the type of extremely fair complexion that sunburned easily. It was obvious she had not yet been in the sun. Not a touch of pink marred her creamy white face.

Jacy gestured for them to come over to their table. "Please, sit with us," she said. "There is plenty of room."

"Thank you, Jacy," the invalid said, to Frank's disappointment. He had hoped to have Jacy to himself. "Don't mind if we do." He smiled at Helen and Poppy and then back at Jacy. "I finally have an appetite. I think the fresh air did me much good."

"I'm so glad," Jacy said. "You do look much improved."

She stood and introduced the man to her aunt and cousin and then to Frank.

Frank only half listened to everyone's name. Who cared who these people were? Inwardly outraged, he struggled not to let it show. He could see what was happening, and it made him angry.

It was obvious, based on the way the cripple and Jacy spoke to each other, that they had been together that morning. While Jacy's aunt and cousin were frantically searching for her, and he was waiting for her to join him for breakfast, she had been with the sick man.

Why? Something was amiss.

Frank decided to find out what.

CHAPTER FIVE

"**S**o what happened…did you get all the way to the lighthouse? It's far, and it was so dark when you left…" Poppy tucked Jacy's arm firmly under hers. Peering at her from under her white wide-brimmed hat, she leaned closer and whispered, "Mother is furious with you, you know."

Jacy reached over and patted her cousin's cheek. "Nothing happened. I did what I told you I was going to do. Walked to the lighthouse, which by the way, is not that far. The sun came up. The sky was a glorious riot of color. I climbed to the top—with the keeper's permission." She sighed. "Of course, I did not see Edmund's ship, which I know does not surprise you."

They were strolling the strand after breakfast, at Poppy's request. Jacy was glad she had suggested it, because it gave them the ability to speak privately, out of Aunt Helen's earshot.

Already mid-morning, the strand was obviously the place to be and be seen at that time of day. Men and women, all stylishly dressed, many arm-in-arm, walked up and down on the beach, nodding at each other, sometimes stopping to face the ocean. It was calm at the moment, nearly as placid as a lake.

Jacy smiled. What a lovely day, she mused. It seemed a perfect day for a swim. She would go that afternoon and perhaps invite Aunt Helen to join her. Picturing her aunt frolicking in the sea made her laugh.

Poppy yanked Jacy to a stop and stared at her. "What, pray tell, is so funny?"

"What? Oh...nothing..." Jacy studied her cousin's face. Despite her shady chapeau, the sun was having its way with Poppy's fair skin. She sunburned easily and would need to be careful.

Two little girls darted past them, screeching with joy, kicking up sand. A harried-looking woman, likely their governess, chased after them. They reminded Jacy of her and Poppy, growing up almost like sisters.

Like many in their social circle, they had been visiting Cape May all their lives. Families had started going there in the early 1800s, coming from Philadelphia, New York City, and other points south. First, they traveled by schooner. Later, by steamship and train. The first visitors stayed in public houses or taverns. Then hotels sprang up. Thanks to its wide, white beaches, refreshing surf, and growing popularity of ocean bathing, Cape May had become America's first seaside resort town.

Poppy did not seem to be enjoying the beach. A refreshing breeze blew off the ocean, but she appeared deep in thought. "You just told me that you did not see Edmund's ship." She shot Jacy a perplexed look. "You left me to face Mother's wrath when you went in search of it. Yet, here you are laughing. At what?"

Jacy's smile faded. She had been trying to forget about Edmund, relax and have fun. She had succeeded, too, thanks to Cape May's festive, carnival-like atmosphere.

As a child, she had spent time there during the summer. But never the entire season. Due to her circumstances, she had not expected to enjoy herself. But the beach, with its clean salt air and rhythmic waves, felt healing.

"You're right, Poppy," she whispered. "I shouldn't be laughing, I suppose. I don't know why I am." Grief suddenly grabbed her. The sun's bright rays seemed to dim. There was not a cloud in the sky, but a heavy darkness descended on her soul.

Edmund.

How could she possibly go on without him? How dare she try?

Yet, she was not a sad person by nature, and Cape May was such a happy place.

"You're right, Poppy," she whispered. "I didn't see his ship. I probably never will. I felt such a fool once I got to the top of the lighthouse and saw nothing but vast expanse of sea."

Poppy grabbed hold of Jacy's hands and squeezed them. "So, don't go back."

"I must."

"No...no...just forget about him. He is no good for you."

"He is. People don't understand him. Papa doesn't—"

"He is no good for you. He's not good enough for you."

"We've talked about this so many times before. He is the perfect man for me."

Poppy stamped her foot. A couple passing by grew quiet, shot her a questioning glance, and resumed their stroll. "He is not the perfect man in any way," Poppy whispered. "For one, he is too old for you. You know that."

"He is not. He is only thirty-six. That's not—"

"It is. And he's a sea captain." Poppy wrinkled her nose. "He sails around the world. Around the world...gone for months at a time."

"So?"

"So? He probably has a woman in every port, as they say. In fact... in fact, many people say he does."

Jacy felt the blood rush to her face. "It's not true. How dare you. It's just something my father says. He hates him."

"For good reason, Jacy." Poppy resumed walking and Jacy reluctantly followed at a distance.

They passed a group of eager young men. One of them counted loudly, "One, two, three," and they raced into the surf, laughing.

"Listen to yourself," Poppy said, turning around to face Jacy. "It's not just your father. It's everyone who knows Edmund Overton. And cares about you. He is not suitable for you. You deserve better. A man closer to your age. And social class. With a respectable profession."

"I don't want anyone else. I want Edmund."

"Well then..." Poppy said, an angry frown darkening her face. She turned and scurried farther ahead of Jacy, then whirled around to face her again. "Well then..." she shouted, "I am glad he's dead! There, I've said it. And I'm not sorry—it's good that he's dead!"

Jacy halted. Feeling numb, her eyes welled up with tears. She watched Poppy walk away. Her beloved cousin's words hurt, but they did not come as a surprise.

No one in her family saw Edmund the way she did. They never had. It was true, he was fifteen years older than she. But what did it matter? Yes, his brown hair and beard were beginning to gray, and he had a ruddy sailor's complexion, but she didn't care. He was so distinguished. In her eyes, he was quite handsome. Most importantly, he loved her. His striking blue eyes warmed her heart whenever he smiled at her—when he used to smile at her.

What if Poppy was right? Jacy squeezed her eyes closed. What if she never saw him again?

Raising her hands to her mouth, Jacy let loose a quiet sob. The delightful squeals of children chasing one another in the surf were drowned out by her desperate inner wailing.

She blinked back her tears and saw Frank Lynch a short distance away at the water's edge, waving to the men who had just run into the waves. He was signaling them to stay close to shore.

Just beyond Frank, the waves were lapping at the wheels of Cole Stratton's wheelchair. His brother, Henry, and his orderly, Samuel, stood next to him, like sentinels in the sun.

"Edmund is not dead," Jacy whispered to herself. A tear ran down her cheek, then another. "He can't be. He cannot be. I won't let him be."

She lifted her chin and turned to stare at the sea.

Closing her eyes, she imagined Edmund's arms around her.

In her mind, she was back in time with him, the night before his last voyage.

She could see him so clearly. He was naked—naked to the waist. He was kissing her face, her neck and her arms. And then, before she knew what was happening, he was completely naked.

And so was she.

She loved him fiercely. He had just asked her to marry him, and she had just accepted.

What she did next was not so wrong, was it? *Was it really so very wrong?*

She opened her eyes and stared at the rolling waves and the foam of the incoming tide. Yes, yes it was. In the eyes of society, it was ruinous.

Fortunately, no one need ever know. That is what Edmund had said, and she believed it. He promised that when he returned, they would wed. They would do so, he said fiercely, with or without her father's approval and she had agreed. She had breathlessly and eagerly agreed.

Then, he never came back. Now, in the eyes of respectable society, Jacy was forever ruined for any other man.

* * *

Bright sunlight burned Cole's eyes as he stared unblinkingly at the ocean. It was a lovely day to be on the beach, but he was not in the mood to enjoy it.

Not normally an envious person, he resented the joyous people frolicking about on the strand, in the water, young and old, healthy all.

Frank Lynch was clearly enjoying himself, Cole noticed sourly as he turned his head to look around. Tan and muscular, the lifeguard struck an imposing figure as he paced up and down the shoreline. Weakly raising his hand to shade his eyes, Cole watched him preen. Lynch appeared ready to dash into the surf to rescue anyone in the slightest danger. Watching the water with the intensity of a man eager to play hero, he squinted against the sun's glare, his jaw set in a determined line.

Cole turned back to the water. Three young women splashed past him who might prove to be promising rescues for Frank. Giggling and holding hands, they repeatedly dipped their fannies into the waves. But they did not seem intent on wading out further than their knees, and the sea was calm at the moment. It did not appear they would need rescuing any time soon.

Too bad for Frank.

Jacy stood a short distance beyond the lifeguard, alone and still dressed in the gingham frock she had worn earlier that morning. Cole smiled. At least she would not need rescuing.

Feeling a rush of pleasure at the sight of her, he smiled. Then his smile faded to a frown. Something about her seemed sad. He could not tell from so far away, but she might have been crying.

Samuel and Henry were standing beside him, chatting, so he turned to get their attention.

"Samuel," he said. "And Henry—I know it won't be easy, since the sand here is so wet, but do you think the two of you could wheel me down that way..." He pointed in Jacy's direction. "I need a change of scenery."

Henry squinted in that direction. "What? Why? The scenery's not any different down there. Same ocean."

Samuel glanced over, too. With an amused grin, he shook his head. "Look closer, Mister Henry. Scenery mighty prettier down there. Least I suspect in Mister Cole's opinion."

"Prettier...?" Henry mumbled, shading his eyes with his hand. "Oh yes..." He nodded. "The fair Jacy James."

Cole sat up straight in his chair. "Very observant, you two. Just wheel me down to her, will you? She looks like she could use some cheering up."

"Why...you sly Romeo," Henry said. "You must be feeling better already. Could it be that you are developing a romantic interest in the lovely Miss James?"

Cole gripped the arms of his chair, annoyed at Henry's observation. "What are you talking about? I am not developing any romantic interest. I just want to talk to her. If I could—and how I wish I could—

I would just walk over there myself. But since I can't, I need your help."

Henry shrugged, went behind Cole's wheelchair, and grasped the handlebars. "Okay, Samuel," he said. "I'll push while you pull. Grab hold under the seat and we'll maneuver our moonstruck friend over to his Juliet."

Samuel grunted and followed Henry's bidding. "No sense arguing with him," he said.

Cole held onto the arms of the chair as it moved in fits and starts, trying to ignore the stares of beachgoers.

"You *obviously* feeling better already," Samuel said, laughing good-naturedly as he scooted backwards across the sand in a half-crouch. "And I don't think it's the sea air."

"Very funny, you two." Cole gritted his teeth. People were looking at him with expressions of polite pity, so he smiled, striving to appear cheerful and nonchalant.

Jacy was not among those looking in his direction, however. Staring at the water, she seemed so wrapped up in her thoughts, she did not even hear him call her name.

Cole called to her again. When she finally turned, it became clear—he had been right. Her cheeks were wet, and her lips quivered when she tried to return his smile.

"Hello, Cole, Henry, Samuel," she said, softly, looking embarrassed. Her voice sounded raspy when she added, "It's beautiful out here, isn't it?"

"Yes, it is," Cole said, embarrassed for her. He probably should not have come over. Why had he been so impetuous? Whatever was bothering Jacy, she most certainly would have preferred privacy. "I saw you alone and thought you could use some company," he blurted. "But if this is a bad time, we can leave."

She pressed her lips together and lightly dabbed her cheek with a finger. Sighing, she put her hands to her face and wiped away the residue of tears. "No. No. That's quite alright." She shook her head. "I'm fine. I really am." She looked down at Cole and gave him an embarrassed smile. "I needed to stop feeling sorry for myself. So, thank you—thank you for coming over."

It was gracious of her to thank him, but he suspected she was just being polite. He steeled himself against a wave of self-pity. Feeling sorry for himself felt worse than other people feeling sorry for him.

It was bad enough that he had attracted attention on his way to speak to a woman he found attractive. Making matters worse, he could not stand up to talk to her face to face. Earlier that morning on the beach, she had sat down next to his wheelchair, kindly putting herself at his level. At the breakfast table, he had also been able to talk to her eye to eye.

Now, Jacy loomed over him, even though she was not unusually tall. He guessed she was about five feet, five inches, of average height for a woman.

Whereas he was six foot, one inch—taller than most men. That is, when he was healthy and could stand.

Unfortunately, when she looks at me now, all she sees is a frail invalid. He suppressed a groan. *Just like the rest of the world.*

He learned forward in his chair. "I'm sorry if you are not feeling well, Jacy. Is there anything we can do to help? That I could do..." He sat back, inwardly cursing himself. What could he possibly do?

When she just shook her head, and turned to stare back out at the waves, he glumly wondered if maybe Henry was right. Maybe he was developing feelings for Jacy. That would be a foolish idea, under the circumstances.

He had to focus on regaining his physical health. A broken heart was the last thing he needed.

Jacy turned back to him. "Thank you, but I am fine. You need not concern yourself about me."

A light breeze caught her bonnet, knocking it sideways. She reached up to re-tie the ribbons under her chin. "It's sweet of you to ask, Cole, but there is nothing you can do to help me. Nothing anyone can do... It's just...that I allowed a sad memory to overtake me...that's all."

Henry cleared his throat. "Hmmm, well... I am sorry to hear it. Hopefully the good cheer of this place will help."

Cole could not see Henry, who was standing behind him. But he could tell that he, too, wished they had not come over.

Jacy met Henry's gaze. "People tell me that I need to heal," she said. "That's what they keep telling me."

Samuel coughed, breaking the silence. Cole could not see his orderly's face either, but he was clearly uncomfortable. If only Samuel and Henry were not there. If only he could talk to Jacy alone, even for a few minutes. He had no idea what to say to her, but having an audience certainly was not helping him.

Lowering his head, Cole stared at his hands in his lap, feeling more helpless than he had ever felt in his life. Whatever was upsetting Jacy was none of his business, and she clearly did not want to talk about it.

The problem was, he could not just turn around and leave her to her thoughts without causing another scene.

The tide was coming in, and the sand was softer and wetter than before. Soon he might need to be carried off the beach.

Jacy seemed to sense the awkwardness of his situation. Pointing to some bathers in the water, she casually remarked, "Look at them."

Cole looked, grateful she had changed the subject. People were screeching and laughing and splashing each other, having a grand time. "Looks like a lot of fun," he said.

Jacy's face brightened. "I know. I know what I need right now. I need to be doing that."

Cole nodded. "Of course. That's a wonderful idea. Henry..." He twisted around to address his brother. "Why don't you and Lydia change into your bathing costumes, so you can join Jacy for a swim."

"That would be delightful," Jacy said. "I had thought about asking my Aunt Helen to join me for a dip." Her green eyes twinkled a little. "But I have a feeling she will decline."

"Bring Poppy. Surely Poppy will come," Cole said.

"I don't know. She is a little perturbed with me right now. But I will go find her and ask her." Jacy nodded at Cole, then Henry and

Samuel. "If you will excuse me, gentlemen, I need to go change. I'll meet you soon, back here on the strand."

"See you shortly," Henry called out. When she was out of hearing range, he added, "I'm glad she cheered up. Didn't know what to say to her."

"Neither did I." Cole patted his thighs with the palms of his hands. Cursing his wasted muscles, he watched Jacy walk off. "I guess we should not have bothered her. I sensed she was upset about something and I convinced myself she needed company. But I don't think she did."

* * *

AFTER A FEW MINUTES OF SILENCE, Henry told Samuel to grab onto Cole's chair again so they could get him onto firm sand and wheel him back to his room.

"Wait," Samuel said. "Look like we got company."

"Lynch," Henry muttered.

Cole widened his eyes when Frank Lynch stepped in front of him. Positioning himself about an inch from Cole's knees, the lifeguard put his hands on his hips and looked down at him with a sneer.

"Hello, Lynch," Cole said in as friendly a tone as he could manage. What did the man want? Whatever it was, he refused to be intimidated.

"Just what do you think you are doing?" Lynch spat the words out.

Startled at his hostility, Cole said, "What do you mean?"

"We get a lot of sick folks here at White Caps, but they know their place."

"Their place?"

"Yeah. Like up on the porch, or out on the lawn."

Cole stared at him. "I don't know what you are talking about. I am enjoying the fresh air coming off the sea. It's—"

"You're supposed to *breathe* the air, not get in the water."

"What? I'm—"

"Look, the wheels of that conveyance of yours are practically in the water."

Cole looked down. Lynch was right. Waves were lapping at the wooden wheels of his chair. Although he failed to see how that was any of Lynch's concern. "So? What—"

"Me and my crew have enough to do without having to worry about rescuing invalids."

"You won't have to rescue me, and anyway we were just leaving."

"Ohhh." Lynch drew the word out, sarcastically. "You're going, now that Jacy has left. I get it."

"What exactly do you get?"

"What makes you think Jacy James is interested in your company? Leave the woman alone."

Speechless, Cole tried to hide his surprise at Lynch's ridiculous demand. Being forced to look up at the man put him at a disadvantage, so he looked out at the sea to stall for time.

His bangs fell into his eyes and he weakly lifted a hand to brush them back, making a mental note to schedule an appointment with the hotel barber.

He stared back up at Lynch while slowly raising his hand to shade his eyes from the sun. "What did you say?"

"You heard me."

"I did, but I don't know what you are talking about."

"I think you are sweet on her. And I'd like to know why you think she would be the slightest bit interested in you."

What?

"See here." Henry stepped over and shoved his face into Lynch's. "My brother's business is none of yours. He can talk to whoever he wants."

"Henry," Cole said. "I can speak for myself."

Lynch took a step back. His face was red, and not just from the sun. "Yeah, but you can't move yourself. Got to have your brother and manservant carry you down the beach. So pathetic."

Cole struggled to sit up as straight as he could, gripping his armrests and pushing down on them to raise himself higher. "I am a guest at this hotel. What I do is not your business. Just leave me alone."

"You need to leave Jacy James alone."

"What business is it of yours whether I talk to her or not?"

"Lynch is sweet on her," Henry said. "Isn't it obvious? That's why he's making it his business."

Cole stared at Lynch. "Oh, so that's it."

Lynch took another step back and folded his muscular arms. He glared at Cole. "Just stay away from Jacy," he repeated. "Don't go using your invalidness to gain her favor. You're making her feel sorry for you. She's obviously a kind woman, and I see what you are doing. You are taking advantage of her graciousness and generosity."

Invalidness? Cole wanted to lunge at Lynch. If he could, he would hurl himself from his damned chair, punch him out, and take him down. His frustration raged. "It's none of your business, Lynch." He waved his hand in dismissal. "So, go save lives, Lynch. Go be a hero, Lynch. The world needs you. Or, at least Cape May does. And leave me alone."

Lynch grunted and opened his mouth, as if he had more to say. But somewhere, out in the water, a bather screamed for help.

He glared at Cole, shook his head, and ran off.

CHAPTER SIX

"Oh, no, no!" Helen Bainbridge vigorously shook her elegantly coiffed head, then in dismay realized what she had just done.

She glanced around to see if anyone was looking, then discretely reached up to position her immense white hat back into its proper place.

Forcing a few deep breaths to calm herself, she pressed a gloved finger to her lips, looked around again and heaved a sigh.

Thank heavens. No one at the croquet match seemed to have noticed her undignified outburst, although in the grand scheme of things it was small comfort.

Jacy was still engaging in extremely embarrassing and unbecoming behavior. With a look of triumph on her face, she was standing in the middle of the croquet course, waving her mallet in the air and shouting, "Victory! Victory!"

Helen groaned. It was bad enough her niece had done that after trouncing her first male opponent, and then her second. Doing it a third time was outside of enough.

Foolish girl. Didn't she realize how it made her look? That it was not the way to charm a man's heart?

Beating men at croquet with such aplomb did nothing but wound their male egos. Jacy was not in Cape May to win games. *She knows that, doesn't she?*

"Poppy." Helen turned to her daughter. She sighed again, exasperated. "Poppy," she snapped.

Poppy pried her head out of her book. "Yes, Mother?" Stylishly dressed in one of the many white dresses she had brought to the resort, she was not paying attention to the game, Jacy, or anyone around her. They were among a large crowd of spectators, but her darling daughter seemed not the slightest bit interested.

Instead, she stood ramrod straight while holding a lacy white parasol over her head in one hand, and a slim volume of poetry in the other.

Poppy blinked at her.

Helen tried to keep her voice low. "Why don't you go out there and join your cousin? Instead of burying your pretty nose in a bunch of silly words."

Poppy scrunched her petite nose and frowned. "I—"

"Jacy is making a fool of herself. And us." Helen held out her hand for Poppy's book, and Poppy slowly and reluctantly placed it in her outstretched palm.

"What is the problem, Mother?"

"She keeps winning; that is the problem." Helen folded her arms and watched Jacy get ready to play another round. "So far, she has declared victory over every man out there, and there are some very fine looking, and by all appearances, suitable gentlemen playing today."

"Mother, really."

"Really? Really what? Am I being old and fussy by insinuating that a woman should try *not* to win?"

"Well, since you put it that way, yes." Poppy shook her head. "Why should Jacy lose on purpose when she is so good at the game? You know, as children, she and I used to play for hours on our front lawn. We both became very good at croquet."

"Then why are you not out there playing, too?"

Poppy gave an exaggerated shrug. "I'd rather read. It's more relaxing. And I don't have to pretend to be bad at something at which I am quite good, just to spare a man's feelings."

Helen tucked Poppy's book into her skirt pocket and watched Jacy's opponent bow, gesturing for her to go first. With thick black hair, a handlebar mustache, and good manners, he was about Jacy's age and appeared to be quite a prospect. Like everyone on the course, he was dressed in white.

The two dozen players had agreed that participants could stay in the game as long as they kept winning. Jacy looked unbeatable.

Helen was growing fatigued. So far, it had proved quite a day. They had spent a couple hours after lunch on the beach, where Jacy and Poppy went bathing with new acquaintances, Henry and Lydia Stratton. Everything went smoothly. No drama unfolded. No one needed rescuing. She even relaxed, chatting briefly with Henry's poor sickly brother at the shoreline.

The convalescent had seemed nice enough. What was his name? She couldn't remember. Then she saw him on the croquet sidelines, watching his brother and sister-in-law. The spacious side lawn of White Caps was decorated with several sets of hoops and stakes, to accommodate many players.

Henry and Lydia Stratton were among them. Why wasn't Poppy?

"Poppy dear, why don't you go offer to play as a foursome with your cousin?" Helen nodded in the direction of a tall, blond, gangly young man standing alone. "He looks eager to join the action. Go suggest it to him."

"Mother." Poppy looked up in horror from under her wide-brimmed bonnet. "I couldn't."

Helen pursed her lips. "Yes, you can. It might be a touch forward, but—"

"No, Mother, I won't."

"Why not?"

"Because, you are right. It would be awfully forward. And I am not that kind of woman."

"Not that kind of woman? Well, what kind of woman are you, my dear? The kind that never marries? Because that is what you are headed for if you don't change your ways."

Poppy stared at her. "What are you talking about, Mother? What are you saying?"

Helen glanced around, afraid to make a scene. She was used to it with her spirited niece, but not with Poppy. Not with her sweet, placid daughter, who was now darkly angry.

"Why did we come to Cape May, Poppy?"

Poppy let out a loud sigh. "Oh, I don't know, Mother. To spend the summer by the sea instead of in the sweltering city? Because we have the financial means? Because everybody who is anybody..." She sighed again.

"And?"

Poppy whispered, "And to get Jacy's mind off Edmund Overton."

"Yes. Of course. That's the most important reason. I promised your Uncle Tobias I would do my best. And as I love my brother—and he is paying most of our expenses—I feel I owe it to him to succeed."

"Yes, Mother, of course, Mother." Poppy blinked several times, fixed her gaze on the croquet players, and began watching the action with exaggerated interest.

Helen was not fooled. She whispered, "But I am also here for you. As much as I am here for Jacy."

Poppy turned to look at her. "Me?"

"Yes, *you*." Really, sometimes her youngest child could be so obtuse. "What could possibly lead Jacy to forget about Edmund Overton, Poppy?"

Poppy raised her chin. "Another man? Falling in love with another man?"

"Yes, of course. We talked about that. And I am delighted there are so many young, eligible gentlemen here." She held her daughter's gaze. "Including for you."

Poppy began to giggle.

"What is so amusing?"

"Mother, I don't care if I ever marry." Poppy covered her mouth with her hand, then let her hand fall to her side. Her eyes were as large

51

as saucers, her expression suddenly serious. "In fact, if you must know, I am beginning to think I would rather not."

Helen gasped.

"I am sorry to have to tell you that now, Mother. But I have been thinking I might rather remain single."

"And be an old maid?"

"If that's what you want to call it, yes. I have my books. I have my poetry. I shall come into a substantial inheritance one day. I don't need a man. In fact, I believe one would get in my way."

"Well." Helen felt as if someone had punched her in the abdomen. Her legs, which ached from standing so much of the day, suddenly felt weak. She could think of nothing to say. The ground tilted under her. She grabbed onto Poppy's arm to steady herself.

Poppy patted her hand. "Now, now, Mother. Let's just see how the summer unfolds. Maybe I shall feel differently by the end of it. Maybe not."

"Yes." Helen nodded. "Let us do see how the summer unfolds."

"Mother," Poppy whispered. "As far as that goes, I hate to be a bearer of bad news regarding Jacy."

"Oh no, what?"

"It seems Jacy is determined not to forget about Overton. Quite the contrary, in fact. She came here because of the lighthouse. She means to climb it every morning to look for his ship."

Helen gripped Poppy's arm. "That can't be." She moaned quietly. "Can't something be done? The foolish, foolish girl. Poppy, what are we to do?"

"I don't know..."

A shout went out. The crowd applauded. Helen could not believe it. Once again, Jacy was declaring victory. The man sheepishly handed his mallet to the next gentleman waiting to play her.

Helen's heart beat faster and she felt a rush of hope. It was Frank Lynch. He was a most suitable, eligible young man, indeed.

Perhaps he could win Jacy's heart. Helen smiled. Tobias would be so pleased.

"Frank Lynch," Poppy said. "She will beat him, too. Just watch."

CHAPTER SEVEN

Tugging the ribbons of her bonnet tighter under her chin, Jacy scurried down the hotel hallway. Taking the stairs two at a time, she yanked open the door leading to the veranda and almost ran into Cole.

He was alone, sitting in his chair next to the steps to the lawn, allowing the sun's early morning rays to warm his face.

His eyes popped open with surprise when he saw her. "Good morning, Jacy."

Drat. She was already getting far too late a start on her daily hike to the lighthouse, and she had hoped to slip away without being seen. After a week in Cape May, she thought she had succeeded in setting out at dawn without anyone noticing.

She smiled politely. "Good morning to you as well, Cole."

He grinned. "You are looking fine this morning. The color peach suits you."

"Thank you," she said, curtseying as she returned his grin. His compliment triggered a warm fluttering in her chest, which surprised her as she self-consciously glanced down at her dress. Softly pleated, it happened to be one of her favorites, with a scooped ruffled neckline that matched the hem at her ankle. "Why, thank you," she said, repeating herself. "I expect today will get rather warm, and this cotton fabric keeps me cool."

He nodded. "I'm glad. Where are you off to so early? You look in a hurry."

She bit down on the side of her lip. "For a walk."

"Oh, where to?"

She hesitated because she knew he would be shocked, and she really needed to get going. "Oh...to the lighthouse." She waved her hand as if it was a short distance away.

"What? Isn't that—"

"Somewhat of a walk. Well, yes...maybe just short of a mile...so I think I better be off. I need to get back for breakfast, before it gets too late."

Frowning, she realized he was alone and wondered why.

"Is that where you go every morning, Jacy? Before breakfast?"

"What? How?"

"How did I know you always go for a walk before breakfast? Because you always enter the dining room a bit winded." He grinned and leaned forward. "And slightly disheveled. I mean...what I mean is...not in an unflattering way, I assure you...No, not that. It's just... your cheeks are flushed and your hair is always a bit askew." He stopped, looking sheepish. "I am not explaining myself very well. I'm sorry, Jacy." He raised his hand. "Where you go is none of my business."

Jacy was tempted to agree. But something stopped her.

She could not help but notice that Cole was looking much better, much healthier. The sun was starting to bleach his thick brown hair and burnish his cheeks. When they had first met, he had been alarmingly pale. After a week in the sun, his face looked tanned and more filled out.

He also seemed to be sitting up straighter.

The sea air must be doing him good. How wonderful.

She still wished she had not awakened so late. The fewer people who knew about her treks to the lighthouse, the better. She did not want to be judged, or to become a source of gossip. She had been rising every morning well before dawn and had established a routine that Aunt Helen and Poppy had begrudgingly grown to accept.

As long as she joined them for breakfast at a civilized hour, they never remarked about where she had been, or what she had seen. Which, so far, was no trace of Edmund.

Since Aunt Helen was interested in meeting as many of the other hotel guests as possible, Jacy never knew where in the dining room she and Poppy would be sitting when she hurried in. They had dined with an interesting assortment of people, including, as her aunt intended, several nice gentlemen around her age.

They had not dined with the Strattons since the first morning and Jacy suddenly wished they had. She liked Cole. She liked his family.

"Don't let me keep you, Jacy. I can see you are in a hurry," he said. "You don't need to keep me company. Henry wheeled me down here and then went back to Lydia. Samuel should be along any minute."

Jacy shook her head. "Oh. No. I am not worried about you. I am just aggravated at myself for sleeping in so late today. I enjoyed the orchestra's concert on the lawn last night a little too much. I got to bed much later than usual."

Cole leaned his head against the back of his chair. He flashed her a smile that crinkled the corners of his eyes. Even sick, he was a remarkably good-looking man. "I think most of us got to bed later than usual. The dancing after the concert was too much fun. Not that I could partake. But I enjoyed watching everyone else."

Jacy nodded. "I did have a good time. I surprised myself."

"I saw you. I bet you never sat down. You must have danced with most of the men there. I think you were by far the most popular belle."

Jacy giggled at the gleam in his eye. "But I never danced with any man twice. I made sure of that. Not even with Frank Lynch, much to his disappointment."

"Oh. And why was that?"

Jacy held his gaze and hesitated. Should she tell him? He was obviously curious about her lighthouse hikes and he did seem to genuinely care about her. She decided to confide in him.

She knelt down to his level. "What I am about to tell you is confidential." She realized she was whispering.

His eyes widened. "Okay."

She put her lips near his ear. "Can you keep a secret?"

"Of course. You can trust me. I pride myself on being an honorable man."

She hoped he was because she could use a sympathetic ear. She pulled back and looked him in the eye. "Do you think it odd that I walk to the lighthouse every morning?"

The corners of his mouth turned down. He shifted in his chair. "Truthfully...yes."

"Do you want to know why I go there?"

He stared at her, unblinking. "Sure, if you want to tell me."

She took a deep breath. "To look for a missing ship."

A deep line formed between his eyebrows. "Oh?"

She tilted her head. "It vanished off the coast last spring. A man was aboard it. A man I cared deeply about. His name was Edmund Overton."

The line deepened. "Oh."

"I loved him."

"Oh."

"People tell me I'm crazy for believing he might still be alive. Or, at least deluded. Foolish."

Cole turned to look at the sea. "Jacy, you don't need to tell me any more. It is not for me to judge you." He lowered his voice. "You must be in a lot of pain."

"Yes. I am."

"I have been sensing a sadness about you that you try hard to hide." He turned back to look at her. "Very well, I might add. Most of the time."

"Yes," she said, surprised at his perceptiveness. "That is why my aunt and cousin brought me here. So I would forget about him. So I would heal."

"To heal your heart."

"Yes."

He gave her an understanding, warm smile. She was glad she had confided in him. He understood her.

"Well, then it seems we have something in common, you and I," he said softly. "You came to Cape May for emotional healing. And I came for physical healing. Aren't we a fine pair?"

She laughed. She could not believe she was actually laughing.

Cole, however, was not. He was staring at her glumly.

"I'm sorry, Cole," she said hastily. "I wasn't laughing at you. Of course, your health problems are not at all funny." She leaned toward him. "Forgive me. I was only laughing at myself."

He shook his head. His bangs fell into his eyes and he slowly reached up to brush them away. "I'm not laughing Jacy, because I think *your* situation is tragic."

He looked away from her again. "I told you I did not want to judge you. But I must speak my mind. I hope you are not on a fool's errand. The likelihood of a ship that has been missing for months just showing up here is...well..."

Cole, too?

Jacy felt blood rush to her cheeks as he leaned toward her. "By summer's end, I intend to be well, Jacy. Completely healed. That is my plan. But as for you?" He slowly shook his head back and forth. "I fear that the chances your missing ship will be found are slim. And then, what? You will have spent a great deal of energy looking for it in vain. And you will remain as broken as you are today."

Jacy blinked back tears. She should not have told him. She thought he was different. But he was like all the rest.

He, too, thought she was a fool. For some reason, that made her pain even worse.

"No, you are wrong," she whispered. "Edmund is alive. I know he is. And now, if you will excuse me, I am off to look for him."

"Good luck," Cole said, lifting his hand.

Shaking her head, she skirted past him, hurried down to the beach, and ran most of the way to the lighthouse.

* * *

COLE WATCHED Jacy disappear from sight.

With a sigh, he leaned his head against the high back of his chair, hoping to return to the relaxed state he had been in before she showed up. It was no use.

Her confession about Edmund Overton disturbed him. He did not know why. He had been dozing off when Jacy found him, relaxing in the sun while waiting for Samuel to come and take him down near the water. In keeping with his morning routine, Henry wheeled him as far as the lawn and when Samuel reported for duty at 7 a.m., he took over from there.

Cole squeezed his eyes closed. Inhaling as deeply as he could, he slowed released his breath, pleased he could do it without coughing.

He was still agitated as hell, though.

Why did he keep thinking about Jacy? He had enough of his own to deal with. Her grief over her missing sea captain was none of his business.

So, damn it, why did he care so much?

"Cole."

He opened his eyes and looked up at Samuel.

"How long you been here?" Samuel's face was wreathed with concern.

Cole grunted. "Long enough."

"I'm not late."

"No, I asked Henry to bring me down early. Woke up and couldn't go back to sleep. Told Henry I would be fine. Told him to go back to his bride."

"You put out 'bout something, Mister Cole?"

"No, why?"

"You look it. Shook up. You feeling okay?"

"I'm fine." Cole lifted a hand and let it fall back in his lap. He decided not to mention Jacy. She had asked him to keep her confession a secret, so it would be best not to bring her up at all. Squinting up at Samuel, he grunted, "Just getting hungry is all. I'm ready to go back to my room, get ready for breakfast."

"You sure? You breathe enough sea air this morning?"

"Enough for now."

"Alright," Samuel reached down to unlock the wheelchair brakes. "Here we go."

Cole finally began to relax when they got to his room. The door between it and Henry and Lydia's suite opened and Henry came in.

"Back already?"

Henry certainly sounds cheerful. And why shouldn't he? He's on his honeymoon. Cole nodded. "I'm back."

"Feeling any better this morning?"

Cole shrugged. "Somewhat."

Samuel wheeled Cole over to his wardrobe. Opening the door, he waited for Cole to choose his clothes for the day.

"What it be, Mister Cole?" Samuel asked as Cole stared at the selection of pants and shirts neatly arranged on hangers. "What you in the mood for this fine morning?"

Cole glanced over at Henry. Behind him, in the adjacent suite, he heard Lydia bustling about.

Cole wished his mood matched the fine weather. A balmy breeze wafted in from the floor-to-ceiling window to the patio, softly rustling the curtains. The sky above the White Caps lawn—and beyond to the sea—was clear blue.

"I don't know," Cole said, trying not to sound as hopeless as he felt. "Do we have plans, Henry?"

"Plans?" Henry looked puzzled. "What do you have in mind?"

Cole rubbed his chin. "Oh, I don't know. Swimming, perhaps? Tennis? Bowling? Let's go bowling. Or, better yet, yachting. That sounds grand." He cringed at the sarcasm in his voice. It wasn't like him, but he couldn't help it.

"Cole." Henry sounded shocked. "I don't know... Lydia and I—"

"You and Lydia." Cole pressed his hand against his forehead. "You and Lydia could do anything you wanted if you didn't have to worry about me."

"Cole."

Cole balled his fists in his lap. "That's the sad truth of the matter, isn't it? I can do nothing. Just sit and take in the sea air. Breathe the sea air in. Breathe the sea air out. All the day long."

Lydia walked in the room. By the expression on her face, she had heard him. "Hello, Cole." She looked radiant, as usual, in a dark-green dress that flattered her dark-blond curls. With her creamy skin, cute plump figure, and sweet nature, Cole thought his brother was a lucky man.

"Hello, Lydia," Cole muttered. "I'm sorry to sound such a bear." Embarrassed that he had let his usually well-concealed self pity show, he attempted a smile. "You look lovely, as usual."

"Thank you. But I am sorry you are not feeling better. You sound agitated."

"Mister Cole put out about something this morning," Samuel said. "Was that way when I found him on the lawn."

"You would all be put out, too, if you were stuck in this chair."

Lydia tilted her head. "You look better than when we arrived here, Cole. We all believed you were getting better."

"That's right," Henry said. He was wearing a dark-green shirt and tan pants. Cole realized his outfit matched his wife's. "You hardly cough anymore, and your color is better."

Cole looked down at his scrawny legs. His muscles were pitifully wasted from disuse. "But I *want* to stand up. I *need* to stand up. How is my health supposed to improve by sitting all day?"

Henry stared at him, his brows knitted together. "Be patient. The summer has just begun."

Cole meant what he had told Jacy. He *would* regain his health by the end of the season. Or, he silently promised himself, he would die trying. "Yes, and you and Lydia are having quite the honeymoon. Father was kind enough to give you three months off from practicing law, so you could accompany me to the seaside. But I am holding you back from the many festivities this fair town has to offer."

"He is giving you time off, too," Henry said. "We are all focused on one thing right now: your health."

Cole nodded. He was grateful for his strong family support, as well as a career that allowed him time to recover. After he and Henry had graduated from the University of Pennsylvania Law School, they went directly to work for their father, William. Their Philadelphia firm, Stratton, Stratton & Stratton, was thriving and could do without them for a while.

"You are not holding us back from anything," Henry insisted. He looked at Lydia, then back at his brother. "We *want* to be here for you. We want to help you."

"Yes, dear," Lydia said. "We both care about you. Very much."

Cole nodded. "I'm sorry. I don't know what got into me." He looked at his wardrobe again. He had many choices of clothes to wear, but in his present condition, what did it matter? He waved his hand. "Anything will do, Samuel." He pointed. "There, that blue shirt. And there, those khaki pants. I'll wear those to breakfast."

"Very good," Henry said.

Cole glanced at his ocean bathing costume hanging on a hook, next to his clothes, a one-piece, black tank top and black shorts in keeping with the style for men. He got an idea. He had brought it to Cape May with the hope of wearing it when he got better.

Why not put it to use now?

"Henry…"

"Yes?"

"After breakfast, I want to get out of this chair. So, I will need to come back and don those." He pointed to his bathing costume.

Henry stared at him and Lydia gasped.

Samuel cleared his throat. "Mister Cole—you gonna swim?"

"Yes, Samuel. I think I will."

Lydia widened her eyes.

"But how?" Henry said, sounding alarmed.

"With your help, and Samuel's." Cole realized he felt more alive and hopeful than he had in a long time. "The two of you are going to lift me up and put me in the water and I am going to move my arms and kick my legs."

Henry frowned. "But the doctor said not to overdo it. Remember?"

"I remember."

"He said your health is delicate. You have finally stopped coughing. Swimming in cold ocean water might set you back."

Cole shrugged. "I am sick of being sick. I need to get some exercise. I won't get better staying in this chair. I have to do *something*."

Henry turned to his wife. "Lydia, dear. Could you please excuse us? Samuel and I need to help Cole dress. We won't be long and then we can go eat."

Henry walked over to Cole, and folding his arms across his chest, glared down at him. "In the meantime, Lydia, we will try to change Cole's mind about going in the water."

"You won't," Cole said, shaking his head. "You won't, so don't even try."

CHAPTER EIGHT

"Jacy, you look marvelous. Poppy, you are a vision." Aunt Helen's eyes gleamed as she entered her niece and daughter's room and found them dressed for the annual White Caps *Hooray for Summer Ball*. "I don't doubt for a moment that a great many gentlemen will vie for the opportunity to dance with both of you."

Jacy curtsied and smiled. "Thank you, Aunt Helen. That is kind of you to say. Although I won't dance with any man twice, because as you know, I am saving my heart for Edmund."

"*Jacy,*" Poppy said, shaking her head. "Don't say that. You might change your mind."

"Indeed, dear," Aunt Helen said, giving Jacy a look of disappointment. "In the two and a half weeks we have been in Cape May, I had believed you were forgetting about that man. I thought you were having a fine time."

Jacy turned to meet her gaze in the mirror above the bureau and gave herself a half smile. Apparently, she had fooled Aunt Helen. She also had to admit there was some truth in her aunt's observation.

Every day had dawned bright and full of promise. After breakfast she and Poppy had a wide variety of activities at their disposal. In addition to ocean bathing, they had played tennis, shopped on Washington Street, taken carriage rides, and promenaded up and down the boardwalk.

Despite her grief for Edmund, Jacy had thrown herself into a whirlwind social life, because she knew her father and aunt had wanted it. She had made it a goal to appear cheerful. At times, she had caught herself actually feeling that way.

Unfortunately, her joyous moments never seemed to last.

Grief for Edmund would well up inside her, and anxiety over his whereabouts would descend on her like fog creeping over a sunny meadow.

She would think about him, ache for him. But no matter how much she tried to get him out of her mind, she could not.

Not knowing Edmund's fate was agony, and she found herself ruminating on the same questions again and again: Could he be marooned on a distant island? Might he be dying of starvation and thirst on his storm-wrecked ship, somewhere out at sea? What if he had washed up, horribly injured, on some unknown shore, in the care of someone who had no idea who he was because he could not speak?

She found hope and comfort hiking to the lighthouse at dawn and climbing its steep steps.

She found purpose at the top, scanning the vast expanse of ocean.

Walking back to White Caps, nursing disappointment, she would console herself that there was always tomorrow.

Sometimes she fantasized that he might sail back into her life and greet her with a smile, then chide her for having been so worried. He would tease her for being so upset about him, and say, "Why didn't you trust me? Didn't you know I would come back to you? Silly woman."

"Jacy."

She whirled around and looked at Poppy, who was staring at her with impatience.

"Are you ready to go?" Poppy's expression softened. "You look beautiful." She gave Jacy an admiring grin. "Don't worry. Your gown and your hair—they're perfection. You have never looked lovelier."

Jacy nodded and turned to face the full-length mirror across the room. Her mood lifted when she realized Poppy wasn't just being kind.

Her lemon-yellow silk gown, low cut with cap sleeves, suited her complexion. She lightly touched her hair. Poppy had pinned it up, tucking small daisies from a local florist throughout. The effect was unique and striking.

Jacy's fingers dropped to the glittering diamond necklace around her neck. It enhanced the sparkle in her eyes. One of Aunt Helen's favorite pieces of jewelry, she had insisted Jacy wear it for the evening.

Jacy sighed. *Dear Aunt Helen has such high hopes for me this summer.*

She turned to face her aunt and cousin. Taking a deep breath, she summoned a wide smile. "I'm ready," she said. "So, let's take ourselves to the ball, shall we?"

* * *

TRAILING behind her aunt and cousin, Jacy entered the White Caps ballroom looking around in amazement.

Garlands of fresh white lilies and pink roses draped the walls, scenting the air with a heavenly perfume. Hundreds of flickering candles cast a golden light, enhancing the romantic atmosphere. Whirling couples filled the dance floor, gliding to the strains of soft music that harmonized with the breaking waves just beyond the open doors.

Dazzled, Jacy stopped to take it all in. Looking around for Aunt Helen and Poppy, she heard a deep voice behind her.

"May I have this dance?"

She turned. It was Frank Lynch. *Oh, no, not him. Anyone but him.* Flustered, she smiled, trying not to be rude. "I...but I have only just arrived."

"I know." He bowed. "I've been waiting for you. I wanted to be the first man to ask you. Please, Jacy, do me the honor of accepting my request."

She stared at him. In truth, he had never looked so fine. With his usual dapper air, he wore a black coat, a blindingly white shirt, and a black tie, carefully tailored clothing that flattered his tall, muscular physique.

Jacy pressed her lips together. He might be the most handsome man in the room, but that didn't mean she wanted to dance with him.

When she continued to look at him, saying nothing, he reached for her hand and firmly led her to the dance floor.

Suppressing a gasp, she allowed herself to be led. *Might as well go ahead and give him his dance and get it over with.* She could tolerate one.

With a grin, he took her in his arms. Trying to relax, she looked around. A lot of women were casting envious glances her way.

She had to admit Frank was a marvelous dancer. He exuded confidence and skill and she had no doubt they looked stunning together. As he twirled her around the dance floor, he didn't miss a step. In his sure arms, neither did she.

When the dance ended, he did not release her.

"Will you please do me the honor of giving me your next dance?" His smile nearly a leer.

She swallowed hard and shook her head. "No thank you, Frank." He was gripping her arm so tight it hurt. When she tried to pull away, he held her firm. She pursed her lips. "I would like to go sit down."

He continued to smile as if he had not heard her.

When the music started up again, he whisked her into the crush of dancers and pulled her closer.

Her shock turned to fury.

"Frank, please," she whispered. "Release me." She leaned her head back and glared up at him. "I said, 'No.' Did you not hear me?"

He snorted a quiet laugh. "I heard you." He whispered in her ear, "But I know you don't mean it."

"Oh, but I do," she said between clenched teeth.

He ignored her again and—gazing arrogantly into her eyes— smoothly led her across the dance floor.

She wanted to scream. He was acting for all the world like a crowned prince who always got his way: regal, extraordinarily self-assured and insufferable.

She would *not* tolerate it.

Fixing a faux smile on her face, she tried to push him away. It did not work. He was too strong; his muscular arms held her firm.

The dance was a slow one. She tried again, to no avail. He did not even miss a step.

Jacy looked wildly around. Other couples, romantically waltzing around them, seemed oblivious to her plight.

She tried to disengage her right hand from Frank's left. But the more she tried, the harder he squeezed.

Pain shot through her fingers.

His right hand was pressing on the middle of her back. It felt hot and demanding.

Feeling her face grow red, she winced.

"Jacy." She turned her head. Henry Stratton bowed and extended his hand. "May I cut in? May I have this dance?"

Thank you, Lord. Relief flooded through her. "Yes," she said, nodding eagerly. "Yes, yes, of course."

Frank still did not let her go. "Go away," Frank muttered. "Go away, Stratton." He quickly turned Jacy around and two-stepped her away from Henry.

Shocked at his audacity, she lost her balance and stumbled. He caught her and resumed dancing as if nothing had happened.

In desperation, Jacy looked around for Henry. To her relief, he did not seem deterred by Frank's rudeness. Weaving through startled couples, he caught up with them.

"Jacy wants to dance with me now," Henry said, raising his voice with each word, as if making sure Frank could hear him over the orchestra's violins. "I asked her, and she accepted."

"Too bad." Frank said, whirling Jacy away, again.

"Frank, let go of me," Jacy pleaded. "I don't want to dance with you."

She glanced back at Henry, who looked as angry as she felt.

As Frank firmly led her around the edge of the dance floor, spectators in chairs watched the action as others chatted amongst themselves.

Then she saw Cole. He was staring at her. Even from a distance, and the flickering light, she could see he was angry, too. *Bless him, he must have seen my distress and urged Henry to intervene.*

She tried to pull away from Frank again, without any success.

She gritted her teeth. She was outraged. Frank was flouting the rules. He had taken a second dance without her permission. He would not release her to dance with another man.

Fury surged through her.

It seemed her only choice was to let him get away with it or cause a scene.

She suppressed a groan.

Aunt Helen would not like it. She would probably be humiliated. Frank, however, was making it necessary for her to cause a scene.

In desperation, Jacy looked around for Henry. She finally saw him, surrounded by dancers, obviously unsure of what to do next. He likely did not want to do anything to cause her embarrassment. Nor, to embarrass his wife. It was sweet of Lydia to let him dance with another woman—one obviously in distress. Causing any kind of socially humiliating scene, however, was another matter.

When Jacy looked back at Cole, Lydia had taken a seat next to him and was leaning over and whispering in his ear. Then they both looked at her and Frank.

Frustrated at feeling so helpless, Jacy tried to stomp on Frank's foot.

He was too fast for her, however, and she missed. Throwing his head back, he laughed.

"Let go of me," she said, firmly. *"Now."*

He laughed again and kept dancing. As he directed her across the floor, he kept a dreamy, romantic smile on his face, as if he was not at all fazed by the situation.

What nerve.

"Let go of me!" she shouted.

People turned. Eyebrows shot up. The orchestra played on.

Henry hurried over, excusing himself as he weaved through

staring couples. When he finally reached Jacy, he held his hand out once again, with his palm up.

She tried to reach for it, but Frank was too quick. "No, my dear," he said, his voice steely as he twirled her away again. "This dance is mine."

Okay, it's time for a scene.

Jacy bent her knees and buckled her legs, hoping that by turning herself into dead weight, he would drop her. Falling to the floor might cause injury, but what else could she do?

Unfortunately, that ploy did not work either.

Frank just propped her up, as if she weighed nothing at all, and dragged her along like a rag doll.

Then, to Jacy's shocked surprise, Cole appeared in front of them. "Stop, Lynch," he growled.

Jacy widened her eyes. Cole was leaning forward in his wheelchair, glaring at Frank, with his hands gripping his armrests. He must have wheeled himself over to them, somehow, weaving through the whirling dancers. His face was red and he wore a furious scowl.

The music finally stopped, although Jacy wasn't sure if it was because the song had ended or for Cole's sake. All the couples stopped dancing and hurried over to stare at him, as if he was some kind of curious fish that had washed up with the tide.

Frank glared at Cole. Then, keeping a firm grip on Jacy's arm, he turned his body sideways and slammed full force into the wheelchair, sending it flying.

Jacy gasped.

Cole, amazingly, remained calm—outwardly, at least. He grabbed the wheels of his chair, slowly propelled himself over to Frank, and stared up at him.

Frank finally released his hold on Jacy. Humiliated, she ran over to Henry, terrified Frank might attempt to snatch hold of her again.

Lydia dashed over and threw her arm around Jacy's shoulder, hugging her close.

"Thank you," Jacy whispered. "Thank you."

Everyone in the room stared at Cole. As onlookers gathered

around him, he held himself erect in his chair, his body rigid as a statue. Narrowing his eyes, he glared at Frank. "The woman did not want to dance with you," he said, spitting out each word. "What did you not understand about that?"

Frank stepped toward him and looked down at him with contempt. "She is no concern of yours." He waved his hand like he was swatting away a pesky bug. "Get out of my way."

Cole did not move. "She wanted to dance with my brother."

Frank's arrogant smile twisted into a sneer. "So what. Get your pitiful body off this dance floor. It's not for cripples."

Clasping her hand over her mouth, Jacy stifled a gasp. Dashing over to Cole, she reached for his hand in a show of support and looked around at the people staring at them.

"I'm sorry. This was all just a misunderstanding, folks." She forced an apologetic smile. "Yes…that's all it was…a mix up…a mix up in communication."

Turning to Frank, she gave him a smile he did not deserve to prevent any social stigma the unfortunate episode might have on the Strattons, or her family. She made her smile as sweet and forgiving as she could manage, silently vowing to show the insufferable bully her real feelings later.

Pivoting back to the sea of faces, she took a deep breath and then let it out, acutely aware of the perspiration forming on her brow and the blood rushing to her cheeks. "You see…Mr. Lynch thought he had this dance…" She shrugged and then turned and nodded at Henry. "And Mr. Henry Sutton…thought he did…"

Jacy looked down at Cole. He raised his eyebrows, but the expression on his face was otherwise unreadable.

She noticed with a start she was still holding his hand. Flustered, she let go. "Thank you, Cole," she said softly. "I appreciate your concern and assistance."

Raising her voice, she again addressed the audience. "Ladies and gentlemen, Mr. Cole Stratton was only trying to help his brother. And me. It took courage and I admire him for it."

Then slowly, holding her head high, in as dignified a manner as she could manage, she walked over to the orchestra. Apologizing for the interruption, she asked them to resume playing.

Henry hurried over, and once again held out his hand. "Now," he said, smiling, his eyes crinkling in the corners just like his brother's. "May I have this dance?"

Jacy beamed. "Yes," she said loudly, over the music. "I would be delighted. Thank you."

When they began dancing, so did everyone else, as if nothing untoward had happened.

It was another slow song, one Jacy had never heard before.

She did not know where Frank had gone. As she tried to relax in Henry's arms, she told herself she did not care.

She looked around for Cole.

He was sitting where he had been before, next to Lydia.

When his eyes met hers, he held up a hand in an encouraging wave.

His smile warmed her heart.

CHAPTER NINE

$\mathcal{H}$elen's head hurt. She placed a cool hand on her forehead and massaged it with her fingers.

Willing herself to relax, the pounding lessened somewhat, until her rented carriage rolled over a crater in the road. Launching its occupants forward, and then back, it took several more bumps as Helen braced herself. "Lord, help us," she wailed.

"Relax Mother," Poppy said, obviously not bothered by the jostling.

Jacy, to Helen's amazement, actually smiled. Leaning forward, she peered out the open window next to her and waved to a carriage clip-clopping by in the opposite direction.

Helen sat up straighter, curious. She massaged her forehead again. "Who are you waving to, Jacy?" she asked wearily.

Jacy was sitting in the seat across from her, next to Poppy. The girls seemed to be having a grand time, but Helen was ready to go back to the hotel and retire to her room. She had enjoyed touring Cape May, but the frenetic pace the young people displayed was exhausting. God willing, Jacy and Poppy could join up with friends.

"I don't know who we just passed," Jacy said with a shrug, dashing Helen's hopes. "Everybody in Cape May waves at everybody else."

Helen sighed and glanced out the window as they turned onto

Washington Street. She stared at the shops as they passed by: Mrs. H. F. Doolittle's Ice Cream Parlor...Isaac H. Smith's Clothing Emporium...the Swiss Store, with a colorful painted sign in the window promoting an exotic offering of "Swiss Carvings, Fancy Porcelains, French Paintings on Wood, Sea Beans & Sea Shells etc."

Washington Street was where everybody who was anybody went to shop, especially when it was raining and there was little else to do. The street was crowded with carriages.

The busyness and traffic made Helen's headache worse. Leaning out her window, she called for their driver to please pull over and park.

Poppy and Jacy looked at each other.

"Where are we going, Mother?" Poppy frowned. "If we get out, won't we get wet?"

Helen opened the door and placed a booted foot on the step. "The rain has stopped and I have seen enough."

As the grizzled, gray-haired driver hurried over to take her hand and help her down, she suddenly had an idea. She turned and gave Poppy a smile. "I think we should go get some ice cream."

"What a wonderful plan," Jacy said.

It was indeed, Helen thought, until they entered the ice cream parlor. The purveyor, Mrs. Doolittle, was nowhere to be seen, but the five young men on her serving staff were hustling to and fro to wait on the sudden hoard of customers.

Since the rain had ceased, everyone in town seemed to want to celebrate with ice cream.

Helen suppressed a groan and looked around. The decor was colorful and exotic, lifting her spirits a bit. "I wonder what inspired Mrs. Doolittle to decorate the walls with elephants?" she remarked as she, Poppy, and Jacy hurried to take the last available table by the front window. Many customers waited in line at the counter, apparently willing to take their goodies with them out to the street.

Helen, however, needed to sit and was grateful to do so.

"They are Indian elephants," Jacy remarked, looking at each of the shop's three painted wall murals with admiration. She pointed to the one next to their table. "See the howdah on the elephant's back?"

"The *what*?" Poppy asked, pursing her lips.

"The howdah," Jacy said. "The giant saddle, if you will. I love its red and white stripes. And that it can fit five men…see them, all wearing red hats, squeezed together? You can't get that many men on a horse."

Helen wondered how Jacy knew such things, since her niece had never been to India. She was not surprised, though. Jacy had an exceptional degree of curiosity about the world—too much, really, for her own good.

"That still doesn't explain why Mrs. Doolittle chose elephants, of all creatures, for wall decorations," Helen said, relieved to see a server heading their way. The pain in her head was lessening already, and she was certain a cold, sweet treat would cure it altogether.

"Oh, but Cape May has an elephant," Jacy said. "Remember? The Light of Asia, on the beach between Cape May and the lighthouse…" She stopped and cupped her hand over her mouth.

Helen frowned and held Jacy's gaze. They had agreed not to talk about Jacy's morning sojourns. Helen knew it would be pointless to forbid her from going because Jacy would do as she pleased. Helen had found it best to ignore the situation. Jacy was discreet, and as far as Helen was concerned, Jacy's father need never know. Why bother Tobias with such a trivial, silly thing? If walking on the beach at dawn comforted Jacy, so be it. Unless, of course, that odious Edmund Overton did reappear one day. Then, Helen told herself, she had no idea what she would do.

The server finally got to their table and Helen ordered a large dish of chocolate ice cream. As Jacy and Poppy placed their orders, Helen smiled in anticipation of the treat and chided herself for worrying too much. Of course, Overton would never return.

Then, shockingly, she heard someone mention his name. Jacy and Poppy heard it too, because they all turned in unison to look for the source of its utterance.

It came from a plump, middle-aged woman seated at the table next to them.

She was dressed in a purple gown and a large hat with black ostrich feathers. Her companion across from her, another matron around her age, wore navy blue with an equally large feathered hat.

Helen wondered if she was mistaken. Why would such women be discussing Overton?

The tables were placed so close together it was impossible to avoid overhearing the conversation. Helen tried not to stare as she listened. She noticed Jacy and Poppy were listening, too.

"It's not such a mystery, Pamela," the woman in purple said in a whiny voice. "Edmund Overton is alive. I don't know why you don't believe it."

"Preposterous," Pamela said with a sniff. "I do not know why you *do* believe it, Addie."

"Because he is not my friend. So, I don't mind believing ill of him, my dear."

"He was not my friend, he was my sister's friend," Pamela said. "And if he was alive, she would know it."

Helen stiffened. She looked over at Jacy, whose eyes were as big as scoops of ice cream. She was staring at the women, who mercifully did not seem to notice.

Poppy reached over and placed her hand on Jacy's.

"I hear he is hiding out," Addie said. "Some people say in New York."

"Where did you hear such a thing?" Pamela frowned. Tilting her head, she regarded her friend with an expression of incredulous disbelief.

Helen knew how Pamela felt. She could not believe what she was hearing either. The server came back with Helen's three scoops of chocolate, a two-scoop vanilla and strawberry concoction for Poppy, and a single scoop of vanilla for Jacy.

Helen did not even pick up her spoon, and neither did Jacy or Poppy.

"Where is his ship, then?" Pamela wanted to know.

Addie leaned forward and whispered loudly, "No one knows."

"That is because he is likely on it," Pamela said. "At the bottom of the sea."

Helen drew in a sharp breath and glanced at Jacy.

Jacy's face had gone ghastly pale. She pushed her chair back, and stood up.

"Jacy, please," Helen said.

"Excuse me," Jacy said to the women. "I couldn't help overhearing you."

Helen shook her head at her niece. She put a finger to her lips.

Jacy, her eyes welling with tears, ignored the warning.

Addie and Pamela stared up at her.

"Yes?" Pamela said. "I'm sorry—"

"I hope you are," Jacy said. "Because Edmund Overton is my fiancé."

Helen gasped. She put her hand over her mouth.

"Jacy," Poppy whispered. "Jacy, please. Sit down. Look, your ice cream is melting…"

"What?" Jacy frowned at her. "Who cares?"

Addie and Pamela continued to stare at Jacy, their mouths agape. Neither said a word. It appeared they had no idea what to say.

Helen pushed her chair back and stood up. Someone had to say something. "I apologize for my niece," she said. Clearing her throat, she kept her voice low. "You see, she was a friend of Edmund Overton. So, when we heard his name, we were surprised. She has never gotten over his disappearance. It is very sad."

"*Fiancé?*" Addie said. "That can't be…"

"I agree," Helen said.

"Believe it." Jacy lifted her chin. "I say he is my fiancé, present tense. Not that he *was* my fiancé, in the past. Because I too believe he is still alive. But I don't believe for a minute he is hiding out."

Jacy was so upset she was almost shouting. Helen reached over and laid a hand on her niece's arm. Jacy jerked it away. Helen felt sorry for her, but she also felt sorry for herself and for her dear brother, Tobias. Was it true that Jacy and Overton had become secretly engaged? If so, it had been a well-kept secret.

"Where did you hear that he is hiding out?" Jacy asked, glaring at Addie. "I want to know."

Addie did not answer. She looked hideously embarrassed; her cheeks turned crimson as her lips set in a stern, thin line.

Helen couldn't tell if she was mortified at having been caught gossiping, or if she was angry because they had eavesdropped on her conversation.

"Pamela," Addie said, her strident, whiny voice suddenly haughty. "We are finished here. Let's go."

Pamela stood up, her eyes darting from Helen to Poppy to Jacy. "Yes, yes," she said. "I think it's best that we end this conversation." She gave Jacy a look of pity. "I am sorry, dear," she said in a loud whisper. "You must excuse my friend. She enjoys spreading stories she has heard. She only wants to entertain. She is quite harmless. Ignore her."

"*Indeed*," Addie said with a huff. Turning, she headed for the door, shoving dollar bills into the server's hands on her way out. Pamela followed, keeping her head down, clearly humiliated. Cape May was, after all, a small town.

Exasperated, Helen knew how she felt. All too well.

Jacy sat back down and stared into her bowl.

Helen sat down, too, and picked up her spoon. Her ice cream looked like brown soup. She ate it anyway. At least she no longer had a headache. For that at least, she was grateful.

In silence, Helen glanced over at Poppy. She was spooning goopy pink ice cream into her mouth.

Helen shifted her gaze to Jacy. She was not eating. Sitting motionless, she was just staring into her bowl.

* * *

Cole was glad to see the sky clearing in time for the arrival of the steamship, *Republic*. The magnificent three-deck iron vessel, with its festive, holiday-like atmosphere, carried passengers daily from Philadelphia to Cape May Point and was scheduled to dock at the pier at 3 p.m.

Cole's primary physician, Dr. Albert Morris, was aboard. The doctor had planned a one-week visit to Cape May to see some of his patients, including Cole. The Strattons had secured him a room at White Caps, and Cole, Henry and Samuel arranged to fetch him in a rented carriage.

Cole smiled as he watched the luxury side-wheel steamer glide up to the dock. The *Republic* always made him smile. The ship, which could carry up to three thousand people, was the most popular way to travel to the seaside resort, and for good reason. Departing in the morning from a wharf in Philadelphia, it docked in midafternoon on the Delaware Bay side of Cape May Point. Breakfast, lunch and supper were served in its dining saloon, and bands serenaded passengers as they sailed down the Delaware River.

In nice weather, many people liked to sit out on the open deck, cooled by river breezes as they relaxed and watched the farms and woodlands roll by.

Since it had rained most of the day, Cole figured Dr. Morris and his fellow passengers likely had been confined indoors. How nice for them that the sun was finally peaking through the clouds.

Cole's wheelchair was too large to fit in the four-seat carriage. So, when they pulled up in time to see the *Republic* dock, he and Samuel stayed put as Henry and the young, sandy-haired driver went to fetch the doctor and his trunk.

"Here they come," Samuel said, peering out the window at the mobs of people streaming off the ship.

Cole looked where Samuel was pointing. Henry and the driver were carting the doctor's trunk down the gangway as the doctor, walking beside them, lugged his big, black medical bag.

"I hope Dr. Morris is pleased with my progress, because I'm not," Cole muttered as he watched them hurry over to the carriage.

After helping Henry set the trunk on the ground, the driver grabbed the reins of the two horses, which he had fastened to a wooden post, and then climbed up onto his seat.

Samuel swung open the carriage door, climbed out, and hurried around to the rear to help Henry secure the trunk onto the back.

Dr. Morris climbed in and took the seat next to Cole.

"Good to see you, my son," Dr. Morris said with a nod, a concerned expression creasing his always-serious face. Dr. Morris had been treating Cole since he was a child. Cole could not remember a time when the doctor did not look seriously concerned about his health.

The white-haired physician wore the same expression with all his patients. Short, with a closely cropped goatee and intense, intelligent eyes, he made house calls. He had visited every member of the Stratton family through the years and had a well-deserved reputation as one of Philadelphia's best.

Cole, however, did not find his doctor's ever-present, grave expression reassuring. Instead, it always made him uneasy.

"It is always good to see you, Doctor," Cole said politely, as Henry and Samuel climbed into the carriage and sat down across from them. "I hope when you examine me, you can tell me I am on the mend."

Dr. Morris studied Cole's face as the driver guided the horses onto Sunset Boulevard, the road leading to downtown Cape May. They eased into a line of carriages going in that direction. "You look tanned, not ghastly pale like the last time I saw you," the doctor said. "But I don't know if that means you are actually getting better. How do you feel?"

Cole frowned. "Frustrated."

"Frustrated?"

"Yes. I want to walk."

"His coughing has subsided a lot," Henry said. "But he is restless. There are too many pretty ladies in this town. And I think he feels left out of all the fun."

"Henry," Cole said, exasperated. "I want to get better. It is as simple as that."

Dr. Morris looked out the window, cleared his throat and turned back to Cole. "Restlessness..." he said. "That could be a good sign. When we get to the hotel, I will do a full examination. I need to listen to your heart and lungs."

"I need to get out of my wheelchair," Cole said, meeting his gaze. "I am weak because I don't get any exercise. That can't be good for my heart, or my lungs."

The doctor frowned. "Now, now, let's not overtax yourself. It could set you back."

"He been swimming in the ocean," Samuel said.

"What?" Dr. Morris' eyes widened. "That could—"

"Not actually swimming, more like floating," Cole said, shooting Samuel a warning look.

Dr. Morris shook his head. "I did not prescribe that. You could take a chill. You could have a relapse. It could be fatal."

Cole took a deep breath and let it out slowly. "I need to stand up. I need to walk. Can you prescribe that?"

Dr. Morris patted Cole's thigh. Cole winced. It didn't hurt, but he knew what the esteemed physician would say.

"Your muscles feel very weak, Cole. You need to take it easy awhile. You came here for the sea air. To allow the fresh breezes to heal your lungs. I think since you are not coughing much anymore, that is a very good sign."

Cole nodded and then raked his fingers through his hair. "Yes, I believe it is a good sign that I'm not coughing as much. But now, I need to do more. Or I will continue to stay weak."

"Perhaps in a month." Dr. Morris looked at Henry, whose expression of concern matched the doctor's. "It is only the end of June. Perhaps by the end of July, you can try standing."

Cole grimaced. "What? No. I do not want to wait that long."

"You might fall," Henry said. "What then? You might break a leg. That would only add to your troubles."

"I will take my chances."

"How?" Dr. Morris stared at him. "How will you stand up?"

"With Samuel's help. And my brother's." Cole looked at Henry. "Right?"

"I don't know." Henry shook his head. "I want to do the right thing. And if the doctor says…"

Dr. Morris leaned toward Cole. "We can discuss all this later. But I do have some happy news for you, my boy."

Cole looked at him. "Oh?"

"Yes. Miss Priscilla Day sends her greetings. I paid a visit to Priscilla's mother about a week ago, and when Priscilla heard I was planning to visit Cape May, she told me to tell you hello."

Cole rolled his eyes, then caught himself. He tried to keep his voice neutral, so as not to sound rude. "She did, did she? That's nice."

"I know the two of you were an item once," Dr. Morris said. "Basically, almost engaged?"

Cole stared at the window. Carriages were passing them, going in the opposite direction, hurrying to pick up *Republic* passengers. "Yes, I guess you could say we were almost engaged. But I got the message she was not interested in pledging herself to a sick man."

"Cole…" Henry said, frowning.

"Which I respected," Cole continued, feeling an urge to let the doctor know where he stood. "I respected Priscilla's dislike of illness. She is a woman deathly afraid of it. So afraid that she refused to visit me. After a month went by, I wrote her a letter and released her from our relationship. I wanted her to feel free to see other men."

"I delivered the letter," Samuel said. "Handed it to her maid, Mavis Allen."

Cole gave his orderly a knowing grin. Samuel was sweet on Mavis. He had been devastated when Cole broke it off with her employer and had taken it a lot harder than Cole.

"Did you see Mavis, Doctor?" Samuel leaned forward. "When you went and saw Miss Day's mama last week?"

Dr. Morris nodded. "Yes. Mavis was there. Why?"

"How she look?"

The doctor shrugged. "Fine. Just fine."

"I miss her," Samuel whispered.

"I'm sorry, Samuel," Cole said.

After several moments of silence, Cole cleared his throat and looked at the doctor. It was time to get back to the unfortunate subject of his health. "I plan to continue ocean bathing," he said, striving not to sound too defiant. "Samuel and Henry don't carry me out very deep. I only paddle around a little. It feels good to move my legs."

Dr. Morris drew his brows together and stared into Cole's eyes. "As I told you, that is *not* a good idea. The water is far too cold this early in the season. I must forbid it."

Cole ran a hand down his face in frustration. He squeezed his thighs. They felt like they were all bone. "I don't know if I can follow your orders, Doctor," he said. "My situation is too dire."

CHAPTER TEN

"Come on, Poppy, let's go for a swim in the ocean." Jacy opened the door to her armoire, grabbed her bathing costume—dress, tights, shoes and cap—and threw them onto her bed. She had not been able to get the rumor about Edmund out of her mind. She needed a physical diversion. Swimming would be the perfect thing.

Lifting her arms high in anticipation, she twirled around, grinned, and looked at her cousin. "After all that rain yesterday, you would think it would have cooled down some. But it's hot as Hades."

Curled up on her bed, reading her favorite book of poetry, Poppy raised her eyes and looked at Jacy. "I'm not hot. A nice breeze is blowing in the window. The ocean is cooling me just fine right where I am."

Jacy sighed. "Poppy…"

Poppy snapped her book shut and stood up. "Okay, I will go. But you know I don't swim. I bathe. I shall only wade out as far as my knees."

Jacy laughed, relieved her cousin had been so easily persuaded. "It's fine with me if you don't go out far. I'm just glad I don't have to go alone."

"Mother would not let you go alone." Poppy walked over to her armoire and pulled out her bathing costume. Her black, ankle-length dress was almost identical to Jacy's. "Alright, let's get ready. But promise me, Jacy, promise me you will stay close to shore. Don't leave me all alone in Neptune's embrace."

Jacy laughed again. "Don't worry. Frank Lynch will be happy to rescue you, if you need rescuing." Sitting down on her bed, Jacy yanked off her boots. "More than happy."

"That's what worries me," Poppy said. "Horrors."

* * *

WHEN JACY and Poppy got down to the beach, Jacy felt hotter than ever in her long, wool dress and tights.

Aunt Helen was waiting for them by the water's edge, wearing a white gown, holding a parasol over her head.

Frank Lynch was on duty. He waved to Jacy, but she did not wave back.

She was distracted by the sight of Cole Stratton's empty wheel-chair at the shoreline. Confused, Jacy looked out at the ocean. Cole was floating on his back in shallow water, with Samuel on one side of him and Henry on the other. Moving his arms and kicking his feet, Cole had a look of determination that made Jacy smile.

Bravo. Good for him.

Cole turned his head and saw Jacy looking at him.

Jacy smiled and waved. Cole flashed her a big grin. She realized he would have waved back if he could have done so without accidentally flipping over. He seemed to be using every bit of energy he had just to stay afloat.

"Well, I never..." Aunt Helen frowned. "Where is Mr. Stratton's doctor? Should he be doing that?"

Poppy nodded. "I was thinking that as well."

"I think it's marvelous." Jacy turned to Poppy. "I'm going in the water. Coming with me?"

"I don't know..."

"Don't go out far," Aunt Helen said, gripping her parasol. "Stay together."

Jacy looked at the sun-sparkled waves. Women, in groups of two and three, were fanny dipping. Men, some in groups and some swimming alone, watched with obvious delight.

Two young women, holding hands, tittered loudly that they needed help.

Frank Lynch dashed in and gallantly led them safely to shore.

Jacy sighed. She yearned to do some actual swimming. She noticed Lydia Stratton, standing knee deep and alone and suggested Poppy join her.

"Alright," Poppy said reluctantly. "But be careful, Jacy. Don't do anything rash."

Jacy grinned. "I won't." Wading in deeper, she dove under a swell and then surfaced, giddy with joy. The water was refreshingly cold.

She swam past all the men. When she got out beyond the breakers, she paddled in place. Then, silently counting to herself, she swam ten strokes north and turned around and swam ten strokes south.

The undertow was a bit strong, but it didn't bother her. She had confidence in her skills.

With a happy sigh, Jacy paddled in place again and looked at the crowd of bathers between her and the shore. She wondered if Cole was still in the water. Glancing around, she saw him and froze. He had floated out deeper, and Henry and Samuel were struggling to reach him.

A large wave formed. Alarmed, Jacy realized Henry and Samuel would not be able to get to Cole before it reached him. She watched in horror as the swell lifted him up and then carried him farther out.

Jacy gasped.

"Cole!" Henry shouted.

"I'll grab him!" Jacy yelled. Floating face up, Cole appeared panicked, thrashing his arms. He was not too far from her. Jacy launched herself toward him, but her heavy costume slowed her down.

Another wave pushed Cole past her, just beyond her grasp. "Jacy!" he shouted.

"Hold on!" she cried.

Another wave lifted him up and pushed him even farther out. Cole began to cough. Jacy tried not to panic. What if he inhaled water into his lungs? What if he started to sink?

She reached down and yanked off her bathing slippers.

Keeping Cole in sight, she reached under her skirt and peeled off her tights.

Then she untied her cap and pulled it off her head.

Freed of some of her constrictive clothing, she swam toward Cole. A wave rolled over him and he disappeared. A moment later, he reappeared, gagging. Hacking and spitting water, he looked at her with fear in his eyes.

Paddling furiously, Jacy splashed up to him and managed to grab hold of one of his hands. "I have you," she gasped.

He groaned.

"Stay on your back, hold on, and I'll swim you to shore."

He moaned and rasped, "Wouldn't think of letting go."

When they got closer to the beach, Frank Lynch swam out to meet them. Signaling to Jacy that he would take Cole from her, she let go and watched Frank take him in the rest of the way.

When Frank reached shallow water, he picked Cole up and carried him onto the sand.

Cole lay face up, staring at the sky, as Jacy stumbled over to him. Barefoot, with her hair hanging in her face and her dress plastered to her body, she remembered how it felt after Frank Lynch had rescued her. It was humiliating.

Kneeling beside Cole, she gave him an encouraging smile. "I'm so glad you are okay. That was scary, but I admire your courage."

Henry and Samuel ran up. Lydia and Poppy did, too, joined a moment later by Aunt Helen and a great many other people.

Cole gave Jacy a wan smile. He lifted a hand and then lowered it back onto the sand. "I was just trying to get some exercise. Strengthen my arms, my legs." His words came out in a croak. His black tank top was plastered to his chest, and he was so thin Jacy could see his ribs through the material as he struggled to take deep breaths.

Cole closed his eyes and then opened them again. A corner of his mouth turned up in a grin. "My doctor advised against ocean bathing, Jacy… I just didn't listen."

Jacy grabbed his hand. She returned his smile. "Nor should you, Cole."

"What?" He stared at her.

"Exercise is what you need to recreate yourself," she said. "And from what I've seen, you have what it takes. Swimming is wonderful exercise. You need to do more." She squeezed his hand. "Once you learn how to do it better, that is."

"Really…" Cole held her gaze. "And who will teach me?"

Jacy grinned. She felt more excited about life than she had in a long time.

"I will, Cole," she whispered. "I will."

PART II

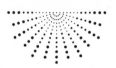

JULY

*T*he next morning, when Jacy returned from her hike to the lighthouse, she looked for the Strattons in the White Caps dining room. She had told Poppy she would not be joining her or Aunt Helen for breakfast, like she usually did, because she wanted to discuss swim lessons with Cole.

"That poor man," Poppy had said. "I was horrified when he almost drowned, and so was Mother. She said she was glad you were able to help save him, despite the impropriety of your actions." Poppy made a face. "But removing some of your clothing and such..." Poppy winced. "All Mother could manage to say about that was, 'well, at least the pitiful soul didn't die.'"

"Indeed."

"But..." Poppy wasn't finished. "I must tell you that Mother is totally against you giving swim lessons. To anyone, especially a man. She overheard what you told Cole—and she is *aghast* at the idea. Says it is most improper. That if Cole wants to learn to swim, he should hire Frank Lynch to be his teacher."

Jacy chuckled. "I'm pretty sure, Poppy dear, that Cole would rather drown than take lessons from Frank."

Jacy confirmed her assumption when she took a seat next to Cole at the Stratton's table. Cole, Henry and Lydia welcomed her with beaming smiles and introduced their new acquaintances, Louis and Ursula Barker, an elderly couple who had checked into the hotel the evening before.

Cole looked none the worse for his ordeal the previous afternoon. In fact, he exuded good cheer. He had obviously just come from the hotel barber. His sun-bleached hair was cropped nicely around his ears, and there was a sparkle in his blue-gray eyes, which looked bluer than usual with his tan.

"My doctor absolutely forbids me from going swimming," he told Jacy with a mischievous grin. "But I told him I plan to do so anyway. I told him that a beautiful woman has offered me swimming lessons. And so, how can I refuse?"

Henry, who was sitting on the other side of Jacy, leaned around her and glared at his brother. "Lydia and I suggested Cole take lessons from a lifeguard, perhaps in a few weeks, when his health improves. Lynch isn't the only one who offers them." Henry cleared his throat. "But Cole insists on starting today." He looked at Jacy. "With you."

Jacy felt herself blush. "Good. I'm very glad."

"Lynch offered lessons—for a price, of course," Cole said. "But I turned him down. Not because I can't afford his fees. But because I can't stand the man."

"Now, now," chided Lydia, who was sitting on the other side of Henry. "He did, after all, help save your life."

"He just helped," Cole said. "Jacy was the one who saved me."

A waiter came over, poured coffee, and then took everyone's orders.

Louis Barker looked across the table at Cole and then at Jacy. Almost completely bald, he had a twinkle in his eye and a kind smile that peeked through his bushy, gray beard. "Young lady," he said in a loud voice, "did this young man just say that you rescued him yesterday? From the *ocean*?"

Jacy nodded.

"Incredible," he said, widening his grin. "This summer is going to be more interesting than I had anticipated."

His wife did not seem as amused. Placing a hand on her husband's arm, she gave him a scolding look. "Really, dear." She sniffed. "I find it difficult to believe a woman would even find herself in a position to rescue anyone in the ocean. Women should be discreet while bathing, not draw attention to themselves."

Jacy smiled. "I need to introduce you to my Aunt Helen. I believe the two of you would hit it off fabulously."

Cole laughed as the waiter arrived with their food. "Let's eat," he said. "We don't want to spend the entire day in this dining room. We need to get out onto the beach."

"I agree," Henry said. He turned to Jacy. "Lydia and I have told Cole that we approve of him taking lessons from you, although we are quite apprehensive about it. We would rather he wait a few weeks to go in the water again, as his doctor advises." Henry gave Cole a pained smile and then turned back to Jacy. "I know my brother well enough, however, not to argue with him. When he sets his mind to do something, there is no holding him back. Might as well not even try."

Jacy smiled at Cole. "There is no holding me back either when I am determined to do something. I believe you and I will make a good team."

* * *

"WHY ARE YOU DOING THIS?" Henry asked Cole after he had wheeled him back to his room so he could get ready for the beach.

Closing the door firmly behind them, Henry pushed Cole's wheelchair over to his bed and stared at him. "Why are you insisting on going swimming today? *Today?*"

Cole felt a flash of annoyance. They had talked about it, and he had thought the matter was settled. It was, as far as he was concerned. He told Henry so. "Just help me put my swim trunks on," he muttered. "They're over there, on that wooden rack by the open window." He pointed. "Must be dry by now."

Henry ignored him and sat down on Cole's bed. Raking his fingers through his hair, he also ignored Cole's frown. "I know I have given you my blessing regarding Jacy teaching you to swim." he said, "but I don't like it. Going against doctor's orders makes me uneasy."

Cole met his gaze. "It shouldn't. Relax. When Dr. Morris examined me, he said my heart is strong. My lungs sound clear. Which is great news. The only thing wrong with me is that I am weak."

"I'm afraid you might get pneumonia again."

Cole frowned. "I don't think I will. And I am willing to take the chance."

Henry pushed himself off the bed and slowly walked over to the rack. Picking up Cole's swim trunks and tank top, he held them out in front of him. "They're dry." He didn't move. He stared at Cole with an odd look in his eye as Cole stared back at him. "I think you are attracted to Jacy," he said. "I think that's the real reason you are doing this."

Cole sucked in his breath. He laughed. Even to his own ears, his laughter was a little too long and a little too loud. "I am attracted to her," he admitted. "What man isn't?"

"But I've heard rumors." Henry wasn't laughing. He looked at Cole with pity. "Rumors about a ghost who Jacy happens to be in love with. I bet you have heard them, too."

Shocked, Cole looked at Henry and then looked away. When Jacy had confided in him about Edmund Overton, she had asked him not to tell anyone, and he had kept his promise. What did Henry know, and how did he know it? "What rumors?" Cole whispered.

Henry walked over to Cole. Leaning over him, he looked him straight in the eye. He dropped the swim clothes in Cole's lap. Taken aback, Cole frowned. His normally easygoing brother looked upset.

"Don't play ignorant with me," Henry said. "From what I've heard, Jacy walks to the lighthouse every morning. To look for a lost sea captain. A man who was once her beau."

Cole stared up at him. "Where did you hear that?"

"It's all over town. Rumors. Whispered talk. Edmund Overton is his name. Disappeared months ago, along with his ship." Henry narrowed his eyes and looked at Cole suspiciously. "Like you didn't know."

"Jacy would be devastated if she knew."

"So, you do know."

"Well…" Cole took a deep breath and let it out slowly. "Well…yes… Jacy told me in confidence. Please keep this to yourself."

Henry widened his eyes and nodded.

Cole stared at his brother as the silence between them grew awkward. "Could you please just help me get my swim trunks on?" he finally asked, trying not to sound as exasperated as he felt. "I would dress myself if I could. The day when I can finally put my own clothes on can't come soon enough."

Henry didn't move, except to put his hands on his hips. "You are falling for Jacy. Which is not a good idea."

Cole groaned. He shook his head. "No. I am not falling for her. I am attracted to her, you are right about that. She is the prettiest, most fascinating woman I have ever met. But I am not falling for her. She is in love with another man and I am not a fool. She could never love an invalid like me."

Henry raised his eyebrows. "Then why has she offered to give you swim lessons? There is something between the two of you. It's obvious."

Cole pushed down on the seat of his chair. Did he have the arm strength to propel himself onto his bed, only inches away? If so, maybe he could dress himself.

He suppressed the urge. He would probably just get hurt.

Gritting his teeth, he said, "Jacy has offered to help me because she is a nice person, Henry. She is kind. She is thoughtful. That is all there is to it. You are imagining the rest."

"You will end up with a broken heart, Cole. To add to your problems."

Cole lifted his eyes and looked at his brother. "Sit down, Henry," he said. "And I will tell you why I am really doing this—if you really want to know."

"I *do*." Henry sat. "Enlighten me."

Cole let out a loud sigh. "I want to help Jacy. She wants to help me. So, by allowing her to help me, I will also be able to help her."

"*What?*"

"Heal. I will be able to help her heal." Cole turned and stared out the window. Hearing the roar of the surf, he smiled. "Jacy is suffering —emotionally. As much as I am suffering, physically. She needs to get her mind off Overton. She needs to recover from her grief. The way I look at it, what better way is there to help her than to give her a project? A worthy project. Me."

Henry shook his head. He stared at Cole with his mouth open. "You are unbelievable."

Cole grinned. "Jacy told me the real reason she came to Cape May was to search for Overton. The man is probably dead. Deep down, I think she knows it. In the meantime, she needs something to do. Other than shallow socializing, that is. Something that involves a worthy purpose. I am going to give her that purpose."

Henry shook his head again. "Amazing. And I think you actually believe it."

A knock on the door between the brother's rooms startled them both.

"Henry," Lydia called. "Are you still in there with Cole? Is he ready?"

"Yes, dear," Henry called back. He stood up, reached for the swim trunks in Cole's lap, and threw them onto a chair next to the bed. "Just give us a few more moments."

Henry went over to Cole. Grabbing him under his armpits, he lifted him up, swiveled, and lowered him down onto the bed. "Let's get you dressed, and quickly."

Cole grinned. "Finally."

Henry did not return his grin. "I have another concern, in light of all this…"

Cole groaned. "Now what?"

Henry stared at him. "What if Overton sails back into Cape May one day? Very much alive."

Cole widened his eyes and chuckled. "I don't believe it will happen. But if it did—it would make Jacy very, very happy."

"Yes," Henry said. "I'm sure it would. But what would it do to you? I think it would be the end of your swim lessons."

* * *

"Fantastic, Cole! You are doing great! Kick your feet more, move your arms..." Jacy watched her student bob up and down in shallow seawater as she stood knee-deep next to him.

Henry and Samuel hovered nearby, in case they were needed.

Cole had attracted an audience. Jacy was surprised so many people were interested in watching him take his first swim lesson. At the water's edge stood Frank Lynch and about a dozen onlookers, including Aunt Helen.

Jacy hoped Cole impressed everyone with his courage and determination. She had expected he would do well, but after only a few minutes of instruction, he was exceeding even her expectations.

Kicking his feet vigorously, he reached his arms behind his head and swam a short distance doing a slow backstroke. Breathing rhythmically, with his eyes closed, he was obviously concentrating all his efforts on doing it correctly while staying afloat.

"Good, very good." Jacy clapped her hands. "Keep going, keep going."

Cole kicked harder and paddled faster.

Then he opened his eyes, met Jacy's gaze with a grin, and with one hand attempted to splash her in the face.

He did not quite succeed—wetting only her already-soaked bathing dress—but Jacy was delighted he even had the energy to try such a prank.

"Very funny, sir," she said, splashing him lightly in return. "You are an exceptional student. Do you want to keep going?"

"You are a wonderful teacher. But I don't know..."

Jacy flashed Cole an encouraging grin. He was not coughing, and he seemed downright cheerful. Suspecting he could do more, she said, "Let's get you turned over for some freestyle strokes."

"Okay," Cole said. "I guess I can do that."

Henry dashed over, shaking his head. "He will have to put his face in the water. What if he accidentally—"

"Breathes some in? He won't." Jacy looked at Henry, then at Samuel. "Not with the three of us helping him. Samuel, please get on one side of Cole. Henry, please get on the other. Stay close and follow him."

She looked down at Cole and demonstrated alternating arm strokes. "All you have to do is turn your head from side to side to breathe. If, at any time, you look like you are having problems I will give the signal to flip you onto your back. Okay?"

"Okay." Cole splashed water at Jacy again. He looked nervous. "Jacy, I know you have faith that I can do this. But I'm not sure I believe I can."

She met his gaze and held it. "If you don't believe you are ready, we don't have to go on. We can stop for now."

He was floating on his back, bobbing up and down to the movement of small waves, with a look in his eyes that simultaneously registered vulnerability and bravery. "If you believe in me, I believe in me," he declared. "I'm ready. Let's go."

"Good." Giving her assistants a nod, Jacy positioned herself at the top of Cole's head. "On the count of three, Henry and Samuel will flip you over. Ready? One, two, three."

Face down, Cole kicked his feet and moved his arms. He turned his head to the right, took a breath, put his face back in the water to exhale, then turned his head to the left and took a breath.

Watching, Jacy realized she was holding her own breath. She willed herself to relax.

Cole was moving his body through the water. He was swimming.

On shore, she saw additional spectators gathering. Frank Lynch, with his arms folded across his chest, watched with a frown. Aunt Helen, her face partially obscured by the shade of her wide-brimmed hat, had a hand over her mouth. The Barkers stood next to her. Ursula's lips were set in a grim line. But her husband was grinning from ear to ear. "Wonderful!" Louis Barker shouted. "Wonderful show!"

Jacy waved to Louis Barker and then felt water splash into her face. Startled, she looked down at Cole. He was swimming with so much enthusiasm that he was getting her wet without meaning to. Not only was he breathing correctly, he was moving faster than she could have thought possible. Hoisting her skirt, she ran against the current to keep up with him.

Samuel and Henry were splashing through the water to keep up with him, too.

"Wow," Jacy said, panting. Beaming, she met Henry's eyes. "Your brother is a natural."

Henry laughed. "We took lessons as children. Cole was a fair swimmer before he got sick. Never thought he would be well enough to swim this summer, though. Now he can. Thank you."

Jacy smiled, feeling a warm rush of pride. Her actions were helping someone else. The self-pity that had plagued her since Edmund's disappearance had lifted, even if only for a little while. She was doing something worthwhile with her time. What did it matter if the sight of a woman giving swim lessons to a man shocked some people? So what if it wasn't socially acceptable in many people's eyes?

Oh well.

No doubt, she would have to endure a lecture from Aunt Helen. Her aunt would probably send her brother, Tobias, a postcard to warn him that his daughter's summer was not unfolding as he had hoped.

So what? Jacy mused. So far, the season was going far better than she had dared to hope. Edmund was still among the missing, but she was getting on with her life.

Jacy watched Cole swim north at a slow pace, one deliberate stroke at a time. "Henry," she called. "Cole deserves a lot of credit for being so brave. I am gratified."

"Yes," Henry said, nodding. "I am suddenly feeling much better about this."

"He is making encouraging progress," Jacy said. "But now we need to do more."

"More?" Henry frowned and looked at Samuel.

"More?" Samuel said, squinting at Jacy.

""More." Jacy gave both men a knowing grin. "We need to get Cole up and walking."

* * *

AFTER SWIMMING FOR ABOUT AN HOUR, Cole returned to his room, exhausted. Henry helped him get into dry clothes and then into bed, so he could take a much-needed nap.

He was too keyed up to sleep, however. Spread-eagled on his back, staring up at the ceiling, he could not get images of Jacy out of his mind. He kept thinking about how she had looked—standing in the ocean, smiling down at him, encouraging him to "kick, kick, kick, paddle, paddle, paddle."

Cole smiled. For the first time in months, he felt good about his life. *Hell, I feel more than good, I feel great.*

"Amazing what a woman can do to lift one's spirits," Henry remarked from his chair next to the bed. "I can tell by the expression on your face, Cole, that you are feeling quite proud of yourself."

Cole grunted in agreement. "I am. I'm proud of what I accomplished today. And I have Jacy to thank."

"You feeling chilled?"

"Nope."

"Feeling okay?"

"Yep."

"Glad to hear it. Because Jacy has a plan."

Cole opened his eyes. He rolled his head and looked at Henry. "Really? What?"

"She wants to get you standing. Wants to help you walk."

Cole widened his eyes. "Oh."

"What do you think?"

Cole wanted to tell Henry he thought Jacy was an amazing woman. He did not, although his heart beat faster just thinking about her. The idea of standing up for the first time in months got his heart racing, too.

"Jacy didn't tell me she had that in mind," Cole whispered. "Yes, yes. I like it."

"She told me. And I'm not so sure…" Henry rubbed his chin. "Might be too much, too soon."

Cole closed his eyes again. Too tired to even move, he could not think about walking. He needed a nap, a long one.

"If she wants to help me walk, I'm ready," Cole mumbled. "I can do it…I will try…"

"For her sake?" Henry asked.

"Yes," Cole said, feeling himself drifting off. "Right now I need to rest. But yes…I am ready to try—for her sake."

CHAPTER TWELVE

$\mathcal{C}$ole woke up several hours later, flat on his back, still feeling drained.

Opening his eyes, he stared up at the ceiling and tried to move his legs. It wasn't easy. He had about as much energy as a giant clump of seaweed that had washed ashore. Deciding to stay in bed for the rest of the day, he asked Henry to bring his meals to his room.

The following morning, sitting up in bed was still a struggle, but not as much.

Most of the muscles in his body had become weak from disuse, he told himself—so, *don't get discouraged. The more I exercise, the stronger I will become.*

He would start again soon—take Jacy up on her offer to help him stand and eventually walk.

The door to the adjacent room opened and Henry strolled in. "Good morning, Cole. How are you faring today?"

Cole smiled. "Better than yesterday."

"That's good to know."

"How is Jacy? Is she worried about me?"

"No. I told her you are fine. Just resting."

"That's good." Cole swung his body around and dangled his feet off the bed. "I want to write Jacy a note." He pointed to the small desk just beyond his reach. "Could you hand me some paper and a pen?"

"Sure." Henry opened the top drawer and found what Cole had requested. Lifting an eyebrow, he asked, "What are you going to write?"

"I want to formally thank her for the swim lesson, assure her I am getting stronger, and ask her to help me stand up tomorrow."

"*Tomorrow?*"

"Yes, tomorrow. And of course, I will need you and Samuel to help me, too."

Henry's eyes narrowed. "Why tomorrow?"

Cole grinned. "It's the Fourth of July."

"So?"

"Otherwise known as Independence Day."

"So?"

"So, I plan to make the day my own personal Independence Day."

A knowing look appeared in Henry's eyes. "I see. You plan to declare your independence from...?"

"From illness. From weakness. I want to stand up. If I can stand, for even a moment, with you and Samuel helping me, that will be a start."

* * *

"Are you ready, Cole?" Jacy's big, green eyes sparkled with enthusiasm. "Are you sure you want to try this?"

"More than ready," Cole said, meeting her gaze. "I am going to stand up. With my brother holding me on one side, and my orderly on the other—I will do it."

"We just gotta make sure we don't drop you," Samuel muttered.

"Right," Henry said.

"Just put as much pressure on your legs as you can—don't worry if it's not much." Jacy gave Cole an encouraging smile. "If we do this every day, you should improve. Slowly, perhaps. But slow is okay."

Cole liked the way Jacy said, "we." He raised his chin and smiled back. "I will improve," he said, "but I don't intend to be slow about it."

Independence Day had dawned bright and clear. They had gathered on the beach, in soft sand, just in case Cole fell. It seemed the safest place.

Dr. Morris had advised against it, of course. The doctor had gone back to Philadelphia, giving Cole one final and very stern warning before he left.

"No more swimming, my son," he had said while examining Cole. Furious, the sage physician did not even try to conceal his anger as he placed his stethoscope on Cole's chest. "Heart sounds strong—amazingly," he muttered. "Lungs are clear. Also good."

Then, with a dark frown, he had added, "But you ignored my instructions, Cole. I warned you not to go into the chilly ocean. So, what happened? Doing so put you back in bed for two days." Glaring at Henry, who was standing over by the window, he tucked his stethoscope back into his medical bag, hoisted the bulging satchel off the bed, and headed for the door. "Heed my advice," he had said, "both of you. Cole is a sick man. He has no business pretending otherwise. He is here for the sea air. He must be satisfied with that."

Yanking the door open, the physician turned around and added, "I will give a full report to your father, Cole. He is most anxious to hear how you are doing. I will return in a few weeks. Hopefully you will have improved—"

"Wait," Cole said. "But what about walking? I want to walk again."

"Patience," Dr. Morris said with a parting frown. "All in good time, my son. All in good time."

Cole smiled as he remembered the doctor's words. All in good time? He looked at Jacy's eager face and knew. *This is it—this is my time.*

"How are we going to do this, Jacy?" Henry asked.

"It's fairly simple," Jacy said. "Henry, you grab Cole under his right arm. And Samuel, you grab him under his left. I will count to three. Then Cole, when I get to three, stand up as they lift you."

Cole nodded. A surge of energy shot through him. "Okay…let's try it."

Everyone got into position. Jacy planted herself in front of the threesome. "Alright," she shouted with a wide grin. "One… two…three."

She raised her arms on "three," Henry and Samuel pulled Cole up on "three"—and Cole stood on "three."

Shaking all over, Cole pressed his feet into the sand. They felt solid against the earth. He was doing it. As difficult as it was, he was *standing*.

One second went by…two…three…four…five…

Cole knew Henry and Samuel were holding him up, but he was also using some of his own muscle power to stay up. It felt fantastic.

Clenching his jaw, Cole looked at Jacy. She was beaming. Her sunny, encouraging smile gave him more strength than he knew he had. Finally, after about a minute, he was not sure because time seemed to stop, he felt his knees buckle.

Henry and Samuel, sensing Cole had reached the limit of his endurance, slowly lowered him back into his chair.

"Congratulations, Brother, you did great," Henry said, patting Cole's shoulder.

"Proud of you, Mister Cole," Samuel said.

Jacy hurried over. For a heart-stopping moment, Cole thought she might lean down and hug him. She looked like she wanted to. He wanted her to.

She refrained. With a shy smile, she gleefully clapped her hands instead.

"Happy Fourth of July, my friend," she said. "You are well on your way to restored health. I knew you could stand. Next, you will walk."

* * *

FRANK TAPPED his foot to the strains of *Yankee Doodle*, caught up— along with the rest of Cape May—in patriotic fervor as Simon

Hassler's Orchestra and The Weccacoe Band entertained guests on the White Caps lawn.

Independence Day was the summer city's favorite holiday, and Frank's as well. Locals celebrated it in grand style with picnics, music from morning to night, and parades up and down the boardwalk.

Fireworks accompanied by jaunty patriotic tunes capped the holiday, illuminating the inky sky with showers of popping color. This was always Frank's favorite part.

Enjoying the show even more than usual, he smiled to himself. *It's probably because of the company I'm keeping.*

Leaning forward, he snuck a sideways glance at the woman on the other side of the woman next to him. He grinned like a silly schoolboy. Bursts of light from the heavens lit her face—and to his delight, her expression was pure joy. It was wonderful to see Jacy looking so happy and carefree.

Frank quickly looked away. He did not want Jacy to catch him ogling her. He had learned his lesson. He needed to be more subtle in his admiration. She was a woman who required careful handling.

He had heard rumors Jacy was in love with a missing sea captain, which explained why she had not yet succumbed to his handsome, heroic charms. He found it comforting that she was in love with a man who was likely dead, whose body was decomposing at the bottom of the deep blue sea. It meant that, sooner or later, she would come to her senses and see him for the catch he was.

In the meantime, unlike most women he had courted, she did not like obvious signs of adoration. Which was fine with him. It made pursuing her more fun. To his surprise, he found he liked the game. What did it matter if Jacy was a challenge? He loved to be challenged. That was why he did not rush to sit next to her at the concert and fireworks. It would have spooked her. That was why he had rushed to sit next to her aunt, instead.

Helen Bainbridge liked him, he could tell. She considered him an extremely eligible bachelor. He glanced at Helen, sitting between him and Jacy, and caught her eye. "Splendid show, is it not?" he asked loudly over the music and fiery explosions. "Wonderfully entertaining."

She nodded, her tense lips curving into a relaxed smile. "I love it. Truly wonderful."

The band finished *The Star Spangled Banner* just as a pause fell between celebratory rockets of red glare. Frank took advantage of the quiet lull. "I trust you are pleased with your decision to stay at White Caps this summer?" he asked Helen.

She looked at him and nodded again. "Why, yes, as a matter of fact, I am. This a marvelous hotel. Jacy's father insisted we stay here. He says it's the best in Cape May."

"Does he? The man has good taste."

"Yes. He considers it the best since that horrid fire in 1878. What a shame that was."

"Yes." Frank frowned, "it was."

"Destroyed so much of the town." Helen leaned toward him. "But I'm glad it has sprung back. Better than before."

Frank smiled. "I'm glad you think so. And I'm glad you and your family are here."

The band struck up another tune, *The Battle Hymn of the Republic,* just as more fireworks exploded in the sky. Frank took that as his cue to settle back and enjoy the festivities and let Helen Bainbridge do the same.

When the show ended with a spectacular round of fiery rockets, he turned back to her.

Jacy, and Poppy were standing up to leave. He did not have much time.

"Mrs. Bainbridge—Helen—this evening has been a pleasure," Frank said, leaping to his feet. Turning, he gallantly reached for her hand to help her up. "I have so enjoyed spending this time with you."

She smiled, obviously pleased to have the attention of a young gentleman. The expression on her face was a mix of amusement and surprise. "Indeed. And I have enjoyed your company as well, Frank. Considering you could have had your pick of pretty young ladies to sit next to, instead of an old matron like me."

He nodded. She had just handed him the perfect opening. "You do yourself an injustice, ma'am. I like you." He held her gaze. "And I like your family...and...and...I was wondering if you...and your daughter and niece...Poppy and Jacy...would take a ride with me on my yacht?"

"Your yacht?"

"Perhaps tomorrow, or—"

"Are you ready to go, Aunt Helen?" Jacy put a hand on her aunt's arm, smiled stiffly at Frank, and nodded at her cousin. "Poppy and I are exhausted. It has been quite a day."

"Yacht?" Helen said again. "You say you have a yacht?"

He grinned, his gaze meeting Jacy's. The minx looked confused, which was good. "Yes, as a matter of fact, I do."

"Well," Helen said, obviously impressed. "Well, well."

"I keep it at the Cape May Yacht Club," he said, striving for the right casual tone. "Don't get as much time on it as I'd like. With my lifeguard duties and all. So, when I give myself a day off, I head for the open sea."

Jacy was staring at him. Something flashed in her eyes. Was it irritation? Maybe he was trying too hard.

"Come, Mother," Poppy said with a whine. "Let's go."

Helen turned to her daughter. "Frank has invited us to go sailing on his yacht. Tomorrow." Her eyes glinted in the gaslights that ringed the hotel lawn. Frank had never seen the woman look so enthusiastic about anything. The poor thing was probably bored to death watching all the young people in town have all the fun.

"Oh," Jacy said. "But I don't—"

"I don't know, Mother," Poppy said. She yawned. "I'm tired. Do we have to decide right—"

"I say we accept," Helen said.

"What?" Jacy widened her eyes.

"In fact, my dears, I insist upon it."

Frank smiled. His plan was working.

"It would be downright rude of us to turn this gentleman down." Helen stared at Jacy. "And I would like to go."

"Well..." Jacy shook her head. "I don't—"

"We accept," Helen said, ignoring her niece. "I hear it is expected to be an exceptionally beautiful day. Sunny and hot. A perfect time to be out at sea, where it will certainly be cooler."

Frank studied Jacy's face. Her cheeks appeared flushed. She opened her mouth and then closed it without saying anything.

Poppy looked at Jacy, wide-eyed, then at her mother and at Frank. "If it will give my mother pleasure, I suppose we should go. Lord knows she deserves it, after putting up with Jacy and me thus far."

Jacy sighed loudly. "I don't think we have been that much trouble, Poppy."

Helen laughed lightly. Frank did not know the woman could laugh and the sound of it warmed his heart. "If your father only knew, Jacy," she said.

Jacy looked away.

Frank hurried to fill the awkward silence. "I am so glad you will do me the pleasure of joining me tomorrow morning, ladies. I will have a carriage waiting to take us to the yacht club at ten o'clock sharp."

Jacy folded her arms and nodded.

Frank smiled at her, but she looked away.

Fine, if that's the way she wants to be. For now. Frank grinned. *Wait until she sees my yacht. She will change her mind about me.*

Jacy turned back to Frank and met his gaze. A tentative smile formed on her lips and his heart did a flip. Could it be she was already softening toward him?

"I look forward to our excursion," she said. "But I think it might be even more fun if a few more people joined us."

His heart fell. He raised his eyebrows. "What?"

"You know what they say, the more the merrier. I was just thinking …perhaps the Strattons could come along as well?"

"The Strattons?" He tried to keep the alarm out of his voice. "The Strattons?"

"Yes. Henry, Lydia and Cole."

Frank felt as if he had been punched in the gut. An angry burn formed in his chest, then slowly expanded to his neck and face. He gritted his teeth. He had to get a hold of himself, calm down. He could not let it show.

"You know, Jacy, I agree with you. I do think it would be fun to invite more people. And I like Henry and Lydia Stratton."

"Good." Jacy's face lit up.

It was time, however, to let her know she was not going to win.

"But as for Cole..." He paused, striving to look genuinely contrite. "I am afraid I cannot accommodate a wheelchair. It would be far too dangerous. A large wave might pitch it overboard, and wouldn't that be a tragedy?"

"Oh." She stared at him.

He chuckled and shrugged. "I wouldn't worry about Cole Stratton. I am sure he won't mind remaining behind. He has a very capable orderly, he won't be alone."

CHAPTER THIRTEEN

*a*unt Helen was right about the weather: it turned out to be a horribly hot day.

Jacy was grateful that, once they sailed off, the air was refreshingly cooler. She stood at the bow and closed her eyes, letting the ocean breeze fan her cheeks as the yacht skimmed the waves.

Angry at first about spending the day on Frank's yacht she convinced herself to relax and stay as far from him as possible. She had to admit the opulent vessel, *Splendid Lady*, was impressive. The yacht was a floating mansion, likely one of Cape May's largest. Aunt Helen would be able to brag about it for the rest of the season.

Henry and Lydia had declined Frank's invitation, and Jacy didn't blame them, considering Frank's outrageous behavior at the Congress Hall dance.

Thus far, Frank was behaving like a gentleman, which came as a profound relief to her. Aside from holding onto her hand slightly longer than necessary when he had helped her board, he had been polite and gracious.

He had wasted no time in giving his guests a tour of the two-masted wooden steamship, beaming with pride at Aunt Helen's compliments. The vessel was at least 150 feet long, must have cost a fortune, and required a full-time crew to sail and maintain. As the daughter of a man who ran a shipping business, Jacy knew her way around ships. She also knew Frank was letting the world know that, when it came to ostentation, he could keep up with the best of them.

"Three guest rooms, in addition to the master bedroom," he had said smoothly, ushering them down a hallway. "A spacious library with mahogany paneling...nothing but the best...hot and cold running water throughout...and, of course, quarters for a crew of twelve."

"Indeed," Aunt Helen had said with a pursed smile. "A crew of twelve. My, my. I suppose we could sail to Europe if we wanted, could we not?"

"That's the idea, my dear." he had said, spreading his arms wide. "With this magnificent vessel, I could literally explore the world... except, I haven't. Yet. I am afraid I would find myself quite lonely... without a wife."

"Oh?" Aunt Helen squealed.

Jacy looked at Poppy and rolled her eyes.

"Is that so? You dear boy," Aunt Helen continued. "Money cannot provide everything one needs in life, now can it? It certainly can't take the place of love."

When a man dressed in a navy-blue uniform joined the tour, Frank introduced him as his captain, Joshua Zane. About forty years old, he had a light brown beard and a distinguished look about him. At first, he reminded Jacy of Edmund, and her heart lurched. She told herself she was being ridiculous. Zane was quite good looking, with feathery lines around his eyes and a wide, honest face. But he was not as handsome as her beloved.

Jacy had hoped that Frank would be focused on steering the ship, meaning he would leave her alone. When Captain Zane at the helm, she realized Frank had other plans.

Relishing the cool breeze on her face, she watched Cape May fade from view.

She heard someone cough. She turned. It was Frank.

Drat.

Sighing deeply, Jacy forced a smile. She was cornered and chided herself for not sticking closer to Poppy. Maybe if she remained calm and coolly polite he would continue to act like a gentleman. "Thank you for inviting us on this excursion," she said, tightening her grip on the handrail to steady herself. "Aunt Helen is over the moon. She loves the sea."

Frank took a step closer and grinned. His teeth were startlingly white against his dark tan. He wasn't wearing a hat, and the wind whipped his dark hair back from his face. "Think nothing of it," he said. "It is my pleasure. In fact, I am hoping you will keep me company aboard this modest vessel many times this summer. I want to get to know you better, Jacy."

I wish he had not said that.

Jacy's purple and white striped dress pressed against her legs, held fast by the wind. Afraid of losing her bonnet, she reached up to tie it tighter under her chin. Then she tried to change the subject. "This is a lovely yacht, Frank," she said, raising her chin. "*Splendid Lady.* What an intriguing name. Is there a woman in your life who inspired it?"

He nodded, giving her a knowing look, as if he knew what she was doing and was happy to play along. "As a matter of fact, yes. My sainted mother, Bettina. Gone these last five years. God rest her soul."

"Oh, I'm sorry. You must have loved her dearly."

"I did. Which is why, in my twenty-seven years, I have not been able to find a woman like her who I would care to marry. When a man has had a mother as wonderful as mine, he tends to compare every woman to her."

Jacy stifled a groan. Frank was clever, she had to give him that. "What about your father—is he still living?" she asked, before he could start comparing her to his mother.

Frank held her gaze and frowned. "No. Sadly he died two years before his beloved Bettina." He looked away, out at the rolling, sun-speckled waves. "Lawrence was his name. Lawrence Lynch." A distant look crept across his face. "Lawrence and Bettina were very much in love. I envied them, growing up. We all did."

"All?"

"My two older brothers, and my younger sister."

"I see."

He stared at her, squinting against the sun's bright rays. "They are all married, with children, and we are not close."

"Oh."

"We each inherited a great deal of money. There were arguments about it, but in the end, the lawyers made sure we each got an equal share. After the family home in Princeton was sold, that is. After that, there was no longer any reason for me to stay in that town."

Jacy suddenly felt sorry for Frank, despite her dislike for him. Perhaps his sad family situation explained some of his flawed character traits.

When he continued to stare at her, she felt increasingly uncomfortable. "So, you live at White Caps all year round? I didn't think it was open in the winter." She did not particularly care where he lived but thought it best to keep the conversation casual until she could make an escape.

He laughed. "It's not open in winter. No, I own an oceanfront cottage." He cleared his throat. "Actually, quite a large cottage—a three story mansion—in Cape May Point. I live there most of the year, but rent it out during the summer, so I can live at White Caps and serve as a lifeguard."

Jacy knew what Frank was doing. He wanted her sympathy. He might be arrogant and conceited, but deep down, he did seem genuinely lonely.

She did not doubt he was on the hunt for a wife—but why did he act interested in her? He could have his pick of many women. "Do you have a profession?" she asked to change the subject again.

He smiled, obviously pleased she seemed to care. "No. Not yet, at least. I inherited enough money that I need never work, if I don't want to."

If he was bragging, she wasn't impressed. "Aren't you bored?"

He shook his head. "No, not yet. I graduated from Princeton and could go into business or law. But right now, I am enjoying life.

Saving people's lives is my hobby. While on a serious quest to find a wife."

He was bringing that up again? Was he so smitten with her that he was hoping she would take the hint?

Or did he talk to every woman that way?

Jacy did not really want to know, but Frank was obviously eager to tell her. He stepped closer, close enough to touch her. She froze.

"You fascinate me, Jacy. You must know that."

Oh, no.

"You are like no other woman I have ever met."

She shook her head.

"You are spunky and headstrong and independent. Wonderful qualities in a stunningly beautiful woman."

She swallowed hard and wondered if she should try to run around him.

"And you can swim. Extremely well. No fanny dipping for you. I find that incredibly attractive. Not to mention singularly unique."

Maybe running would be a good idea. But what if she fell on the slippery deck?

"And you are really difficult to court. Which somehow makes you even more exciting."

Jacy had enough. He was being too bold, and what good would running do? She would have to let him know the truth. "I am in love with another man," she said firmly, lifting her chin and looking him straight in the eye. "I am sorry to disappoint you. But, I am."

"I know."

He knows? She narrowed her eyes. "What do you know?"

"Edmund Overton is his name, am I right?"

She stared at him. "How…?"

"Silly Jacy. All of Cape May knows you go to the lighthouse every morning to look for the missing sea captain. A more useless endeavor I cannot imagine."

She glared at him. "How dare you."

He shrugged. "Overton doesn't bother me. Because he's dead."

Frank stepped closer. Jacy grasped the rail behind her so hard her fingers hut. He leaned forward to whisper in her ear. She felt his breath on her skin. "Sooner or later—and I hope it is sooner—you will realize that you are in love with a ghost. And you will turn to me."

Time to run.

Darting around Frank, Jacy felt her feet slip. She righted herself and turned to face him, backing farther away. "Never, sir, I regret to inform you. I will never turn to you."

He gave a harsh laugh. "Why not, Jacy? I am a catch. Many women would love to be you. It would make your aunt so very happy. Likely your father, too."

Now it was her turn to laugh—bitterly. "Leave my father out of this. You don't know him, and he is no concern of yours."

"I hear he hates Overton. He would love me."

"I doubt it."

"What do you—*did you*—see in Overton? I heard he's much older than you."

"*So?*"

"Was he a replacement for your father's affections? Your father and your stepmother have a passel of children, do they not? Competition for your father's love?"

"How dare—?"

"Did that make you turn to an older man? One your dear papa heartily disapproved of?"

Jacy felt the blood rush to her cheeks. Anger surged through her. Frank had gone far too far. He was also scaring her. "How do you know so much about me?"

He didn't answer. They locked gazes.

"As I said, you fascinate me, Jacy. I made it my business to find out everything I could about you, and I like what I have found. Despite your flaws."

"My flaws?"

"Your obvious blindness to the truth. About yourself. And Overton."

"I don't know what you are talking about." She should *not* have agreed to come on his yacht, not even for Aunt Helen's sake.

"You do know what I'm talking about," Frank said. "So, think about it. And ponder this, while you are at it—why Cole Stratton?"

Cole? Jacy widened her eyes. "What did you say?"

"You heard me. Why have you taken such a fancy to Cole Stratton, of all men?" Frank continued to hold her gaze. When she did not answer, he said, "I know why."

She shook her head. "Leave Cole out of this. He has—"

"Because, he's *safe*," Frank said, his voice a snarl. "He's sick. He can't court you. How could he? Believe me, he would like to. But as he can't even stand up…he's safe. You can get close to him, you can be his friend. And it's no threat to your relationship with a dead sea captain."

"How dare you," Jacy whispered. The sun felt hot all of a sudden.

She turned to the door that led into the interior, yanked it open, and stopped. "You are wrong about me, Frank," she said, facing him with her chin up. "And you can stop trying to court me. I am not, and never will be, interested in you."

He laughed. Unbelievably, he laughed. "I will never give up on you," he said. "You will be mine. And your Aunt Helen be so pleased."

CHAPTER FOURTEEN

*S*leep was fitful for Jacy after her excursion on Frank's yacht. She woke up again and again during the night, haunted by Frank's mocking words. What he had said about Edmund. What he had said about Cole.

Tired of tossing to and fro, she finally just got up, much earlier than usual, and set out for the lighthouse.

She was exhausted mentally and physically, so the walk seemed to take much longer than usual. When she arrived, the climb seemed more laborious.

On the balcony, her hands gripping the rail as she looked out at sea, Jacy kept thinking about how the rest of the day had gone on Frank's yacht, when she had made certain she was never alone with him again.

Of course, she had not enjoyed herself, and she was sure Aunt Helen or Poppy had not, either. Although they did not mention it, they seemed to sense the strain it had put her under.

Jacy exhaled a sigh of relief when she finally got back to White Caps shortly after sunrise.

Surprised to see Cole and Samuel on the beach, she smiled and waved.

The sight of Cole, sitting cheerfully in his wheelchair, with the golden light of dawn illuminating his face, brightened her mood.

"You are up extra early today." Cole flashed his boyish grin.

"You, too," Jacy said. She suddenly felt awkward, thanks to Frank's snide comments the day before. She heartily disliked the lifeguard, now more than ever. Silently, she cursed him for making her feel self-conscious around the brave, kind man in front of her.

She forced herself to stop thinking about Frank. In any case, he was wrong about what he had said, and she would not let him interfere with her friendsip with Cole. What did it matter if Frank was jealous of Cole? Jacy found the notion amusing.

"I'm glad you are up and about so early, Jacy," Cole said. "Because I am eager to begin my exercise session today."

"Oh?" Jacy looked at Samuel, who just shrugged.

"Mister Cole wants to walk some today," Samuel said. "So excited about it, didn't want to eat first."

"That's right." Cole nodded. "I have not felt this good in a long time. I'm ready."

"Really?" Jacy smiled. "I'm truly glad to hear you are feeling so well. But—"

"He mighty restless yesterday." Samuel grinned. "Wants to use his legs. Wants to get strong again."

"Oh…" Jacy smiled at the twinkle in Cole's eyes. "I'm sorry I was not available. I was out at sea, aboard Frank's yacht. I tried to convince him to invite you, but…"

"I know. Henry told me. I appreciate you thinking of me. Most people don't think about people in wheelchairs."

Jacy turned and looked around. The beach was empty, save for the three of them. She looked back at Cole, confused. "Where is Henry?"

Cole shrugged. "Likely still asleep."

"Seems so," Samuel said.

Jacy frowned. "How are we supposed to do this? We need Henry. Samuel can support you on one side, Cole, but we need someone strong on your other side."

"What about you, Jacy?" Cole smiled.

"Me?" She raised her eyebrows, then her voice. *"Me?"*

"Nobody else here," Samuel muttered.

She pursed her lips. "Yes, but—"

"You can do it, Jacy," Cole said. The twinkle was gone from his eyes. He looked deadly serious.

Jacy's heart did a flip in her chest. He desperately wanted to walk, and she truly did want to help him.

"I probably won't be capable of going more than a few steps," he said. "Please."

"You might fall, Cole. I don't think I'm strong enough to hold you up if you start to."

"Samuel won't let me fall. I just need you to lean on."

Jacy looked at Samuel. He just nodded and shrugged.

Shaking her head, Jacy took a deep breath and let it out. "I don't think it would be proper."

"Proper?" Cole sounded genuinely surprised, as if he really had not considered that. "What do you mean?"

"What do I *mean*? I mean...I will have to put my arm around your...waist. You will have to put your arm around me. Uh...I don't think..."

Cole drew his brows together, as if perplexed by what she was saying. Their gazes locked, and a glint of amusement crept into his eyes.

There was a lot more than a glint in Samuel's eyes. He seemed to be struggling not to laugh.

"Jacy," Cole said softly. "It wouldn't be any different than dancing. Men and women dance together all the time. Someday—soon, I hope— I would love to dance with you. Let's just pretend we are dancing now."

Jacy looked at the rolling waves, swallowed hard, and sighed. He had a point. She looked back at Cole. "Well...I suppose..."

Cole nodded eagerly. "Yes, yes, yes. Let's get going. It's not like there is anyone on the beach to see us, anyway."

"Okay." She looked at Samuel. "Are you ready?' She looked at Cole. "Are you?"

"Yes, ma'am," Cole said. "I'm ready to walk all the way to the light-house and back."

"I'm not," Samuel said and grunted. "You heard Doctor Morris. He won't like this."

"He's not going to know about this," Cole said. "Now, Jacy get on my right and Samuel get on my left and when I count to three, lift me up. Then I'm going to walk. As many steps as I can go."

"And then what?" Jacy said, her pulse quickening as she got into position. What was she doing? How could she let him talk her into this?

"When I can't go any farther, just lower me to the sand," Cole said. "Slowly, if possible. Don't drop me." He grinned. "Then, Samuel, you bring me my chair. And help me get back into it, with Jacy's help if need be."

When Cole stood up on the count of three, Jacy was surprised he was not as heavy as she had assumed. Or maybe his legs were stronger, which was encouraging.

Her left arm firmly around his waist, she was also surprised by Cole's height: he was about a head taller than Samuel. Cole seemed to tower over her. Used to looking down on him, it came as a pleasant surprise.

His right arm securely around her waist, she was suddenly barely conscious of how many steps he was slowly managing to take. She was too distracted by the heat of his body against hers. Unnerved, she felt herself blush. They were pressed together, melded as one.

Time seemed to cease as Cole took one step, then another, then another.

Jacy felt him start to shake, his muscles quivering from the phys-ical exertion. She began to shake, too, because she was terrified he might topple over at any moment. He might break an arm, or a leg, or, even worse, his neck. Everyone would blame her. They would be right to. It would be all her fault.

She felt Cole tiring. He began leaning on her more and more, and she assumed he was doing the same with Samuel.

She would keep going, though, as long as Cole desired. If he could do it, so could she.

Finally, after what seemed a very long time—but no time at all—his knees began to buckle. She looked at Samuel, who gave her a nod.

"Cole?" Jacy said. "Are you—"

"Stop...stop," he said, panting. "That's all I can do."

"Lower...slow," Samuel said calmly as he and Jacy eased Cole down onto the sand. Samuel's face lit up in a wide grin. "You did it! You did it, Mister Cole. You must a took ten steps. Maybe more. You did real good."

Cole was beaming, too. Sweat streamed down his face, but she saw pride in his eyes—and, for the first time—hope.

She dropped to her knees and sat next to him. Reaching over, she gently placed her hand on his. "Samuel's right," she whispered. "I am so proud of you, Cole. You did good. Real good."

* * *

HELEN TOOK a bite of poached egg, raised her cup of honey-laced tea to her lips and then froze.

Jacy, wearing a big smile, was sauntering into the dining room, slightly earlier than usual, but not alone. She was pushing Cole Stratton in his wheelchair as Henry and Lydia Stratton, smiling and chatting with each other, followed behind.

Helen set her tea down, rattling the saucer. "Poppy..."

Poppy, munching her grape-jellied toast, swallowed and looked at her. "Yes, Mother?"

"Why is Henry Stratton letting Jacy push that heavy chair?" Helen nodded toward the foursome. "Shouldn't he be doing it? It is no chore for a woman."

"What?" Poppy looked over. A smile tugging at her lips, she watched her cousin and friends make their way to their table. "They all look rather cheerful this morning," she remarked. "I could use some good cheer. As I suspect you could, too."

Helen did not disagree with that, after their disappointing tour the day before. She had so hoped it would go well, that Frank Lynch and Jacy would spark. Instead, something happened between them that put a damper on the entire outing.

Whatever had transpired, it was obvious Jacy wanted nothing more to do with the man. Jacy and the wealthy lifeguard would never become an item, meaning Frank would not be replacing Edmund in her niece's affections.

How unfortunate.

Almost as unfortunate, Poppy and the Cape May hero would never become an item either. Not that Frank had shown the slightest interest in her daughter, but a mother could always hope. No, Poppy had informed her, after they returned from their adventure, that she wanted nothing to do with "the braggart" either.

"Mother, in case you have any ideas, I want you to know I would rather marry a pauper who hawks rags for a living than Frank Lynch," she had declared. "And anyway, as I told you, I would rather not marry at all."

Poppy was being ridiculous about never marrying, but Helen decided not to worry about it. A dance hop was slated to take place on Cape May's iron pier that afternoon. Eternal optimist that she was, Helen harbored hopes that Poppy—and Jacy—would meet nice, suitable gentlemen there.

She also decided to ignore the impropriety of Jacy pushing Cole's wheelchair across the dining room. With a polite smile, she greeted her niece as they approached the table. Helen nodded at the convalescent as Jacy positioned his wheelchair to Helen's left and took a seat on the other side.

"Hello, Aunt Helen," Jacy said cheerfully as she unfolded her napkin, shook it out, and placed it in her lap. "You are looking well this morning."

"As are you," Helen said, not entirely meaning it, because in truth, Jacy looked tired.

Helen smiled at Cole. "Nice to see you again, young man."

"And you, Mrs. Bainbridge—Helen," he said. "Do you have an exciting day planned?"

She was delighted he had asked. "Yes, indeed. I am looking forward to the hop today." She looked around the table. "I assume all you young people are as well?"

They all indicated they planned to attend, even Cole Stratton.

Talk turned to the reason they had entered the dining room looking so happy. It seemed Cole had managed to walk a few steps on the beach before breakfast.

"A marvelous accomplishment," Jacy gushed, that "boded well" for his recovery.

Surprised, Helen didn't press for more details, although it did strike her as odd that no one volunteered to give her any.

* * *

AFTER BREAKFAST, Helen elected to spend the rest of the morning resting, secure in the knowledge that her maid, Florence, would help Poppy and Jacy dress for the dance.

Florence did a wonderful job, because both girls looked lovely when it was time to go. Both wore their hair pinned up, their sun-kissed cheeks framed by dangling curls. Jacy was a vision in pale-green chiffon, the color of the sea. Poppy was equally stunning in tangerine, which accentuated her hair.

At three o'clock, the threesome set out for the open-air dance pavilion.

When they arrived, Helen sat down with other matrons her age, observing with pride that her girls were the loveliest ones there.

It did not take long, however, before Helen grew uneasy. Tapping her toes to the orchestra's third song, it occurred to her that while Poppy had been dancing since they arrived, Jacy had not been out on the dance floor even once.

Pretty and perky, she sat next to Cole Stratton, chatting away with him. Deep in conversation, the two young people were laughing and obviously enjoying each other's company.

A man came over to ask Jacy to dance, but she shook her head.

Helen kept watching. Three more fine young gentlemen bowed before her niece, but she turned them all down.

By all appearances, Jacy seemed content to refrain from going out onto the dance floor at all.

Helen pressed her lips together. Jacy's behavior would not do, *not do at all.* Dealing with the ghost of that awful Edmund Overton was bad enough. Must she now endure watching her niece waste precious opportunities to find a man she deserved?

Cole Stratton was clearly not that man. He was ill, weak. Why, he might even take a turn for the worse before summer was over. In all her many years visiting Cape May, Helen had seen many unfortunate souls seeking the sea-air cure die before the season ended. She had attended more funerals than she cared to remember.

What was Jacy thinking?

Helen decided to find out. She rose, walked over to her, and requested a word in private.

Jacy looked alarmed, as if Helen might be bearing bad news. Helen felt guilty about letting her think that, but only a little, as she ushered her charge out of the pavilion and onto the pier.

They found a bench overlooking the ocean, and Helen got straight to the point. Frowning, she reached for Jacy's hand and looked her straight in the eye. "What are you doing?" she asked. She had tried to keep frustration out of her voice, but failed. *So be it, this matter is important.*

Jacy's eyes widened. "Aunt Helen, whatever do you mean? Is something wrong?"

"I don't know, Jacy. Please tell me."

Jacy shook her head. "Tell you what?"

"Why you are not dancing."

"What?"

"You heard me. Why are you not dancing today? Why are you just sitting there with Cole Stratton?"

Jacy's eyes widened even more, and she was silent for a moment, seemingly shocked at the question. Then she shrugged and said, "Because I want to."

"Many men have asked you to dance. Why have you turned them all down?"

Jacy pursed her lips. She stared at the ocean and then turned to meet Helen's gaze. "Why is who I dance with—or who I do not dance with—any of your business?" She looked angry, which was most unlike her.

Helen felt her own face grow red. She did not like to feel angry, either, and rarely needed to because life usually gave her what she wanted. At least it had until Captain Overton came along, throwing the entire family into a tizzy. "Why…why?" Helen answered. "Because you are my business, Jacy. Your father sent you here with me, remember? I am your chaperone. And not only that, I am the only mother you ever really had. Since you were a toddler, at least. You know that, and I know that, and Tobias knows that." She was raising her voice louder than was socially acceptable, but she could not help it. "*That*, my dear Jacy, is *why*."

"Oh." Jacy stared at her, unblinking. "I see." Her voice was a whisper. She reached over and patted Helen's arm. All traces of her anger were gone. "I'm sorry. I am truly sorry. You are right. It was rude of me to speak to you as I did. Please forgive me."

"Of course," Helen said. "I love you."

"I know you do. And I love you, too."

Helen smiled. She felt her lips quiver, but she would not let herself cry, not in public. She took a deep breath. "Then believe me when I tell you I am concerned for you, Jacy. First, Edmund Overton. Now, Cole Stratton. I am concerned about your choice of men."

Jacy shook her head, looking confused. "My choice…whatever are you talking about? What do you mean about Cole Stratton?"

"You are spending more and more time with him."

"So?"

"You seem to have appointed yourself as his nurse."

Jacy scrunched her eyebrows together. "What?"

Helen sighed. "I believe you are attracted to him, my child. Him of all men. A more unsuitable man for your affections in all of Cape May, I cannot conceive of. He is *sick*."

Jacy stared at her.

"I fear for you, my dear. A woman needs a good husband. Women have few options in life, as you well know. Poppy might believe she will be fine with her poetry alone, but you are not Poppy. You need a man who loves you and will cherish you. One who will provide a good home for you and your children."

Jacy squeezed her eyes closed and shook her head. "Aunt Helen—"

Helen put her hand on Jacy's shoulder. "You are not getting any younger, and good men are rare. Sadly, I wish that were not so. But it is. And you are wasting valuable time."

Helen held her breath, hoping Jacy would not get angry again. She studied her niece's countenance. It was difficult to tell how she felt. Sitting motionless, Jacy sighed and said nothing.

Inside the pavilion, the orchestra struck up a lively tune. Waves broke under the pier, below their feet. Jacy's silence stretched on.

"Jacy?"

Jacy met her gaze. "I am sorry, Aunt Helen," she said. "I am sorry to cause you so much trouble as far as Edmund Overton is concerned."

She placed her hand on Helen's and patted it affectionately. "I am almost sorry that I am in love with him. Because, believe me, it would make my life easier if I wasn't."

Helen widened her eyes. *Finally...some hope.*

"But..." Jacy picked up Helen's hand and squeezed it. "You are wrong about Cole Stratton."

Helen stared at her.

"Cole is a nice man, and he has become a wonderful friend, and it's true I want to help him. I like him. I like him a lot. But I am not attracted to him in the way you believe. Please. Believe me. I am not."

Helen swallowed hard, reached over, and embraced Jacy in a hug. She held onto her like she did when Jacy was a little girl. It felt wonderful and right to hug her, and to be hugged by her. It had been far too long.

When they pulled apart and stood up, Jacy's eyes were misty. Helen knew hers were, too.

"Okay, my beloved, let us go back to the dance," Helen said. "I will try to believe what you tell me about Cole. I will try."

But Helen did not believe Jacy, not for a moment.

Jacy might believe she was not attracted to Cole Stratton, but Helen knew better.

She was indeed attracted to him, and no good would come of it.

CHAPTER FIFTEEN

*J*acy pondered Aunt Helen's words as she walked back into the pavilion. Couples crowded the dance floor. The air felt warmer than it had outside, despite the sea breeze wafting in between the iron pillars supporting the roof.

Cole was sitting alone where she had left him. With a serene, dreamy expression on his face, he watched the men and women as they glided by.

"I was just thinking how I will be out there, doing that, before long," he said as Jacy sat down beside him. He waved his hand. "Dancing with beautiful women."

"I hope so. I hope you get to dance with many beautiful women."

He broke a smile that caused her heart to skip a beat. "You do?"

"Yes, of course." She smiled back and remained silent for a moment. "I hope that includes me."

He laughed. "Especially you."

The orchestra began a new song, and an auburn-haired man with a goatee strolled over and asked Jacy to dance.

"Dance, Jacy, dance," Cole said. "Go, have fun. Don't worry about me."

Jacy sighed. "Alright." She extended her hand to the red-haired gent and waved to Cole as the man whisked her away.

She allowed herself a smile. Her partner danced extremely well. It felt good to be moving, after so much sitting.

She danced with about a dozen other men after that, only once with each.

During the last song, she glanced over at Cole and wished she were dancing with him.

The truth hit Jacy hard. *I would rather sit with Cole than dance with any man here. Or any man at all, even Edmund.*

The realization took her breath away.

Something about Cole made her happy. In his company, she felt complete. When she was around him, she felt like she was where she was supposed to be. It did not seem to matter where they were—on the beach, in the dining room, or sitting and watching other people dance.

It had not been like that with Edmund. Being with Edmund had made her happy—but in a naughty kind of way. Being with him had allowed her to defy who she was, or who society expected her to be. Maybe that had made him attractive. He had been her way of turning her back on the world: her father, her family, her limited choices as a woman. He allowed her to rebel against a world where everyone thought she should marry a man of a certain class, with an acceptable pedigree, with impressive wealth.

"Damn the world," Edmund would say. "It's just me and you, Jacy. Me and you. You and me. We are all we need."

She would laugh and melt into his arms. She had loved that he loved her and delighted at the brave way he cherished her in defiance of society. When she was with him, it had been easy to believe what he told her, again and again: "I love you, Jacy. More than anyone else loves you. More than anyone else will ever love you. You belong with me. I belong with you. You belong to me. I belong to you."

Then one day Edmund was gone. It was no longer him and her. It was just her, alone. She had worried he might have left her with child, and she was profoundly relieved when her time of the month came.

She shuddered to think what might have happened. She had been such a fool.

Gliding across the dance floor, Jacy glanced over at Cole. He was not looking at her. Disappointed, she chided herself for being silly. She studied his profile. He looked regal. Even in his weakened state, he was the best-looking man in the room.

The orchestra leader announced they had time for one more dance. Jacy accepted the hand of a gangly youth who could not have been any older than sixteen.

As soon as the music stopped, she hurried over to Cole. "Congratulations, Jacy," he said, giving her a wide smile. "You managed not to dance with any man twice."

She grinned. "You noticed."

Henry and Lydia, who had danced exclusively with each other, joined them.

Lydia's face shimmered with sweat, as did Henry's. They held hands. They were always holding hands. Jacy smiled. Why would they not? They were on their honeymoon. They were deeply in love. *Lucky them.*

"I have a great idea," Lydia said, panting because she was still out of breath from two hours on the dance floor. "Let's go fishing tonight. After an early dinner. Let's go at sunset. On this pier. It will be such fun."

Exhausted, Jacy stared at her. It had been a long day, and she had slept little the night before. The last thing she wanted to do was fish. She did not particularly enjoy it and always felt sorry for the poor creatures dangling from her hook.

"Please. Let's the four of us go. The hotel has poles and bait and it would be good for Cole," Henry said. "Something he can participate in, for a change."

Jacy looked at Cole and smiled. He did appear eager. For him, she would go.

"Okay," Jacy said. "Sounds like it could be fun."

* * *

It did not take Jacy long to discover why Lydia wanted to go fishing. Within thirty minutes, she hooked half a dozen big ones. It was clearly an activity at which Henry's bride excelled.

Henry didn't seem to care if he caught anything or not. Instead, he appointed himself as the remover of hooks.

Cole did well, catching about half as many fish as Lydia.

Jacy caught nothing. Bored, she declared a desire to take a quick walk down to the end of the pier. So tired she was nearly delirious, she hoped the exercise and view would revive her.

"Don't topple off," Cole said with a smile as she dropped her pole down next to him. "You don't want Frank Lynch on the scene."

"Heavens." Jacy made a face. "No, don't worry. I'll be careful. And I won't be long. It will soon be getting dark."

By the time Jacy reached the end of the pier, the setting sun had painted the sky with glorious brush strokes of red and orange. Two men, working-class locals clad in loose-fitting gray pants and brown short-sleeve shirts that appeared to be uniforms, fished alone.

The younger one, perhaps in his twenties, was blonde, while his middle-aged companion was bald. Neither of them seemed to notice Jacy as they chatted with each other.

Happy to have a moment to herself, Jacy eased onto a bench and stared out at the ocean. The men's conversation grew louder, so she closed her eyes and tried to ignore them.

Then she heard one of them mention *The Largo*.

Edmund's ship? She opened her eyes, suddenly wide awake, and listened.

"Yeah, ya know, that steamer disappeared maybe in February or March?"

Jacy glanced over. The bald one was talking. "That's what I'm talking about," he insisted. "I'm talking about that ship."

"Right," the blond man said. "I remember now."

"Yeah, yeah."

"We was supposed to keep an eye out for debris washing up on the beach," the blond man continued. "Cause they thought it mighta wrecked around here. Never saw no debris, though. Nothing. Was hoping to, Clyde. Was really hoping to. Case there was a reward or something."

"Weren't no reward, Tim," Clyde said. "But I know what happened to it all the same."

Jacy held her breath. She pressed her hands against her chest in a vain effort to calm her pounding heart.

"What?" Tim sounded as if he didn't believe Clyde knew anything about anything.

"It wrecked, all right. Went down in a storm. Real fast. Took most the crew with it."

"How do you know?"

"Cause it didn't take everyone."

Jacy put her hand over her mouth.

"What you mean?"

"I mean I was in Philadelphia a couple weeks ago. Spotted my buddy, Hal. Walking down the street. I was shocked. Cause Hal worked on that ship. When he sees me, he gets real scared. Tries to run away. But I caught up to him. Told him I was sure glad he was alive."

"And?"

"And he swore me to secrecy. But I'm telling you."

"Telling me what?"

"What I said. The ship went down in a storm. Only Hal and the captain made it off in a lifeboat. And they been hiding out ever since. Cause they don't want to be blamed for the loss of the vessel and crew. Hal swears it weren't their fault. But they don't want to be blamed all the same."

Jacy jumped to her feet.

Shaking, she stared at the men. Numb with shock, she started over to them, to find out more.

She stopped. Was she crazy? The men were rough looking characters and one of them had just sworn the other to secrecy about a supposed scandal. She was a woman, alone. What might they do to her if they knew she had eavesdropped on their private conversation?

She didn't want to find out.

Besides, she scolded herself, she did not believe Clyde. He was just spinning a dramatic tale to entertain his friend.

Jacy swallowed hard. She returned to the bench and sat down. Clyde's story had to be a lie. It was a whopper of a lie. It had to be.

What if it's true? Jacy put her hands to her cheeks. They felt like blocks of ice.

Clyde's story reminded her of what she had heard in the ice cream parlor, when she, Poppy and Aunt Helen overheard two gossips discussing Edmund. She had nearly dismissed that incident from her mind.

Jacy shook her head. She no longer knew what to believe.

Edmund loved me. That's what he said.

If he is alive, where is he now?

CHAPTER SIXTEEN

*T*he next morning, Jacy raced to the lighthouse. Bounding up the stairs, she stopped to catch her breath upon reaching the top, opened the door to the balcony, grabbed the iron rail, and stared at the vista before her.

She did not see Edmund's ship, or any ships for that matter. However, just as it did every day, the spectacular aerial view reminded her of the largeness of the world and how small she and her problems were. Still reeling from what she had overheard the night before, that gave her little solace.

Instead, she was overcome by a profound emptiness.

Far to her left, lay the city of Cape May. Its oceanfront cottages and hotels, which looked so grand and ornate closeup, appeared tiny.

She turned to the right and stared at the pier where the *Republic* would dock that afternoon. Scores of passengers would stream ashore, giddy with anticipation of the summer's joys. She sighed. *What did it matter? Happiness is so fleeting.*

Below, stretched the long, gentle curve of beach between Cape May and the lighthouse. Glancing down at where the sand met the sea, Jacy smiled for the first time that day. She walked that beach every morning, alone with her thoughts, contemplating her life: what it meant, Edmund, her abiding love for him.

Where are you, Edmund?

Jacy thought about the gift she had given him so freely, in the heat of passion.

Aunt Helen had warned her. Warned her to save "her treasure" for her husband on her wedding night. On Jacy's sixteenth birthday, she had taken Jacy aside to explain the "ways of the world." Virginity "is a flower," she told her. "A treasure that once given away is gone forever."

Jacy could tell, by the way her aunt whispered and stammered, that it wasn't easy for her to talk about. Jacy could not imagine having such a conversation with her stepmother. She appreciated her aunt making the effort.

Aunt Helen had scared her, though, by relaying what had happened to a woman she once knew—"a poor soul" who had allowed her flower to be plucked before marriage. The story put terror in Jacy's heart.

"The scoundrel didn't love her, although of course he professed to, prior to the deed," Aunt Helen had whispered. "Shortly after, he proposed to and married another woman. My friend was ruined. Mortified. Betrayed. She never got over it."

"What happened?" Jacy had to know.

"Her family became suspicious, because she seemed so sad. She confessed to her father. Fortunately, she was not with child. But she was shamed. Her father sent her to live with relatives in another state. She lives with them still, I believe, in a room on their third floor. She was a disgrace to society. No self-respecting man wanted her."

"Oh," was all Jacy said at the time. She promised herself such an awful fate would *never* befall her.

Then, five years later…

How *could* she?

What if…

She tried to push the awful thought away.

What if… what if Edmund is alive and well?

What if he is staying away because he doesn't love me anymore?

What if if he never really loved me?

Jacy closed her eyes. They burned with unshed tears—tears she refused to release.

No, no, no.

How could she think such things? It wasn't fair to Edmund. It was a betrayal of what they had meant to each other.

Jacy rubbed her eyes. She squeezed them closed and opened them again. She scanned the sea for ships and still saw none: No yachts, no fishing vessels, no sailboats. She saw nothing…nothing…but an empty expanse of sun-speckled water.

"Edmund!" She wailed. "Edmund…"

She stared down at her beach again. She scanned the empty stretch of sand.

Beacon Beach.

She had never walked it at night, when the lighthouse beam surely illuminated its sands. But the name seemed to fit.

Cole thought it did. He had helped her name it. He had asked her if the strand, where she went every morning, had a name.

"I never heard one mentioned," she said. "But it sits under a beacon, so…"

"Beacon Beach." He grinned. "How's that?"

"Perfect," she said. Remembering it made her smile.

Cole.

Just thinking about Cole lessened her grief for Edmund. Before long, Cole would be well.

Cole…healthy. Cole…ready to resume his life. Then what?

Jacy felt her mood plunge. *Then*…every pretty girl in Cape May—and beyond—would vie for his heart. He was attractive, professionally successful, wealthy. He came from a wonderful family. He was kind, generous, fun to be with.

He would be able to court any woman he wanted.

But, would such a self-respecting man ever want her? Wanton, soiled Jacy James? No, he would not. Not once he learned the truth about her.

Jacy's breath caught in her throat. A tear rolled down her cheek.

Closing her eyes again, she tried to blot out the world. Looking was too painful.

She gripped the rail and willed herself to calm down. She stood there a long time.

The past cannot be changed. Aunt Helen was right. Once a woman gives her treasure away, it is gone forever.

Jacy lifted her chin. She opened her eyes. She would just have to soldier on, pretend. Pretend she was the woman everyone believed she was. How long could she do so? She had no idea.

In any case, she could not stand there all day. People would start to worry about her. Aunt Helen and Poppy would worry. Cole would worry.

Jacy opened her eyes and took in the wide, wide ocean. Still, nothing. There was nothing to see.

There was nothing to see, except an unbroken expanse of glistening water, beautiful and awe inspiring in the morning sun.

* * *

"Are you sure Jacy walked to the lighthouse this morning?" Henry wiped perspiration from his forehead as he gave Cole a look of exasperation. "Because it seems to me she would have returned by now."

Samuel, sitting cross-legged on the sand, nodded. "Seems so to me, too. Probably in the dining room, chowing down eggs and bacon. We musta missed her."

Cole shook his head. "Don't see how we could have." He didn't blame Henry and Samuel for losing patience. They had been out on the strand for two hours, since sunrise. He had walked well that morning, with their help, and wanted to show Jacy.

Where was she, though? As he sat in his wheelchair, waiting for her, he worried something was amiss.

"Do you really think you have the strength to walk more, anyway?" Henry dropped down next to Samuel and stretched his long legs out in front of him. "You must have walked about a hundred steps. I doubt you could do that again, even for Jacy's sake."

Samuel grinned. "I think you ready for your cane, Mister Cole."

Henry's eyes lit up at that suggestion. He jumped to his feet. "I think you are, too." He brushed the sand off his hands. "Samuel's suggestion gives me an idea, Cole. Let's go back to your room so you can practice that. You packed a cane. It's in your armoire."

"But what about Jacy?" Cole looked at Henry and then at Samuel. "Better to wait for her. I can try the cane later."

Henry groaned.

"I am sorry, but I want to wait," Cole insisted. "Maybe something happened to Jacy. She might be in some kind of trouble."

"I'm sure the fair Jacy is fine," Henry said, emphasizing the word "fine." He was clearly losing patience. "Did it ever occur to you that maybe she was tired this morning? That after we got back from fishing, maybe she was just too excited to sleep?"

Cole stared at him. "Excited? About what? She didn't catch a single fish."

"Oh." Henry looked at Samuel, who just shrugged. "I didn't notice. Sorry. I was too busy helping my bride. My pretty little angler…who by the way, is probably starting to worry about where I am."

Cole drew in a deep breath and let it out slowly. "I apologize, Henry. You're right." He frowned. "Did Jacy seem upset to you?"

"Upset? When?"

"Last night, when she returned from her walk."

"Walk where?"

"Down to the end of the pier and back."

"Oh." Henry shook his head. "No. I don't think so."

"She seemed upset, unusually quiet. But I don't think she wanted to talk about it."

Henry frowned. "Did you *ask* her?"

"Didn't want to pry."

"Maybe it had something to do with her missing sea captain." Henry shaded his eyes with his hand and studied Cole's face. "But that doesn't make any sense." He put his hands on his hips and held Cole's gaze. "I think you are falling for her. That's what I think. Falling for a woman obsessed with another man. Which is a bad idea. We should go."

Samuel stood up. "Yep. It's getting hot."

A knot of frustration formed in Cole's throat. Squinting, he looked down the beach but saw no signs of Jacy. He turned toward the rolling waves. Maybe Henry was right. He tried to push the thought to the back of his mind, but it wouldn't stay there. Maybe his feelings for Jacy *were* evolving into something far beyond friendship.

Then, he saw her, in the distance, walking toward them. Her head was down and she seemed deep in thought.

Cole waved to her, but she wasn't looking.

When she reached them, a puzzled look came over her face. "What are you doing here?"

"Waiting for you," Henry said. "Aren't you rather late?

Jacy didn't answer. She shrugged.

Cole leaned forward in his chair and grinned. "I just walked about a hundred steps with Henry and Samuel. We were waiting for you so I could do it again. So I can show you."

Jacy's eyes widened. "Really?"

"Really," Cole said softly. Something was amiss. She looked sad, teary-eyed, even more upset than she had the night before. "Jacy, what's wrong?"

"I'm fine." She waved her hand in the air. "Don't fret about me. I am glad you waited to show me, Cole. I do want to see what you can do."

Cole nodded. "Henry and Samuel, are you ready? Let's show her. Because I know I can do this. And after that...I'll be ready for my cane."

CHAPTER SEVENTEEN

*C*ole's legs grew stronger over the next few days, and he steadily increased his walking distance.

His progress did not surprise Jacy. She knew Cole was a strong and determined man. He proved it next by insisting he was ready to use a cane.

At first, he walked with his cane—an elegantly carved walking stick—while holding on to Henry or Samuel's arm.

When he was ready, he used the cane alone, with his brother or orderly walking beside him, in case he started to fall.

When he was ready to walk without a cane, holding onto someone's arm for support, he asked Jacy if he could try it with her.

"You don't need to hold me up. I just need your arm for support," he told her. Relaxing on the White Caps veranda, they were socializing with several other hotel guests, with Samuel present. Cole insisted, however, that he wanted Jacy to do the honors.

Jacy shook her head, both flattered and flustered. "Samuel," she said, "maybe you should...you are his orderly. I don't want you to think I am trying—"

"No worry, Miss Jacy," Samuel said with a knowing smile. "Mister

Cole want to walk with you. Okay by me. I think he likes you better." He gave her a wink.

If Cole caught the wink, he didn't let on. "Please, Jacy," he said, flashing her his handsome grin, "walk with me."

Jacy stared at him. "Okay…I suppose…if you insist."

He pushed himself to his feet. She gave him her arm. They strolled the length of the porch and back. Jacy suppressed a giggle when the hotel guests applauded.

After that, when Cole walked around White Caps, he did it while holding onto Jacy's arm. They met in the lobby and walked into the dining room together. They meandered around the grounds together. They walked down to the beach together.

Standing near the water's edge, only three days after he first walked holding onto Jacy's arm, Cole announced he was ready to stroll the boardwalk.

Jacy raised her eyebrows. "You are? Only a week ago you…"

He met her gaze and grinned. "I have made so much progress, thanks to you, that I am ready for the boards."

Jacy beamed. "Okay, Let's make an afternoon excursion of it with Henry and Lydia."

An hour later, Jacy gasped when she saw Cole waiting for her in the lobby. Wearing a navy-blue suit with a matching top hat, he looked positively dapper. Everyone who was anyone dressed in their finest to walk Cape May's boards. Jacy was glad she had donned her pale-pink dress and matching bonnet. She felt pretty.

Passing boardwalk shops with Henry and Lydia, Jacy realized, with a rush of pleasure, that she and Cole looked like all the other couples strolling past. Cole radiated good health, and people greeted him with nods and smiles instead of pitying stares.

Jacy no longer felt like Cole's nurse, either. Women glanced at him and then gave her envious looks. *They think we are a couple because we are arm-in-arm.* She smiled to herself. Pretending that was fun.

Henry tucked Lydia's arm tighter under his and gave Cole a wink. "You are doing so well, I believe it's time for Father to pay us a visit. What do you say? He will be pleased with your recovery."

Cole looked at Jacy and nodded. "I think he will. Let's send him a postcard."

Jacy widened her eyes. She would get to meet Cole's father. Then it occurred to her how awkward that might prove to be. What would his father think of her? Would he ask questions about her role in his son's life? If so, what would Cole tell him?

Jacy winced. *What is my role in Cole's life? We are not really a couple.*

Pressing her lips together, Jacy tried to dismiss the dread creeping into her thoughts. When Cole didn't need her anymore—didn't need her arm to lean on, didn't need her at all—what would happen then?

"Father should bring Dr. Morris with him," Henry said. "I think he will be pleasantly surprised."

Cole gave Jacy a knowing grin. "I think he will."

* * *

"I can't get over how well you look, son," William Stratton said. Folding his arms over his chest, he looked at Cole, sitting across the room on his bed. He smiled. "Our family's prayers have been answered."

Cole nodded. "Yes, I don't even need my cane."

"You are indeed much improved, my boy," Dr. Morris said as he stuffed his medical supplies back into his satchel. Lifting it off the bed, he walked over and dropped it by the door. "Your temperature is normal, your heart sounds strong, and I don't need anything but my own eyes to tell me you are almost recovered. When you walked across the room just now, holding onto nothing but your father's arm, I confess I almost fainted. I am pleased. Very, very pleased."

Cole gave his father a satisfied grin. People told him he resembled his father, which he took as a compliment. In his fifties, with graying hair, striking blue-gray eyes, and a tall, sleek physique, William Stratton exuded confidence and good cheer—that is until his son had returned from Europe practically on his deathbed.

Cole hated being sick, but he also hated worrying his father. He had not seen him smile in months.

"You have no idea how much it pleases me that you are looking more yourself," he told Cole, beaming. "I am vastly relieved, as your mother will be when I relay to her how well you look. She sends her love and promises to come to Cape May at some point this season. You know how busy her garden keeps her this time of year."

Cole laughed. "Yes, you don't have to tell me. Rose Stratton detests sand and hates salt water. Not everyone loves the seaside. I understand. She knows I am in good hands." He looked up when Henry opened the door from the hall and came into the room. "Henry and I are just glad you and Dr. Morris were able to visit so soon, Father."

William Stratton and the good doctor had boarded the *Republic* two days after receiving Cole and Henry's postcard. Cole was eager for them to meet Jacy, so he could relay how she had helped him.

"Cape May is proving to be the cure we had hoped for," William Stratton said. He walked over to Cole and put a hand on his shoulder. "I must admit I had my doubts about whether breathing fresh, clean air would do the trick, but I am now a believer."

Henry laughed. "I wouldn't give Cape May's salty vapors all the credit. Or maybe any."

"Henry," Cole said. "Let me tell them."

"I give the credit to a beautiful woman." Henry grinned at Cole. "One who believed in him and helped him believe in himself."

Dr. Morris' eyebrows shot up. "Really?"

William Stratton looked at Cole and held his gaze. "A woman? Most interesting."

Cole shook his head at Henry. "The woman and I are just friends. She saw my determination to get better and so she offered to help."

"Turns out she had some good ideas." Henry cleared his throat. "Jacy has been extremely supportive. And she has a strong arm."

Cole wanted to throttle him.

"Jacy?" William Stratton said.

"Her name is Jacy James." Cole met his father's quizzical gaze. "She is staying here at the hotel with her aunt and cousin. I was planning to introduce you."

Dr. Morris rubbed his chin. "Sounds risky—a woman helping you walk. I don't know if I—"

"Henry and Samuel have been helping me, too." Cole stared at his doctor. "And you must admit, the results speak for themselves. I am convinced it won't be long before I can get around on my own, without leaning on anyone's arm."

William Stratton nodded. "I'm proud of you, Son. And I would very much like to meet your Jacy—"

"By the way," Dr. Morris interrupted. "Priscilla sends her love."

"What?" Cole stared at his physician. Why had he brought Priscilla Day into the conversation? And she was sending him *love*? She certainly had nerve. Cole nodded. "You don't say."

"Yes." Dr. Morris looked surprised at Cole's dry response. "Yes, truly. She comes to my office quite frequently, in the company of her maid, Mavis, and asks about you."

Cole had no idea what to say. "She comes to your office often? Is she ill?" Not that he cared.

William Stratton frowned. "No, Cole, she misses you. Your mother has been telling her how your health is improving. And, it seems to us that she truly regrets—"

"Never once visiting me when I was ill?" Cole realized he was raising his voice. He glanced at Henry, who looked confused.

"She is afraid of germs." Dr. Morris explained, as if it was perfectly understandable.

Cole let out a brittle laugh. "So that excused her from staying away from me for weeks? Communicating solely by letter?" He shook his head. "No. Other people visited me. People who truly cared about me. If everyone had been afraid of my so-called germs, I would have died of loneliness."

Dr. Morris stared at Cole. "Some women are queasy around sickness. I see that all the time. Although I must admit, Miss Day displays more queasiness than most."

Cole was surprised how annoyed he felt. He looked at his father. "I broke it off with her, you know that. I made it quite clear when I wrote to her and told her she was free to seek other suitors. You read the letter before I sent it. Whatever understanding existed between us —I ended it. I did not want to be a burden to her in any respect, and I haven't been."

William Stratton only nodded. He held Cole's gaze in silence.

His face burning, Cole turned away and looked out the window. The sea sparkled. It beckoned. He longed to be out on the beach, where it was surely cooler than in his increasingly stuffy room. "I never heard back from Priscilla, which told me all I needed to know," he said. "She was relieved."

William Stratton whispered, "I believe she still loves you."

Cole looked at Henry and rolled his eyes. "Ridiculous."

"You know how much your mother and I loved Priscilla. And we still do. The two of you were perfect together. Everyone expected that you would propose to her. Not write her off. Literally."

Cole said nothing.

"I believe Cole has said all he plans to about Priscilla Day," Henry said.

Cole shot his brother a grateful smile. "I have," he said. "And now, Father, Dr. Morris, let me take you to meet Jacy James."

CHAPTER EIGHTEEN

The mid-afternoon sun burned hot on Jacy's cheeks, but she was too lazy to move.

She dozed on and off for hours as she and Poppy relaxed on the White Caps porch. The bright sun gave her an excuse to keep her eyes closed, and Poppy didn't seem to mind her less-than-chatty companion because she was composing a new poem.

Every time Poppy finished a line to her satisfaction, she read it aloud, and the sound of her voice roused Jacy to listen.

Her cousin's current masterpiece was about the sea, a natural topic in Jacy's opinion, given that it glistened in all its glory.

Jacy loved Poppy's poems. She had true talent. "Marvelous," she assured her with every line.

Nodding off after a stanza that began with "dawn's golden hour and the sea nymph's power," Jacy had no idea how long she had been asleep when she heard her name called again.

Prying her eyes open, she discovered it was not Poppy's voice she had heard.

It was Cole's, and he was not alone.

Startled, Jacy rubbed her eyes and struggled to sit up. She gave

Cole an embarrassed smile and switched her gaze to the tall, older, pleasant-looking man beside him.

"Father, this is the woman I have been telling you about—Jacy James." Cole gestured with his hand. "Jacy, meet my father, William Stratton."

"Nice to meet you, Mr. Stratton," Jacy said.

Cole seemed to sense her embarrassment. The corner of his mouth lifted in amusement.

Patting her lips, Jacy felt a line of drool on her chin and discretely tried to wipe it away. Must she meet Cole's father under such awkward circumstances? She glanced at Poppy, who appeared almost as amused as Cole.

William Stratton gave her a kind smile. He looked like an older version of Cole. "So this is the beautiful woman I should thank for my son's miraculous recovery," he said. "It is an honor to meet you." Turning to Poppy, he said, "And this equally lovely woman is...?"

"Poppy Bainbridge." Poppy grinned. "Poet and cousin of the remarkable woman who volunteered to be Cole's nurse." She held up her notepad. "It just occurred to me that I need to compose a poem about that. About Cole getting better, and Jacy helping him. It has been most inspiring to observe."

"I am sure," William Stratton said. "I look forward to reading such a poem."

Jacy looked at Cole and smiled sheepishly. She feared she must look a mess. She put her fingers to her cheeks. Already burned by the sun, she could tell she was blushing. Her face was probably crimson.

She put a hand to her head. Where was her bonnet? Glancing down, she saw it on the floor beside her chair. Her hair was up in a bun, but a lock seemed to have come unpinned. She tucked it behind her ear.

The air felt hot and still. What happened to that lovely ocean breeze that had been cooling her all day? A sliver of sweat slid down her face.

She gave Cole's father an embarrassed grin. "I am pleased to meet you, Mr. Stratton. But you need not thank me. Your son should get the credit for his fast recovery. He is a very determined man. When he puts his mind to something, it seems nothing can stop him."

William Stratton widened his smile and tipped his hat to her. "You are a perceptive woman, Miss James. And why do I get the feeling the same can be said for you?"

He pointed to the chair next to her. "Would you mind if I sit here for a bit? Cole's physician and I just recently arrived. When Cole showed us how well he could walk, we were flabbergasted—and over-joyed. We wanted to meet you right away. Dr. Morris should be along any moment."

Poppy stood up. "Here," she told Cole, "take my seat. I must be going."

Gathering up her pen and reams of writing paper, she scurried off with a cheerful wave.

$$* * *$$

COLE TOLD his father about his recovery process. William Stratton listened, looking back and forth between Cole and Jacy.

When Cole described his first swim lesson with Jacy, his father looked shocked, then bemused. When Cole told him how he had taken his first few steps while holding onto Samuel's and Jacy's arms, he widened his eyes, then nodded.

To Jacy's relief, he did not become angry or scold Cole for disregarding his doctor's orders.

"Fascinating," he said, when Cole finished. "But I find myself confused about one thing." He cast a questioning gaze at Jacy. "How did you meet my son? Why did you offer to help him recover? Are you a nurse? You do not look—"

"Jacy is not a nurse," Cole said. "She just happens to be a kind person."

Raising his eyebrows, the older man looked at Jacy. Swallowing hard, she met his gaze. "Cole is a man of some wealth," he said. "You are attractive and close to him in age. Forgive me, but I could not help but wonder."

"Father." Cole's voice was sharp. "We are friends."

"Friends. I see."

"Father, you are embarrassing me..." Cole glanced at Jacy. "You are embarrassing *us*."

"Son, you know I am a curious man. Jacy seems like a fine woman." He gave her a smile. "The type of woman who many men would love to court."

Jacy wished she could crawl under her chair. Her chest felt tight. What would Cole say? Would he—heaven forbid—bring Edmund Overton into the conversation? To her relief, he did not. "We are friends," Cole said again, with a tone of finality in his voice. "Could we please change the subject?"

William Stratton leaned back in his chair. To Jacy's relief, he did so with an accepting smile and waved his hand. "Alright. Alright. I understand." Leaning over, he patted Cole's knee. "To tell you the truth, son, I was thinking about Priscilla Day." He paused and pressed his lips together. "You know how much I like Priscilla. You know how much your mother and I love her. After all...the two of you seemed devoted to each other..." He glanced at Jacy, then back at Cole, and shrugged. "I was just wondering if another woman had stolen your heart."

Cole's face grew red. Jacy couldn not tell if he was angry or embarrassed. He stared at his father but said nothing.

Jacy realized she, too, was staring at William Stratton with her mouth open. Who was Priscilla Day? Cole had never mentioned anyone named Priscilla. She felt a chill come over her, despite the heat. Folding her hands, she looked down at her lap.

The silence stretched on. Jacy glanced at Cole. His expression remained stony. *Is Priscilla his sweetheart?*

Surely, Cole would have mentioned her.

Jacy's heart pounded in her chest as her mind raced. Where was Priscilla? Did she live far away? Why hadn't she come to Cape May?

Jacy studied Cole's face out of the corner of her eye. His expression was unreadable. She realized there was a great many things about him she did not know.

Footsteps interrupted the silence. A man carrying a black medical bag walked toward them.

Looking relieved, Cole stood and smiled.

William Stratton stood too, also looking grateful for the interruption.

"So glad you could join us, Doctor," Cole said. "I want to introduce you to my friend, Jacy James, the woman who helped me heal."

CHAPTER NINETEEN

*W*hen Jacy returned from her lighthouse trek the next morning, Samuel was sitting on the hotel porch steps, resting his elbows on his knees.

Jacy waved to him, happy to find him alone. Chances were good he knew Priscilla Day, and she longed to find out more about the woman.

After Cole's doctor had joined them on the porch the day before, Priscilla's name had not come up again. Stiff and professional, the physician had formally thanked Jacy for helping Cole, indicated he was pleased with his progress, and kept the conversation focused on Cole's health.

As she greeted Samuel, Jacy realized she had thought about Cole more than Edmund as she hiked to the lighthouse and back. She had also spent an inordinate amount of time contemplating the mysterious Priscilla Day.

"Good morning, Samuel," Jacy said with a smile, hoping she sounded more cheerful than she felt. "Are you waiting for Cole?"

"Yep. Should be along any minute, Miss Jacy." He stood. "You have a good walk?"

"Yes, thank you."

He nodded and gave her a sly grin. "Mister Cole want to go with you one a-these days. To the lighthouse."

"He *does?*"

Samuel's grin widened. "What he told me."

"Wow." Jacy looked at him wide-eyed. "That would be wonderful. If he could walk that far and back, that would be wonderful."

"He mean to do it." Samuel held her gaze and smiled. "He like you, Miss Jacy."

Jacy felt herself blush. Did Cole think about her as much as she thought about him? A rush of warm pleasure washed through her. Then she reminded herself how he would feel about her if he knew her truth.

Maybe Priscilla Day was the type of woman Cole deserved. It seemed likely, since his father spoke highly of her. But did Cole love her?

Striving to keep her voice casual, Jacy asked Samuel if he knew the woman.

Samuel's eyes lit up. "Sure do. I know Miss Day." He stopped and looked over at the hotel porch, as if looking for Cole. Not seeing him, he whispered loudly, "I know her maid, Miss Mavis Allen, too."

"Her maid?"

"Yes. I'm sweet on Mavis. And she is sweet on me." His eyes held a twinkle.

"Oh." Jacy smiled.

Samuel laughed. "Miss Priscilla and Mister Cole, they was sweethearts. But ain't no more."

"Oh. I see."

"Don't worry 'bout Miss Priscilla, Miss Jacy."

Jacy stared at him. "I'm not worried."

Samuel laughed again. "Sorry. You look it."

She lowered her voice. "Cole's father just happened to mention Priscilla Day. So, I was just curious. That's all."

Samuel gave her a knowing look. He put his hands on his hips and squinted in the direction of the hotel. There were still no signs of Cole or Henry. He looked back at Jacy. "Tell you the truth, I sure do wish

Mister Cole was still seeing Miss Priscilla. Not cause I like her all that much. I like you a lot better. 'Cause you're nice." He shrugged. "It's just...I miss Mavis. I ain't seen her since Mister Cole sent Miss Priscilla a break-up letter."

"A letter?"

"Yep. I delivered it. Few months back. When Mister Cole was real sick. And Miss Priscilla wouldn't visit."

"She wouldn't visit him?"

"Nope. Like I said, not a nice woman."

Jacy widened her eyes. "Oh. I see. Hmmm."

"I told you too much," Samuel put a finger to his lips and nodded in the direction of the porch. Cole and Henry stood in the doorway. When Cole saw Jacy, he headed toward her, lightly holding onto Henry's arm. Before long, he wouldn't need anyone's arm.

"Shhh. I got a big mouth. Don't tell Mister Cole what I told you," Samuel whispered. "Please."

"Don't worry. I won't. I like you, too, Samuel. Thank you so much."

"For what?" Samuel's voice was so soft she could barely hear him.

"For the truth," she whispered back.

Knowing truth about Priscilla Day, she felt oddly better.

* * *

Frank Lynch slapped the oars of the lifeguard rowboat into an oncoming wave, launching the white, wooden craft into the air. Hovering over the rolling sea, it slammed down onto the next oncoming swell.

Rowing was always a thrill for Frank, especially when he was irritated, and he was beyond irritated.

Flying over the waves relieved his stress. He rowed faster and harder—drenching himself and fellow lifeguard Pete Potter as they paddled parallel to the hotel's beach.

Frank usually enjoyed patrolling from the water, but seeing Jacy and Cole strolling up and down the strand together ruined what should have been a fine summer day. Arm in arm, they were hard to miss. Jacy was dressed in a lacy white dress, holding a parasol over her head, while Cole wore a white suit and straw hat.

Have they started dressing alike on purpose? How obnoxious.

Grinding his teeth, Frank fumed. In their get-ups, they obviously would not be swimming. Suppressing a growl, he rowed harder, unable to take his eyes off them. The prig Stratton was holding onto Jacy's arm like a lover.

Splash! The boat crashed down onto a wave. Buckets of sea water flew in, covering the bottom of the boat with sloshing water.

"Egads! Watch it!" Potter yelled. Crouched in the seat across from Frank, he shot him an angry look. "What are you doing? We are supposed to be patrolling the beach, not practicing for the Cape May Hotel Lifeguard Competition." He squinted at him. "You know we win that damned race every year. What are you worried about?"

Frank slowed his pace and shouted back, "I'm not...worried... about that." Raising the red oars in the air, he allowed the boat to coast, forcing himself to settle down.

Besides, it was time to turn around and head back in the other direction to keep within White Caps territory. Every large oceanfront hotel had its own volunteer lifeguard crew and entering another crew's waters was not considered gentlemanly.

It was also Potter's turn to take the oars.

Frank gestured for them to switch seats. Potter was one of Frank's best guards. They had worked the beach together for years, and he was a good friend.

Potter rowed at a leisurely speed as Frank shaded his eyes with his hand and scanned the crowd of bathers between the boat and the shore.

The beach was crowded. Saturdays in July usually were, but everything in the water looked fine.

The situation on the sand, however, was another matter.

Cole and Jacy were still together. Strolling, chatting, laughing—they obviously enjoyed each other's company. They acted as if they were the only two people in the world.

"Bloody hell..." Frank muttered. "Bloody, bloody—"

"What? Someone in trouble?" Potter ceased rowing, in case Frank needed jump out to rescue someone. "Where? Where?"

"No. No. Sorry." Frank waved his hand. "No one is going down. Nobody is drowning."

"So...what are you yelling about? Why are you so..." Potter dipped the oars back in the water. He gave Frank a confused squint, looked at the beach, paused a moment, and began to laugh. "Ohhh. I seee," he said. "The lovebirds are making you crazy."

"*Lovebirds?*"

"Yeah. *Lovebirds.* You know who I mean. That Jacy woman you are so obviously infatuated with and her patient, the rapidly recovering Cole Stratton."

Potter laughed louder, which got on Frank's nerves. "That man has suddenly made a mighty impressive recovery, got to admit." Potter snickered. "Being sick sure wrangled him the attention of this summer's prettiest belle. Got to admire his luck."

Luck? Frank tore his gaze away from the "lovebirds" and glared at his friend. There was nothing funny about the situation—and Stratton certainly wasn't lucky. He was clever. Oh, no doubt his illness was real. He had arrived at White Caps in early June looking like he was on death's door. But he was taking advantage of it.

The invalid did look much healthier. He had gained weight. He had developed muscles in his pitifully skinny arms and legs, and he had acquired a tan almost as golden as Frank's. Stratton also wore his hair longer than what was in vogue—probably to show off his sun-bleached locks. He had a habit of pushing his bangs back from his forehead when he smiled. Which, now that he obviously felt better, was often.

Then again, Frank fumed, what man would not be smiling from ear to ear with Jacy James on his arm? *Blast Cole Stratton. Blast him all to hell.*

"Frank!" Potter shouted. "Calm yourself down, pal. You look like you would like to punch Stratton's face in. But I doubt that convalescent has any more chance of winning Jacy's heart than you do. You must have heard the rumors—or, by now, the open secret. She's in love with missing sea captain extraordinaire Edmund Overton. He's the one you need to be jealous of."

Frank growled. Of course, he had heard. "There's only one problem with that scenario," he said through clenched teeth. "The man's dead." He leaned forward and folded his hands together, squeezing his fingers so hard they hurt. Pressing his feet against the bottom of the boat to brace himself against the rolling waves, he added, "I don't think he's any competition to Stratton in that condition."

Potter flashed him a sly smile. "Except maybe he's not."

"What?"

"*Dead*. Except maybe he's not dead."

"What do you mean?"

"What I mean is that maybe, just maybe, he's hiding out somewhere."

"What makes you think that?"

"Cause that's the latest rumor going around." Potter's eyes held a mischievous gleam. "And I happen to know it might be true."

Frank leaned forward. "What do you know?"

Potter rowed slower, turning to look at the people in the water. "You're supposed to be watching the bathers," he muttered. "It's your job when I row. You're allowing yourself to get distracted."

"*Damn it.* What do you know, Potter?"

"Huh?"

"What do you know about Edmund Overton? And how do you know it?"

Potter grinned. "Had a nice chat with a fellow on the hotel maintenance squad the other day. Clyde Smathers. Know him?"

"I've met him. Local. Works at White Caps year-round."

"Right. Well, he told me he ran into a buddy in Philadelphia not long ago. Bloke who worked on Overton's ship. Was shocked to see him alive. The man tells him Smathers he and Overton were the only survivors of a wreck. Ship went down in a storm. Months ago. How do you like that?"

157

Frank frowned. "I don't. It doesn't make sense. Why are they hiding out?"

"Because if the story is true, they obviously let the rest of the crew go down with the ship. Or, at least they didn't succeed in rescuing anyone. If they even tried. They sure aren't heroes."

"Unbelievable," Frank muttered. "And if true, unforgivable."

"And maybe criminal." Potter shook his head. "Sounds like whatever happened, it's their word against what authorities might believe. Guess they don't want to take the chance. Or face the wrath of the families of the souls they failed to save."

"Scoundrels," Frank growled. "Cowards."

"Sounds like it to me. But there's hope there for you."

"What? How?"

"Think about it. If a very-much-alive Edmund Overton could be located, and brought back to Cape May, dear Jacy would go running into his arms. Her dream of his return would be realized. And Cole Stratton would be plum out of luck."

"Hmmm." Frank stared at Potter. "Hmmm." He ran his hand over his chin. "But why would Overton not have come back to her by now? How could he stay away from such a wonderful woman?"

Potter guffawed. "Maybe he got what he wanted from her, Frank. Maybe…just maybe… he was bored."

Frank almost choked. "What do you mean he got what he wanted?"

Potter stared at him like he was the dumbest man in the world. "What every man wants from a woman," he said with a sneer. "Do I need to paint you a picture? Come on…"

Frank felt blood rush to his face, shocked at Potter's suggestion. "No," he said. "A man of honor would respect a woman like Jacy. If he loved her. If he truly cared about her. If he wanted what was best for her. She is no prostitute. She is a woman from a respectable family."

Potter gave him that are-you-stupid-look again. "Yeah. Well. I don't think we are talking about an honorable man, Frank."

Frank narrowed his eyes, imagining the sea captain he had never laid eyes on. He formed a fist and punched his imaginary face. "*Blackguard…I'll kill him!*"

"You will have to find him first," Pete said. "So why don't you try?"

Frank grinned at the thought. "Maybe I should..." He nodded. "Except... I cannot try to find him now. It is peak bathing season. I will have to wait until fall. I will have the time then. Right now, I am needed here."

Potter grinned. "Yes, you are. But remember, you do have a crew of lifeguards under your command. Men like me that you can trust. Go. Take a week off. Go find Overton. We will watch the beach."

"Maybe...that might work." Frank paused. "But wait a minute. Why should I bring that creep back into Jacy's life? I want her for myself."

Slapping the oars hard into a wave, Potter aimed water at Frank's face. "*Think*. Think about it. What story could the creep give to explain his long absence, the reason he stayed away from her—let her suffer alone in her grief? Your beloved Jacy is an intelligent woman. It would not take her long to see him for the low life he really is. Then... then you could be there to comfort her. Especially if she learned you were the one who found Overton and brought him to light."

Frank wiped stinging salt water from his eyes. "Well...that does sound like an interesting plan..." He shook his head. "But it is one that can wait. If Overton is in hiding now, he will still be in hiding come September."

Potter shrugged. "You might be right, my friend. But let us hope that September is not too late." He nodded toward shore. "Because those lovebirds...if you ask me, they look like they were made for each other. Wouldn't surprise me if they were married by September."

* * *

"Your romantic life is becoming rather interesting," Henry remarked to Cole. "Which, under the circumstances, I find delightful *and* amazing. A mere six weeks ago, we were all afraid you were going to die. Now, we get to watch you tumble into Cupid's snare."

"I do not know what you are talking about." Cole pulled his bedcovers up to his chin and closed his eyes. He knew exactly what

Henry was talking about, but he was not ready to talk about it. "Please go," he mumbled. "Thank you very much for helping me get ready for bed. But I am exhausted and really need to go to sleep. Good night."

Henry laughed. "Nice try. But we need to talk."

Cole squeezed his eyes closed tighter. "And if I do not want to?"

"Then I will talk." Henry coughed as he lowered himself down into the chair next to Cole's bed. "And you will listen."

Cole groaned. He knew his brother. There was no arguing with him. "Okay, if that is the way you want it, I will try not to doze off." He yawned loudly. "But if you hear me snoring, do not wake me up."

It had been a long day, but one of Cole's best so far that summer. Physically, he was exhausted. Emotionally, however, he was on fire. Chances were, he would not be able to sleep at all.

The last thing Cole wanted was to discuss his feelings with Henry. He had spent the entire day with Jacy—and he was in love with her.

Finally able to admit it to himself, Cole knew he was being a fool.

He could no longer fight his romantic feelings, though, and as God was his witness, he had tried.

He had first come to the realization at breakfast. She was quietly eating a poached egg while he was sipping coffee. He knew in that instant. He had fallen for Jacy the very moment he first laid eyes on her. And there was nothing he could do about it.

After they had finished eating, she had inquired if he wanted to walk with her on the strand.

"Of course," he had said with more enthusiasm than he intended.

"Wonderful. Meet me in thirty minutes by the water's edge. I need to go freshen up."

She had done more than freshen up. When they reunited, she looked so dewy and fresh-faced, he found it hard to breathe. She was dressed in white, and laughed when she saw that he, too, had changed his clothes and was wearing white.

When she had gazed up at him with her gorgeous green eyes, he had found the energy to walk with her on the strand for what had seemed like a mile holding her arm.

After lunch, they had taken a swim together in the ocean. They went far beyond the breakers, earning Frank Lynch's ire. The lifeguard had not tried to hide his feelings, watching them from the beach with a dark frown.

Later in the afternoon, they had spent hours together on the porch. Poppy sat in the chair between them, reading some of her favorite poetry aloud.

Henry coughed again. Cole opened his eyes, remembering that he was in bed. He would never get any sleep if Henry didn't leave.

"Since when do you like poetry?" Henry asked. "I understand Poppy has written a poem about you and Jacy."

Could Henry read his mind? Cole sat up. "*What?*"

"Lydia told me. She says it is very sweet. It is about Jacy helping you get well."

Cole eased himself back down and stared at the ceiling. The room was dark, but the window was open for the breeze, and a full moon threw soft light into the room. He listened to the low rush of the ocean's waves. "It is a great poem," he muttered. "I need to ask her for a copy."

"Cole?"

"Yeah?"

"You falling for her?"

"Jacy?"

"I'm not talking about Poppy."

Cole hesitated. "Yes."

"I was afraid of that. Does she know?"

"Of course not. But she probably suspects."

"Why don't you tell her?"

Cole sat up and stared at Henry. In the moonlight, he could see his eyes. They held a look of concern. "I don't think she is ready," Cole said softly. "I don't think I am ready. I don't want to lose what we have."

"And what is that?"

"True friendship."

"Is she in love with you?"

"I don't know." Cole was silent a moment. "I would like to think so. But…"

"But what?"

"Edmund Overton. That's what."

"You need to ask her how she feels about Overton." Henry sounded exasperated. "How does she feel about him now? After all this time, climbing the lighthouse every day to look for him? For God's sake. With rumors flying around that he might still be alive, what is she thinking?"

Cole collapsed back onto his mattress. He frowned. "I know. I need to talk to her about it. About him. About us. But I'm not sure I am ready."

Henry stood up. "You better get ready. Because you are going to end up with a broken heart if you are not careful. I have never, ever, seen you really and truly in love with a woman. Until now. It is scaring me."

"Me, too," Cole said with a wry grin. "Me, too."

CHAPTER TWENTY

*H*elen smiled at her image in the mirror as her maid, Florence, fitted her new blue hat over her freshly crimped gray curls. Tilting her head to make sure her stylish chapeau stayed on, Helen turned around.

"Do you think I am over dressed for a carriage ride on the beach?" she asked.

Florence shook her head. "No, ma'am," she whispered, her pale, thin face expressionless, as usual.

Helen gave a prim smile, and silently thanked her good fortune for having found such a perfect maid for the summer. The plain, middle-aged woman came and went quietly and efficiently. She arrived on time every morning to help her dress for the day, returned at the designated hour in the evenings to help her prepare for bed, and came when needed for Poppy and Jacy.

"Have you ever visited the Light of Asia?" Helen asked her. "That is where Jacy says we are off to. Although I'm not sure why my niece is so excited about visiting a building shaped like an elephant."

Florence's eyes lit up in a way that Helen had not yet seen. "Yes, ma'am. We locals like to go inside for fun during the off-season.

There's stairs that take you into the head and there's windows where you can look out."

Helen nodded. "So I understand. Well, I am looking forward to our ride there. But I think I will wait in the carriage if Jacy and Poppy decide to go inside. Mr. Cole Stratton is coming along, too. And I know he will not be able to climb any stairs. I will need to keep him company."

"Yes, ma'am," Florence said.

Helen was pleased Jacy had invited her to go along on the excursion, and she was even more pleased when she learned Cole Stratton would join them. In fact, it was his idea, Jacy said. He planned it and was paying for the carriage.

Helen liked the charming and polite Mr. Stratton better every day. Jacy's interest in him had confused and troubled her at first. Of all the fine, eligible gentlemen in Cape May, Helen did not understand why Jacy had set her sights on someone so ill.

She had to admit that Mr. Stratton appeared vastly improved. More importantly, he was helping Jacy forget about Captain Overton. The more Helen thought about Cole as a suitor for her niece, the better she liked the idea. He came from a good family. Helen had discretely asked friends and acquaintances about him, and Jacy could do no better.

Helen smiled at Cole as he stood waiting in the hotel lobby. The two-horse carriage pulled up to the White Caps' front door and the driver took Cole's arm and helped him in first. Jacy eagerly sat down next to him. Her face was flushed, and she was beaming, which Helen took as a good sign that Jacy felt something for the man beyond friendship.

A very good sign, indeed.

With any luck, Helen mused, she would be able to tell her brother the sea captain was out of their lives for good. Taking a seat next to Poppy, Helen smiled at her daughter and at Jacy and Cole across from her. The driver cracked the whip, and they were off.

At low tide, the carriage bounced along on the sand at a leisurely pace. They arrived quicker than Helen expected.

Pulling up to the exotic pachyderm, they were not the only visitors that day. A line of people snaked across the sand, waiting to go in.

Jacy looked disappointed, but Helen was glad. It would give her time to speak to the intriguing Mr. Cole Stratton.

"Don't worry about me, girls. Go ahead and get in line," Helen said. "Mr. Stratton and I will be happy to wait in the carriage. Won't we, Mr. Stratton?"

"Cole," he said, giving her a warm smile. "Cole to you, and of course I don't mind waiting here with you. I have climbed the Light of Asia in the past. No need for me to explore it today."

Jacy frowned. "Are you sure?"

"Absolutely." He looked at Poppy, who appeared as eager as Jacy. "I look forward to getting to know your mother better. So, go and don't worry about us."

"Thank you." Poppy exited the carriage and turned to take Jacy's hand. "Let's go."

Helen watched her charges saunter over to the crowd then turned to smile at the handsome man across from her. She held his gaze as he returned her smile. He had a confident, self-assured air about him. No wonder Jacy liked him.

Cole leaned forward. "I am pleased to be able to spend some time with you, Mrs. Bainbridge."

"Helen. If I am to call you Cole, then…"

"Of course." His eyes twinkled. "Helen."

Helen smoothed her skirt. Blue and gray striped, it matched her hat. She took pride in looking her best. "And I am most happy to spend time with you," she said. "I like you and your family very much." She knew what she wanted to discuss with him, but for some reason felt tongue-tied. Peering out the window, the line was moving faster than she had anticipated. Poppy and Jacy were almost to the door.

She admonished herself and took a deep breath. "I must tell you how pleased I am that you and Jacy are becoming an item," she said, her words spilling out in a rush. "I think the two of you suit."

Cole's reaction surprised her because he appeared surprised. A strange, shy look came over his face. "Oh?"

She waited for him to elaborate on his strangled, one-word comment. When he said nothing more, she plunged ahead. "Well, yes." She cleared her throat. "If you are looking for my approval as far as my niece is concerned...that is...if you are interested in courting her...you have approval."

Oh dear, have I overstepped my bounds?

He looked out the window then turned back to her. His lips twitched, as if he was trying to find the right words to say. A deep crease formed between his brows. "Why thank you, Helen. That means a great deal to me." He held her gaze. "But...but I don't believe Jacy is ready to be courted. By me, or any other man. Unfortunately. And you know the reason."

"You mean..." Helen choked at having to say the man's name. "Edmund Overton? Are you concerned about him? I hope you aren't. Because he is dead. And I believe Jacy is finally beginning to accept it."

Cole nodded. "That may be. But is she still in love with him?"

"What do you mean?"

"If she still loves him, there is no room in her heart for me."

"Do you want there to be room in her heart for you?" Helen put her hand to her mouth. She *was* overstepping her bounds.

"Jacy is a wonderful woman." Cole's voice was soft. "What man would not desire her love?"

"I'm afraid you are not answering my question, which I apologize, was a bit forward." Helen looked down at her hands in her lap. "When someone is desperate, they find themselves doing things they would not ordinarily do. I am sorry. You don't need to tell me anymore."

"I can't. Because I don't know the truth about how Jacy feels."

Helen shook her head. All her life, she had prided herself on her ability to be discrete, composed, and in control of her emotions.

Something in her snapped. "The truth?" She stared at him. "Do you want to know the truth? The truth, my good sir, is that Edmund Overton was an awful man. He took advantage of a lonely, vulnerable young woman who didn't have a mother to take her under her wing the first few years of her social life. He cared not a fig that he was ruining her life."

Cole frowned. "I don't understand. Jacy ...lonely and vulnerable? She seems to have a wonderful family and is very sociable."

Helen stared at him. She sighed. If he was to understand, she must tell him. Every family had problems. If he were to understand, she must tell him everything.

She told him Jacy's mother had died when Jacy was only three, about Jacy's subsequent close relationship with her father, and how her father's second marriage brought many more children into the family. Stripped of her father's undivided attention, "The poor child must have felt it more deeply than any of us realized," she said.

After graduating from Miss Pennington's Academy for Young Ladies, Jacy seemed adrift and directionless, Helen continued. Her family assumed she would meet a nice young man and marry, like her friends, so they did not become overly concerned. It did not occur to them that an older, wily man like Overton would come along to charm her.

"My brother, Jacy's father, blames himself in a way," Helen said. "Because he introduced them to each other. Overton was in his office on business, and Jacy stopped by to visit. Jacy has a bit of an independent streak, which I am sure you have noticed, and Overton took advantage of it. He apparently convinced her to keep their relationship a secret for a long time, as some kind of madcap adventure." Helen shook her head. "She was a young girl. Naive. Inexperienced in the world. He was a monster."

"So, the family didn't know?"

"Not until it was too late," Helen said softly. "Not until she had already fallen in love with him. Then, she started bringing him to family functions. We don't know what he was planning, and we were relieved when his ship disappeared."

"But Jacy was devastated," Cole said. He rubbed his chin, the expression in his eyes unreadable.

"Yes. We felt badly for her but thought she would get over him. For some reason, she didn't. We brought her to Cape May to take her mind off him."

"Hoping she would meet someone else."

Helen nodded.

Cole lowered his head. He sat motionless and silent, and Helen wondered if she had told him too much.

She stared out the window. "You have given me hope," she said. "If you care for Jacy at all, and she cares for you, then maybe…"

She stopped.

Jacy and Poppy were walking out of the Light of Asia, laughing and chatting as they headed toward the carriage.

Helen leaned forward, and Cole looked up. "I implore you," she said. "Forgive me if I am being too forward. But if you love Jacy, tell her how you feel."

Cole stared at her. "Do you think it's possible she could ever love another man?"

Helen's eyes widened. "Yes, yes, I do," she said. "I know my niece. Her involvement with Overton was just a silly infatuation. She has a pure heart. She has much to give a man who deserves her."

Jacy and Poppy stepped up to the carriage. The driver hopped down from his seat, opened the door, and helped them into their seats.

"Did you have a good time?" Helen asked, striving to sound casual.

"Yes, yes," Poppy said, her eyes bright.

Jacy grinned. She looked at Helen and then at Cole. "I hope you two were not bored waiting for us."

Helen shook her head. "Cole and I had a grand time getting to know each other better." She glanced at him out of the corner of her eye, and to her relief he nodded in agreement.

"We were not bored in the slightest," he said.

* * *

JACY GASPED when Cole entered the dining room holding on to no one's arm.

Henry and Lydia strolled in behind him, holding hands and beaming as if in a triumphant parade.

As Cole walked past tables, friends and acquaintances applauded.

Holding his head high, he acknowledged each with a knowing smile. Many people in the room had watched him strive to regain his health this summer. They were proud of him. Her eyes welled with tears.

When Cole saw Jacy, he slowly and confidently headed to her table, halted and bowed.

"Mrs. Bainbridge, Miss Bainbridge, Miss James," he said, looking at Aunt Helen, Poppy and Jacy in turn. "Would you mind if we join you this evening?" His eyes twinkled.

Jacy jumped to her feet, clapping her hands. "Please do! Yes, indeed, please do!"

Flustered, she grabbed the chair next to her and pulled it out for him, then realized her faux pas. He didn't need her, or anyone, to do that for him anymore.

Cole caught her eye and laughed. "Thank you, my dear, but it is my pleasure as a gentleman to help you to your seat." He reached for her hand as she nodded and sat down. He sat next to her, waited for Henry and Lydia to get settled, then turned back to face her. "As you can see, I seem to have recovered my health completely." He gave her a heart-stopping grin. "With half the summer still to go."

She laughed. "Congratulations. I am so happy for you."

He leaned over to whisper in her ear. "Thank you. I could not have done this so quickly without you."

Jacy nodded, feeling everyone's gaze on her. Blushing, she whispered back. "Helping you was my pleasure, sir."

She could not think of anything else to say. Overcome by a wash of emotions, she found Cole's closeness unsettling. Acutely aware of the heat of him, his masculine energy, she felt her mouth go dry. Slightly dizzy, a rush of warmth surged through her, making her tingle all over. Snatching up her napkin, she fiddled with it and placed it in her lap to hide her trembling hands.

Her heart leapt with joy. Cole was well. He was healthy. He had achieved his goal. He was essentially a new man.

The dream he had shared with her had come true.

So. She swallowed hard. *What now?*

Nervously smoothing the napkin in her lap, Jacy looked around the room. As Cole had triumphantly pointed out, summer was only half over, and he could partake in the social activities like everyone else. She pressed her lips together. Now healthy, women would surely flock to him.

She would be forced to share his attention with other women. It would be awful.

Jacy drew in a deep breath as she glanced at the other diners. As Cole conversed with Aunt Helen, pretty young things cast admiring glances his way.

Jacy let out a quiet sigh. Was she surprised? In any case, what right did she have to discourage him from socializing with any woman who struck his fancy?

It was not as if she had given him any hope of winning her affections.

She had made it clear to him, and most everyone, that Edmund Overton had her heart. But did he? Did he still? *Did Edmund ever really have it?*

Jacy had flash of insight. Beginning as a whisper, it grew louder and louder. Was it possible she had used Edmund's ghost to hold other men at bay? Because she feared he had ruined her for any other man?

Tears welled in her eyes. She steeled herself to avoid crying and struggled to maintain an appearance of normalcy.

"Are you alright, Jacy?" Leaning over, Cole peered at her with a concerned frown. "You look upset about something."

"I do?" She tried to smile and managed only a pained grin.

"You looked worried." He leaned closer and lowered his voice. "What's wrong?"

He knew her well. Too well to fool him for long. Attempting another smile, she failed and sighed. "I was just thinking...I was just thinking that you will be very popular with the ladies. For the rest of the season."

"Really?" He laughed. "You think so? You really think so?"

Nodding, she said, "Look around, Cole. Some are batting their eyes at you already."

He laughed again. "They are?" With slow deliberation, he looked to his right, to his left, and behind him. Turning to face her, a corner of his lips turned up in amusement. He reached for her hand and she gave it to him. She was still shaking. Could he feel it? He whispered, "Jacy, are you jealous?"

She withdrew her hand. "Do you want me to be?"

His eyes widened, and she silently cursed herself for asking the question. How could she have? How could she have been so impetuous? So brazen?

She held her breath. A slow grin spared across Cole's face.

He held her gaze and she couldn't look away.

Vaguely aware she might faint if she didn't resume breathing, she swallowed hard and took a deep breath.

Then she knew.

The truth washed over her as strong and powerful as a crashing ocean wave.

She was not just attracted to Cole, she was falling in love with him. Actually, she wasn't just *falling* in love.

I love him. Fiercely. With all my heart.

She loved him more than she had ever loved any man. Including Edmund.

Jacy looked deep into Cole's eyes as he gazed deeply into hers. She could not lie to herself any longer. There was no use trying. She had been falling in love with him all along and she no longer had the strength to deny it.

Tearing her gaze away, she stared down at her lap, feeling too frozen to move.

He had not answered her question. Finally, after what seemed an eternity, he did.

"I do want you to be jealous, Jacy," he said softly. "I would very much like it if you were."

CHAPTER TWENTY-ONE

*C*ole and Samuel waited for Jacy on the beach the following morning at dawn. As usual, she was happy to see them, but after what had unfolded the evening before, she also felt shy as a moonstruck schoolgirl.

As Cole strolled toward her, she scolded herself for being silly.

It wasn't as if any other romantic pronouncements had passed between them. After their jealousy conversation, Cole had seemed as hesitant to push the subject as she. Instead, they had chatted about a variety of inconsequential things. Cole went off to play cards with the men after dinner, and Jacy retired to her room, emotionally spent.

Informing Poppy she was going to bed early, she threw herself onto her bed and stared at the ceiling for hours before mercifully falling asleep.

Cole played a starring role in one of her dreams. Although she couldn't quite recall what it had been about, she woke up with a smile on her face.

Now, in the semi-darkness of dawn, he was with her in the flesh, and she smiled again.

He hurried toward her, walking faster than she thought possible. "We'd like to go part of the way with you to the lighthouse," he said.

Samuel had warned her he would want to do that one day. She just never imagined it would happen so soon, if ever. "I am amazed at your courage," she said. "But do you really think you are ready? For something so strenuous?"

Jacy glanced over at Samuel, who gave her a knowing shrug.

The situation suddenly struck Jacy as slightly odd. "Do you want to go with me to look for Edmund Overton?" she asked, trying not to sound incredulous.

Cole grinned. "Not exactly." His eyes held a mischievous gleam. "If you want to know the truth, I would rather he not be found."

Jacy opened her mouth, but no words came out.

"You heard me. If you are going to be jealous of other women flirting with me...then... I have the right to be jealous of your sea captain." He looked sheepish. "Please understand, I'm not..."

"Ahh..." Jacy said, holding his gaze. "That's quite alright. I understand." She felt shy again. She hated feeling awkward in Cole's company.

Changing the subject, she blurted, "So why do you want to walk with me?"

Samuel grinned. "To get stronger. He can walk, but not far. Not yet."

"That's right," Cole said. "Samuel and I came up with a plan. If we walk with you every morning, it will build my endurance. Then, by the end of the week, maybe I can make it all the way there."

"And back," Samuel muttered.

Cole smiled. "Right. And back."

Jacy put a hand over her mouth. "Hmmm," she said, excited but also worried. What if Cole pushed himself too far, and had a setback? "Alright," she said, meeting his gaze. "I am happy for the company. Let's go."

Cole walked beside her, and Samuel walked next to him. The sun rose over the horizon. Already, the morning felt hot and muggy.

The threesome walked in silence, but Jacy didn't mind. She was used to doing the route alone, with only her thoughts for company. It was best that Cole conserved his energy and didn't try to carry on a conversation, anyway. He clearly seemed focused on just putting one foot in front of the other.

His tall, quiet, masculine presence gave her enough nervous energy to walk to Maine and back, but he soon tired.

Cole walked farther than Jacy thought he would be able to, but after about ten minutes, his breathing grew labored, and his face was dripping with sweat.

Jacy stopped. "You are doing great, Cole. But you need to rest."

"Yep," Samuel said. "Don't want to carry you back."

Cole gave Jacy a look of relief. Nodding, he eased himself down onto the sand. "I agree this is a fine enough beginning." Running a hand across his brow, he looked up at Jacy and flashed her a brave smile. "A few minutes sitting here and I should be fine. Samuel and I will head back. You can go on without us."

Jacy hesitated. Cole did look as if he would be okay. She wasn't, however, ready to leave him.

Dropping down beside him, she arranged her skirts around her legs. A knowing look passed between Samuel and Cole and then the orderly meandered down to the shoreline.

"Good man," Cole remarked.

"Samuel?"

"He knows I want to talk to you."

"You have been rather quiet."

Cole inched closer. Sitting side-by-side, they were close enough to touch. A sliver of sweat ran down Jacy's cheek. She removed her bonnet and placed it in her lap.

She smiled at Cole. He wasn't wearing a hat, so why should she? A breeze blew in off the ocean and ruffled his hair. The cool air caressed her forehead.

"I have a question I have been wanting to ask you." Cole's voice was husky.

Jacy's pulse begin to race. "Oh…" She cleared her throat. "What is that?"

"I was thinking about something. When I was walking next to you just now."

"Oh? What?"

Cole gave her a crooked grin. "I was wondering if you still make this hike every day to look for Edmund."

Jacy went still.

"Or, has it by chance just turned into a habit? Or...perhaps something else?"

Cole leaned back and searched her face. His perceptiveness amazed, flattered, and frightened her a little.

She took a deep breath and let it out. "You understand me, Cole."

"What does that mean?"

"For a long time, I walked to the lighthouse to look for Edmund. Walking Beacon Beach calmed my nerves. It gave me an outlet for my nervous grief."

She couldn't believe she was telling him, but it felt good to unburden herself.

Cole lifted an eyebrow. "And then?"

"And then I began to walk it for me. The beach became a place I could go to think. To think about my life."

"And then?"

She stared at him. "And then I realized climbing to the top of the lighthouse gave me a clearer perspective."

"On?"

"On life."

"What did you see?" Cole's voice was soft. "From up there?"

What did she see? *Not Edmund, not his ship.*

She saw herself. With each passing day, the woman she once was, and the woman she was becoming came sharply into focus. Dare she share that with Cole?

No, she should not.

She could not tell him about her scandalous behavior. Nor could she tell him that, when she contemplated her future, it was a very lonely one.

The last thing she wanted was his pity.

"What do I see up there?" She gave him a wistful smile. "It's beautiful," she whispered. "You need to see the view for yourself."

Cole's eyes lit up. "Of course," he said. "As soon as I am strong enough, I will climb the steps with you."

* * *

THE NEXT DAY, Cole walked about fifteen minutes before he and Samuel needed to turn back and let Jacy go on alone to the beacon.

Every morning for the next five days he managed to go farther than the day before.

On the fifth day, he made it all the way to The Light of Asia. Jacy was delighted. "The lighthouse is just over the dunes." She pointed. "Maybe tomorrow, you can make it all the way."

"Real likely," Samuel said, sounding surprisingly sad.

Cole shot Samuel a look of concern. "You don't sound happy for me."

Samuel stared at him, his usual upbeat mood gone. "You won't need me soon, Mister Cole. Healthy men don't need no orderlies."

Jacy's breath caught in her throat. Mired in her own concerns, she had not thought about Samuel's situation. He would have to find a new employer. She struggled to think of something to say to him, but nothing came to mind.

Cole gave Samuel a broad grin. "Nothing will change for the rest of the summer." He held Samuel's surprised gaze. "I would like for you to keep working for me as you have, but going forward, as my companion and assistant. I hope it doesn't happen, but it's possible I might take a turn for the worse and get sick—"

"You won't." Samuel shook his head.

"You're right," Cole grinned. "I feel great." He glanced at Jacy then looked back at Samuel. "But you know what? I have been feeling so good it's caused me to think about my future. For a long time, I wasn't sure I would have one. Now, that it appears I will, I was thinking about looking for a larger house. Come September. My townhouse is nice, but I would like something larger. A mansion, perhaps. Maybe close to the river."

Jacy suppressed a gasp.

Samuel looked as surprised as she felt. "Mister Cole, that—"

"That means I will need to hire a household staff, you are right," Cole's eyes gleamed. "So, Samuel, if you would like to continue to work for me, I could use a head houseman."

"I'd like that, Mister Cole."

Cole looked at Jacy, and a sly smile spread across his face. "It's time for me to settle down. As soon as I find the right woman."

Blood rushed to her face. She couldn't pull her eyes away from Cole's. She couldn't move, her mind became a blur. Cole was healthy again, so naturally he would want to make plans for his future. In the prime of his life, he was ready for a woman worthy of his affections.

She grieved that she could not be that woman.

She looked away. Her heart pounded so hard she feared he might hear it. Out of the corner of her eye, she saw Cole looking at her as if she was the woman of his dreams.

In truth, she was a respectable man's nightmare.

Cole sensed her distress. He looked confused, but he politely did not press. He changed the subject. "I am tempted to go ahead and haul myself over that dune right now and get it over with," he said, his tone jovial. "Go all the way to the damned lighthouse already."

Jacy turned back to face him. "No. You look exhausted. Tomorrow. Maybe tomorrow."

He nodded, sat down on the sand, stretched his long legs out in front of him, and leaned back on his hands. "You're right. Jacy, you are the voice of wisdom. Besides, I need to conserve some of today's energy for tonight." He winked at Samuel.

"Tonight?" Jacy stared at Cole. "What about tonight?"

"Have you forgotten? Tonight is the Midsummer Ball. One of the most anticipated events of the season."

"Oh, yes…at Congress Hall." Jacy had forgotten. "Thank you for reminding me."

"You are welcome." Cole gave her a knowing smile. "I am looking forward to it. Now that I can walk, I can dance. I plan to do so with you, Jacy. One dance, if that is all you will grant me. But I would very much like it if you will give me more."

177

* * *

"This is certainly an evening to celebrate," Henry declared as he and Lydia entered Congress Hall with Cole.

Cole nodded as he admired the festively decorated lobby, where tuxedoed men and bejeweled women mingled and greeted each other near the potted palms. "At last, I don't have to be a bystander," he said, beaming. "I get to be a participant."

Lydia touched his arm. Radiant, in a pale pink gown that flattered her sun-kissed face, she stood on tiptoe to whisper in her brother-in-law's ear. A tendril of her swept-up hair brushed his cheek and a wisp of gardenia perfume tickled his nose. "You will get to dance with Jacy, finally," she said in a giggly, breathy voice. "Aren't you glad?"

Henry gave his wife a mock frown. "Are you demanding Cole dance with you?" he asked in faux horror. "I was hoping to keep you to myself the entire night."

Lydia batted her eyelashes at him. "Which you shall, dear husband. I was asking Cole if he planned to dance with Jacy."

Cole cleared his throat and slapped Henry on the shoulder. "Of course I do. Greatly looking forward to it. Hope she will give me her first dance."

"And after that?" Lydia fingered the pearls around her neck.

"I am wondering the same thing," Henry said.

"Well, after that we shall have to see," Cole said. "I wouldn't mind dancing with Jacy the entire night, but it will be up to her."

Feeling physically better than he had for a long time, Cole also felt good about his appearance as he sauntered into the ballroom. His tuxedo fit him well, thanks to a trip to a local Cape May tailor. He had gained some weight and was nearly back to looking as fit as he had before he had gotten sick.

A group of four young women meandered over to him, clutching their dance cards. Three more young ladies followed, giggling and whispering amongst themselves as they hovered nearby. Cole smiled. It seemed Jacy was right. Women were competing for his heart.

"Cole, it looks as if you will have a good time regardless of what

Jacy decides to do." Lydia grabbed Henry's hand, pulling him toward the dance floor. "I hope you don't mind if we leave you for now."

Henry shrugged and nodded. "I see Jacy over there," he called out, pointing with his free hand to one of the wide doors leading to the hotel's lawn. "Best of luck, Brother. Go dance."

Cole gave Henry an understanding smile and waved him off with a salute. Watching Henry and Lydia slip into the crush of dancers, he smiled politely at the young women around him, excused himself, and hurried over to Jacy.

Chatting with Poppy, she looked over at him, and when their eyes met, his heart slammed to a stop. She was wearing a satin, sapphire blue gown. She had never looked lovelier, which for her was saying something. Her dark hair, stylishly pinned atop her head, was adorned with blue and green ribbons. Long, loose, wavy tendrils framed her face.

"Hello, Cole." Poppy, dressed in a striking peach gown, greeted him in a cheerful, sing-song voice. "You look wonderful." She tilted her head and peered behind him. "And I can see a great many pretty young ladies think so, too."

"Thank you, Poppy." Fixing his gaze on Jacy, he said. "I'm surprised I am suddenly so popular. I don't believe I will be sitting down at all this evening."

"I don't believe you will." Jacy's smile sent Cole's heart racing.

He grinned at her. "Have you just arrived?"

"Yes," she said, her face flushed.

"Good. Then may I have your first dance?"

She handed him her dance card, beaming. "Of course."

When she gave him her hand, and he drew her close, a jolt of electricity shot through him.

Merging into the crush of dancers, he suspected she felt it, too. She was quivering. When he tilted his head to peek at her face, he noticed tiny beads of perspiration on her brow. Very flattering beads, they were.

He didn't recognize the slow waltz and was relieved his feet remembered what to do. Holding Jacy, it was if he had never been sick.

They whirled across the dance floor as if they had been together all their lives.

Jacy leaned back and gazed into his eyes, and he knew she felt it, too.

"You are a fabulous dancer, Cole," she whispered. "I never would have guessed."

With a chuckle, he gave her a knowing grin. "Why do you act surprised? You had more faith in me than I had in myself."

Her head fell back as she laughed. He felt the heat of her body against his and her soft, dewy skin and womanly curves. Suppressing a groan, he wondered how he would ever let her go.

He did not think he could.

Cole remembered when Lynch forcefully whisked Jacy across the dance floor to keep her all to himself. Now he knew how Lynch had felt, not wanting to let her go.

Cole frowned. Would Jacy do the same with him? Give him only one dance? He would, of course, respect her wishes. But he hoped he was more to her than Frank had been.

Of course I am.

"What's wrong, Cole?" Jacy gave him a worried look. Their fingers interlaced, she tightened her grip on his hand. "Do you feel okay? Do you need to sit down?"

He shook his head and looked deep into her beautiful jade green eyes. They sparkled with concern, but that was not what he wanted. He wanted her love. He wanted her. He wanted her to want him.

He suspected she did, but he felt a flicker of alarm. Something seemed to be holding her back. Something haunting, a sliver of a shadow, flashed in her eyes as they danced.

Is Jacy still pining for Edmund Overton? He winced. *Even slightly?*

He had to know, as much as he dreaded her response. "You mesmerize me, Jacy," he whispered in her ear. He body tightened, and he summoned the courage to continue. "I know we are friends. But I think you can see how I feel. So, I need to just come out and say it. I can't hide it any longer. I feel much more than friendship for you. I have for a long time." He rushed his next words: "Could I please have the next dance?"

She drew her head back. He held his breath as her eyes widened. Parting her lips, she said nothing, but gave him a silent nod. He felt as if she had handed him the entire world.

Halfway through the next dance, Cole sensed something was wrong. Jacy was tensing up. When he looked into her eyes, she seemed sad.

Sad? Why should she be sad?

He slowed their steps as the other dancers whirled around them. "What's wrong?" he whispered into her ear. Her skin smelled sweet, like a fresh-picked rose. "Is it Edmund Overton? Are you still in love with him? Because if you are…" He stopped and gripping her hands, studied her face. A couple, so wrapped up in each other they weren't looking where they were going, almost bumped into them before darting around.

"If you are still in love with Overton, I understand," Cole said, almost choking on his words. "I won't pressure you. I am a patient man. I can wait. I can wait until you are over him, if that's what it takes."

Jacy gasped. Her eyes filled with tears. She took a step closer, and grasping onto his tuxedo, burrowed her face in his chest. He held her tight.

Time stopped. So did the music. Cole could hear Jacy's breathing as the other dancers swirled around them.

"Cole…" Jacy lifted her face. The despair in her eyes confused him, triggering a sense of foreboding.

"I…I want you to dance with other women. I…I think it would be best." She swallowed hard and looked away.

"*Why*? Tell me *why*? You're not making—"

"I am not good enough for you." He could barely understand her words. Her voice was breaking, and he felt as if his heart was, too. A single tear ran down her cheek. Reflected in the candlelight, it resembled a precious jewel. "You need to have a chance to meet someone else," she whispered.

"What?" Cole let go of her hands. He could not think. Nothing made sense. Not good enough for him? She was perfect.

The orchestra stopped playing, and hand-holding couples wandered off the dance floor. Cole longed to ask Jacy to explain herself, but sensed the time was not right. He reached for her hand and guided her to a chair where they could get some fresh air. An ocean breeze cooled his face. He took the seat next to her.

"I don't understand, Jacy," he said, inching closer. "But I can see you are upset about something. Maybe we can talk about it later."

She turned to him, held his gaze, and nodded. "Thank you. I think that's best. But for now, please go dance, Cole. *Please*, please, go dance."

Nodding, he glanced around. Several pretty young women were looking his way. But he was in no mood to twirl any of them around the dance floor. Right now, he could not act carefree and debonair.

Looking up, he saw Poppy standing in front of him , giving him a quizzical look.

Cole stood and reached for Poppy's hand. "May I have this dance?" He didn't sound as cheerful as he knew he should. His heart felt far too heavy.

Obviously surprised, Poppy glanced at Jacy, who wordlessly nodded her consent.

Poppy handed Cole her dance card. "I'm honored to dance with you," she said. "I am confused, I will ask Jacy later what is going on. But in the meantime, thank you. For asking me."

CHAPTER TWENTY-TWO

*J*acy sobbed into her pillow that night, finding relief from grief only in sleep.

When she awoke, she lifted her face off the damp and clammy linen, sat up, and let out a deep sigh. Staggering as she stood to dress, she wondered in despair how she would get through the day. Turning Cole away had been the hardest thing she had ever done. The loss she felt rivaled anything she had ever felt for Edmund.

Stumbling down the hallway, the stairs, and onto the porch, she headed for the beach.

Cole stood there, in the semidarkness, waiting for her.

She gasped.

"Hello, Jacy," he said, his voice almost inaudible against the sound of the surf. Had she really heard him?

Was he really there?

Dazed and confused, Jacy walked toward him. Her heart skittered in her chest. She had assumed Cole would never want to speak to her again. Who could blame him? The way she had treated him at the ball had been inexcusably rude.

She had kept her eye on Cole for the rest of the evening, even as she half-heartedly danced with other men. After taking a turn with

Poppy, Cole had escorted one woman after another around the dance floor, never sitting down, not even once.

So, why is he here now? Does he still want to walk with me all the way to the lighthouse?

If Cole wanted to prove to himself, and to her, that his recovery was complete, he had certainly done that at the ball.

Jacy glanced around for Samuel. Not seeing him, she assumed he would be along shortly.

She looked back at Cole. He stood as motionless as a statue, his hands hanging by his sides as he silently watched her walk toward him.

Feelings of shame coursed through Jacy.

Then she stopped, shocked. She did not deserve the crooked smile Cole gave her when she reached him. He slowly raised his hands and held them out to her. Biting down on her lip, she placed her hands in his. They were as warm as the expression in his eyes.

Frozen, barely able to breathe, Jacy stared at him.

"If there was music, I would ask you to dance." Cole's voice was soft. "Will you dance with me anyway, Jacy? To the rhythm of the waves?"

"I'm sorry, Cole," she whispered.

"Don't be."

"You must think me an idiot. The way I behaved...you didn't deserve it."

He released her hands. "It's not about what I deserve, Jacy. I thought we had a connection, that's all."

How could she make him understand? She longed to explain, but how could she without revealing the truth about herself? Inwardly, she cursed society's stupid rules.

She swallowed hard and almost choked on her words. "You are a wonderful man, Cole. It's just that I don't deserve you."

"So you said. Which, forgive me, makes no sense."

"I—" Jacy stopped. He was right. What a mess she was making of things. She tore her gaze away and looked around. "Where is Samuel?"

"He's not coming today."

"What? Why?"

"Because I don't need him. I know I can make it all the way to our destination and back without his help."

"But—"

"But what?"

"Just you and me?"

"That's right. We need to talk. Just you and me."

"But…it's not proper."

Cole ran his fingers through his hair and laughed. "Really? Was it proper for you and me to walk together all those mornings with only Samuel as chaperone? Did he make it proper? I think many people would say not. I think you were supposed to have another woman with you, if I am correct in my interpretation of social etiquette."

He was right, of course. Shrugging, she gave him a rueful smile.

"Let's go, Jacy," Cole said. "We are wasting time. The sun will be up before we know it."

"That is true." She shrugged again. "Okay."

They walked in step, at a clip so fast it took Jacy by surprise, and Cole reached for her hand.

Hesitating at first, she gave it to him.

He laughed and so did she. Being with Cole felt right, as it always did, when she did not think about the past.

"You amaze me, Cole," she said, panting as she struggled to keep up with him. "I knew you would regain your health, and clearly you have." She shot him a sly grin. "Why, last night, you danced every dance. To the delight, I might add, of a great many beautiful women."

He slowed his pace. "You noticed."

"Yes."

He stopped and turned to face her. "I am *glad* you noticed."

"Again, I'm sorry for how I acted."

"You should be sorry, Miss James. Because you never sat down the rest of the evening, either. After me, you danced with a great many *handsome* men."

"You noticed."

"Of course, I noticed."

Turning toward the ocean, she glanced at him out of the corner of her eye and squeezed his hand. "After me, you didn't dance with any woman twice. Not even with Poppy."

"I was following your lead."

She drew in a breath and met his gaze. "Why, Cole?"

"Because I want you." His voice was a whisper. "Only you. It's only, always, ever been you." He paused, then continued. "You might think I'm crazy. And I am beginning to think I might very well *be* crazy. But I believe a part of me somehow always knew you would come along. That's why I never fell in love before, Jacy. Because you were with me even before you were with me."

Goosebumps tickled Jacy's arms as she stood in the warmth of the rising sun. She felt the same way. What Cole had said about time was true. Time meant nothing when she was with him. It did seem as if Cole had always been with her.

She shook her head. If only he *had* been. If only she could go back and erase her mistakes. If only she had not been such a fool with Edmund.

It hit her hard. If only she had not been fooled *by* Edmund. If only she had not been tricked by a man much older than she, a man wise to the ways of the world who had sensed her desperate need for love and took advantage of it.

Feeling dizzy, Jacy lowered her head and squeezed her eyes closed.

If only she had realized the love she craved would arrive in due time—if she had been patient and trusted in fate.

If only she had waited for Cole.

If only she could go back in time and erase her scandalous folly.

But I can't.

Weak-kneed, Jacy felt herself start to fall.

Cole grabbed her under her arms and pulled her upright. "What's wrong? Please tell me."

Opening her eyes, she looked into his kind and concerned ones.

Then she knew. She and Cole *belonged* together.

Destiny had brought them together.

She could not erase her feelings for him and did not want to. She would not fight them any longer. She would let him love her, and she would let herself love him.

Someday, she would find a way to tell him the truth about herself. When that day came, if and when it came, she would hope and pray for his forgiveness. If he could not and would not forgive her, she would just have to find a way to go on.

Jacy reached for Cole's hands, squeezed them, and gave him a beaming smile. "Nothing is wrong." She felt her smile turn into a giddy grin. "In fact, everything is suddenly and wonderfully right."

"It *is?*"

She let go of Cole's hands and raised her arms in the air. "Yes, I have just realized what a fool I have been."

"You *have?*"

"Yes. And how wonderful it is that I finally realized it."

A corner of his mouth lifted up. "Well, if you say it's wonderful, I am very glad to hear it. Care to enlighten me?"

Jacy shook her head. "Not now." She turned and pointed to the lighthouse. "Look, we are getting close. Come on. Let's go. You can make it."

He laughed. "I know I can. Come on, hold my hand. I'll take the lead."

Running together like happy children, they raced down the beach, scampered over the dunes, and sprinted onto the beacon's grounds.

Skidding to a stop, Cole let go of Jacy's hand. Bending over, he inhaled deeply to catch his breath. Straightening, he pointed to the top of the lighthouse and declared, "I'm going up with you."

Jacy ran over to the entrance door and yanked it open. "I was hoping you would say that, sir. Follow me."

Climbing the winding stairway, Jacy heard Cole breathing hard behind her. Thankfully, he could keep up.

When they reached the observation deck door, she waved him through first. Nodding, he stepped out and grabbed the rail.

Pressing her bonnet onto her head, Jacy scurried over to him, admiring his face in profile. He wore a look of triumph, grinning from ear to ear.

She looked down at the long ribbon of sand they called Beacon Beach. Overcome with happiness, she let go of her bothersome bonnet and reached for Cole's hands.

He turned to her as the wind whipped the bangs off his forehead. His expression a mix of delight and desire, Jacy caught her breath.

"I love the view," Cole shouted against the roar of the wind and the rush of the sea.

"I knew you would."

"And I love the person I am seeing it with."

Their gazes locked. She felt his desire. She could not fight it. She did not want to fight it, not anymore.

"Jacy?"

She swallowed hard. The ribbons of her bonnet pulled against her neck. The wind was trying to take it. The wind could have it. Reaching up, she untied it and let it go.

"Jacy, your—"

She lifted her chin and laughed. "I'm not worried about it. Maybe I'll find it down on the beach, and maybe not. It doesn't matter."

"It doesn't?"

"No."

"What matters, then?" Cole's voice was husky.

"You. And us."

Cole reached over and cupped a hand around Jacy's head. Pulling her closer, he lowered his lips to hers in a kiss so passionate, so filled with longing, it set her soul on fire.

Jacy's heart soared with the wind.

CHAPTER TWENTY-THREE

"So...does this mean you are over Edmund?" Cole, his eyes gleaming, looked at Jacy. He gently lifted her chin and caressed her cheek with his thumb.

Still flushed with desire, the question did not register.

"Edmund?"

A corner of Cole's mouth turned up in amusement. "Yes, you know, the man who for many weeks has brought you to the top of this beacon every morning. The man you said you loved. Whose return you have been awaiting for many, many, many days. That man."

She did not want to think about Edmund.

Holding Cole's gaze, she said, "I thought I loved him. Now, I know better."

"What?"

"I thought what I felt for him was love." She winced and turned to stare out at the sea. "But I was wrong. Very, very wrong. What I felt for him in no way resembled what I feel for you. It couldn't have been love. It wasn't."

"Ah..." Cole stared unblinking into her eyes. "And what you and I have is..."

"Love."

"Yes." His voice was a soft whisper. Reinforcing that single word, he placed his lips over hers again. Tingling all over, she threw her arms around his neck and lost herself in sweet passion.

After a while, they pulled apart. They looked at each other and kissed again.

An unmarried man and woman alone together on top of a lighthouse was beyond improper. It was, in fact, scandalous. She did not care. She had done worse. Blissfully caught up in the moment, she would not allow herself to think about it.

Then one thought entered her love-fogged brain: she would not make the same mistake with Cole as she had with Edmund. They would go no further than kissing, as difficult as that would be, given how they felt about each other.

She doubted he would try to take advantage of her, but she would prove to herself, and to him, that she was an honorable woman.

The sun was getting hot by the time Cole put his head back and looked deeply into Jacy's eyes.

"I think we need to go," she whispered.

He lightly touched the tip of her nose. "I think you are right. People are going to start wondering where we are. They're probably doing so already."

She gave him a saucy grin. "And what shall we tell them, if they should pepper us with questions when we get back?"

"That I am completely and officially restored to health." He matched her grin. "And that you won't be looking for Edmund Overton anymore."

"Ha," Jacy said as she yanked open the door to the stairs. "I think many people will be glad to hear that."

Cole went first on the way down and then reached for Jacy's hand as they turned in the direction of White Caps.

The trek back was a blur for Jacy because she and Cole kept stopping to kiss. That is, when she was not giggling with joy and he was not laughing and remarking at the wonder of them being together.

How is it that two people who met as strangers and quickly

became friends could become sweethearts, he mused aloud. To which she replied, it was the best kind of romantic love of all.

They discussed how they should act when they got back to the hotel. Jacy wasn't even sure what time is was. Cole said he didn't care.

They decided to just act nonchalantly, "as if that will even be possible," Jacy declared.

Entering the lobby with Cole at her side, she was relieved to see no one there. Certain her cheeks must be flushed and her hair a mess, she suddenly realized she had completely forgotten about her bonnet. It was probably back on the beach, or bobbing up and down on a wave somewhere.

Catching a glimpse of herself in the floor-to-ceiling mirror in the entryway, she gasped.

"Cole…I look a fright."

He flashed her his boyish grin. "Well…your hair is a wild tangle of curls. Quite fetching, actually."

"Cole…" she whispered. "What are people going to say?"

"Too late to worry about that now," he whispered back. "Shhh…I hear voices, people coming down the stairs. I think one of them might be your aunt."

He was right. Aunt Helen rounded the last turn of the grand stairway leading from the upper floors and when she saw them, her mouth dropped open.

Poppy, bounding down the steps right behind her, stared at them, wide-eyed.

Jacy heard a voice behind her, near the hotel's entrance. She didn't recognize the strident, high-pitched voice. It sounded like a child.

Why would a child be calling Cole's name?

She and Cole turned at the same time. It was no child. The voice belonged to a very tall, slender, extremely well-dressed, stunningly beautiful woman who looked to be in her early twenties.

"Priscilla," Cole said.

"Cole, darling," she cooed.

CHAPTER TWENTY-FOUR

*J*acy felt invisible.

The woman named Priscilla did not even glance at her as she click-clicked her way toward Cole in pointy-toed white boots.

Cole stood frozen, his mouth slack as if in shock.

Jacy glanced at him, then back at the stranger. Was *she* the woman Cole's father had mentioned? Priscilla. Wasn't that the name of Cole's former sweetheart?

Cole said he had ended their relationship. Why was she calling him "darling?"

A vision of regal haughtiness, she minced across the lobby floor inches at a time. Her tight black-and-white-striped gown made it almost impossible to walk any faster because it was layered with a great many bustles.

Her alabaster skin was strikingly smooth and unblemished, as if the sun had never touched it.

Jacy studied the woman's locks. She had never seen hair quite that shade, so blonde it nearly matched her white skin. Three corkscrew tendrils on each side of her face peeked out from under a most ornate hat. Like its matching gown, the zebra-striped chapeau was elaborately adorned. Jacy had never seen so many ribbons and feathers in one place.

"Priscilla." Cole's voice sounded strangled. "What are you doing here?"

"Darling, I came for you." The vision smiled, and as she did, her cherry-red lips moved upward without making a single crease around her mouth. Her eyes, the color of cornflowers, widened as she fanned her porcelain cheeks with long, black eyelashes.

"You came for me?" Cole did not sound pleased. Jacy turned to stare at him. His face turned almost as pale as Priscilla's. It reminded Jacy of the way he had looked when she first met him, when he was sick.

"Yes, you, my dear. Why do you doubt it? You look wonderful, simply wonderful," she said in a gushy, sing-song voice.

Cole looked at her as if she had lost her mind. "Thank you. I am feeling quite well, finally. I believe I will live. But it is no business of yours, Priscilla. Because we ended our relationship some time ago. I believe you got my letter?"

It was a question, stated sarcastically, but Priscilla ignored it. "I love you, Cole," she said. "I never stopped loving you. And now I have come to Cape May for the rest of the season, to be near you."

Jacy heard someone gasp and turned around. It was Aunt Helen. Standing beside her mother, Poppy had a hand over her mouth.

Blinking, Jacy turned to look at Priscilla. She hated feeling invisible. "Hello," she said, forcing a smile as she stepped forward to shake the woman's hand. "My name is Jacy James. I don't believe we have met."

Priscilla did not so much as look at her. Extending both her hands toward Cole, she click-clicked closer to him, paused, and gave him a wry smile. "Darling," she said. "Could we talk privately, please?"

* * *

"WHAT DO YOU WANT, PRISCILLA?" Cole couldn't believe she had the nerve to act as if they were still a couple. It was so ridiculous, he thought he must be having a bad dream.

He had taken her by the arm and guided her outside. He did it for Jacy's sake, not for hers. The quicker he could set Priscilla straight about the finality of their relationship, and get her to leave him alone, the better.

But she was having none of it.

"I have rented a cottage with Mother and Mavis," she told him with a bright smile. "I thought you would be happy to see me."

"And why would I be?" Cole stepped away from her and folded his arms across his chest. He suspected Jacy and her aunt and cousin were watching them from inside the lobby. If they were, he hoped they saw how perturbed he was by Priscilla's reappearance. In no way did it gladden his heart.

He hoped Priscilla noticed as well, but if she did, she did not let on.

"I have been praying fervently for your recovery, Cole, and I can't tell you how relieved and grateful I am that my petitions to the Almighty were heard and answered."

"Are you taking credit, or giving it to God?"

"Darling, really. Don't be cross."

"Darling? Since when did you ever call me that? I don't recall you ever calling me by that cloying moniker. I would have ended it with you far sooner than I did if you had. What are you trying to do? Make Jacy jealous?"

Priscilla's rudeness to Jacy had annoyed him to no end. As the daughter of one of the wealthiest men in Philadelphia, he knew Priscilla had been educated from birth in the proper rules of politeness. She knew better.

"Who is Jacy?" Her voice was frosty.

"She introduced herself to you. And you ignored her."

"Oh, that woman."

"What do you mean, 'that woman?'"

"The disheveled slut in there." She nodded in the direction of the lobby. "The woman whose hair is hanging down her back in untamed curls. Uncovered. Loose and wild. Where did you pick her up?"

194

Furious, Cole felt his face grow hot. "She's—"

"Is she a local you were trying to sneak into your room? My, my. You really must be feeling better."

Cole tightened his jaw.

Priscilla took a step back. "What? What? I'm sorry, is she your newfound love?"

He glared at her. "Yes. As a matter of fact, she is. And she is no slut."

Priscilla tossed her head back and snorted a brittle laugh. It was a most unbecoming sound from a woman who had always taken pride in her gentility. He had never seen her act so maliciously.

Then he knew. Not only had she heard he heard was healthy again, she had learned he had a new sweetheart and had hurried over to see for herself.

Priscilla was clearly furious that the story was true.

Giving Priscilla an icy stare, he said, "Jacy is a wonderful person and a woman from a fine upstanding family. I don't appreciate you calling her names."

"Oh, excuse me." Priscilla narrowed her eyes and met his stare. "By the way she's dressed...a rather flimsy dress...a bit damp with perspiration. Flushed cheeks and slightly swollen lips. Really, Cole. What was I to think?"

He felt his face grow even redder. Realizing that any explanation he could offer at the moment would make the situation worse, he clamped his teeth together and looked away. It was time to change the subject. He forced himself to look back at Priscilla. "Where are you staying? Did you say you rented a cottage?"

"Yes." She brightened at his interest. "A few blocks from here. It's a marvelous place. Three stories. A wide, wrap-around front porch. And a room for Mavis on the first floor, behind the kitchen."

"Mavis. Interesting. Samuel will be happy to see her. I will have to tell him she is in town."

Priscilla pursed her lips. "Oh, yes, I forgot your orderly has a crush on my maid."

"They got to see quite a lot of each other during my convalescence.

You know, when you sent Mavis to my house to deliver all those get-well-soon letters. Instead of visiting me in person."

She sighed and tilted her head. "I did send you a lot of letters…"

"I wanted to see *you*."

"I'm sorry. You know how I am around sickness."

"I certainly found out. It opened my eyes to the type of person you really are. You did me a favor. Thank you."

She took a step toward him. He stepped back away from her. Shaking his head, he pointed to the lobby. "I need to go. Jacy is waiting for me."

"Cole." Priscilla's voice was pleading. "Don't leave me, I have more to say."

HE SHOOK HIS HEAD. "I left you long ago, Priscilla. And there is nothing you can say that I want to hear."

CHAPTER TWENTY-FIVE

*N*umb, with a cold, sinking sensation forming in her chest, Jacy dashed over to one of the windows that framed the hotel's front door. She peered out at Cole and Priscilla. Cole looked angry. At least he wasn't happy to see his former flame. *But why has she come to White Caps?*

"What on God's green earth is happening?" Aunt Helen demanded. "Jacy, where have you been? And who is that woman?"

Jacy whirled around and looked at her aunt, who was gripping the stairway banister so hard her knuckles had turned white. Unable to come up with a reply that wouldn't make the situation worse, Jacy just shook her head.

"I would like to know as well," Poppy insisted. Rushing over to the window, Poppy looked out and then turned to Jacy with a perplexed frown. "You and Cole missed breakfast entirely. And Mother and I have been beside ourselves with worry."

"I'm sorry," Jacy mumbled. Meeting Aunt Helen's furious, questioning gaze, she added in an almost-whisper, "We were at the lighthouse."

"What?" Aunt Helen put a hand to her cheek. "You and Cole went there together? Who was your chaperone?"

Jacy glanced at Poppy's shocked face and then stared at the floor. "No one," she whispered.

Aunt Helen gasped. "No one? Please tell me that's not true. All summer I have suppressed my displeasure and worry about you going there alone. But going there with *a man*, alone, is far worse."

Despondent, Jacy kept her eyes on the floor. Nothing she could say would make it right in her aunt's eyes.

The door opened and Cole rushed in. To Jacy's relief, Priscilla was not with him.

"I'm sorry," he said, giving Jacy an apologetic smile. "I owe you an explanation."

"I am the one who needs an explanation, young man," Aunt Helen said, her voice rising to a shriek.

Cole nodded, his expression contrite. "I agree. As Jacy's guardian this summer, this must be awfully confusing for you. I assure you that I will explain. But first, I must speak to Jacy, alone."

"Alone—*again?*" Aunt Helen looked like she might faint.

"Mother," Poppy said, hurrying over and grabbing her arm. "I think you need to sit down." She narrowed her eyes and looked at Jacy and Cole. "I believe we all need to sit down. We should go somewhere quiet and private, where Jacy and Cole can talk, and you and I, Mother, can chaperone from a respectable distance."

Relieved that at least Poppy was thinking clearly, Jacy nodded and suggested the porch. Cole agreed it would be the perfect place and ushered the women to go ahead of him.

They found four vacant chairs at the far end of the veranda. Cole seated the women before taking the one beside Jacy.

Glancing at her aunt's thin, pursed lips, Jacy stared down at her hands. The angry older woman was the least of her problems. Priscilla's sudden appearance bothered her more. Where had Priscilla gone? And what had transpired between her and Cole?

"I think you know, Priscilla and I were once sweethearts," Cole said, turning to face Jacy directly. "I'm afraid she has rented a cottage a few blocks from here, through August, with her mother and maid.

Although you have nothing to worry about. I broke it off with her months ago."

Jacy stared at him. "What? She is planning to stay in Cape May through the rest of the season?"

Cole heaved a loud sigh. "Yes."

Still reeling from her passionate encounter with Cole, she was flustered by the way things looked to her aunt and cousin and blind-sided by Priscilla's sudden appearance.

If only she could speak to Cole in private.

On her way to the porch, Jacy hastily twisted her hair back into a bun, pinning it up as best she could. A piece of hair fell down over her eye. Quickly tucking it behind her ear, she used both hands to smooth her rumpled skirt, then blurted out, "But *why* is Priscilla here? If you ended your relationship with her? Does she think she can win you back?"

"I'm sorry. I believe so. But—"

"I never expected to meet her. I thought she was a part of your past."

"She was. She is." Cole took a deep breath and let it out slowly. "I think she does want me back. I think that is the reason she has come to Cape May. I wish she had not come, but I have no control over what she chooses to do."

Jacy widened her eyes. "I still don't understand."

"I don't either," Aunt Helen murmured. "This entire situation is—"

"Shhh, Mother," Poppy said. "Don't interfere."

Cole looked over at Aunt Helen and then back at Jacy and asked, "What don't you understand?"

"The nature of your relationship with Priscilla."

"We no longer have one."

"She obviously doesn't believe that."

"No."

"She is very beautiful." Jacy swallowed hard. Something rancid and bitter burned her throat. She swallowed again. "I can see why you loved her."

"No."

"What?"

"You don't see anything, Jacy. I never loved her. I know that now."

"Oh." Jacy glanced over at Aunt Helen, who was wringing her hands. Poppy, her eyes unblinking, stared at Cole and then at Jacy.

Jacy did not want the conversation to turn to the subject of her relationship with Cole. Her romantic feelings for him were too special and too raw. What had transpired between them was too new. She caught Cole's gaze. Raising a finger to her lips, she shook her head, praying he understood her silent message: *Our feelings for each other need to remain private for now. Please.*

Cole nodded, flashing her a smile that brought tears to her eyes.

He understands.

Turning to look out at the ocean, Jacy was overcome with gratitude for having Cole in her life. *He is so intelligent and so kind and so brave—and he loves me.*

Then her breath caught in her throat. Who was she fooling? She did not deserve such a man.

The memory of Priscilla waltzing into White Caps, calling Cole's name, flashed through Jacy's mind. Lovely Priscilla, haughty Priscilla —did *she* deserve Cole? Jacy suppressed a groan. The woman almost certainly did. She was clearly a socially respectable woman from a fine, upstanding family. Women like her saved their virginity for the men they hoped to marry. Priscilla had hoped and expected to marry Cole.

Jacy went numb with despair. Cole's father had said he and Cole's mother still had fond feelings for Priscilla. In fact, William Stratton had made a point of telling Cole so. Doctor Morris had also spoken highly of her, even defending her fear of germs.

Priscilla obviously believed she and Cole might still have a future together. Perhaps she was right.

Jacy turned back to Cole and took a deep breath. "About Priscilla..."

"Yes?" A wary look came over Cole's face. "What about her?"

Jacy glanced at Aunt Helen. She was staring straight ahead, trying to give the impression she was not listening to Jacy and Cole's conversation, but obviously hearing every word.

Jacy swallowed hard and plunged ahead. Having an audience of chaperones was unfortunate, but she *had* to tell Cole how she felt. "Maybe a part of you does still love Priscilla," she whispered. "Maybe you need to give her another chance, Cole."

A look of disbelief crossed Cole's face. He leaned closer. "What? What did you say?"

"It's just that...just that...the two of you once suited." Jacy almost choked on the words. "And perhaps...perhaps she is better for you than I am."

Cole widened his eyes. He opened his mouth, then closed it. He looked at Aunt Helen and Poppy. They stared at him and then turned to stare at Jacy.

Cole broke the silence with a laugh. Leaning toward Jacy, he gave her his heart-stopping grin. "Nope. It's you, Jacy." He reached over and touched her hand. "It has always been you."

* * *

"WELL, I never...What am I to think? What am I to tell your Uncle Tobias?" Helen slid a handkerchief out of her gown's pocket and blotted her forehead with it.

"I don't know," Poppy answered softly.

Jacy had left, with the excuse that she needed to go up to her room to wash her face and change her clothes.

After a few minutes of awkward silence, Cole had also excused himself, saying he needed to go find his brother.

Helen hoped Jacy did go straight to her room. She prayed she was not having a rendezvous with Cole in a corner somewhere. She did not have the energy to get up and find out, however, even though it was probably her duty to do so. *Really, one can only do so much.*

Blotting her neck with the handkerchief, she stared at Poppy. "Jacy has always been a bit free-spirited. But to go on a long walk with a man, unchaperoned, and then return from said walk looking like *she* did? I am beside myself."

Poppy nodded. "I don't blame you, Mother. But I am sure nothing scandalous happened. Jacy is not that kind of woman. And Cole is not that kind of man."

Helen hoped Poppy was right. Helen liked Cole Stratton—very much. Still, what had transpired between him and her niece? She didn't want to think the worst, but Jacy had already proved she did not have a bit of sense when it came to men. Carrying on with that ridiculous sea captain, as if he had been a serious contender for her heart, had almost ruined her. What if Jacy had run off and married him? Most likely only his disappearance had prevented that.

Cole Stratton, on the other hand, could offer her a wonderful future, if she did not ruin her reputation in the meantime. Waltzing into White Caps alone with him, looking like she had just…looking like they had just…Helen pressed a hand to her heart just thinking about it.

"I am far more worried about Priscilla Day," Poppy said.

Helen stared at her. "What? Whatever for?"

"Think about it, Mother. Now that Cole has recovered his health, he is obviously interested in courting Jacy. And Jacy is obviously romantically interested in him. Which is what I have been hoping for."

"As have I. But Jacy needs to think about her reputation."

"I agree. But she also needs to think about Priscilla Day. I believe the woman could genuinely threaten Jacy's future. I wish she had not come here."

Helen sighed. "It is unfortunate. The Day family is one of Philadelphia's most socially prominent. And one of the city's wealthiest. The Strattons do not strike me as social climbers, but I am sure Cole's parents greatly approved of Priscilla."

Poppy pressed her lips together. Nodding, she asked, "So, what should we do?"

"*We?*" Helen cupped a hand over her mouth and looked around. She had spoken too loudly. The porch was getting crowded, and a few people were indeed glancing in her direction. "What *can* we do,

Poppy?" she whispered. "Jacy is an independent-minded woman and Priscilla is a wealthy heiress and Cole is a man with a mind of his own. What do you mean what should we do?"

Opening her mouth, then closing it, Poppy stayed silent for a moment. "Cole Stratton has answered our prayers, Mother. He has cured Jacy of her grief for Edmund Overton. We need to encourage her to consider Cole her new beau. For some reason, she seems to believe she is not worthy of him. And we need to reassure her that she is."

Helen nodded. Her daughter was wise beyond her years, which was most fortunate considering the way the summer was unfolding. She studied Poppy's face. It would be nice if pretty Poppy had a romantic interest of her own, but perhaps it was just well she did not. Romance often brought drama, and the family already had enough of that.

"I think your idea is a sensible one," Helen said, patting Poppy's hand. "For now, I will refrain from telling your Uncle Tobias anything at all about Cole Stratton."

"I think that is wise, Mother."

"I will, however, give him some good news."

"Oh, and what is that?"

"I am going to tell him that Jacy seems to be recovering nicely from her infatuation with Edmund Overton."

CHAPTER TWENTY-SIX

$\mathcal{J}$acy dreaded seeing Priscilla Day again. She did not have to wait long for the pleasure. The next afternoon, the entire town buzzed with excitement over a concert featuring John Philip Sousa and his Marine Band.

Beginning at noon on the wide front lawn of The Chalfonte Hotel, Jacy and Cole went an hour early to secure good seats. Among the first to arrive, they found some in the front row.

Jacy happily watched other people arrive as she sat beside Cole, with Poppy and Aunt Helen on her other side. It was a delightfully sunny day, with a breeze blowing off the ocean, and she looked forward to the music.

Then Priscilla walked up.

Stiffening, Jacy glanced at Cole. His face turned to a dark frown.

Holding onto the arm of an older woman, Priscilla flashed Cole a beaming smile. Sliding into the unoccupied chair next to him, she waved her hand and gestured for her companion to take the one next to her.

Jacy gasped. Those seats were reserved.

"Cole darling," Priscilla said in a cool drawl. "It is so good to see you again. Say hello to Mother. She has missed you so."

Cole shot to his feet. "Priscilla, Mrs. Day." He gave a bow. "I am afraid I have been saving those seats for Henry and Lydia. They should be along any moment."

Priscilla gave a girlish giggle. "Well, indeed. I am sure they won't mind if Mother and I sit here."

"But…" Cole shook his head. "If you *wouldn't* mind, I would rather you find seats elsewhere."

Not moving an inch, Priscilla held Cole's gaze. "As you know, Lydia is one of my best friends. And Henry is one of the kindest men I have ever known. Except for you, of course. They would *want* us to sit here."

"Still, Priscilla—"

"Still nothing, Cole. Mother has been greatly looking forward to this concert. And she has been absolutely dying to see you again."

Jacy leaned over and studied "Mother." An older version of Priscilla, she did not look at all happy to see Cole. Turning her head, she gave him a cold smirk.

Jacy switched her gaze to Priscilla. As she had the day before, she wore a fashionable gown. Silver blue, it drew attention to her unusually light eyes. Her hat, of course, matched. Wide-brimmed, it framed her white-gold ringlets, which jiggled when she tilted her head.

"Mrs. Day," Cole said, his voice tight. "I trust you have been well."

Glaring at him, she gave a prim nod. "I have."

Cole introduced Jacy, Poppy, and Aunt Helen.

Ignoring the two younger women, the matron leaned over, glanced down the row at Aunt Helen, gave her a thin-lipped smile, then turned away.

"It is good to see you again, Zinnia," Aunt Helen remarked loudly. "It has been a long time since we last met. I believe it was at the reception—"

"Yes, I believe it was," Zinnia Day called back, without looking her way.

Jacy's jaw tightened. Priscilla was taking advantage of Cole's easygoing and generous nature. She knew he would let them keep their seats because he was not the type of man to create a scene.

Not wanting to embarrass Cole, Jacy said nothing. She tried to think of some socially polite comment to make to Priscilla but was too furious to think clearly. Priscilla was purposely ignoring her.

Henry walked up, with Lydia on his arm.

As Priscilla had predicted, the gracious couple assured the Days they would not mind taking seats elsewhere.

Unbelievable.

Pointing to the back, Henry said some empty chairs were still available there. "How nice to see you again, Priscilla," he added, his voice a bit strangled. "Cole informed me yesterday of your arrival. I hope you and Lydia will be able to play some tennis. Just like before."

Priscilla's face lit up. "I certainly hope so. I am so looking forward to spending time with the Stratton family again. Especially Cole."

Lydia opened her mouth, glanced at Jacy, and closed it. She whispered to Henry, "Dear, I think we should go get those seats you pointed to. Before someone else gets them."

A pained look crossed Henry's face as he patted her arm. "I agree." He turned to Cole. "We will see you during intermission. Enjoy the music."

Cole nodded. Watching them leave, he slowly sat back down. In all the time she had known him, Jacy had never seen him look so agitated. "We will *not* be spending any time together, Priscilla," he said through clenched teeth. "But I do hope you enjoy your Cape May visit."

Jacy leaned over and looked at Priscilla. She did not return her gaze. Holding her head still and erect, her expression was oddly serene. In the sunlight, she was even prettier than Jacy had thought. She had a petite, dainty nose, a dimpled chin and fine, patrician features. Undoubtedly, she attracted men in droves.

Unfortunately, the only man she appeared to want is Cole.

Smoothing her skirt, Priscilla turned back to Cole and remarked on the "fine" weather. Then she launched into a conversation about friends she and Cole had in common.

Cole said nothing.

Priscilla raised her voice. "You must know that the Browns send their—"

"Stop." Cole turned to her. "I really don't want to hear it." He switched his attention to Jacy. "My good friend, Jacy, and I are excited to hear Sousa's band. Aren't we, my dear?"

Priscilla looked at Jacy for the first time. Her gaze was hostile. Jacy returned it with the most cheerful grin she could muster. "Yes, we are very excited. Mr. Sousa comes to Cape May quite often, although I've never had the pleasure of—"

"His band played at the reopening of Congress Hall in 1882." Priscilla titled her head and her ringlets danced. "After it was rebuilt after that horrid fire." She sniffed. "I was there."

Jacy kept her smile in place. It wasn't easy. "Really? How nice."

"And he honeymooned here in 1880," Priscilla said, raising her chin. "Did you know that?"

"I certainly did not." Cole gave Jacy a wink. "*Most* interesting."

Priscilla leaned over and put her hand on Cole's. "I always dreamed of spending my honeymoon here as well. I cannot think of a more romantic spot, Cole, can you?"

Cole pulled his hand away.

Jacy felt the blood rush to her face. Turning away, so Priscilla could not see her, Jacy caught Poppy's eye.

"I cannot believe that woman," Poppy whispered, with a stiff grimace. "She is horrid."

Aunt Helen leaned toward her daughter and gave her a warning look. "Hush," she said, pressing a finger to her lips. "The band is about to begin."

Thank the Lord. Jacy sighed. *Now Priscilla Day will have to hush, too.*

The audience grew quiet. They applauded when Mr. Sousa stepped up to conduct and murmured in appreciation when he announced the band would begin with "The Gladiator," his newest march.

The Chalfonte lawn became a place of tapping feet and beaming smiles.

Jacy lost herself in the music.

Cole reached for her hand. They held hands until intermission.

When the music stopped, Jacy went to untangle her fingers from Cole's. Tightening his grip, he would not let go.

Jacy glanced over at Priscilla. She was staring at Cole. She flashed him a furious look. She understood his message all too well: Mr. Stratton and Miss James, holding hands, were now publicly an item.

Cole stood and helped Jacy to her feet. "Come, Jacy, let me buy you a lemonade. Priscilla, please excuse us."

Priscilla dropped her jaw. "*Excuse* you? Where are you going?"

"I am going to buy Jacy a lemonade during intermission. We shall return."

"But...what about *me?*"

"What about you?"

"Are you just going to let me sit here, thirsty?"

"I believe you are capable of getting your own refreshment."

Priscilla jumped to her feet to block his way.

Cole smoothly guided Jacy around her. "I hope you enjoy your time in Cape May, Priscilla. I really do."

Priscilla stared at him, her mouth agape.

"Go play tennis. Go boating. Go dancing every night if you wish," Cole added. "Just keep in mind that you won't be doing any of those things with me."

CHAPTER TWENTY-SEVEN

*I*diots! Frank Lynch shook his head and bounded into the surf. *How can some people be so dumb?*

"Stop!" he shouted. "Don't go out any farther. Turn around, turn around..."

With thunderous waves crashing onto shore, Frank and his crew did not have many bathers that morning. Which was a damned good thing, because anyone with a brain could tell there was a storm out at sea. Most beach-goers seemed content to cool themselves off by wading no deeper than their ankles.

Except two buffoons who thought it would be fun to go deep.

Paunchy, late-middle-aged, and likely drunk, Frank had watched in shock as they sprinted into the roiling ocean, started swimming and kept swimming.

They ignored his warnings. Which left him no choice but to go get them and haul them in.

Ducking under a huge wave, he surfaced and surveyed the situation. Miraculously, the two men were still close together and not too far out. But, by the looks on their faces, they knew they were in over their heads and in serious trouble.

"Help!" the bald one with a goatee yelled, his eyes bulging with fear. Splashing wildly, he flailed his arms in wide circles, struggling to stay above water. He would not be able to keep it up for long. Sure enough, a huge swell washed over his head and he disappeared.

The other fool screamed. He had gray hair, a full beard and dark eyes that flashed extreme panic. As Frank swam toward him, the man thrust out one of his hands for Frank to grab. He was not close enough. A giant wave swallowed him, too.

Frank groaned. Treading water, he looked around. He had lost both of them. *Damn.* He would *not* let them drown. *People don't call me the hero of Cape May for nothing.*

Paddling furiously in place, ducking under the waves, he scanned the churning surf. Then, amazingly, they reappeared. Fate, in the form of a monster wave, had deposited the lucky duo, spitting and gasping, right in front of him. Both were well within his reach.

He swam to the bald one, grabbed him around the chest, and growled, "Got you. Relax."

Swimming one-handed, he reached for the other man, pulled him closer, then wedged his free arm around his chest.

Kicking in the direction of shore, Frank heaved a sigh of relief when two lifeguards rushed out to help.

"I got 'em," Frank shouted. He rode a large swell into shore, set the men on their feet, then let the two crew members take them in. He watched as, staggering and coughing, the two fools collapsed on the sand.

Frank followed, holding his head high as the crowd of spectators applauded. Someone tossed him a towel. He used it to dry his hair, then patted down his arms and legs. Another day and two more rescues under his belt. He returned his admirers' cheers with his customary only-doing-my-job-folks grin.

He had hoped to see Jacy among those cheering. Looking around, he felt a twinge of disappointment. She was probably off somewhere with the miraculously recovered Cole Stratton. They were probably playing tennis or croquet or something.

"That was impressive."

Frank whirled around. He dropped the towel.

A woman he had never seen before stood behind him. He knew he never set eyes on her before. He would have remembered. Stunningly gorgeous, she had big, pale blue eyes, thick dark lashes, fine-boned features and a rosebud mouth. The smile she bestowed on him with that mouth did not look entirely sincere, but that had to be his imagination. He impressed women; it could not be helped.

"Thank you, ma'am," he said, drawling out the words. "All in the line of duty." He wiped stinging salt water out of his eyes and returned her gaze. "I don't believe we've met. Name's Frank Lynch. Whole town calls me Frank. And you are?"

"Priscilla Day. Nice to make your acquaintance."

"The pleasure's mine."

"Do you have a few minutes?" She batted her long lashes at him from under a wide-brimmed pink hat. "I have been hearing about you ever since I came to town three days ago with my mother. I never imagined I would meet you under such dramatic circumstances."

Really? Interesting. Frank flashed her his sure-to-melt-a-woman's-heart grin. "What have you been hearing about me, pray tell?"

"That you are popular with the ladies."

"True. Very true. So?"

"So, I would like to ask you about one in particular."

That's curious. "What's her name?"

"Jacy James."

He drew in a breath and tried to keep his expression neutral. "Oh. Yes. I know her. Is she a friend of yours?"

"No. I only met her shortly after I arrived. Under, I might add, less than pleasant circumstances."

Frank studied the woman's pretty face. The day was proving more interesting by the minute. "Miss Day—"

"Priscilla, please."

"Priscilla. What do you want to know about Jacy James? How can I help you? I am confused."

She gave him a petulant pout. "Aren't you going to ask me what the unpleasant circumstances were?"

Lifting an eyebrow, he said, "If you insist on telling me, I'm listening."

"She was with Cole Stratton."

"Oh." Frank stared into Priscilla's eyes. The look in them was a mix of anger and humiliation. "I see," he added, rubbing his chin. He coughed and stifled a smirk.

"You know him, too?"

He rolled his eyes. "Yes, of course I know him. Or, should I say, yes, unfortunately I know him. And if it upset you to see him with Jacy James, then get used to it, my dear. They are always together."

"That is precisely the problem," she hissed.

"Oh, and why is that?"

"He and I were courting. And we would have become engaged, if he hadn't taken ill and almost died."

Planting his hands on his hips, Frank let out a loud sigh. "I am sorry, but I don't understand. What does any of this have to do with me?"

Priscilla turned and looked around. Apparently satisfied that nobody else on the beach was close enough to overhear, she pivoted back to Frank and gave him a sly smile. "I understand that you have a crush on Miss James. Is that right?"

He took a step back and frowned. "What? How do you—"

"Never mind how I know. I'm good at finding things out about people. And suffice it to say that you have not exactly been keeping it a secret. Isn't that right?"

He studied her face. "Right." He let the word out slowly. Why deny it?

"So, you and I might want the same thing." Folding her arms, she looked him straight in the eye.

"The same thing?"

"Yes. To force Cole Stratton and Jacy James apart. Break them up. End their budding relationship."

Frank blinked. What audacity. What a woman. "Right," he said, nodding. "I suppose."

"So, let's team up, you and I," she said. "And together, let us come up with a plan."

* * *

"I DON'T UNDERSTAND why you need another bathing costume." Lydia smiled at Jacy as they walked past shops on Washington Street. "Don't you already have two?"

Nodding, Jacy stopped. She pointed to Isaac H. Smith's Clothing Emporium. American flags mounted above the entrance of the narrow, brick building flapped in the breeze. "This is the place. I am told they have a fine selection of the latest fashions." She returned Lydia's smile. "Humor me, I value your advice."

"My advice is that you don't need any more—"

"Oh, but I do." Laughing, Jacy reached for Lydia's hand and pulled her into the shop. "Don't you understand? The costumes I have take forever to dry. The wool is so thick and heavy. I need something lighter."

Shrugging, Lydia said, "Okay, let's see what they have." Leading the way across squeaky wooden floorboards toward racks of readymade women's fashions, she halted and turned back to Jacy. "This is fun. I'm enjoying spending time with you."

"The feeling is mutual, Lydia. I am so glad you feel that way."

Jacy had in fact arranged the outing because she wanted to get to know Lydia better. She liked Cole's sister-in-law. Vivacious and sweet, she never had an unkind word to say about anyone.

Which is why Jacy found it surprising that she and Priscilla Day were friends. Their friendship gave Jacy pause. It made her a tad nervous. Cole had made it clear that he and Priscilla were through. Jacy hoped Lydia would not take up Priscilla's cause.

Priscilla had been in Cape May a week, and during that time had visited White Caps at least four times to see her "dearest and best friend," Lydia.

Jacy quickly found a bathing costume she and Lydia liked. She arranged to have the green-checkered outfit delivered to the hotel. Then they walked outside and sat down on a bench under a tree.

"You will look fetching in your new bathing get-up," Lydia said. "Cole will love it." Giving Jacy a sympathetic smile, she lightly touched her arm. "Don't worry, if indeed you are, about Priscilla. She and I are good pals. But I believe you and Cole are wonderful together. I've never seen him so happy."

"I'm touched," Jacy said, swallowing hard. "Thank you for saying that."

"You are welcome. But…" Lydia's expression turned serious. "I still worry about Cole. His health was fragile for so long. Henry and I had become engaged before Cole went to Europe, and Priscilla had confided in me that she had expected Cole to propose to her before he left. She had hoped to use the time he was away to arrange their wedding. And when he didn't ask her to marry him, it was a devastating blow. Then, when he came home sick, she was furious."

"Furious? It wasn't his fault."

"No, of course not."

Jacy pursed her lips and glanced at Lydia out of the corner of her eye.

"You are wondering why I am Priscilla's friend, aren't you, Jacy?"

"Truthfully, yes. You are nothing alike."

Lydia sighed. "She's changed. When Cole didn't propose to her before going on his trip, I think she was humiliated. She had hinted to too many people that he would. She became bitter."

"Did he love her, do you think?"

Lydia hesitated. "No. I don't believe he ever really did. Not when I see the way he is with you."

"Oh."

"That is the reason I am worried about him."

"What? Why?"

"Your former sweetheart, Edmund Overton. That is why."

Jacy flinched. She had not expected Lydia, of all people, to bring up the name of a man she had finally convinced herself was no longer among the living. He was gone. It was good thing, too. He had stolen her purity and chasteness, the most valuable attribute a woman of her station possessed.

"Edmund," she whispered. "Why does he concern you?"

"I hope you are not still in love with him."

Jacy looked away, unable to meet Lydia's gaze. "He is dead, as I'm sure you know."

"That wouldn't stop you from—"

"No, don't worry. I no longer love him."

"I know it's probably none of my business, but did you ever?"

Jacy turned to her. "No. I realize now, compared to the way I feel for Cole, that I never truly loved Edmund."

"Really?" Lydia's eyes widened and she grasped Jacy's hands with both of hers. "I feel so much better knowing that. Thank you for telling me. Because Cole is crazy in love with you and I was terrified you might someday break his heart."

Jacy released Lydia's hands and looked down at her lap. Not knowing what to say, she twisted her fingers together and looked up at Lydia, giving her a reassuring smile.

"I feel I must warn you about Priscilla." Lydia held Jacy's gaze. "She is extraordinarily determined. I always admired that about her. Although, now it concerns me."

Jacy felt a sense of foreboding. "Oh. Why?"

A deep line formed between Lydia's brows. "She has been in love with Cole for a long time. Her family and the Strattons' have been friends for years. She set her sights on him when she was a child. I don't know if he knows that, but it's true."

"Since she was a child?"

Lydia nodded. "And she is not about to give up on him now. Just because you have come into his life. *Especially* since you have come into his life."

CHAPTER TWENTY-EIGHT

*T*he next morning, Priscilla arrived at White Caps, declaring she had come to see Jacy.

"Are you sure?" Jacy asked Poppy when her cousin found her on the porch and conveyed the unwelcome news. "She wants to see *me?*"

"Quite sure, she made it quite clear." Poppy gave her a quizzical smile. "She wants to speak to you. She is with her maid."

"Where are they?" Jacy asked, apprehensive and curious.

"Follow me," Poppy said. "I came upon them in the lobby when I returned from a stroll around the grounds and asked them to wait there."

It was immediately clear Priscilla's call was not a social one.

The lobby was decorated with several lovely sofas upon which the socialite could have taken a seat. Instead, she stood with her arms folded across her chest, tapping one of her booted feet when Jacy and Poppy arrived.

As usual, she was dressed in the latest fashion. Her stunning gown was deep purple, almost black. Her hat, which featured an array of large black bows, sat perched to one side of her head. At first, Jacy thought it might be falling off, then realized it had been set that way on purpose, with the use of a great number of pins.

Jacy looked at the only other person in the lobby, Priscilla's maid. Dark-skinned and pretty, she sat with her hands folded in her lap, looking as calm as her employer looked agitated.

"Hello, Priscilla," Jacy said. "Poppy said you wanted to see me?"

"She certainly did," Poppy said. "So, now, if you will excuse me, I will give you some privacy." Launching herself up the stairs to the upper floors, Poppy stopped and called over her shoulder: "I will be in our room if you need me, Jacy."

"She won't," Priscilla called back loudly. "I will only need a few minutes of her time."

A few minutes? Jacy took a deep breath and let it out slowly. *What can she possibly want?*

Jacy glanced at the young woman on the sofa.

"My maid, Mavis," Priscilla said, her voice tight. She pointed to an adjacent, larger sofa. "I suppose you and I can sit there."

Jacy nodded, gave Mavis a nervous smile, and went over and sat down. Mavis returned her smile. Frowning, Priscilla plopped down inches from Jacy and stared at her. "I'll get to the point," she said. "Did you know that I was practically engaged to Cole?"

Priscilla was so close, Jacy could see the pores in her flawless skin. The woman's nearness unnerved her, but she would not to be intimidated. "*Practically*, yes," Jacy said. "I have heard that from more than one person, actually." She tried to stifle a grin.

Priscilla deepened her glare. "Do you find that amusing?"

Jacy widened her eyes and felt her cheeks grow hot. "No, not at all. I'm sorry if I appeared rude." After a moment of awkward silence, she added, "I'm afraid I don't understand why you are here."

"Here in Cape May or here at White Caps?"

"Both, actually. But more pointedly, why are you here at White Caps? I don't understand why you have come to see me."

"I'm curious is all." Priscilla fixed her with a look that said curiosity was only part of what she felt. "Are you a nurse? I understand you had a lot to do with Cole's recovery. Or, so many people tell me. Lydia included."

"Then Lydia must have told you I am not a nurse."

"Oh, I didn't ask her." Priscilla gave Jacy a sly smile. "You see, I have been asking everyone I meet about you, and what I have learned is far more interesting."

Jacy felt the hair on the back of her neck stand on end. A shiver went down her spine. She slid a glance in the direction of Mavis, who was staring into space, her face expressionless.

In trepidation, Jacy looked back at Priscilla. "Far more interesting? I am not that interesting."

"Oh, you are."

"Really? How so?"

"Edmund Overton. Edmund Overton makes you interesting. Very."

Edmund? Jacy suppressed a groan. If Priscilla had been inquiring about her around Cape May, of course people would have mentioned him. At least, the gossips would have. Stories about Edmund still being alive somewhere had been circulating all summer. Too many people knew of Jacy's grief for him. She had not exactly kept it a secret.

Jacy struggled to remain calm but knew her burning cheeks gave her away. Anger and alarm surged through her. What could Priscilla possibly want? Staring at her, Jacy held her gaze. "Edmund? Why do you bring up his name? As you must know, since you have made it your business to know, his ship disappeared long ago and he is presumed to be deceased."

"You were in love with him. Oh, so very much in love, despite the misgivings of your family."

"I am not in love with him anymore, if you must know. Even if he is somehow still alive, Cole is now—"

"I don't believe you. From what I hear, you—"

"What do you want, Priscilla?"

"I wish the man were *not* dead," Pricilla snapped back. "I wish you could run into his arms. And then I could run back into Cole's."

Jacy stared at her, shocked. "Why are you telling me this?"

"Because, there are rumors that he is alive. I might try to find him."

Priscilla looked at her with a gleam in her eye. "And then, my dear, you can thank me."

* * *

"You know I dislike tennis. I'm no good at it." Cole gripped his racket and playfully took a swing at Henry, just missing his chest.

Henry jumped back and grinned. "Very funny." He shook his head and kept walking toward the hotel tennis courts. "You're in fine form it seems. Looks to me like you are ready to play again."

"You just want to play me because you know I'm easy to beat."

"True. But so what? You can use the exercise now that you and Jacy are no longer hiking to the lighthouse every morning."

Cole shrugged. He could not dispute that. He sliced another swing at Henry and chuckled. "No need. She's given up looking for Overton. And anyway, we were hearing too many whispers about the two of us going there unchaperoned. Something about it being scandalous."

Henry barked a laugh. "Right. Scandalous. You and Jacy are the talk of White Caps right now. Everyone thinks you are adorable together. 'Meant to be,' they say, and I agree."

When Henry had suggested an after-lunch tennis match, Cole acquiesced. Although he genuinely disliked the sport, he wanted to pay Henry back for all he had done for him. Henry loved tennis.

The courts were busy when they arrived, and Cole groaned, hoping he did not make a fool of himself. His skills had been mediocre before he got sick. Now, they were likely pathetic. It had been months since he had whacked a ball over a net.

It looked like they would need to wait for a court. Settling down on a bench next to Henry, Cole watched men and women, all dressed in bright white, dash back and forth, chasing balls. All were much better players than he could ever hope to be.

Cole turned to Henry. "Where's Lydia? Surprised you didn't invite her to join us. She's the best player in the family."

Henry shot him an amused grin. "Then you could have invited Jacy for a foursome. But what would we do with Priscilla?"

"Priscilla?"

"Yes, she and Lydia have played almost every day since she blew into town last week. Thought you knew that."

Cole winced. "I've been trying to ignore her, and mostly succeeding. If she thinks she can get me back, she is horribly mistaken. Truth is, her presence in Cape May is making me nervous."

"Really? Why?"

"I'm not sure why."

In truth, he did know why, he just was not ready to discuss it with Henry. Priscilla made him nervous because of Jacy, and he was not yet ready to talk about his powerful love for Jacy. His feelings for her were too raw, too intense. He needed to shelter them from the world, until he got up the nerve to ask Jacy to marry him.

Part of his hesitation involved Jacy herself. He needed to be sure she was completely over Edmund Overton. She insisted she was, but seemed unsure of herself for some reason that Cole could not fathom.

Why doesn't she believe she deserves the kind of love I could give her?

If he were to convince Jacy she did deserve his love, and if they became engaged, Priscilla would become spitting mad. Might she turn vengeful?

Wiping beads of sweat off his forehead, Cole glanced around and was relieved to see Priscilla was not on the courts. Priscilla was no longer the woman he used to know. She had changed, and not for the better.

She had always been somewhat haughty, but outgoing and fun-loving as well. They had enjoyed many of the same activities: sailing, horseback riding, reading Shakespeare.

The friends and activities they had in common had proved insufficient, however. Observing what Henry and Lydia had together, it became obvious his relationship with Priscilla paled in comparison.

Cole thanked the heavens he had held off proposing marriage. Priscilla's true character revealed itself after he took ill: she was clearly more deeply flawed than he had suspected.

Her rudeness toward Jacy shocked and disturbed him. Jacy told him Priscilla had paid her a visit and tried to intimidate her by bringing up Edmund Overton. It made him furious. He would never have courted Priscilla if he had known she was that type of person.

Henry bopped him lightly on the head with his racket. "Get up. It's our turn."

Cole bounded to his feet, wiping sweat off his forehead again. "Okay."

"You alright?" Henry frowned. "You were deep in thought about something."

"What?" Cole shook his head and grinned. "No...yes...I'm fine. Let's get this over with."

Henry laughed. "Okay. Love your enthusiasm."

Cole groaned. "I'm going to look like an idiot. But guess I'll get over it."

* * *

Frank Lynch tipped his driver and told him to wait. He had no idea how long his visit would take, or even if the woman he intended to see was home.

He was impressed with her lodgings, though. "No question she has money," he muttered to himself as he alighted from his carriage and sauntered up the sidewalk to the three-story Queen Anne. In the heart of Cape May, a few blocks from the beach, the grand house had to be the largest on the street.

Surprised it was still available as a rental mid-season, he mused. *Must cost a fortune.*

He knocked loudly and held his breath. The door opened and the woman he had hoped to see stood at the threshold. She gave him a tight-lipped smile.

"Mr. Lynch. Frank, so good to see you again," Priscilla said. "Although you could have sent me a message that you were coming."

"Didn't want to go to the trouble. Also didn't want anyone to know." He anxiously glanced behind him. "Still don't. Can I come in?"

"Please do." She waved him off the wide front porch and into the vestibule. Ahead, he could see a large sitting room, furnished with overstuffed furniture and too many nicknacks. He hated the current style of filling every inch of one's home with stuff. More was better, and there was no such thing as too much.

"Come in, come in," she whispered. "Mother is asleep upstairs, but my maid, Mavis, is here and will serve as my chaperone." She gave him a sly smile and raised her voice slightly. "Mavis can be trusted to keep everything she hears to herself. She knows without me even having to tell her that she will not hear a word we say."

As Frank slowly entered the sitting room, he saw Mavis sitting on a small sofa in one corner. Obviously within earshot, she immediately impressed him with her ability to be discrete. She gave not the slightest indication she had overheard anything Priscilla had said about her.

Dark skinned, with high cheekbones and intelligent brown eyes, she nodded as Frank was briefly introduced as "a new friend." Folding her hands in her gray-uniformed lap, she fixed her gaze there.

"I have been busy since last we met," Priscilla said as she motioned for Frank to sit in a black leather chair near the room's immense fireplace. She took the matching chair on the other side, facing him.

"So I have heard." Frank nodded. "That's why I am here."

"Oh?" She lifted an eyebrow. Even though she could not have known he was coming to call, she was dressed as if expecting company, in a cream-yellow gown that flattered her light hair and flawless features.

"Yes." He shifted in his seat. "I am hoping you have good news."

She tilted her head and stared at him. "I don't know if you would call it good. I call it interesting."

"Really? Maybe that's a start."

She patted her hair, which was swept loosely up in a bun. "I inquired all around town about the man you mentioned to me that day we met on the beach. Edmund Overton."

"Discretely, I hope."

"Of course."

"And what did you find out?"

"I believe it's highly possible the rumors are true. That he is still alive."

Frank felt his pulse pick up. "Ah. And why is that?"

"Because there are so many of them. So many rumors."

"And?"

"Unfortunately, that is all I have for now."

Frank's heart sank. That was it?

Priscilla leaned forward. "I said my news was interesting, I didn't say it was good. Were you listening?"

Frank glanced over at Mavis. If she was listening, she gave no sign. She was still staring at her hands in her lap. Relieved at that, at least, he fixed his gaze on Priscilla and smiled. "What rumors did you hear?"

"Probably the same ones as you. He's hiding out somewhere. New York seems to be the consensus."

"Do you believe that?"

She frowned and sat back in her chair. "I want to."

"So do I."

"If he's in hiding, he must have good reason. He doesn't want to be found. He must have taken a different name." Priscilla sat forward and snickered. "No wonder Jacy's family didn't like him. What an unsavory character."

"An unsavory halfwit. But he was the love of Jacy's life. She was obsessed with him. Until Cole Stratton got her un-obsessed, that is."

"Which is truly unfortunate." She sighed. "I believed I had Cole's heart. I really did. I believed Cole might recover his health in Cape May. I believed if he did, he would come to his senses about me. About us. I never imagined he would fall in love with someone else."

"As you say, 'truly unfortunate.'"

"I went to see her, you know."

"Jacy?" *That must have been interesting.*

"Yes. And I have bad news there." Priscilla frowned and lowered her voice to a whispered hiss. "She claims she no longer loves Overton."

"What?"

"Yes." She raised her voice. "She doesn't believe he is alive. But she no longer loves him, in any case."

"I don't believe it. I think if he came back from the dead, she would feel differently."

"So do I." Priscilla stared at him with defiant eyes. "We have to believe that, don't we? Or what is the use of looking for Overton? He is the key to breaking Cole and Jacy up. I can't think of a better way."

"Nor can I. Then, when Jacy finally sees Overton for the scoundrel he is, she will thank me. She will finally see me as her hero."

Leaning forward, Frank cradled his head in his hands, closed his eyes and reflected. He remembered his conversation with Pete Potter in the lifeboat. Potter had dared him to investigate the rumors about Overton. At the time, he did not want to leave Cape May in the middle of the busy summer season to try to find the man. He was beginning to feel differently, now that he had an ally.

"I have an idea." Frank stood up enthusiastically, rubbing his hands together as he looked at Priscilla.

"Yes?"

"Let's hire a private investigator. You and I."

Priscilla leapt to her feet. Her pale eyes sparkled with amusement and hope. "Of course. Of course. Why not hire a detective?"

"It could be expensive," he warned. "We need a good one. And I happen to know one."

"You can afford it, Frank. I've inquired around town about you as well."

Why was *that* not a surprise? "And you? Will the money be an issue for you?"

She pursed her lips and then put her hands on her hips. "You insult me, sir. We will split the detective's fee. Whatever it is. Money is of no concern."

"Of course. Didn't *mean* to insult you."

Priscilla sat back down. Frank did the same. He stared at her and grinned. "I know just the man and I can give him a lead. He can take it from there."

Sniffing, Priscilla raised her dainty chin. "Really? What is the lead?"

"I know of a local who claims he ran into a friend, a crew mate of Overton's, in Philadelphia. This crew mate claimed they were the only two survivors of a storm that sank the ship. Our man can start there."

Priscilla flashed him a conspiratorial grin. "I like the sound of that. *Our man.*"

"So do I, actually." Frank stood to go. "I believe you and I will make a very good team."

"I agree."

As Priscilla showed him to the door, Frank glanced back at Mavis. She was still staring down at her hands.

CHAPTER TWENTY-NINE

*J*acy handed her croquet mallet to Poppy and ran over to Cole, who had been watching her from a spectator bench.

"You *lost?*" Cole drew his brows together and gave her a look of mock horror. "Jacy James, Cape May's Queen of Croquet, *just lost?*" He raked his fingers through his hair. "Why, what will happen to us all now, my dear? I'm afraid the world might come to an end."

Wrinkling her nose, Jacy gave him a playful swat on the arm. "Okay, okay, that's enough. I can lose sometimes, you know."

Cole laughed. Jacy loved it when he laughed, even if he was teasing her.

He slapped his forehead. "You lost on purpose, didn't you?"

Was it that obvious? "Well..."

"Why? Why did you let that handsome red-haired devil beat you? So Poppy could play him? You haven't taken on the role of match-maker for your cousin, have you?"

A smile tugged at Jacy's lips. "No, Poppy doesn't care about that. Poppy has made it clear she doesn't care if she ever—"

"Your aunt cares."

"True. But I didn't lose for her." Jacy gave him a saucy grin. "I lost for you."

Cole had warned her he was no good at croquet. That was an understatement.

Gripping his mallet far too low, he hit almost all his shots much too hard, launching the balls past the wickets and sailing off to parts unknown.

"Me? You lost for me?" Cole gave Jacy a look of pretend surprise.

"Yes." She inched closer. "You lost the first game you played, which means you are out for the afternoon, even among the beginner set. And since I would rather sit next to you than win, I lost for you."

Cole inched closer to her, until they were as close as socially permissible. He put his hand on hers. "I do declare, that is the most loving thing anyone has ever done for me, Miss James. I shall be beholden to you for the rest of our lives."

Jacy's heart did a flip. "Very funny, Mr. Stratton," she said in a choked whisper. "Very funny. Now hush up, we need to watch Poppy and cheer her on."

Poppy did not need any cheering. She was beating her flame-haired opponent handily with quiet confidence, concentration, and skill. Jacy just needed time to still her heart, to clear the jumbled thoughts that had been causing her pulse to race. Watching Poppy was a handy excuse.

Now that Cole was healthy, and they were publicly courting, they were spending more and more time together. It was heavenly. They swam, they went sailing, they went on carriage rides, they danced.

They stole kisses when no one was around.

Henry told Jacy almost daily that his dream for his brother's summer had come true. Lydia thanked her again and again. Aunt Helen was over the moon.

Jacy tried to embrace her joy. But her shameful secret would not let her. The harder she tried to push the memory of her tryst with Edmund into some dark corner of her mind, the larger it loomed.

She longed to confide in Cole. To end the secret's tyranny over her soul. If only she could be sure Cole would forgive her. And she could not be sure of that at all.

Her secret was too shocking. Too shameful. Cole would see her differently. He would not love her anymore.

Cole's words echoed through Jacy's mind: *I shall be beholden to you for the rest of our lives.* He had said it jokingly, in reference to croquet, but he was sending a signal. He planned to propose.

And then? She would have to tell him. And then all would be lost. The rest of the summer, not to mention the rest of her life, would be ruined.

She would have to tell Cole one day, of course. But the longer she could delay it, the more joy-filled days they could have together.

A shout went up among the spectators and Poppy raised her mallet in victory. Jacy applauded her cousin as Cole jumped up and ran over to her. He shook Poppy's hand, then turned and gave Jacy a huge smile.

Jacy waved and beamed. Then she ran over to congratulate Poppy, too.

* * *

HELEN SLID the elegantly written invitation out of its envelope and read it a third time. She sighed. She could not decide whether to be flattered, or worried.

Zinnia Day was requesting her company for tea the following afternoon. "At my home on Ocean Street," the summons proclaimed. "I would be delighted, Dear Helen, if you would join me at 4 p.m."

Dear Helen? Helen shook her head, dangling the card between her thumb and index finger as she slowly sat down on the bed. Staring at a seascape painting on the wall, she tried to think. *What in the world does Zinnia Day want? Why is she inviting me to tea?*

She and Zinnia ran in the same social circle, but they were not friends. Zinnia was much too uppity to be her friend.

She must want something. Maybe it's about her daughter, Priscilla. Helen glanced at the envelope again. "Helen Bainbridge," it read.

Clearly Poppy and Jacy were not invited. If it was about Priscilla, then it was about Jacy, too.

Helen stood up and tossed the card onto the desk near her bed. She walked over to the door connecting the two bedroom suites and knocked.

The door flew open and Jacy greeted her with a smile. Dressed in one of her bathing costumes, it was clear where she planned to spend the rest of the afternoon.

"Aunt Helen." Jacy waved her in. "Have you heard the good news? Poppy was today's croquet champion. She had to beat quite a few male opponents to stay in the game and she played magnificently."

Helen looked around the room. "Where is Poppy now?"

"Down on the porch, I believe. Why? Do you want me to go fetch her?"

"No." Helen shook her head. "It is actually you I want to see, my dear."

"Oh. Is something wrong?" Jacy's forehead creased with worry. "You look a bit perplexed about something."

"Actually, I am."

"Oh?"

"Yes." Helen sighed. "I have received a most curious invitation to tea. At Zinnia Day's home. And I do not know why. Or whether to accept."

Jacy frowned. "That is odd. I didn't think you two were friendly."

"We are not."

Jacy gave a tentative smile. "Well, maybe she wants to become your friend."

"I doubt it."

Jacy shrugged. "Then decline her invitation. I'm sure she is not inviting you because she's lonely. With her social contacts, she must know a great many people summering in Cape May."

"I don't know. I am curious as to what this is about. I am also concerned. Because I think she might want to talk to me about you."

Jacy widened her eyes. "Me?"

"Yes, well you and Cole Stratton. And Priscilla. And what good would come of such a conversation? I would have no idea what to say if she blamed you for stealing Cole from her daughter."

"I didn't." Jacy sighed and walked over to the window overlooking the beach.

Helen had to know. "Jacy?"

"Yes?"

"I wrote your father a postcard. I told him about Cole Stratton."

Jacy turned away from the window and returned her gaze. "You did?"

"I don't think it will be long before he proposes to you. The man is besotted. It would be delicious if I could hint such a thing to Zinnia Day."

"Aunt Helen." Jacy sounded shocked. *"Please*, why would my relationship with Cole be any of Zinnia Day's business?"

"I don't know. I guess it is not. It's just that I don't really want to accept her invitation to tea. But if f I do, I would like to give her some good news about you and Cole. It would effectively end any conversation she might try to start about Priscilla's hopes where he is concerned."

"Aunt Helen." Jacy frowned. "What are you really asking me?"

"Well…"

"Are you asking me if Cole has proposed?"

"Yes!" Helen's heart jumped. *"Has* he?"

"No." Jacy shook her head. "Although it doesn't mean he won't. I suspect—"

"That he might, any day now? I hope you say 'yes.' You must, of course, accept." Helen gave her a beaming smile. "He is by far the most eligible man in Cape May. He is a successful attorney, from a wonderful family. You couldn't do better."

Jacy stared at her with her mouth open. Red circles formed on her cheeks. "What matters to me is that I love him. It's nice that he seems to have a bright future, now that he has been restored to health. But I love *him*. Not his money or his social status."

"Yes, yes, of course." Helen nodded and waved her hand. "When do you think he might propose?"

"What? I don't know. And I haven't told you I will accept." Jacy's entire face was turning as red as a ripe apple. "I don't want to talk about this right—"

"You what!?" Helen rose to her feet. "You might not *accept?*"

"I...I...I didn't say that. Or...I didn't mean that. I..." Jacy looked as if she might cry.

Helen stared at her. Seconds ticked by, measured loudly by the clock on the wall.

"Jacy," she whispered. "Jacy, dear, what is wrong? You are clearly distraught about something. I know you love Cole and that he loves you. You believe he might ask you to marry him. You should be deliriously happy, but instead you look like you are about to break into tears. I don't understand."

Jacy opened her mouth, as if she was about to say something but then closed it and turned back to look out the window. "I can't talk about this right now, Aunt Helen. I'm sorry, but I can't."

Helen gasped as an unwelcome thought entered her mind. "Edmund Overton. You are not still in love with him, are you? I thought you had accepted that he is no longer among the living."

Jacy turned and looked back at her. "I have accepted it. But there are rumors, of which you are well aware, that he is alive."

"*So?* I am sure they are not true. And anyway, if he were to make a miraculous appearance someday, he would have a lot of explaining to do. And you would *not* have to accept him back into your life."

A tear slid down Jacy's cheek. She reached up and delicately dabbed it away. "I suspect Zinnia Day might want to talk about Edmund, and that is why she has invited you to tea. I would not be surprised."

"*Really?*" Helen felt a surge of indignation. "Why would she want to talk about *him?* What could I possibly tell her?"

"I don't know," Jacy whispered.

"Do you think I should accept her invitation?"

"Yes." Jacy lifted her chin. An odd, defiant look came into her eyes. "Yes, Aunt Helen. I think you should."

CHAPTER THIRTY

a light mist of raindrops dampened Frank's face as he stood at the end of the Cape May Point pier watching passengers disembark from the *Republic*.

Steamship passengers streamed past him, most wearing sunny expressions that defied the weather. With growing impatience, Frank searched the faces for "detective extraordinaire," Ernest Zeller.

Zeller deserved to bill himself as extraordinary. The crafty private investigator had done quite a bit of work for the Lynch family, mostly involving lawsuits, and he had proven himself well worth his fee.

If Edmund Overton still breathed, Zeller would find the bastard.

Finally, just when Frank was afraid Zeller might have missed the ship, his craggy face came into view. Frank shook his head. Leave it to Zeller to be one of the last off the steamer. He had probably been talking to someone and did not even notice they had docked. Zeller was a talker, one of the reasons he was so successful. That, and the fact that he was a superb listener.

Rather ordinary in appearance, he also blended into the crowd. In his early fifties, slightly portly, his brown hair and mustache were streaked with gray and he wore a perpetually amused, slightly cynical expression on his face.

He had once confided to Frank, after solving a particularly complicated case for Frank's father, that he liked people. He just did not trust most of them. "Everyone has a secret," he said. "I have a habit of looking for the worst in people, and I usually find it."

Zeller also walked with a self-confident swagger. When he saw Frank, he picked up his pace, dropped his valise and clapped him on the shoulder. "Good to see you again, my boy," he said, his brown eyes twinkling. "Always good to see my favorite Lynch."

Frank laughed. "And why am I your favorite?"

Zeller squeezed Frank's shoulder. "Because you and I are a lot alike. Determined. Persistent. We know what we want, and we find a way to get it. Don't get me wrong. Your father was my favorite, God rest his soul. But now that he no longer walks the earth, you are."

"I think you also like my money."

"That, too, my boy. That, too. And from what you have told me about this case, it might cost you plenty."

"And from what I told you before I booked you passage on the *Republic*, money is not an issue. All I care about is finding Edmund Overton. If you do, you will have earned your pay. If you can go one important step further, and persuade him to come to Cape May, you can look forward to a very generous bonus."

Frank filled Zeller in on Overton as they took Frank's carriage to Priscilla's house.

Frank had secured a room for the detective at The Chalfonte but wanted to introduce him to her first. "Priscilla Day is my partner on this," he explained, then elaborated on the reason.

He gave Zeller the pertinent facts about Cole Stratton and his miraculous recovery, about Jacy James and her role in that medical miracle and everything he knew about Priscilla's relationship with Cole until Jacy came along.

"So, this James woman is the real reason you are hiring me? Is that right?" Zeller sat across from Frank as the carriage made its way down the boulevard to Cape May. He regarded Frank with a gleam in his eye. "You fancy her for yourself? That's what you said in the letter you sent telling me my services were needed immediately. Made it sound like an emergency. Another reason why it's gonna cost you. Had to hand a case I was already working on over to another private eye."

Frank returned his grin. "You know me, and as you said, I go after what I want. Yes, I have fancied Jacy James from the moment I hauled her out of the ocean, thus saving her life. Unfortunately, on that fateful day, she was obsessed with Overton. With finding him. She made it clear to everyone he was the one who had her heart. Even dead. Until, for some reason, she took a liking to a pathetic invalid named Cole Stratton, who played on her sympathy. Then it was him and only him. Nauseating."

Zeller leaned forward. "So how will finding Overton help you? Seems to me he'd add more competition to what you already got."

Frank flashed him a sly smile. "Overton will come between her and Stratton—that's my hope and I'm betting on it. From all I hear about Overton, he's an ass. If he's hiding out on purpose, it's a certainty. Jacy is a smart woman. When she realizes the truth about him, she'll be devastated. But when she finds out I am the one who located him, I'm hoping she'll be grateful."

"Why's that?" Zeller smirked. "She's gonna be grateful you brought a moron back into her life?"

"Yes. Because she has been obsessed with finding him. Really obsessed. If he is alive, she deserves to know it, and knowing it will close a chapter in her life. Allow her to heal. And she will see I cared enough about her to do it for her."

"In the meantime, before she figures out what a cad he is, Stratton will go running back to his precious Priscilla? Is that the plan?"

"That's what Priscilla is counting on."

The carriage stopped, and Frank pointed to Priscilla's house. "We're here." As he threw open the carriage door, he stopped and turned back to Zeller. "One more thing—Priscilla's a beauty. Don't let that distract you."

Zeller grunted. "It won't. Might make the job more enjoyable, though."

Priscilla was indeed looking mighty fine, dressed in a stunning eggshell satin gown, when she opened the door and ushered them in. She informed them her mother was resting upstairs. As before, maid Mavis sat on a sofa in the corner, hands folded, still and silent. Priscilla assured them that Mavis would not be listening.

"Ernest Zeller, nice to make your acquaintance," he said, giving Priscilla a bow. "Let's get started, shall we? Where shall we sit?"

"Over here." Priscilla led them to a table and chairs on the other side of the room from Mavis. The socialite batted her eyelashes at Zeller and smiled. "I never met a detective before. I have high hopes you can help us."

"Of course," Zeller said. "Now we just need to figure out where to start. And to establish my fee, of course." He named it.

Pricilla gave a small shrug of one shoulder and smiled. "Fine. Frank and I are going to split it." Obviously eager to make an impression, she then relayed to him the rumors she had heard about Overton during her discreet enquiries around Cape May, when she was trying to learn more about Jacy James. "He is possibly holed up in New York City," she said. "Probably changed his name. And he might be working a job outside the shipping industry in order to make a living."

"The most credible story I heard came from a local who works at one of the hotels," Frank said. "Claims he ran into Overton's buddy in Philadelphia. Apparently, Overton and the buddy were the only survivors of a shipwreck. Somewhere off the coast of New York."

Zellers eyes sparked with interest. "And who is this local? Have you spoken to him personally?"

"No." Frank held his gaze. "Thought I'd let you do it."

"So, how do I find him? What's his name?"

"It escapes me at the moment. But my lifeguard pal, Pete Potter, knows. Potter's the one who told me the story. Potter's the one who encouraged me to look for Overton. Potter's the man who gave me the idea to hire you."

"Smart man," Zeller said. "I'll start with him."

* * *

"MOTHER HAS A SURPRISE FOR YOU TODAY." Poppy caught Jacy's eye in the mirror and smiled as her maid Florence tightened a ribbon in her hair. "I wasn't supposed to tell you, but you know me…it's hard for me to keep a secret. Anyway, I think you will be pleased."

"What is it?" Jacy lifted a corner of her mouth in a curious smile. "Or, should I say, *who* is it?"

They were on their way to a special picnic on the hotel lawn, billed as a sumptuous feast of cold roast chicken, fruit and potato salads and a variety of decadent desserts.

Has Aunt Helen invited Father? Jacy hoped so. She missed him.

"Your father." Poppy flashed her a grin. "He took the train instead of the *Republic* and Mother went to fetch him from the station."

"Hooray." Jacy beamed. "How long does he plan to stay, do you know?"

Turning around, Poppy thanked Florence, dismissed her, then grabbed Jacy's hands after the maid left and closed the door. "I don't know how long he will stay. All I know is that he's got a room at Congress Hall and he wants to meet Cole."

"Oh. Oh, my."

"Yes. Did Mother tell you she had tea with Zinnia Day yesterday?"

"She told me she had been invited."

"Well, apparently Mrs. Day insinuated awful things about Edmund Overton. And that you stole Cole from her daughter. Mother had already invited Uncle Tobias to visit. Now she is glad she did."

Jacy frowned. "Zinnia Day's opinions are nonsense."

Poppy flashed her an encouraging smile. "I agree." She opened the door and ushered Jacy out. "Let's go. We don't want to be late for the picnic."

* * *

JACY'S FATHER was waiting for her on the lawn, where the croquet wickets had been replaced by a dozen round tables covered with starched white tablecloths. Handsome as always, with a sea breeze ruffling his thick gray hair, he stood beside Aunt Helen, serenely regarding the cheerful people around him.

Jacy dashed over, threw her arms around his neck and squeezed tight.

Laughing, he stepped back and regarded her with a gleam in his eye. "You look wonderful, my dear. I am so pleased you are making the most of your summer."

"I know Aunt Helen has been telling you all about it." Jacy reached for her aunt's hand and gave it an affectionate squeeze. "You probably know more about how I'm doing than I do."

He laughed again, warming Jacy's heart. Her father truly wanted what was best for her, although for a long time she had not been willing to admit it.

"I wanted you to meet Jacy's new beau—well, there is Mr. Cole Stratton now, waving for us to join his table." Aunt Helen's cheeks were pink and her voice was higher than usual. "Let's go over. His brother and his wife are there, too."

Feeling almost as nervous as Aunt Helen sounded, Jacy met Cole's gaze with a shy grin and took the seat to his right. Her father sat next to her and she introduced him to all three Stattons.

"I am so happy to meet you at last," her father said, reaching in front of Jacy to shake Cole's hand. "I have heard so much about you."

"All good I hope," Cole said, raising an eyebrow.

"Indeed. All good."

Henry, sitting to Cole's other side, bounded to his feet. "Here, Mr. James, switch places with me, so you and my brother can chat and get better acquainted."

"Thank you, sir, that's very gracious of you." He turned to Jacy. "You don't mind, do you?"

Jacy swallowed hard. "Of course not, Father. I think it's a wonderful idea."

Fiddling with the napkin in her lap, Jacy could not eat. As the two most important men in her life chatted and laughed, she slid a bite of chicken salad into her mouth and nearly choked trying to swallow it.

She listened as Cole told her father how she had rescued him from the ocean during his first ill-fated swim, then later encouraged him to stand and guided his first steps. The two men seemed to get along fabulously.

Pleased, but also flustered, Jacy nervously glanced at Cole. What if he impetuously asked for her hand in marriage right then and there? Would he do that? Surely not. Surely, he would propose to her first.

Her father seemed to sense her anxiety. Pushing his chair back, he stood, went over to her, leaned down, and whispered loudly in her ear: "I would like to speak to you privately, Jacy. Do you think we could excuse ourselves for a father-daughter walk?"

Relieved, she gave Cole a smile and said, "Of course. I would like that."

They strolled down to the beach. Her father took her arm when they reached the water's edge. They faced the sea, where a few people bathed in shallow surf.

Frank Lynch was on duty, of course.

Jacy steered her father away from Frank. "What do you want to discuss with me, Father?"

Please, not Cole. Not yet.

"My will."

"Your will?" Jacy looked at him in surprise.

"Yes. I have been thinking about it for a while, my dear. And I have decided to give you your inheritance now, instead of when you reach twenty-five, as was previously arranged."

Jacy stared at him, wide-eyed. "My inheritance? Why do you want to give me my inheritance early? You are not ill, are you?"

"No, no, no." Regarding her with affection, he let go of her arm and faced her. "No, no indeed. Don't worry your pretty little head about my health. I am perfectly fine. It's just...just...you see...my original intent was to give you the money when you turned twenty-one last October. But Edmund Overton was in your life then."

Jacy felt her cheeks grow hot. Money had never been a concern of hers. She had never given her inheritance much thought, and it had never occurred to her that her father had changed his will because of Edmund.

"I was hoping that you would tire of him at some point. Surely long before you reached twenty-five. But now that he is gone for good, I feel confident in giving you your trust now. Life is unpredictable, Jacy. I feel it is better this way."

Jacy did not know what to say.

"Your stepmother agrees with me. We are united on this."

Jacy nodded. "Father, I am touched. Thank you." She stared at the breaking waves. "Is Ethel well? And the children?"

"They are all splendid. Ethel sends her love, as do Theo, Tim, Thomas, Ellie, and Eliza."

"Even baby Eliza?"

He smiled. "Yes. They may pay a visit to Cape May sometime this season. Although managing so many young ones might prove difficult."

"I can imagine."

Her father eyed someone approaching from behind. Jacy turned and suppressed a groan when she saw it was Frank.

"Excuse me, Jacy, I hope I am not interrupting anything important." Frank flashed her a hearty smile. "I just thought I would come over and say hello."

"Frank," she said stiffly. She turned to her father and introduced the two men to each other. "Mr. Lynch is the hero of Cape May. He has saved many lives."

"Including your daughter's," Frank said. "You might ask her to tell you all about it. Now, if you will excuse me, I must get back to my job."

Her father watched Frank run off and then turned to her with a worried frown. "What was he talking about?"

"Oh, nothing, Father. Frank Lynch just enjoys exaggerating his exploits."

"I see."

Jacy pursed her lips and watched Frank dash into the ocean to rescue a squealing fanny-dipper. An uneasy feeling overcame her. He was up to something.

CHAPTER THIRTY-ONE

Frank stepped up to Ernest Zeller's door at The Chalfonte and gave it a hard rap.

The door opened and Zeller waved him in.

"I got your message, that you have information for me." Frank gave him an appreciative smile. "You work fast."

Zeller nodded but did not ask Frank to sit down. Folding his arms across his chest, he held his gaze. "It was easy, all I had to do was start with Pete Potter, as you suggested. He put me onto Clyde Smathers, the White Caps janitor who supposedly ran into a crew mate of Overton's in Philadelphia. Smathers gave me the name of that crew mate, man by the name of Hal Higbee. My next step is to head back to the City of Brotherly Love and find Higbee. Shouldn't be hard."

"Hope not." Frank frowned. "Then what?"

"Simple. Higbee tells me where Overton is. The name he's using now, if he changed it. And I go find him."

"Sounds too simple."

"We'll have to see. Anyway, I'm checking out of The Chalfonte today. Give me a ride to the train station and I'll be back in touch."

"How?"

"Soon as I get the information I need, I'll send you a postcard about what I've learned about Overton's whereabouts. I'll head there, and you and your lady partner can reimburse me the travel expenses."

"No." Frank folded his arms to match Zeller's stance. He shook his head.

"No? What you mean, no?"

"I want to go with you."

"Not the way I operate, son."

"I don't care. It's the way I want to do it."

"Best if you don't."

"I insist. I'll pay you an additional fee for putting up with me. But I'm going."

Zeller took a step back and rubbed his chin. "An additional fee, huh?"

"Yep."

"But why? Why do you want to go with me?" He pointed a finger at Frank's chest. "You don't trust me."

Frank shook his head. "Of course, I trust you. But if and when you find Overton, I want to see the idiot with my own eyes. Where he's living, what he's doing. And I want to make *damn sure* he comes back with us to Cape May."

Zeller stared at him but said nothing.

"Besides, I can help. I can be your assistant."

"*Besides*, you might hinder me. And I don't need an assistant."

Frank shrugged. "You got one anyway."

"How much of an additional fee?" Zeller shot him a calculating look.

Frank named an amount Zeller could not refuse.

"Alright. First, we'll go to Philadelphia and wrangle the information we so desperately need. But won't your lifesaving skills be missed while you are away? How you going to explain your absence?"

Frank shrugged again. "I'll just say my mother has taken ill. That she needs me. And that as a dutiful son, I must go where I am most needed."

Zeller laughed. "Yep, that should work. Will only add to your reputation as a hero."

"What? How do you know about that?"

Zeller snorted. "Think, my boy. I'm a detective. I have a way of finding out everything I want to know about everybody. And you sure got an *impressive* reputation in this town."

"Yes, I do." Frank stepped forward and patted Zeller on the shoulder. "I love this plan. This is going to be fun." Stepping back, he gave Zeller a wide smile. "I think you're going to find it enjoyable, too. We'll take my yacht. To Philadelphia and then to New York, if that's where we need to go."

"Your yacht, huh? I was gonna take the train."

"No. I keep my *Splendid Lady* at the Cape May Yacht Club. Got a full-time crew. Might as well put them to work. Plus, it will be a much more efficient way to travel."

"Not gonna argue with you, son." Zeller went over to his bed and picked up his luggage. "Let's not waste any more time." He waved Frank out the door. "After you."

* * *

HOISTING her skirt above her ankles, Jacy dashed into the ocean, grabbed the ribbons of her bathing bonnet, and dove into an oncoming wave.

Surfacing, she wiped water from her eyes and looked around for Cole, who had assured her he would be right behind.

He was not anywhere to be seen.

Frowning, she looked toward shore. He was still on the beach. He was talking to Priscilla Day.

Drat. Priscilla?

Ducking under a wave to avoid getting knocked down, Jacy popped back up, frowned, and made her way back to shore.

Cole gave her a wry smile as she walked up to him. "I'm sorry, Jacy, Priscilla wanted to ask me a question. She says she wants to do more than just wade in and duck down to cool off. She wants to learn how to swim, like you."

Jacy widened her eyes and looked at Priscilla, who shrugged and gave her a suspicious smile. She had on the fanciest bathing costume Jacy had ever seen, a get-up that certainly could not be found in a shop such as Isaac H. Smith's Emporium on Washington Street. Pink-and-gray-striped, it fit her like it had been custom made.

Priscilla's eyes twinkled from under her pink bathing bonnet. "That's right. I do want to learn to swim. I was hoping Cole could teach me."

"Some of the lifeguards give lessons, Priscilla." Cole folded his arms and frowned. "I just told you that."

"Oh, yes. So, you did."

Cole nodded in the direction of the lifeguard on duty, who for once was not Frank Lynch. Shorter than Frank, he had blond hair, a wide handlebar mustache, and was gazing out at the bathers in the water with his hands planted firmly on his hips. "Maybe you can go ask him."

Priscilla gave a petulant shrug. "I suppose I could," she said, her voice tinged with doubt. "I don't know…maybe later."

"Suit yourself," Cole said. He turned to Jacy. "You ready to go back in the water?"

Flashing him a wide grin, Jacy said, "Yes, let's go." She waved Priscilla a cheerful goodbye as she and Cole sprinted toward the waves. They splashed into the water together, ducked under a wave together and resurfaced.

It was a particularly hot day and the water was crowded with bathers. They swam farther out than everyone else, then treaded water as they gazed at each other and grinned.

"I can't believe Priscilla asked *you* to give her lessons." Jacy wrinkled her nose. "She sure isn't giving up on you."

Cole laughed as he pushed wet hair out of his eyes. "She is wasting her time. She won't get me back. I'm spoken for, as you know."

"I do know." Jacy giggled.

A piercing scream split the air. They turned toward the beach. Priscilla, chest-high in water, was flailing her arms and screeching for help. A wave rose up and engulfed her. She disappeared, resurfaced without her bonnet, and screamed again.

The blond lifeguard dashed into the water. But before he could reach Priscilla, a wave rose up and pushed her toward Jacy and Cole.

Cole swam to Priscilla, grabbed one of her hands and pulled her to him. "Calm down, you're okay," he muttered. With his arm around her shoulders, he guided her to shallower water.

Jacy watched in shock as the lifeguard took Priscilla from Cole's arms and led her onto the beach. *Did Priscilla just risk her life to get Cole's attention?* Or was she so desperate to swim that she took a foolish risk? Grimacing, Jacy suspected both things were true.

Cole waded onto the beach. Jacy swam in. She saw Priscilla's cap floating on sea foam and snatched it up.

The lifeguard sat her down on the sand and nodded thanks to Cole. Priscilla's hair was a tangled mess. Gasping for air, her chest heaved as she spit water out of her mouth. She peered up at Cole, her eyes shining with gratitude.

"You saved my life, Cole," she said, gasping. "Thank you."

"I'm proud of you. You *are* a hero, Cole," Jacy said, barely suppressing her disgust as she tossed Priscilla's soaking wet cap onto her soaking wet lap.

* * *

COLE TURNED AWAY FROM PRISCILLA. Suspicious of her intentions, but happy he was able to save her life, he reached for Jacy's hand. "I couldn't have done what I just did if it wasn't for you," he said. "You helped restore me to health. You deserve some credit, too."

The lifeguard walked over to Cole and introduced himself. "Caleb Whitehouse. Thanks for the assist just now."

"Cole Stratton. Glad to help."

"Hmmm. Cole Stratton. I've heard of you. Weren't you sick or something?"

"Was. I *was*."

"Well, you certainly look great now."

"Thank you."

"And you are a hell of a swimmer. You should think about joining the lifeguards. We can always use another volunteer."

Cole lifted his chin and smiled at Jacy. "Thanks. It did feel good to help somebody else when other people have helped me. I'll think about it."

"Do," Whitehouse said. "We'd be glad to have you."

Jacy looked around. "Where is Frank Lynch? I am surprised he is not on duty today."

Cole tried not to laugh. Lynch would not be happy if he joined the lifeguards, and she knew it.

"His mother took ill. Had to go home to Princeton to see about her." Whitehouse said. "He's a dutiful son. And he knows he can count on the rest of us guards to keep folks safe while he's away. Like I just did. With your help."

Priscilla sat motionless with her head down, staring at the sand.

"As I said, I will think about joining the White Caps lifeguards." Cole squeezed Jacy's hand. "Ready to go back to your room and change?"

"I suppose," Jacy said.

Waving goodbye to Caleb and Priscilla, Cole led Jacy toward the hotel.

She drew him to a stop "Wait. Why was Priscilla on the White Caps beach? She is not a guest here."

"I don't know, and I'm not going to concern myself with her." Cole turned and looked back at Priscilla. "Her mother is with her now. They probably came together."

Jacy frowned. Her wet face was streaked with sand, but she had never looked more lovely. "I'm annoyed she interrupted our swim, but I'm glad you saved her life. If she *really was* in any danger. I think she thought she was."

Cole nodded.

"But, Cole. What that lifeguard said about Frank—it struck me as odd."

"How so?"

"He said Frank went to see his ill mother."

"That's right."

"But Frank told me his mother died five years ago."

Cole frowned. "That is odd."

"I wonder where he really went?"

"I don't know," Cole studied Jacy's concerned face. "I don't know."

CHAPTER THIRTY-TWO

*S*o, what now?" Frank removed his black-brimmed hat and wiped the sweat from his forehead with the back of his hand. New York City sure was hot in the summer. No wonder people of means flocked to seaside resorts.

The brownstone was nondescript. Three-storied, the front stoop was spotless and the windows were open to let in the hot, humid air.

Frank smiled. *Whoever lives here, they must be home. Sure hope it's the idiot Overton.*

With any luck, they could wind up their mission quickly and sail back to Cape May.

Zeller shoved his hands in his pockets and eyed the residence. "Must be the place. This is the address Hal Higbee gave us."

"Now, we wait." Zeller said. "Welcome to the life of a private eye. Lots of waiting for something to happen. In usually less than desirable circumstances. Can get boring. Sure you can do this?"

Frank fitted his hat back on his head and nodded. "Of course. Don't worry about me. But don't we look a bit suspicious, just standing here, *waiting?*"

Zeller chuckled. "That's why we're standing a half block away. Can't see us from any of the windows of that place. Somebody comes out the door, we start walking slowly toward them, deep in conversation. Got it?"

"Yep." Frank grinned. "Got it. Worried about the neighbors though." Homes identical to the one they were watching lined the Brooklyn street. "Won't someone notice us loitering?"

Zeller shrugged. "Maybe. Ain't worried about the neighbors though. Hoping at least a few will be able to provide us valuable information about the occupants of 1344 Highland Avenue, if it comes to that."

The front door opened. A man stepped out and looked up and down the street. Zeller immediately began walking in his direction, signaling Frank with his eyes to do the same. "I agree the weather's damn hot. I like New York, but not this time of year."

Frank nodded and studied the man on the stoop out of the corner of his eye. In his mid-to-late thirties, he looked the right age to be Overton. Sporting a well-trimmed brown beard and a somewhat handsome, weathered face, he matched his description, too. His complexion was pale, as if he had been spending a lot of time indoors.

The man barely glanced at Frank and Zeller as he bounded down the steps onto the sidewalk, headed in their direction, then passed them by.

"Looks like he could be our man," Frank whispered loudly. "Aren't we going to turn around and follow him?"

"No. Be too obvious." Zeller didn't look at Frank. "Just keep walking slow."

"But—"

"But nothin. Soon as he's out of sight, we go knock on the door. See who else lives there. By his demeanor, he obviously does, so he'll be back. Right now, I'm curious as to who he might be living with."

"Oh." Frank pressed his lips together. "Guess I got a lot to learn about this detective business."

"Just do what I say if you wanna be of any help." Zeller halted and turned his head to look back. "Okay, he's gone, must have turned the corner. Let's go."

When they returned to the house, Zeller instructed Frank to stay close and act as lookout while he did the talking. "Let me know if you see our man coming back," he said as he climbed the steps and motioned for Frank to follow. "Start coughing, that will be our signal."

"For what?" Frank whispered. "By the time I see him, he will see us and it will be too late to do anything about it."

"At least having a warning will give me time to think of something," Zeller hissed. "Best if you don't question me, son. Just do what I say."

Zeller knocked on the brown wooden door and Frank—as instructed—turned to fix his gaze down the street. It was a quiet afternoon. Two pedestrians came around the corner and entered a home a few doors down. Across the street, three young girls jumped rope. Near them, two little boys played marbles.

No one answered. Zeller knocked again.

Frank wet his lips and swallowed to moisten his parched throat. He could use a cold ale. So far it had been quite a day—quite a few days.

After finding Higbee in Philadelphia, thanks to a tip from Clyde Smathers, they sailed back down the Delaware River, entered Delaware Bay, passed Cape May and headed up the Atlantic Coast to New York. Frank's crew dropped them off at a dock in Brooklyn. From there, it was a short walk to the brownstone.

Smathers and Higbee had both proved extremely talkative when Frank offered money. For a hundred bucks each, they coughed up every piece of information they had.

Realizing he had been holding his breath, Frank tried to relax as Zeller knocked on the door a third time, loudly to convey a sense of urgency.

The door opened. A middle-aged woman, looking annoyed, stood there. Plain-featured and neatly dressed, she moved her gaze to Zeller and pursed her lips. "Can I help you?"

"Yes." Zeller nodded. "Is the woman of the house at home?"

Widening her eyes, she said, "I am she."

"Excuse me ma'am. I thought you might be—"

"The maid? No. She has the day off."

"Oh, well…we apologize for bothering you, ma'am." Zeller's voice sounded more personable and polite than Frank had ever heard it. He was good. The woman was almost smiling. At least she was not trying to slam the door closed.

"Can I help you?" she asked again, looking perplexed.

"Actually ma'am, we were hoping to speak with you husband." Zeller cleared his throat. "We saw him hurrying down the street a few minutes ago and couldn't catch up to him. Do you know when he will be home?"

"My husband?" The woman looked shocked. "I don't have one. You must have the wrong house."

"Oh, I'm terribly sorry." Frank's tone matched his words. "Is this not the home of Edward O'Toole?" That was the name Higbee had provided, saying Overton chose to keep his real initials.

The woman let out a quiet gasp. "Edward O'Toole is my brother, sir, not my husband. And, as you already know, he is not here."

"I see." Zeller turned to look at Frank and then back to the woman. "Well…Mrs…Miss…?"

"Martha Kent. Mrs. Martha Kent." Impatience crept back into her voice. "I am a widow, if it is any of your business, and I am beginning to wonder what your business is. You have not said."

"Well, Mrs. Kent. We are here about some money owed your brother." Zeller gave her a wide smile, as if he assumed she would be happy about that.

Dark lines formed between her brows. "I'm sorry. You will have to speak to him about that."

"We would very much like to," Zeller said. "When do you expect him back?"

Martha Kent looked suddenly nervous. She opened her mouth but said nothing, as if she was not sure what to say. She shook her head. "I'm afraid I have no idea what time he will return."

"Alright," Zeller said. "Perfectly understandable. Again, we are sorry to disturb you. We will just come back at a later time."

"Yes, do." She started to close the door, then stopped. "Who should I tell him came calling? What are your names, gentlemen?"

"Earl Zane," Zeller said. "And my friend here..." he nodded at Frank. "Felix Lennon."

"Mr. Zane and Mr. Lennon. I will go write that down before I forget. Good day." The door closed with a firm click.

"Clever," Frank chuckled as they headed down the steps to the sidewalk. "You used our real initials, just like Overton used his when he forged himself a new name."

"Easier to remember. And at this point, we're only hoping O'Toole is Overton. Don't know for sure."

"I'm betting he is." Frank laughed. "So, while we're waiting for him to return home to his sister, let's go find a pub."

"Good idea." Zeller said. "I believe we have found Overton. And, mark my words, if we have—that woman he's living with is not his sister."

CHAPTER THIRTY-THREE

*P*ulling hard on the oars of the White Caps rowboat, Cole struggled to maneuver the vessel through choppy waves. He groaned. His arms were weaker than he had realized.

During the many long months of illness, he had been acutely aware of how weak his legs had become.

He had not worried so much about his arm strength—until joining the lifeguards. His energy spent, he stopped rowing, and the boat slowed.

Cole flashed an embarrassed grin at the lifeguard sitting across from him as they bobbed up and down on the swells. "I didn't realize this would be so hard," he said, gasping for breath. "I'll do better next time, Pete."

Pete Potter laughed and shook his head. "You did well for a first attempt. You were sick for a long time, and rowing this heavy boat is hard work. It's understandable that it would be a challenge. Glad you joined the crew, though. We can use you."

The two men switched seats. As Pete grabbed the oars, Cole scanned the crowd of bathers as they headed back toward shore.

Cole raked his fingers through his hair, taking deep breaths as he concentrated on watching for people who might be in trouble.

Other than the rowing part, lifeguard training was proving to be fun.

When Jacy had encouraged him to join, he had immediately done so, offering his services two days a week.

"Glad to be of assistance," he told Pete, not taking his eyes off the people in the water. "Too many folks have no idea how to swim. And drownings are tragedies that need not happen."

"That's what Frank says," Pete said with a grin.

"Where is Frank?" Cole remembered Jacy's remark about the lifeguard captain's mother. "I'm surprised he is taking time off now, when people need him the most."

Pete laughed. "His mother needs him more. She took sick, and the family called him home. He'll be back soon."

"Oh…okay." Cole glanced at Pete, and Pete responded with a good-natured smile. Pete had accepted him into the lifeguard crew without hesitation the day before. The more time Cole spent with him, the more he liked him.

He did not, however, think Frank had told Pete the truth. According to Jacy, Frank's absence could not have anything to do with his mother.

"Hey," Pete shouted as he pitched the boat into a wave and maneuvered it with the dexterity of a baker slicing bread. "Don't tell me you're missing Frank? I can't believe that. I don't know you well, yet, Cole. But I know the two of you are not exactly friends."

"No, that's true." Cole decided to keep what he knew to himself. Whatever Frank Lynch was up to, it was not any of his business—and what could it possibly have to do with him, or Jacy?

* * *

WHEN COLE TOLD Jacy what Pete Potter had said about Frank, she shook her head, perplexed. "The hero of Cape May is up to something. I wonder what?"

Cole edged closer, lifted her hand, and kissed it. "I don't know, but let's not let it ruin our day."

Sighing contentedly from her seat in the one-horse carriage, she agreed. "So far it has been glorious." A warm tingling rushed through her as she stared into his eyes. "This is such a romantic idea. I'm glad you thought of it."

They were taking a carriage to Cape May Point along the beach at high tide. Henry and Lydia

their companions and chaperones, sat across from them.

"You have walked this way so many times, Jacy. I was afraid you might find it boring," Lydia said as she leaned her head on Henry's shoulder. "Yet, you have the look of a young girl on Christmas morning, with eyes brightly aglow."

Jacy nodded and giggled. "That's because we're going to the Point to hunt for Cape May diamonds. Poppy and I used to do it all the time when we were children. But searching with Cole will be even more fun, because he has promised to have a necklace made for me out of our finds."

"Ah...brother, how gallant of you," Henry said.

Cole laughed.

"It will be as beautiful as a real diamond necklace," Jacy declared. "And far more special."

Everyone in town knew about Cape May diamonds, the small quartz crystals that washed up on the beach where Delaware Bay joined the Atlantic Ocean. The translucent stones—polished by the tumbling waves at the junction of those two bodies of water—had been prized for centuries, even when Indian tribes had inhabited the land.

The rugged stones had little monetary value, but they were often made into jewelry. When cut like real diamonds, they had a unique sparkle.

The diamonds would be easy to find. They only had to look for shiny stones glittering in the sun near the water.

Looking with Cole would be an adventure. She would remember it all her life. She would treasure the necklace, always. No matter what came of her and Cole's relationship, she would have a piece of jewelry to remember him by. She would wear it close to her heart.

The lighthouse came into view. They were getting close to their destination. Passing a grand oceanfront hotel, the driver brought the carriage to a halt on the beach dotted with Cape May diamond-seekers.

Henry and Lydia clambered out first and Cole helped Jacy step out. Tucking Jacy's arm in his, Cole whispered, "Let's you and I go our own way, shall we?"

Jacy's heart skipped a beat when she met Cole's gaze. *What should I do?*

She would have to tell him the truth about herself, and the sooner she did, the better. Not telling him was unfair to him and torturous for her.

Wetting her lips, Jacy summoned a smile. Telling him was too terrifying to contemplate. Blinking back tears, she whispered, "Do you think Henry and Lydia will mind if we go off on our own?"

"Jacy." Cole's voice was husky. "Of course, they won't mind. Anyway…" He pointed at the tideline, where Henry and Lydia were headed. "Looks like they've staked out their territory. Let's go find our own."

"Let's." Slipping her arm out of his, she grabbed his hand. He laughed as she led him toward the water.

"I love you, Jacy," Cole sang out when they were well away from all the other diamond-seekers.

"I love you, too, Cole." She listened to the breaking surf swallow her words and then whispered, "And I always will."

CHAPTER THIRTY-FOUR

The man calling himself Edward O'Toole was sitting alone in The Rat's Tail Pub when Frank and Zeller strolled in.

The neighborhood joint, around the corner from O'Toole's residence, was dimly lit and just barely clean enough for Frank's sensibilities. He winced as his eyes adjusted to the gloom.

O'Toole was in a rear corner, holding a mug to his lips while staring into space.

Zeller led Frank to a table near the entrance and they sat down. A wide grin spread across the detective's face. "What luck," he said. "We won't have to wait outside his house for hours and hours for him to come back. Finding him here is a hell of a lot easier." Squinting, he studied their prey. "Will be much easier to strike up a conversation with him this way, too. And if you ask me, the man looks lonely."

Frank returned Zeller's grin. The private eye business was proving to be fun, after all. It was almost as exciting as being a lifeguard. Tracking someone down was thrilling— finding them even more so.

Then he remembered who they were tracking down and why.

Clenching his jaw, Frank hoped he would be able to refrain himself from strangling O'Toole, if he did indeed turn out to be Overton. Jacy's dear Edmund had caused her many months of misery.

"Conversation?" Frank tore his eyes off the man and looked at Zeller. "Did you say we were going to strike up a conversation?"

Zeller gave Frank a bemused look. "Next step on our agenda. Soon as we order our drinks. We'll carry them over to his table and introduce ourselves."

"Oh, okay." Frank's pulse began to race. *Hell, this is more fun than lifeguarding.*

A server took their order and returned a moment later with two dark ales. Zeller withdrew his wallet from his pocket, plucked out a couple of dollar bills for the server and stood up, beckoning for Frank to follow.

"I'll put these on my expense account," Zeller said, grabbing an ale in each hand and handing one to Frank. "Let's go. Just remember—let me do most of the talking. Just listen and nod. Follow my lead. Don't mention Cole Stratton *at all*. And remember what I told you about the James woman. Don't let on you have any romantic feelings for her *whatsoever.*"

Frank nodded. "Right. She and I are just very good friends. I care about her as a friend. Which is why I went looking for Edmund Overton. So distraught has she been over his disappearance that when I heard rumors about his being alive, I had to see if there was any truth to it. As a friend."

"Yeah, yeah. Make it convincing," Zeller mumbled. "So far you ain't convincing me."

As they reached O'Toole's table, Zeller asked in a friendly voice, "Hey, buddy. Use some company?"

Plunking down his ale on the table, Zeller did not wait for an answer. Smoothly reaching behind him, he grabbed two unoccupied chairs and slid them—squeaking and screeching across the hardwood floor—to the table. He plopped down in one of them and with his eyes, signaled Frank to the other.

Frank swigged a few sips of his ale, lowered his mug, and mustered a friendly smile for his new pal.

O'Toole stared at Frank and then at Zeller and laughed. "Alright, gentlemen, seems like I got your company whether I want it or not.

So...buy me a drink and you can sit at my table. I don't think you came over here to admire my pretty face, so I'm thinking you want something. I'm thirsty, so you might be in luck."

Zeller chuckled. "What are you having?"

"What you got."

Zeller waved the server over, ordered, then sat back. "What a deal."

"Hope you think so. Edward O'Toole's my name. And you gentlemen are?"

"I'm Earl Zane," Zeller said. "And this is my friend, Felix Lennon."

The server came back with O'Toole's ale. "So how can I help you?" O'Toole asked with mild curiosity, fixing his gaze on Zeller. "Although I have to warn you, I doubt that I can. I'm new in town. Don't know too many people."

Without blinking, Zeller said, "We're looking for a man named Edmund Overton. Ever heard of him?"

Frank stifled a gasp. He grabbed his mug and took a few noisy swallows, trying not to choke. *Zeller sure doesn't waste any time.*

O'Toole just shook his head. "Sorry. Don't know that name."

"You sure about that?" Zeller asked. "We were sure you would."

"Sorry. Thanks anyway for the drink."

Zeller leaned toward him. "We believe *you* are Edmund Overton."

The man widened his eyes. "Me? What gives you that idea?" He turned to look at Frank, who just shrugged.

"You fit his description," Zeller said.

"Really? That's interesting, but I don't know the guy. And to my knowledge, I don't have any long-lost twins."

"You know Hal Higbee?" Zeller took a swig from his mug and watched O'Toole begin to fidget and shift his weight on the chair.

Even in the dim light, the man looked a few shades paler to Frank than he had moments earlier.

"You look like you might know Hal Higbee," Zeller said. "He a friend?"

"How do you know Hal?"

"Let's just say a guy in Cape May, New Jersey introduced us."

Zeller sat back and folded his arms. "I know you've heard of Cape May."

"Of course. So?"

"So, we just came from Cape May. And you—or rather, Edmund Overton—are the talk of the town this summer. Because of a woman named Jacy James. Who is so distraught over a missing sea captain named Overton that she is beside herself with grief. Does the name Jacy James mean anything to you?"

O'Toole's mouth dropped open. Frank no longer had any doubt: the man's face had turned almost white. Even his lips were colorless. "Jacy," he said softly. "Jacy."

"So you do know her?" Frank stood up. He couldn't help himself.

Zeller shook his head in warning. Frank slowly sat back down.

"Jacy," the man said again. "How is she?"

"I told you..." Zeller growled. "She is grief stricken. Distraught. In a great deal of emotional anguish."

O'Toole stared at Zeller. "I'm sorry to hear that."

"So you do know her." Frank stood again, feeling the blood rush to his face.

"*Sit*," Zeller said.

Frank sat.

O'Toole stared at Frank. "Yes, I know her. I loved her once."

"Once?" Frank went to stand up, but seeing the furious look in Zeller's eyes, refrained.

"Yes. Not so long ago." O'Toole kept his gaze on Frank. He looked puzzled. "How do you know Jacy James?"

Frank glanced at Zeller. "She is my friend. I am so concerned about her that I decided to look for her missing sea captain beau, Edmund Overton." Then he added, unable to resist: "*Are you he?*"

The man picked up his mug, drained it, and set it down. "I am."

Frank shot to his feet.

Zeller grabbed Frank's arm and lowered him back into his chair. "Let me handle this," he said. "Do as we agreed."

"You got me," Overton said with an expression of defeat and relief. "You found me. I'm tired of hiding. What do you want with me?"

"Why did you go into hiding?" Zeller gave him a cold stare. "Tell us that first."

"What did Hal Higbee tell you?"

"That you and he were the only survivors of a wreck. One that wasn't your fault. Is that true?"

"It is."

"So why—"

"Shame." Overton shrugged. "We saved ourselves. Nobody else."

"Did you *try?*" Frank stood and put his hands on the table, leaned over, and looked Overton in the eye.

"We *tried.*" Overton said. "But the ship sank too fast. We were afraid nobody would believe us. And that I would be blamed for the loss of vessel and lives. Better and easier to just start a new life in a new city."

"Too bad Higbee returned to Philadelphia. Where people know him." Zeller smirked. "By the way, in case you are wondering, Higbee was willing to give us your new name and address for a hundred bucks. So much for friendship."

Frank snickered.

"And just who is Martha Kent to you?" Zeller asked. "She's not your sister."

"A friend. Who was willing to take me in. Leave her out of this."

"A friend." Zeller winked. "Okay."

Frank balled his fists, furious. "What about Jacy? Didn't you think about her when you decided to start your life over again? You just decided to let her believe you were dead?"

Overton pushed his chair back and looked Frank in the eye. "I believed it was better that way. For her and for me."

Bringing his fist within inches of Overton's face, Frank glared at him, shaking with rage.

Zeller jumped up and grabbed Frank's wrist and told him to stand aside.

"It has not been better for Jacy James," Zeller said. "She has been mourning you. She cannot let your memory go. She believes you are

still alive. We need to take you to Cape May so you can be reunited—
for the sake of her happiness, if nothing else."

"What about *me?*" Overton stared at him. "The authorities will
investigate the wreck. I might be arrested."

"Not if you tell them the truth." Zeller said. "They will investigate,
and the truth will win out. I'm sure of it."

Overton shook his head. "But what will I tell Martha? And then
what will I tell Jacy?"

"We will go see Martha now and you can explain to her that you
are going back to Jacy. While you pack your things." Zeller's voice was
steely.

"And if I don't?"

"We will get the police involved and then you probably will be
arrested on the spot," Zeller said. "Your choice."

"Okay, okay. I will do as you say. I truly do miss Jacy. But what
should I tell her? What excuse can I give for being gone so long?"

Zeller flashed Frank a wink. "We have a plan all worked out. Just
trust us and do what we say."

CHAPTER THIRTY-FIVE

*J*acy closed her eyes and relished being in Cole's arms.

It seemed most of Cape May was attending the *Farewell to July Ball* at the grand oceanfront Stockton Hotel. Jacy was thrilled to be there on this romantic, starlit evening with the man she loved.

With a contented sigh, she leaned her head back and gazed into Cole's eyes. She gave him a dreamy smile. She had attended many soirees that summer when she could only dream about dancing with Cole. This time, she intended to drink in every precious moment.

"So far, you have given me three dances," Cole whispered in her ear. "Will you allow me to claim all the rest?"

Lowering her chin, she looked up at Cole. "Of course, sir. You didn't even have to ask."

"Oh, but etiquette says that I do. Which you well know."

"I suppose we *should* worry about etiquette…"

Cole leaned his head back and laughed. "I have been thinking about what is socially proper a lot of late."

Jacy's breath caught in her throat. "You have?"

"Yes." Words rushed out of him, as if he could not stop them. "There is something I wish to discuss with your father and I hope you don't mind…but I have asked your Aunt Helen to write him to ask if he might consider returning to Cape May for another visit."

Was Cole blushing? Jacy did not think men blushed, but his face was red.

"Cole." Jacy's heart was pounding so hard she feared it might burst.

She missed a step. Cole caught her and pulled her closer. He held her in his arms with an intensity that took her breath away. "Cole," she said again. "What did Aunt Helen say?"

"She was delighted." His eyes gleamed with desire. "Said she would send him a postcard right away."

Feeling weak in the knees, Jacy stumbled again and Cole caught her. "I imagined you would be happy to see him. I know I will be."

"Cole…I…" Jacy swallowed hard and looked away. Her gaze landed on the spectators encircling the dance floor.

Priscilla, dressed in filmy white, was one of them. Jacy stared at her and frowned. Why was Priscilla—the gloriously gorgeous socialite —not dancing?

Cole twirled Jacy around. Priscilla came back into Jacy's view. Jacy pursed her lips. Cole's former flame was gazing at Cole in undisguised admiration.

Jacy clenched her teeth. Cole's former flame had not given up on him. *Incredible*. The woman obviously thought she still had a chance to win him back. How could she? *Cole has made it clear where his heart belongs*.

Cole means to propose to me. The thought took Jacy's breath away and she closed her eyes. She would accept. How could she not? Then, she would have to tell him the truth. She would tell him immediately after agreeing to become his wife. She would not be able to put it off any longer. And what would happen then?

Swallowing hard, Jacy glanced back at Priscilla. The haughty beauty was no longer looking at Cole. Her oddly serene gaze had shifted to Jacy.

A tall, elegantly clad man walked up to Priscilla and asked her to dance. Priscilla shook her head, without taking her eyes off Jacy. She was smiling, but why? Why would Priscilla be smiling at her?

It's as if she knows my dilemma. But how could she?

Jacy forced herself to return Priscilla's smile and then looked deep into Cole's eyes.

He put his lips to her ear. His breath was warm against her skin. "What's wrong, Jacy? You look like a scared rabbit."

She looked at him, wide-eyed. "I'm fine," she whispered.

"You don't look fine."

Jacy gave Cole a beaming smile. "How could anything be wrong? I am having a grand time." Tilting her head, she gave a light laugh, as if she had not a care in the world. "I love dancing with you."

"And I love dancing with you." He drew her closer than was proper. "And I want to dance with you the rest of my life."

Jacy could feel the rapid beating of his heart. It was in harmony with her own.

* * *

"Who are you writing to Mother?"

"Your Uncle Tobias."

"Why?"

Helen looked over at Poppy, who was staring at her as she tapped a black quill pen against her teeth.

Helen had enjoyed spending a rare morning alone with her daughter on the White Caps porch. Most guests, it seemed, were keeping to their rooms, exhausted from the Stratford ball the evening before.

Jacy was among them. She had danced far into the night, and as such, was much on Helen's mind.

Helen did not even try to subdue her excitement. "I am asking my brother to come back to Cape May for another visit."

"Oh." Poppy held her poetry pad to her chest and grinned. "And why?"

"Because Cole Stratton asked me to invite him. He has something important he wants to discuss with him. About Jacy, I'm sure. Isn't that wonderful?"

Poppy set her pen and pad down on the table. Sitting forward, she gave a happy sigh. "He wants to ask Uncle Tobias for permission to marry Jacy. How marvelous."

"I am sure that must be it."

Poppy frowned. "Do you think Jacy will accept?"

Helen widened her eyes. "Of course. Why do you even question it?"

"I don't know… It's just that she seems nervous about something lately. Very anxious. Which is not like her. She is usually so cheerful and sunny. Except, of course, when Captain Overton disappeared. She was distraught then."

"Oh my," Helen whispered. "You don't think…"

"That she is still in love with that sea captain? *No.* She loves Cole. That is very clear."

"Then what could be bothering her?" A feeling of foreboding came over Helen. Admonishing herself for being silly, she tried to push the feeling away. Poppy was right. Jacy *had* been acting nervous lately.

"I don't know, Mother. But I do think it's a good idea for you to invite Uncle Tobias back for another visit." Poppy waved her hand. "Go ahead and finish writing your postcard."

Helen nodded. "Yes, dear. I shall. I want to get it posted today."

She glanced down at what she had written. "Dear Tobias," she read. "Your presence is requested in Cape May." Keeping her hand steady and her writing neat, she added, "Jacy misses you and would love to see you."

Best not to mention Cole Stratton at all, she decided.

Best to surprise dear Tobias when he gets here.

CHAPTER THIRTY-SIX

The more time Frank spent in Edmund Overton's company, the less he liked the man. He was arrogant and dumb, an irritating combination.

Fortunately, Overton had been able to execute a swift and tidy exit from the home of the widow Kent. As Frank and Zeller watched, he hastily threw a few clothes into a large duffel bag, gave his female companion a cold peck on the cheek, and waved goodbye to her as she sobbed and pleaded for him to stay.

Unfortunately, at the very hour Frank and Zeller hustled Overton aboard the *Splendid Lady*, a dark storm descended on the city. The horrendous weather was not a problem as far as sailing was concerned. Frank was confident his crew could get them safely back to Cape May. But the slashing rain forced all the passengers to stay inside the cabin. Frank had to restrain himself from pulling his hair out as he endured Overton's company.

As they sailed south, and the New York skyline faded from view, Frank told himself the forced confinement was just as well. He, Zeller, and Overton had to come up with a plausible story to explain Overton's long absence, and they did not have a lot of time to do so.

"Amnesia," Zeller muttered, comfortably ensconced in the largest, black leather chair in *Splendid Lady's* main lounge.

Rain pelted the yacht's windows and rough seas made the going choppy. But Zeller appeared not the slightest bit concerned as he took a swig of whiskey soda and set it down on the small table next to him. All the yacht's tables were fitted with brass cup holders, so glasses did not roll with the waves, a detail of which Frank was proud.

Zeller looked over at Frank and then at Overton. Both sat across from him, nursing drinks. "Amnesia," Zeller said again. "It's a rare and melodramatic affliction—but I've seen it work before. I also can't think of any other excuse, except that you lost your memory, Overton. For a while, at least. Until we found you. And miracle of all miracles, reminded you of who you really are."

"Genius." Frank took a swallow of his whiskey on rocks. "I like it. Explains the whole sorry mess."

Overton looked incredulous. "Are you suggesting that I pretend that I couldn't remember who I *was*?"

Zeller picked up his glass and took a sip. He slowly set it back down. "That's exactly what I am suggesting."

Frank rolled his eyes. Overton was obviously a doofus, without a brain in his head. For the hundredth time, he wondered what Jacy could possibly have seen in him.

"A loss of memory would be easy enough to explain, and the story would include some truth, which is always helpful." Zeller said. "Your ship wrecked in a storm, which you say is true. You hit your head on something—or something fell on you—during the wreck. Which you will *claim* is true."

"Okay…" Overton said.

"The ship went down with all but you and one of your crew mates. Right?"

"That's right."

"Then the two of you got into a lifeboat and made your way to New York City, where you were rescued. Is that what you say happened?"

"Yes."

"Then the only other thing you need to *claim* is true is that you could not remember who you were after you were rescued," Zeller said. "Simple. Done."

Overton looked pensive, then gave a half smile. Sitting with his ankles crossed, drinking his whiskey straight, he exuded the air of a man who could easily get used to the yachting lifestyle. He lifted his glass, downed the contents, and held it up, signaling he needed a refill.

Frank gritted his teeth. He reached for a large brass bell on the table next to him and rang it. A server hurried into the room and filled Overton's glass to the brim.

Overton drank half the whiskey, spilling a few drops on himself. "You must think I am a pretty good actor, gentlemen. Unfortunately, I am not."

"Too bad. Start practicing." Zeller slammed his glass down. "Now, if you'll excuse me, *gentlemen*, I will leave you to it. Overton, rehearse your lines. Frank—help him."

Zeller bounded to his feet. "If you don't mind, Frank, I am going to avail myself of one of your guest rooms and go lie down. I'm exhausted."

"That way," Frank said, pointing. "Through the door and to the right. And I don't blame you. It's been a fatiguing trip."

Frank watched the detective amble off, then turned back to Overton. Several moments of silence passed.

Finally, Frank could not stand it anymore. Leaning forward, he planted his elbows on his knees and narrowed his eyes. "How did you fool Jacy? Before we get started, that's what I want to know."

"What? What do you mean?"

"What I mean is—how did you get her to fall for you?"

"Is that meant to be an insult?"

"Take it however you want. But I'm puzzled. You are rather old for her, and from what I can tell, you don't seem to have any money. And from what I have heard, her family hated you."

Overton smirked at Frank. "I'm a handsome devil."

"I hardly think so."

"*She* thought I was." Overton said, leaning back in his chair, crossing one leg over the other. "If you think so little of me, why are you so hell-bent on bringing me back to her? Seems to me you want her for yourself."

"Jacy loves you. I don't know why, but she has been grieving for you all summer. She has been climbing the Cape May Lighthouse every morning, looking for your ship."

Overton's jaw dropped. "You don't say?"

"I do say." Frank glared at Overton, giving him time to think about what he had just said. It was only partially true, but Frank liked Zeller's strategy of using half-truths.

Dumbfounded by the revelation, Overton turned to look out the window.

"You're right. I do care about Jacy," Frank admitted. "But only as a friend. One who can't stand to see her in pain. Who has the financial means to help her. When I heard rumors you might be alive, I had to find out if it was true. If you were alive, I had to bring you back to her."

Overton picked up his glass, drained it, and set it down.

"Didn't you love her? How could you just abandon her?"

"I loved her." Overton said, his voice flat.

Frank wanted to strangle him. Restraining himself, he stayed seated and stared him down. "You had a strange way of showing it. Why did you let her think you were dead?"

A pained expression crossed Overton's face. "I told you. I didn't want to be blamed for the shipwreck."

"So, you thought it was better to let Jacy *suffer*? And go on living without her?"

"Yes. Exactly. She was better off without me." He arrogantly raised his chin. "And, anyway, Martha Kent met my needs."

Frank gripped both armrests. "What do you mean by that?"

Overton smirked. "What do you think I mean? Do I need to give you the details?"

"And what about Jacy?"

"I got what I wanted from her."

"*What?*" Frank jumped to his feet. Balling his hands into fists, he stared into Overton's bloodshot eyes.

"Do you want the details?" Overton whispered loudly. "I don't think you do."

Furious, Frank exhaled like a mad bull.

Overton appeared unfazed, except for his snide grin. "For some reason, you want to reunite me with Jacy. Okay. I was tiring of Mrs. Kent, anyway. You and Zeller came along at the right time. I had assumed Jacy's father hated me so much I didn't stand a chance with her. I think he had delayed her trust fund because of me."

"Trust fund? You were after her money?"

"I didn't say that."

"What are you saying?"

"I had stayed away too long. How could I go back—how could I possibly explain my absence? Now, you and Zeller have convinced me that I *can* go back. That Jacy wants me back. Lucky, lucky me."

"You'll be lucky if you don't get arrested." Frank said. He was starting to wonder if he and Priscilla had made a terrible mistake bringing this man, who was more dangerous than he had initially thought, back to Jacy.

"Arrested?" Overton snorted. "How could police arrest someone who had amnesia? You and your detective have given me a way to clear my name. I'll end up looking like a hero. I don't know how I'll ever be able to thank you."

Frank eased back down in his chair as the gravity of Overton's last remark soaked in. Dolt that he was, Overton knew why he was being taken to Cape May and that Frank would not lay a hand on him. Stifling a groan, Frank hoped Jacy did not end up getting hurt. Breaking up her and Cole's relationship was one thing. But Overton was crass and cruel.

Digging his nails into his palms, Frank promised himself Jacy would not get hurt. He would watch Overton split Jacy and Cole up. Then, he—Frank Lynch, Cape May's finest hero—would swoop in and save her. Somehow, he would help her see Overton for the scoundrel he truly was.

Overton snickered. "Don't you think we should get started?"

Frank shook his head to clear his thoughts. "Started?"

"Practicing. I need to practice what I am going to say to Jacy when I see her. Remember?"

Frank nodded. "Right." He raked his hands through his hair and reached for his whiskey. "So, what do you think you should say? Any ideas?"

Overton grinned. "I know exactly what I'll say. I will tell sweet, sweet Jacy how much I love her—that I love her still. Then, I will remind her about the last time we were together. Remind her that I had asked her to marry me. Remind her that she had agreed."

Reaching across Frank, Overton grabbed the brass bell and rang it.

"What are you doing?" Frank asked.

"I'm still thirsty. Do you mind?"

"I do mind."

"Too bad. And by the way, I am going to tell Jacy that when my memory returned, the first thing I recalled was our last night together."

A server hurried in and poured Overton more whiskey. "I am going to tell her that when you and Detective Zeller tracked me down, and reminded me of my real identity, it all came back to me. All at once. Clear as a bell. As clear as that sweet bell I just rang."

Frank swallowed hard. He took a sip of his drink and tried not to gag.

CHAPTER THIRTY-SEVEN

"*I* received a telegram from my brother, Tobias, today." Aunt Helen smiled at each of her dinner companions, resting her gaze on Cole. Delicately inserting her fork into her roast leg of lamb de White Caps, she paused and looked at Jacy. "We can expect him to arrive on the *Republic* in a few days."

Cole beamed. "Wonderful. I look forward to seeing him again. There is something I need to talk to him about. Jacy, I imagine you are looking forward to seeing your father again as well."

Jacy put her fork down. Her mouth suddenly felt dry. If she tried to swallow even a morsel of dinner, she would probably choke. Smoothing the napkin in her lap, she forced herself to appear cheerfully nonchalant. "Of course," she said softly. "I love my papa. Dear, dear Papa."

As they had most evenings of late, Jacy, Aunt Helen and Poppy were dining with the Strattons. They had become an informal family group, joined at times by other hotel guests, including Cole's new lifeguard friends.

Pete Potter sat at their table that night and Jacy was grateful. Witty and talkative, he changed the subject from her father's impending visit to a tale about a rescue Cole had made that afternoon. "Saved a woman in distress," Pete said. "Since I helped train him in the ways of ocean lifesaving techniques, I was quite proud."

Poppy giggled and covered her mouth with her hand. Her eyes gleamed with amusement. "I witnessed it as well," she said. "It seemed the dear lady went out too far—beyond her *ankles*. She stepped in a hole and stumbled, and Cole scooped her up and led her to shore. And then, she was *so* grateful."

"Poppy." Aunt Helen shot her an embarrassed look. "Where are your manners? Mr. Potter was praising our newest lifeguard, but you—"

"It's quite alright." Cole smiled modestly. "Poppy is correct. It wasn't the most daring rescue in the world. But it did feel good to help someone else for a change. Rather than be the one needing help."

Jacy leaned over and whispered to Cole that she was proud of him. Across the table, her aunt was whispering something to Poppy, who was sitting next to the very eligible Mr. Potter.

The extremely eligible Mr. Potter wasn't paying any attention to Poppy at the moment, however. "Well, look who just walked in," he announced, looking toward the entrance. "Frank Lynch. Frank has come back—hooray."

Widening her eyes, Jacy turned to Cole. He met her gaze. Was he wondering the same thing as she? How would Cape May's esteemed hero react when he learned Cole had joined his lifeguard crew?

And where had Frank been?

Pete Potter waved Frank over. Jacy looked down at her lap, hoping Frank would just bypass their table. Maybe if she did not look at him he would get the message.

"Wait, it seems he has two other men with him," Pete said. "I wonder who they might be."

Curious, Jacy turned around—then froze.

One of Frank's companions was an older man with a graying goatee. The other was Edmund.

Edmund.

Jacy's heart skipped a beat. She felt the blood drain from her face. She grabbed onto the table cloth, afraid she might faint. It couldn't be, but there he was heading straight toward her.

Cole touched Jacy's arm. "What's wrong? You look as if you've seen—"

"A ghost," Poppy squealed. "It's—"

"Edmund Overton!" Aunt Helen shrieked. "It can't be. It can't be. No...no...no..." She moaned. "Smelling salts...someone get me some smelling salts..."

Cole grabbed Jacy's hand. He looked deeply into her eyes and slowly turned to the visitor.

Swallowing hard, Jacy turned back to face Edmund and told herself she must be dreaming.

But there he stood, in the flesh. Still handsome, he looked a tad older. His hair and beard were scruffier. He looked taller than she remembered.

The thing she had once wished for most in life had come true— and now her life was ruined.

"Jacy," Edmund said.

Jacy stopped breathing. The dining room began to spin. Murmuring voices roared in her ears. The gas lights dimmed.

She closed her eyes to steady herself. When she opened them again, she looked at Cole. "I'm so sorry," she whispered. "I am so, so sorry."

"Jacy." Edmund said her name again, louder. His low-pitched, reso- nant voice had not changed. He pronounced her name with a caress, a habit she had once found endearing, but now, in Cole's presence, made her wince. "Jacy," he said again. "Jay...seee. I've missed you so much. Please, please forgive me."

"Forgive you!" Aunt Helen screeched. The matron shoved her chair back and stood up. "Lord God in heaven," she shouted, "save us all, save us all!"

Pandemonium ensued.

Everyone in the room stood up.

Everyone turned to see what the loud wailing was about.

Poppy stood up too, took hold of her mother's arm, and quickly hustled her out of the room.

"Dead man come to life," a man called out.

A woman, her voice loud and high-pitched, shouted, "The missing sea captain."

"Unbelievable," a chorus of voices murmured.

Cole looked as if he had been shot.

Shock, anger, and humiliation raged through Jacy all at one. Everyone was staring at her, waiting. Waiting for her to say something.

She forced herself to look Edmund straight in the eye. "Where have you been all these months?" she hissed. "How dare you...to just show up like this. With much of Cape May watching." Trembling, she pushed her chair back, stood up, and faced him. Narrowing her eyes, she felt her lips quiver, heard her voice waver. "Were they true? Were all those rumors true?"

He shrugged and gave her a contrite smile. "I can explain. Please, Jacy, please forgive me and allow me to explain."

Forgive him? Allow him to explain?

How could she could ever forgive him? She did not want to hear him explain anything. She felt nauseous.

"Can we talk, Jacy?" Edmund pleaded. "I have much to tell you."

Jacy turned to look at Cole. With a stricken stare, Cole nodded. "I think you need to hear his story."

Henry stood and helped Lydia to her feet. "Under the circumstances, brother, I think you should stay here. My wife and I will escort Jacy and Captain Overton to the music parlor, so they can talk privately. Don't worry, we won't leave Jacy and this man alone."

Cole held Jacy's gaze and nodded. "I suppose that's as good a plan as any," he said, his voice hollow.

"Come, Jacy," Edmund said, holding out his hand. She ignored it. "Again—I'm truly sorry. I can and will explain."

She did not believe him. She did not believe he was truly sorry. How could she believe anything he said?

She did not know what to believe.

After one last look at Cole, she numbly followed Lydia, Henry, and Edmund to the parlor.

As she did, a tear ran down her cheek.

PART III

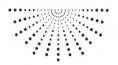

3 8

AUGUST

*I*n bed, with an icepack covering her eyes, Jacy moaned. She had gotten little, if any, sleep.

She could not see anything, but knew it was morning. Poppy had informed her of such when she came over with more ice. Not caring to open her achy, swollen eyes, Jacy had thanked her but said nothing else.

Minutes ticked by. Jacy's head pounded. Her mouth felt as dry as sand. If she tried to move, she was sure she would vomit.

Edmund's miraculous return was a nightmare. Why did he have to come back?

Why?

Jacy heard Poppy's footsteps approaching her again. "Cole wants to see you," she said. "He sent word. He is waiting on the porch."

Jacy groaned. "I can't."

"Can't what?"

"I can't see him. Not now."

"You cried most of the night." Poppy's voice was soft.

"I'm sorry if I kept you awake."

"Was it that awful?"

"Yes."

"Do you want to talk about it?"

"No. Not now."

Poppy sighed loudly. "Okay. I will be out on the balcony if you need me. Just call, the door is open."

"Thank you."

"Are you sure you don't want to talk to Cole?"

"I can't. I have no idea what to tell him."

"Rest," Poppy said. "Call me when you are ready to get up."

Jacy groaned in agreement. She would have to get up eventually, but what then? She had made a complete mess of her life. With no idea how to fix it.

The night before, when she had entered the music parlor with Edmund, she had been confident she could straighten things out. Struggling to remain calm, she told herself she would listen to his story and then end their relationship right there.

She had planned to tell him her heart now belonged to another man.

But their conversation had not gone as planned. As soon as she and Edmund sat down in a corner of the parlor, he questioned why Henry and Lydia needed to be in there with them.

"Because they are our chaperones," she said, irritated at the question. "They are sitting in the opposite corner of the room. They won't be able to hear anything if we speak quietly."

"You and I never needed chaperones before."

"We should have had chaperones, Edmund."

"My, my. You certainly have changed, Jacy."

"Yes. I am not the woman I was before."

"But, who *are* those people?" Edmund asked, pointing to Henry and Lydia, who were sitting quietly, with their hands in their laps.

Digging her fingernails into her palms, Jacy had whispered. "Friends. They are friends."

"Of who? The man holding your hand at the table? Who was he?"

"His name is Cole Stratton. But I don't want to talk about him. I want to talk about you. Where have you *been*?"

He had not answered right away. For several minutes, he only contemplated her in silence, his expression unreadable. He had always been the one in charge. How could she have forgotten that?

"I will tell you where I have been," he said, finally. "After you explain who Cole Stratton is."

So, she told him. She explained how she and Cole had become friends and how their friendship had evolved into something more. "I know this may come as a shock to you," she whispered. "But when you didn't come back... I'm sorry..."

How could she have said she was sorry?

Readjusting the ice pack on her eyes, Jacy let out a deep sigh. She should not have apologized. She had nothing to be sorry for.

Edmund had taken it badly, in any case. "Cole Stratton..." he growled. "They didn't mention him at all."

"They?"

"Frank Lynch and Ernest Zeller. The men who found me. The lifeguard and detective who brought me back to you."

Edmund told her that his ship had wrecked in a storm off the coast of Long Island. That he was knocked out and tossed overboard. That a crew member, Hal Higbee, had dragged him into a lifeboat, which saved his life. And that they had been the only survivors.

"I was delirious as I watched the ship sink," he told her. "Me and Higbee drifted to shore. Apparently, I was unconscious when they found us. Higbee, I later learned, had run off without answering any questions. Police took me to a New York City hospital. When I woke up, three days later, I couldn't remember who I was."

"You couldn't remember?"

He told her he could not recall his name or anything about his life. That an elderly widow in Brooklyn, a friend of one of the nurses, had taken him in. "Her name was Martha Kent," he said, "and she was very kind."

His story did match some of the rumors. But something did not make sense: Frank Lynch's involvement.

"Frank Lynch found you? How? Why?"

"He and the private detective he hired, Ernest Zeller, found me at Martha's house."

"But why did Frank *want* to find you? Frank, of all people?"

"He said he was your friend."

Jacy had laughed at that, incredulous that Frank had pretended to be her friend.

Edmund had seemed genuinely surprised at her reaction. "He told me you still grieved for me. That, as your dear friend, he couldn't bear to see you suffer. When he told me about you, it suddenly came back," he said, snapping his fingers. "I remembered who I was. I remembered my name. I remembered you. It was a miracle."

A miracle? Perhaps. But she and Frank were not friends, and Jacy told him so.

"You're *not?*"

"No. Frank wanted to court me, but when I met him, my heart belonged to you. Then, I fell in love with Cole Stratton." She rushed on, before he could stop her. "I am glad you are alive, Edmund, I really am. But as far as you and I are concerned, I am ending our relationship. What we once had is no more."

Confessing her love for Cole had come as a profound relief. Ending her relationship with Edmund had felt right and honest.

But Edmund had not seen it that way. Enraged, he jumped to his feet and balled his fists.

As Jacy lay on her bed thinking back to the scene in the parlor, she winced at how frightened she had been, despite Henry and Lydia's presence. Playing the role of inconspicuous chaperones, the couple didn't seem to notice just how angry Edmund had become.

Jacy had never been afraid of Edmund before, so she stood and faced him down. "I think you should go to the authorities," she whispered loudly. "Tell them what happened, that the accident wasn't your fault. The crew members' families need to know what happened to their loved ones. I am sure you will be cleared of all wrongdoing. Then you can go on with your life."

"No, Jacy. *No,*" he had hissed. "You cannot just *end* our relationship. Don't you remember, my dear? You pledged yourself to me. I asked for your hand in marriage and you gave it."

"But I have changed my mind," she whispered.

Scowling, he shook his head. "You pledged yourself to me with your body as well as with your words. Don't you *remember*? You made yourself mine that night. And mine you shall always be."

He reached for her hand, but she snatched it away. Then she saw the truth. It was not love that he had felt for her, but lust. Stepping back from him, she cried, *"No."*

He closed the gap between them. "No? My dear, it does no good to say that now. I will not release you from your pledge to marry me." Grabbing her hand, he pulled her to him. "I want you, still. We're going to marry as soon as possible."

"No." She twisted, trying to try to break free from him. "No."

"Yes."

His next words had filled her with terror: "You will agree to restore our relationship, or I will tell everyone who you really are."

"Who I really am?"

"Yes. A woman who acts like she is pure and virginal, when the truth is, she is anything but."

"You *wouldn't*."

"But I would," he had replied, "and Cole Stratton will be the first person I shall tell."

* * *

COLE LEANED FORWARD, propped his elbows on his knees, and cradled his face in his hands. He knew it was around noon because the sun was directly overhead, putting the entire porch in shade.

It was hot. Sitting up, he used the back of his hand to wipe the sweat off his brow.

"We been here a long time," Samuel muttered. "How much longer you think 'til Miss Jacy comes down?"

"I don't know." Cole let out a loud sigh. "Thanks for keeping me company, though. If you want, go get yourself something to eat."

"What 'bout you?" Samuel had been sitting with Cole all morning. His face dripping with perspiration, he looked as hot as Cole felt. "You hungry?"

"No. Have no appetite."

"Women," Samuel grumbled.

"You're right about that, Samuel. You're right about that."

Cole glanced down at the other end of the porch. Jacy was not the only woman on his mind. Priscilla Day and her maid, Mavis Allen, were sitting by the steps leading down to the lawn. They had been there for about an hour—unnerving Cole but delighting Samuel.

Cole knew that if he asked Priscilla why she was there, she would claim to be waiting for Lydia. So he did not go over.

He knew Samuel wanted to, however. Samuel snuck a glance at Mavis and she returned his grin.

"Go sit with Mavis a spell," Cole said, nodding in her direction. "I know you've missed her."

Samuel shrugged. "Don't want to leave you by your lonesome, Mister Cole. You—" Samuel stopped, his eyes widening.

Cole followed Samuel's gaze. Jacy had finally stepped onto the porch.

Samuel jumped to his feet and looked at Cole. "Never you mind, Mister Cole," he said. "This be a good time for me to go."

Cole nodded. "Yes. I agree."

Samuel hesitated.

"Go," Cole urged. "Go say hello to Miss Mavis *and* Miss Priscilla. It would be great if you could keep them both company while I talk to Jacy."

Samuel flashed him a grin. "Can do that. Thanks."

As Cole watched Samuel make his way over to the love of his life, he watched Jacy—the love of his life—slowly make her way toward him. With a start, he realized she did not look well.

Dark smudges under her eyes gave her a haunted look. Her cheeks were puffy. Tendrils of her hair, most of which was fastened atop her head in a loose bun, hung askew down the sides of her face.

Cole had never seen her look so undone and it alarmed him. She appeared to be in a daze as she passed Priscilla and Mavis, not even acknowledging their presence. She gave Samuel a nod and then focused on Cole.

Cole stood quickly and reached for Jacy's hands. "Jacy," he whispered. "Are you okay?"

She nodded yes, but her eyes said no.

He helped her sit down, pulled his chair close to hers, and without taking his eyes off her, slowly took his seat. "Tell me," he whispered.

Jacy swallowed hard and looked away. "Edmund claims he had amnesia. That he couldn't remember who he was."

"*What?*" Cole had braced himself for a wild tale. But not that.

Jacy met his gaze again. "He said his ship went down. That he was injured and then rescued. That he couldn't remember his own name." She sighed. "That's the reason he didn't come back to me." Her lower lip quivered. "I don't know whether to believe it or not."

Cole frowned. The story, although rather dramatic, could be true. Parts of it did match the rumors circulating around Cape May. But something was not right. Jacy was obviously distraught. *Why?* She had kept him waiting for hours. *Why?*

"There is something you are not telling me," Cole said gently, reaching for her hand. She was shaking.

"I..." Jacy's face crumpled as she pulled her hand away. "I..." She cradled her head in her hands and muffled a sob. "I never told you something, Cole. I thought I would never need to tell you...but..." She looked up. Her face was streaked with tears.

"But what?" A chill ran through him.

"Edmund proposed to me the last time we were together," she said in a choked whisper. "And I...and I said, 'yes.'"

Cole sucked in a breath. He felt as if he had been punched in the gut. Still... "So, what did you tell him last night? Did you tell him about us?"

Jacy sniffed. "Of course."

"*And...?*"

"And I told him I had changed my mind. That I didn't want to marry him anymore."

"And?"

"And he got angry. And he insists on holding me to my pledge."

Cole stared at her. "That's outrageous. How can he?"

"Cole." Jacy's voice was pleading. "I need to give him some time."

"*What?*"

She sniffed again. "I am afraid so."

Cole shook his head in disbelief. "Because you still love him?"

She gave a soft sob. "No. But…I need to give him some time."

"Before what?"

"Before breaking it off with him for good."

Cole went numb. "Why?"

She did not answer his question. "He will be staying in Cape May for the rest of the summer," she said so softly he could barely hear her. "I'm sorry."

He stared at her, not knowing what else to say.

Jacy drew in a deep, shaky breath. Cole was afraid she would start crying and not be able to go on. He waited in agony for her to find her voice again.

"We have agreed to not announce our engagement. It had never been publicly announced before he disappeared, anyway. He never even asked for my father's blessing—"

"Then it wasn't official…" Cole felt a sliver of hope.

"It doesn't matter."

Cole's heart fell. "Why?"

"Because I am a woman of my word. And he came back to me."

Cole could not believe what he was hearing. It did not make sense. What was clear, however, was that Jacy was suffering. Terribly. He needed to give her some time. He needed to be patient. As difficult as it would be, he had to remain calm.

Glancing over at where Priscilla, Mavis and Samuel sat, Cole noticed Priscilla was not looking in their direction. Good. His obviously emotional conversation with Jacy was none of his former sweetheart's business. At all costs, he would keep it that way. Turning back to Jacy, he asked, "How will Overton be staying here?" His voice broke. "Does he have any money?"

"I don't think he has a penny." Jacy looked down at her lap. Her hands were folded so tightly together her fingers were white. "Frank

Lynch got him a room here at White Caps. The room next to Frank's just happened to become available, and Frank is paying for it."

Cole leaned back in his chair. "Why does *that* not surprise me?"

"Cole—" Jacy put her hand to her lips. "Cole," she whispered, "he's here. Edmund. He just walked onto the porch. He is coming our way."

Cole managed to give Edmund a half smile when he walked up to them. He longed to punch the man in the mouth. Refraining, he stood to face him.

"Hello, Jacy," Edmund said, his voice confident and smooth. He extended a hand to Cole. "I know who you are. Cole Stratton, right? I don't believe we have been formally introduced. I, of course, am Edmund Overton. Although I doubt I have to tell you that."

"I know who you are." As difficult as it was, Cole shook Edmund's hand. It was as cold as the man's smirk. Turning to Jacy, Cole helped her to her feet. "Jacy has told me much about you."

Overton flashed a snide smile. "She has told me quite a bit about you, too. How you overcame being an invalid and all."

"And all..." Cole smiled thinly. "Yes, and with Jacy's help, I recovered."

"Jacy is a wonderful woman." Overton gave her a smile that was probably supposed to convey love and tenderness. It made Cole's skin crawl. "I am so very happy to be back with her at last," Overton continued. "What a tragedy we were ever separated. So many wasted months."

Jacy, clearly distraught, looked back and forth between Edmund and Cole. "I am afraid you will have to excuse me. I must go."

"Jacy," Cole said.

She did not look at him. Lifting her skirts, she dashed down the porch, scurried down the steps to the lawn and then ran onto the beach.

In shock, Cole watched her turn in the direction of the lighthouse. Frowning, he turned his gaze to Priscilla. She was watching Jacy, too.

Priscilla turned back to look at Cole. He did not like the satisfied smile on her face.

CHAPTER THIRTY-NINE

*J*acy ran toward to the lighthouse. She stopped to catch her breath when she had to, then hurried on.

She reached the grounds, waited for a group of tourists to leave, then climbed the steps to the top.

Yanking the balcony door open, she stepped out. Grabbing the railing, and gasping for breath, she drank in the view of the sea and silvery sky. This was her view. And it brought her comfort.

Memories flooded her mind—all those mornings she had come to search for Edmund's ship, alone and grief-stricken. How many times had she anxiously scanned the empty expanse of sea, only to have been met with disappointment and sorrow?

Those days seemed long ago. Once she brought Cole to the lighthouse, the beacon became a place of joy.

When she climbed to the top with Cole, it was as if the sea itself shimmered with wonder at their love. Remembering, she smiled.

Remembering, she let the wind blow her hair back, unravel her bun and whip her locks into knots.

Cole. I love him.

I never loved Edmund. Why did I believe I did? What did I feel for him, if it wasn't love?

Jacy let the strong breeze cool her cheeks and dry her tears.

Squeezing her eyes closed, she opened them again. It was early afternoon. At that time of day, vessels of all sizes plied the waters.

Off the horizon, she saw a fleet of fishing boats. She watched as a large yacht pulled out of the yacht club and turned north. In the other direction, three sailboats cruised past the pier where the *Republic* would soon dock.

Jacy sighed. The tranquil panorama held no answers to her fevered questions: What should she do about Edmund? What should she do about Cole?

How could she escape Edmund, the man she had sought for so long? How could she tell Cole, the man she had never expected to love, the truth about herself?

I will probably end up disgraced and alone.

With a cry, Jacy yanked open the door to the lighthouse steps. Flying down them, she flung the bottom door open and ran down to the beach. Her beach. Beacon Beach.

Half blind with tears, she stumbled onto the sand. Her legs knew the way. She had walked the route so many mornings alone, or joyfully with Cole.

She lifted her face to the sky. She and Cole had named the beach together. It, too, had become a place of reflection. It was a place to collect her thoughts. A place to cry. A place to kiss. A place to laugh.

The fevered questions mocked her as she walked back to White Caps.

She slowed her pace and began to stumble. Through a stream of tears, she looked down at the sunbaked sand, which faded to a hazy white.

Turning to look at the ocean, all she could see was a blur of blue-gray waves.

Jacy dropped to the ground, gathered her skirts around her, and hugged her knees to her chest. She had to rest. She could not go on. She couldn't see.

* * *

COLE HAD no doubt Jacy was headed to the lighthouse. He longed to chase after her. But it might make her situation worse. She probably needed time alone.

Overton glared at him in silence. Then he turned and walked down the porch.

Priscilla looked up as Overton passed her and disappeared into the hotel.

Cole smiled to himself. Priscilla appeared miffed. Men did not usually ignore her.

Priscilla caught Cole's gaze. She grinned, apparently mistaking his smile for an invitation to come over. She waved. He groaned. He was not in a conversational mood and certainly did not want to talk to *her*.

Priscilla did not seem to notice, or care. Whispering something to Mavis and Samuel, she stood, smoothed the skirt of her lavender muslin gown and sashayed down the porch. When she reached Cole, she extended her hand, so he could help her sit in the chair vacated by Jacy.

"Cole, you poor dear. I couldn't help but notice that you seem to be having a rather difficult morning."

Cole shrugged. Was it that obvious?

She put a finger to her lips, tilted her head, and pointed to the hotel door. "That was Captain Overton, was it not?"

He did not answer, so she answered for him. "I know it was him. I heard he caused quite a scene in the dining room last night. So sorry I missed it."

Cole studied Priscilla's face. Lovely as ever, she somehow looked none the worse in the heat. She had a way of remaining cool and calm in most situations. Not a hair appeared out of place, no sweat marred her brow. "What are you doing here, Priscilla?"

"Waiting for Lydia, of course. We have plans to play tennis."

"Oh, and where is your racket?"

She smiled. "I plan to borrow one of hers."

"You are not dressed for tennis."

Her smile widened. "I plan to borrow one of her outfits as well."

"She's kept you waiting a long time. That's not like her."

Priscilla's eyes brightened. She pointed to the walkway from the beach. "Here she comes now, with Henry." She waved, and Lydia waved back. "I suppose they must have gone for a walk and forgotten all about me. I should be upset, but I'll forgive her."

"Priscilla," Lydia said as she and Henry stepped onto the porch. "Were we on for tennis? I'm sorry, I think I forgot."

Priscilla laughed. "It's fine. I have enjoyed keeping Cole company. He has had to deal with a shocking turn of events. I assume you know that Edmund Overton came back from the dead?

"Yes." Lydia glanced at Cole.

"Well, I believe the man's reappearance has rattled Jacy James," Priscilla said. "She ran off a little while ago."

Henry looked at Cole. "Jacy was here? She finally came to see—"

"She sure did," Priscilla said. "Edmund Overton was just here, too, and Jacy introduced him to Cole. Poor Jacy, she appeared horribly confused. I suppose having two men vying for one's heart must be rather overwhelming." Priscilla fixed her gaze on Cole "Most women content themselves with one man."

Cole looked at Henry and shook his head. "Henry," he muttered, "may I have a word with you in private?" He nodded at Priscilla and then Lydia. "If you could excuse us, ladies? We will leave you to your tennis."

A flicker of understanding crossed Henry's face. "Yes, dear," he said, patting his wife's arm. "Run along with Priscilla. Cole and I need to talk."

Nodding, Lydia reached for Priscilla's hand. "Let's go see if we can arrange a court. We didn't reserve one that I recall, but perhaps we will get lucky."

"Perhaps…" Priscilla looked back at Cole as Lydia pulled her along. "But in my experience luck favors those who make their own."

Henry watched the women leave. "What is Priscilla up to?"

Cole waved a hand in front of his face, as though swatting a fly. "I don't know, and I don't particularly care."

"You don't?"

"No. I have bigger problems right now than Priscilla. Edmund

Overton to be precise. He claims he had amnesia." Cole studied Henry's face. "You and Lydia were in the room with Jacy and Overton. What did you hear?"

"They were whispering most of the time. I could only hear snatches of what was said." Henry sighed. "Amnesia, you say? Outrageous."

Cole filled Henry in on the rest of Overton's story.

"Do you believe him?" Henry asked.

"I don't know what to believe. But that's not the problem. The problem is that he plans to spend the rest of the summer in Cape May. And that Jacy is giving him time. Because they were secretly engaged."

Henry sucked in a breath. "What are you going to do?"

Cole folded his arms. "The only thing I can do. Give Jacy time. And, in the meantime, try to ferret out the truth. Because I don't believe Overton's story. Not at all."

CHAPTER FORTY

$\mathcal{J}$ acy found her father waiting for her in the hotel lobby when she returned from her solitary trek to the lighthouse, exhausted and disheveled.

"Your aunt sent me an emergency telegram regarding Captain Overton, telling me to come immediately," he said, wrinkles of concern creasing his forehead as he took in her appearance. "I just came in on the *Republic*. Hailed a coach-for-hire. Paid the driver extra to hurry." A dark frown came over his face. "So, your friend is not dead, it seems. How wonderful for him."

Jacy nodded. She barely had enough energy to stand, let alone discuss the awful turn her life had taken. "I am sorry you had to come back to Cape May under such circumstances, Father." She let out a deep sigh, then saw Aunt Helen coming down the stairs.

Aunt Helen stopped midstep. Pressing her lips together, she looked at her brother, then at her niece. "I am glad you are both here," she said, her voice shaking and shrill. "Let us go up to my suite, where we can talk in private."

Jacy brought up the rear, fighting back tears, as Aunt Helen led the way. Ushering everyone into her room, her aunt firmly closed the door and took a seat at her desk.

Jacy sank into a chair by the window overlooking the balcony.

Her father paced the room. After what seemed an eternity, he asked for details.

Jacy listened sadly as Aunt Helen told him everything she knew.

"So, he claims to have lost his *memory*?" His voice rose an octave on the word.

Jacy could not meet her father's eye. She looked down and brushed fine grains of sand off her skirt.

"I am mystified," he said. "First, why is he here?"

"Frank Lynch is paying for his room," Aunt Helen said. She sniffed. "He plans to stay through the month. He is a floor above us. Our summer is ruined. And just when it was going so well."

"Jacy, why is he here?" Her father walked over to her. His hands-on-hips stare forced her to look up at him.

"I—" Jacy found more sand on her skirt and brushed it to the floor. How could she make him understand? When she could not tell him the truth?

"I do not understand," he said. "I thought you loved Cole."

"I do."

"So, send Captain Overton away. Banish him from your life. Banish him from all our lives. *Please*."

"I can't."

"Why not?"

"I'm sorry, Father." Jacy almost choked on the words.

"About what?"

"I didn't tell you, but before Edmund disappeared, I promised him I would marry him. We were secretly engaged."

Her father put his hands to his head. "*What* did you say?"

Jacy lifted her chin and fought back tears.

"You didn't have my permission. He didn't ask me for it."

"He knew you wouldn't give it."

"Break it off, Jacy. Cast him away."

Jacy bowed her head. "I can't. I gave him my word."

Aunt Helen gasped.

Jacy had never seen her father so angry. "He needs to go to the authorities. *Now*. Overton must go to the police. Tell them what happened. Let them investigate. How do we know anything he says is true?"

"Father, I don't think he—"

"If he doesn't go to the police, *I will*."

Jacy leaned over and buried her face in her hands.

"Tell Captain Overton to go to the police, Jacy," he said, his voice tight. "And tell him if he doesn't, I will."

* * *

"DAMN IT, Jacy, why can't your father mind his own business? I am not ready to go to the authorities." Reaching over, Edmund placed his index finger under Jacy's chin, lifted it, and forced her to look at him. "It will cause me problems."

Pulling away, Jacy stopped and turned to face the ocean. The day after her father's ultimatum, she had invited Edmund to go for a short walk, and he had eagerly agreed.

But within minutes of setting out, he obviously realized it would not be the loving stroll he had envisioned. Edmund expected Jacy to put on an act—to, if nothing else, pretend to be happy about his return. But it was not possible. Her stomach churned, and her nerves were so fraught with anxiety, she wanted to jump out of her skin.

"Father said he will go to the police if you do not, Edmund," she said. It was a cloudy day, threatening rain, so few people were out and about.

Edmund stepped next to her and reached for her hand. She snatched it away.

"We need to be seen together as a loving couple," he said through his teeth. "I have agreed not to go public with our engagement. But people need to see us together. We need to become reacquainted. I need to regain your trust and your love."

Jacy almost choked. "We have the beach almost all to ourselves, Edmund." She made a show of glancing around. "No one is looking our way."

"Blast it, Jacy." Edmund grabbed her hand, pulled her to face him, then tucked her arm into his. Resuming a slow stroll, he fixed a contented smile on his face.

"Let go of me," she hissed.

"No, my dear." Edmund widened his smile, tightened his grip, and kept walking. "Tell your father *not* to go to the police. He will listen to you. I know he will. You are his beloved daughter."

"It's too late, Edmund. I'm surprised the police have not called upon you already. The story about your miraculous reappearance is the talk of Cape May. If my father doesn't go to the authorities, it won't be long before someone else does."

"Cole Stratton?"

"Leave him out of this."

"Why should I, he—"

"Damn it, Edmund—" Jacy halted, forcing Edmund to stop. She yanked her arm out from under his and rubbed her elbow.

Edmund scowled. "Really, my dear, *you* cursing? I thought I would never see the day." He quickly resumed a smile. "I sort of like the new woman you have become. Quite saucy."

"If you don't go to the police, my father will." Jacy glared at him. "Please believe me. I am not exaggerating when I say he is furious that you are back in my life. *And*, that I have accepted you back. He will not listen to anything I have to say in the matter."

Edmund folded his arms across his chest. With a huff, he said, "Fine. I'll go. I will go to the police."

Jacy nodded curtly. "Good. Thank you."

"Oh, don't thank me." Edmund reached for her hand and patted it. His expression slowly changed from suppressed anger to a man deeply in love. A teasing grin spread across his face. It was an expression that once made her swoon.

She pulled away and walked as fast as she could back to the hotel. "Alright, I won't thank you for doing the right thing, Edmund," she shouted over her shoulder.

"Stop."

She halted in her tracks but did not look at him.

He came up behind her. "My dear, my dear, you see, I will be thanking *you*."

An ominous tingling crept up her spine. "*What? Why?*"

"Because you will come with me when I go to the authorities."

She turned and faced him. "No, I will not. Why should I?"

"Because you need to tell them you believe me. You will tell them, with sincerity in your voice and a sweet, pleading expression on your face, that you know my story must be true."

"Edmund, no—"

"You will tell them that the *only* way I would have stayed away from you was because I couldn't remember who I was. That we were in love. That clearly a cruel accident of fate took my ship, along with my memory, and that I am blameless."

Jacy put a hand to her mouth. She shook her head.

"You *will* come with me." His voice was hard.

"Why should I?"

"Why should you? I will tell you why." Edmund grabbed for her hand again, squeezing it so hard she could not pull away, and continued toward White Caps.

Resisting was futile. He would pull her along if he had to.

"Because if you don't do as I say, I will tell the whole town about you Jacy," Edmund said. "And don't think for a minute that I won't."

CHAPTER FORTY-ONE

*F*rank raised his hand to knock on Priscilla's door, but she yanked it open before he could. She had obviously been watching for his arrival from the window.

With a serene smile, she waved him in and gestured for him to take a seat at one end of her sofa as she settled herself on the other.

"So far, things are going far better than I could have hoped," she said, leaning over to arrange her light-green skirt around her ankles. Straightening, she met his gaze. "I commend you, my hero. Not only did you locate Overton and bring him back to Jacy, you also found him accommodations at White Caps at the height of the season. *Bravo.*"

Frank gave her a sly grin. He did deserve her praise and was glad she appreciated his efforts. "I'm also *paying* for his room, if you must know. But I won't ask you to share in that expense. I am happy to foot the penniless fool's bill in order to keep him in town. For now."

"Our plan is working beautifully."

"So far."

Frank shifted in his seat and noticed Priscilla's maid sitting as usual in the far corner. Still and silent as was her custom, dressed in her drab gray uniform, she blended into her surroundings.

She was, of course, there as Priscilla's chaperone. But something about her presence that day made him uneasy. He had not come for pleasantries.

"You remember Mavis, my maid," Priscilla said. "Don't worry. She can be trusted."

"I should hope." Frank cleared his throat. "And your mother? Is your mother well?"

"She's napping upstairs, as usual." Priscilla tilted her head and gave Frank a quizzical look. "I must say I was surprised when you sent me a note that you wished to visit. I assume your detective friend went back to Philadelphia?"

"Yes. Paid in full. Happy."

"He did a marvelous job. Everything is going splendidly. Everything is evolving as we had hoped." A wrinkle formed between Priscilla's pretty eyes. "So why have you come calling? Has there been a setback?"

"A setback?" Frank shook his head. Under different circumstances, he would have found Priscilla mesmerizing. Now, she was getting on his nerves. She was not doing her part.

"I wouldn't call it a setback," he said. "More of a delay."

"A delay?"

"Yes, you need to move faster. Edmund Overton has been in town for three days. Jacy seems to have accepted him back into her good graces, for the time being at least. I heard she even went with him to the police station. She is supporting his story and using her social clout to soften the upcoming investigation as to what happened to his ship."

"*So?*" Priscilla frowned. "Isn't that good? Isn't that what we wanted?"

"We wanted to break Jacy and Cole up."

"So? This is a start."

"A start?" Frank shook his head. "I need you to finish the job. Whisk Cole back into your life. Make him fall in love with you again. Make him forget about Jacy."

Priscilla winced and fingered a curl. "It's not that easy. I have been trying—"

"Not hard enough, I am afraid."

"What do you mean?"

"I mean the sooner you get Cole to forget about Jacy, the sooner I can get her away from Overton. That was also the plan, remember? My ultimate goal is to convince her that I am the man for her."

"Oh." Priscilla sighed. "But what is the rush? As you say, it has only been three days."

"Three days too many. Overton is more dangerous than I thought."

Priscilla's eyes widened, but she said nothing.

"I know you don't care what happens to Jacy," Frank growled. "But I do, and I need to get her away from that bully she used to fancy herself in love with. The sooner you secure your relationship with Cole, the sooner I can do that."

"Yes, yes. Of course, of course."

"Isn't Cole upset about Overton? I would think he would be."

"Yes, he is. Of course, he is."

"I would think he would be confused, hurt, devastated."

"As far as I can tell…"

"Then comfort him, woman. Be there for him every moment you can. Be the sweetheart he remembers. The gorgeous, understanding woman he once loved, who his family loved. They adored you, right?"

"And still do. Why wouldn't they? I am the woman for Cole. I am the woman he needs and deserves."

Frank stood up. Priscilla was finally talking sensibly. She was saying what he had come to hear. "Then act like it. I know you can. And I know you shall."

* * *

COLE DASHED INTO THE OCEAN, swam out past the crowd of bathers, then turned around and surveyed the beach scene. The hot August sun had drawn a lot of people to the cool refreshing water. So far, however, Jacy did not seem to be among them. And Jacy was the only person he wanted to see.

Frustrated, Cole swam freestyle laps parallel to the shore, back and forth until exhausted.

Treading water, he searched for Jacy again. Then he saw her, standing alone at the shoreline. At last. She was in her bathing costume, a positive sign.

Jacy had been keeping her distance from him, as well as Henry and Lydia, since Overton came back. And it pained him. As she had requested, he was granting her time to decide what she wanted to do about her secret pledge to Overton. But Cole had not realized how difficult that would be.

Seeing Jacy at the beach gladdened his heart. She had been making herself scarce around the hotel and town, taking meals in her room and avoiding social activities. At least he assumed that was the case, because he had not seen her around.

His heart fell. Jacy looked sad, even melancholy.

Swimming toward the beach, he rode a wave in. Pushing his dripping bangs back from his eyes, he waded out of the water and hailed her with a grin. "Hello, Jacy. I haven't seen you around. I've missed you."

"Cole."

He hurried over, longing to reach for her hand but refrained.

She gave him a shy smile. "I have missed you, too." Her voice was a whisper, almost lost in the breaking surf.

"Want to swim out with me? Like old times?"

Her lips tugged up at the corners. "You mean like last week?"

"Yes." He laughed. "And the week before that. And the glorious week before that…"

"Before Edmund." Her tentative smile vanished. "I can't."

"Can't what?"

"Swim out with you." Lips pressed together, she looked around. Was it his imagination, or did he see fear in her eyes?

"What are you afraid of?" Cole felt a gnawing emptiness inside. His

Jacy was gone. He did not know how to reach her. She was curled up inside her lovely self, hiding from him and the world.

"I'm not afraid. It's just…Edmund…I told him, I promised—"

"Jacy, it's me, Cole. I love you. I understand you need time to sort things out. But please, I still want to be your friend. If I can't be anything else…for now at least, let me be your friend."

Standing awkwardly, with her arms hanging by her sides, a glimmer of hope appeared in her eyes at the word "friend."

"Jacy!"

Overton, dressed in bathing trunks and a tank top, had appeared from nowhere. He called her name again.

Cole groaned.

Jacy turned to look at Overton, then turned back to Cole. "I'm sorry," she said. "I am really sorry, Cole. I wish…" She turned back to Overton. He swaggered toward her and whispered something in her ear. She shook her head. She began to cough.

Aunt Helen hurried over to her. Where had *she* come from? Cole had not noticed the older woman on the beach. She must have been hovering nearby, clearly as concerned about Jacy as he was.

"Aunt Helen," Jacy cried. "I am afraid I am not feeling well. Please take me to my room. I need to go lie down."

"Yes, dear, yes, yes. Come with me." Helen put an arm around her, shot Overton a withering look and led her quickly away.

Cole watched the women go, then turned to see Overton giving him an angry stare. Folding his arms across his chest, Cole looked the former sea captain up and down. For a man who had arrived in Cape May without any obvious financial resources, he wore what appeared to be brand new bathing clothes. *No doubt Lynch is paying for his wardrobe as well as his room. But why?*

Overton sauntered over. Positioning himself inches from Cole's face, his smile slowly transitioned to a sneer. "Stay away from Jacy. Now that she has me back, she doesn't want or need you."

Cole dug his teeth into his upper lip. Anger surged through him, but he was determined to remain calm and in control. "I don't know about that. From the looks of things, you are making her sick."

"That's not—" Overton raised a fist and Cole stepped back.

Lynch, who had been patrolling the beach, ran over, grabbed Overton's arm, and shoved him away from Cole. "Remember your reputation, *Edmund*," he said. "You want to be seen as the gentleman you really are beneath that rough sea captain exterior of yours. The type of man worthy of Jacy James' affections. Otherwise, you might as well leave town now."

Lynch pointed to Cole. "This man is not worth getting upset over. He and Jacy were friends. That is all—and that is all they will ever be."

Overton looked ready to swing a punch, but one glance at Lynch changed his mind. "Right. *Friends.* Well, Jacy doesn't need your friendship anymore, *Stratton*. From what I heard, she took pity on your for being *so very ill*—and you somehow manipulated that to your advantage. Congratulations. Now it's time to go away. Leave her alone. She was in love with me, and she loves me still."

Cole glared at him, too shocked to speak.

Shaking his fist with barely controlled rage, Overton added, "Jacy and I will marry, mark my words."

Cole opened his mouth to challenge Overton, but before he could say a word Lynch grabbed Overton's arm and hustled him away.

Hands on his hips, Cole watched them go. Oddly, Overton's bragging gave him hope. The man was trying too hard to convince himself, and everyone else, that Jacy still loved him.

It was clear Jacy was afraid of him. *But why?*

"Cole, darling."

Cole turned. Priscilla, garbed in a green-and-yellow-polka-dotted bathing costume, waltzed toward him, flashing a wide smile.

Oh, great. "Hello, Priscilla."

"Could you use some company?"

"No. I think I will go back to my room." Priscilla had likely witnessed his encounter with Overton. He had no desire to discuss it with her.

"I'm sorry that Jacy threw you off. You didn't deserve that. You don't deserve to be treated the way she is treating you."

"I am in no mood for sympathy, Priscilla."

"But—"

"And I don't *need* sympathy. Jacy wasn't feeling well. Which is no concern of yours."

Her eyes flashed. "I am concerned about you, Cole."

"Don't be."

"Remember how we once loved each other? I have never stopped loving you. Please..."

Cole shook his head and turned his eyes to the bathers, men and women whose biggest challenge at the moment was ducking the next wave. They splashed about with abandon, their squeals and laughter nearly drowning out the ocean's soft, low-pitched roar.

"Please, darling," Priscilla said. "Come bathe with me. We were good together once, and we can be again. I can make you forget all about Jacy James. Come on..." she held out her hand, her eyes pleading with him to take it.

"No, Priscilla," he whispered. "I am going back to my room."

Turning, he walked away and did not look back.

* * *

"SHOULD I CALL FOR A DOCTOR? You look ghastly, my dear." After helping Jacy don a nightgown, Helen helped her niece into bed.

Placing a hand on Jacy's forehead, Helen sighed. She glanced at Poppy, who was frowning with concern.

"I don't need a doctor," Jacy murmured. "Just let me rest."

"In the middle of the afternoon? It is most unlike you." Poppy walked over and lowered herself onto a corner of Jacy's bed. "You look as white as a sheet, except for those gray smudges under your eyes—which by the way, are red."

"Poppy." Helen put a finger to her lips and shook her head. "Hush."

Jacy closed her eyes and pulled the blanket up to her chin. Helen shook her head. It was a hot day, and Jacy did not seem to have a fever. Something was terribly wrong.

"It's Captain Overton, isn't it?" Poppy asked. "What is he doing to you?"

Holding her breath, Helen hoped Jacy would answer. She had been terribly secretive since Overton had reentered her life. Jacy was pushing everyone she loved away, including Cole, which was tragic.

Jacy had been over-the-moon-happy with Cole. The situation with Overton did not make any sense. Why didn't Jacy just end it with him? Something was *horribly* wrong.

Helen walked over to a chair by the window and collapsed into it. She sighed. Tobias had gone back to Philadelphia on an urgent business matter, promising to return as soon as he was able. He needed to hurry.

"I don't want to talk about Edmund," Jacy whispered. "Please. Just leave me be. Just let me rest."

"He is making you ill," Helen said. "Just send him away. Tell him you don't love him anymore."

"You don't understand..." Jacy closed her eyes and gave a low moan. "I can't. I must give him time. We had an understanding. And I did love him once."

"*Loved.*" Jacy kept her eyes tightly closed, but Helen did not let that stop her from speaking her mind. "You loved him in the past. *Fortunately,* you have since come to your senses. I am convinced of that. When you are in his company, you have the look of a frightened bunny. He seems to have some kind of power over you. What is it?"

Jacy opened her eyes a slit and stared at the ceiling. "I don't want to talk about it."

"*Please,*" Poppy said.

"No. I'm begging both of you to just let me sleep. Don't press me on the matter. Just give me time."

"Time? I don't understand all this talk about time. Time for *what,* pray tell?" Helen asked.

Jacy did not answer.

Helen looked at Poppy and gestured that they should go. Jacy wanted privacy, she would get it. Hopefully, after she felt better, she would be willing to talk about what grieved her.

"We're going now. We will be in my room if you need us," Helen said, reaching for Poppy's hand and leading her to the door. Her hand on the doorknob, Helen turned to look at Jacy. Sweat was beading on her forehead as she clutched the blanket to her chin.

Helen put a hand to her mouth. Her heart felt heavy. "Jacy," she called out. "Just remember that I love you. And that Poppy loves you. Whatever is bothering you, it can't be so bad that we will stop loving you. Ever."

"Thank you," Jacy said, her voice a croak. "That means a great deal to me."

CHAPTER FORTY-TWO

*J*acy forced herself to get up the next morning. Aunt Helen would call for a doctor if she did not at least get out of bed.

Feeling stiff and empty inside, she wandered out onto the balcony.

Poppy was there, reading a novel. Poppy tossed the book onto an adjacent chair and jumped up when she saw Jacy. "Finally. Mother and I thought you would never—"

"Rise? Resume my life? Go on living as if nothing is wrong?" Wincing, Jacy shook her head. A lock of tangled hair fell into her eyes. She pushed it away.

"Something is clearly wrong." Poppy reached for Jacy's hand and led her back into the room. "One can tell by looking at you, but it won't do for people on the beach to look up and see what a fright you are."

"Thanks." Jacy sat down on the chair next to her bed. "You just made me feel oh so much better."

Poppy tilted her head and gave Jacy a sympathetic smile. "Do you want to talk about it? I want to help you. Please let me."

Leaning her elbows on her knees, Jacy bent forward and put her face in her hands. "You can't help me," she mumbled. "Nobody can."

"Jacy, please. Together, we can deal with whatever is bothering you. I am your best friend as well as your cousin. Remember?"

Poppy's words touched her. Jacy lifted her head. "You can help me with something. You can bring my breakfast to the room. I don't feel like—"

"Again? Why?"

"I don't want to see Edmund. I don't want to see anyone."

"You want to see Cole."

"I can't see Cole."

"Why?"

"It hurts too much."

"*Why?* Why are you turning him away?"

Jacy did not answer. *I can't tell you, Poppy. I wish I could.*

Poppy let out a loud sigh. When she did not say anything else, Jacy frowned. "Poppy, what?"

"I hate to tell you this, but..." Poppy went over to her bureau and picked up a light blue envelope. "This came for you last evening, from Edmund. Mother and I didn't want to wake you to give it to you. We didn't believe you would be happy to receive it."

Poppy walked over and placed the letter into Jacy's outstretched hand. With trepidation, she opened the envelope and withdrew the card inside.

Remember the afternoon hop on the pier tomorrow, it read. *I am looking forward to dancing with you, my beloved. With you, and only you. It will show everyone we are together again. Be there, and be with me, or... Love, Edmund.*

Jacy stared at the words, unblinking, until her eyes burned. The dance would begin in a few hours and she must get ready. "The hop on the boardwalk...Edmund wants to make sure I attend." Jacy gripped his missive and let out a quiet groan.

"Don't go."

"I must. Don't you see?"

"I don't see," Poppy said. "But I will go with you."

* * *

"MY DEAR, MY VISION, MY LOVE." Edmund hurried to greet Jacy when she entered the open-air pavilion with Poppy.

Jacy tensed up. The iron pier's dances were always crowded, but Edmund had found her immediately in the crush.

She tried to give her former lover the smile he expected. But she could not. Her lips would not move in the right direction. "Hello," she said. A lump in her throat made it impossible to say anything else.

Avoiding Edmund's eye, Jacy turned and looked around. Women, their faces wreathed in smiles, greeted each other, complimenting one another on their attire. Fresh-faced gentlemen, gathered in groups, carried on cheerful conversations as the orchestra warmed up.

Jacy glanced down at her pale lavender, lace-trimmed day dress. It was pretty, but she did not feel pretty. She wished she had not come. She only had because Edmund insisted.

To lighten her mood, Poppy had tucked white daisies into her upswept hair. She still felt ugly. She felt ugly inside: dirty, stained, soiled.

"Come, my lovely," Edmund said as the orchestra began to play. "You don't need a dance card because I am claiming every dance." He reached for Jacy's hand and held it firmly in both of his.

Poppy remained by Jacy's side, withstanding Edmund's glare. "Jacy?" she whispered loudly. "Are you alright? Are you sure you want to dance with—"

"She is sure. She is alright. And she is with me." Edmund's tone was smooth. "Does that set your mind at ease, Miss Bainbridge? Run along."

Jacy wanted to run. Run away. She felt as trapped as a wild animal in a cage, one of her own making. "Poppy," she whispered. "Edmund is right. I will be fine. Go dance. Enjoy yourself. Don't worry about me."

Glancing at the row of spectators around the dance floor, Jacy saw Aunt Helen and pointed to her. "Look, your mother is keeping an eye on me. All is well."

Nodding, Poppy shrugged. "If you say so."

Only, all was not well.

Waltzing around the room with Edmund, Jacy struggled to

breathe. She felt dead inside. Edmund expected her to play the part of a woman whose most fervent dream had come true. Her lost love had against all odds come back to her. But she could not do it.

"Smile. Look happy," Edmund murmured as he pulled her closer. "You are the luckiest woman in the world. You need to act like it."

I can't.

Jacy looked over at Aunt Helen. She suppressed a gasp. Cole was sitting next to the older woman, deep in conversation.

Cole looked up. He saw Jacy looking at him. He and Jacy locked gazes.

The music stopped. Cole stood. He walked over to Jacy and extended his hand. "May I? May I have the next dance?"

Jacy felt as if someone had plunged a dagger into her heart. She shook her head. "I'm sorry," she mouthed, pleading with her eyes for him to understand.

The orchestra struck up another number.

Edmund whisked Jacy away.

When the music stopped, Jacy looked for Cole. The chair next to Aunt Helen was empty. Her eyes searched the room.

Where is he?

The orchestra resumed playing, a slow, dreamy, romantic tune. Edmund pulled Jacy back to him.

Then she saw him.

Cole was dancing. With Priscilla Day.

CHAPTER FORTY-THREE

*C*ole slammed the White Caps rowboat oars into the surf. The vessel flew over a wave and splashed down, spraying Samuel, perched on the seat across from him, with salt water.

"You enjoying this, Mister Cole?" Samuel laughed as he wiped his eyes. "Not sure I am."

Angling the right oar deeper, Cole spun the boat around and headed them in the other direction. Squinting, he looked east, toward the rising sun, and growled. "Enjoying this? No. Is it helping my mood any? Maybe a little."

"You be in big trouble if they catch me out here with you." Samuel grinned. "Why bring me?"

Cole held the oars up in the air, breathing deeply to catch his breath. He had been rowing for an hour, sneaking the craft out in predawn darkness so they would not be seen. They drifted for a few moments and Cole resumed rowing at a slower pace. "I needed to talk to someone. And you're a good listener."

"Thanks." Samuel trailed his hand in the water. "The least I can do for you now you no longer need me as your orderly."

"I told you, I want you to stay in my employ. Don't worry, come this fall, when I purchase a larger home, there will be plenty for you to do. I'm even going to have to add to my staff."

Samuel raised his eyebrows. "That so? I thought maybe...since Miss Jacy...well, I thought you and Miss Jacy might get hitched. But things ain't..."

"Looking good?"

Samuel nodded, holding Cole's gaze. "Right."

Cole grunted and let the boat drift again. Leaning forward, he looked toward the still-empty beach. He was not worried about getting caught in the rowboat with Samuel, now that they were out at sea. Damn the rules that forbid non-lifeguards, not to mention people with dark skin, in the boat.

Clenching his jaw, Cole gave himself a shake. He would get into just as much trouble if he got caught bringing a female into the boat. Like Jacy. But so what? He was a volunteer with the corps. They could not fire him.

"'Bout Miss Jacy." Samuel cleared his throat. "She's what's bothering you, right?"

"Yes. But more so, Edmund Overton. I know Jacy doesn't love him."

"No?"

"No. Even so, she never left his side yesterday at the pier hop. Danced every dance with him. Turned me down...which hurt. Real bad." Cole grimaced. "It hurt so bad, in fact, I asked Priscilla to dance. Then, she wouldn't let me go. Swooned in my arms. I ended up leading her around the dance floor for far longer than I'd planned."

"Oh." Samuel raised a corner of his mouth in a sympathetic grimace. "Uh-oh..."

"It didn't make me feel any better. Dancing with Priscilla. It made me feel worse."

"How's that?"

"The look on Jacy's face. Stark devastation."

Samuel frowned. He turned toward the brightening horizon, then back to Cole. "You think maybe you and Miss Priscilla..."

Cole stared at him. "No. Although I know you might like that, seeing as how it would bring Mavis back into your company on a regular basis."

Samuel's lips curved into a sly grin. He shook his head. "I like Miss Jacy better. Anyway, Mavis and me *been* seeing each other. On her days off. Miss Priscilla gives her Sundays. We been going to Poverty Beach—you know, the strand reserved for servants. It's a fine place."

Cole widened his eyes. "That's great, Samuel. I'm happy for you. As a matter of fact, I will need to hire a maid for my new household. And I have been thinking—"

"Of asking Miss Mavis?"

Cole nodded.

Samuel's eyes lit up. "That be wonderful." His smile faded. "Miss Priscilla be angry...but about you getting yourself a bigger house. Why? Why do it if you got no bride in mind?"

Cole lifted his chin. "I have not given up on Jacy. That is why. There is a reason she is letting Edmund Overton stay in Cape May as she gives him time. But for what? To prove himself? But prove what? That he is telling the truth about why he stayed away for months? I don't think she believes he lost his memory. There has to be something else. I believe it has something to do with Frank Lynch."

Samuel went still. Leaning forward, he gripped his knees. "That hero lifeguard. Did you know he is friends with Miss Priscilla?"

"What?" Cole stared at him. "I didn't know they even knew each other beyond the acquaintance stage. What are you talking about?"

"He visited her house. Three times Mavis knows of."

"*What*? How do you know that?"

"My Mavis told me."

Cole widened his eyes in disbelief.

"Mavis heard everything they say. They thought she turned her ears off, but nothing wrong with her ears. Or her eyes."

"Her eyes?"

"Yep. First time that lifeguard paid a visit, he comes with a man. A mysterious man.

"I need to talk to Mavis."

"Yep. I believe you do."

The boat drifted closer to shore. Cole sat up straighter. In his shock over Samuel's revelations, he had forgotten to row, and the tide was taking them in. It was just as well. He needed to find Mavis. And fast.

Lynch was the one who had gone in search of Overton and brought him to Cape May. The lifeguard was paying for Overton to stay in the room next to him. But as for being friends with Priscilla? That was news. If they were courting, surely the whole town would know. Why keep their relationship a secret?

A wave grabbed the boat and propelled them in. Cole jumped out, Samuel followed. Together, they hauled the heavy vessel up onto the sand.

Dragging it back to the lifeguard shed, Cole flashed Samuel a happy grin. "We didn't get caught," he said. "Now let's go find your Mavis."

* * *

"It ain't Sunday, it's Tuesday. Mavis is working. How we gonna talk to her?" Samuel gave Cole a perplexed look as they walked toward Priscilla's cottage. "Knock on the door and announce we there for the maid?"

Cole stopped. "You're right. We need a plan." He looked down at the sidewalk, thought about it, then looked at Samuel. "I will give you a note to take to the door, asking Miss Priscilla if she could please, *for my sake*, allow Mavis a few hours off. Priscilla will do anything I ask at this point. To win back my love."

"For *your* sake, Mister Cole?"

"Yes. Because it's your birthday, Samuel. And I want to give you a gift. Time with your sweetheart. A picnic lunch..."

A smile tugged at Samuel's lips. "It ain't my birthday, Mister—"

"Well..."

"My birthday ain't 'til next week."

Cole laughed. "Perfect. Close enough so it's not a flat out lie. Now let's go over to Washington Street. I need to buy some paper and a pen."

Cole had been so eager to talk to Mavis, he had considered skipping breakfast until Samuel talked him out of it. Better that they eat and change clothes, Samuel insisted. Especially since he was soaking wet from Cole's enthusiastic rowing.

Washington Street was only a few blocks from Priscilla's house. It was mid-morning by the time Samuel knocked on her door, with Cole waiting out of sight at the end of the block.

About fifteen minutes later, Cole grinned when he saw Samuel and Mavis walking toward him. Mavis still wore her gray uniform. She had not even taken the time to change.

Cole hailed a carriage-for-hire. When it pulled over, he opened the door and hustled Samuel and Mavis in. "We need a ride to Cape May Point, to the steamboat pier," he told the driver. "Since the *Republic* will not arrive for a few hours, take your time getting there. Just keep driving around, give us a nice tour." He pulled a wad of dollar bills out of his pocket.

"Yes, sir," the driver said as he took the money. Cole climbed in behind Samuel and Mavis and took the seat next to Samuel.

Cole smiled across at Mavis as he slammed the door shut and the carriage took off.

Mavis gave Cole a knowing look. "Samuel told me what this be about soon as we got out a Miss Priscilla's hearing range. You want to ask me 'bout her friendship with Mr. Lynch."

"Yes." Cole leaned forward. "I am eager to learn what you know."

Mavis told him how surprised she was one July day, when a "slick and fine-looking dark-haired man" first came to call. Miss Priscilla answered the door herself. She seemed to be expecting him. At first Mavis thought he had come to court her employer, especially when Miss Priscilla told her she needed her to serve as chaperone. When they started to talk about hiring a detective, Mavis realized it was no ordinary social visit.

"A real handsome man, he was. But not acting sweet for Miss Priscilla. He talked 'bout you," Mavis said.

"Me?" Cole pointed to himself, letting the word trail off.

"And Miss Jacy. And some missing sea captain a hers. 'Bout finding him."

Cole swallowed hard. Things were beginning to make sense. The dark fog that had descended when Overton came to Cape May was starting to lift. And he did not like what he was seeing.

"Why?" Cole ran his fingers through his hair. "Why did they want to find him?"

"To get you away from Miss Jacy," Mavis said softly. "So you'd look at Miss Priscilla again."

Cole stiffened. Shocked, but not completely surprised, he asked, "Did Mr. Lynch call on Miss Priscilla more than once?"

Mavis nodded. "Brought a detective fellow the second time he came. Kind of old but looked smart. Except he wasn't so smart. Just like Miss Priscilla and Mr. Lynch, that detective thought my ears didn't work. They work just fine."

Lowering her chin, she glanced at Samuel out of the corner of her eye and apologized for not telling him sooner. Afraid of losing her job, and feeling loyal to Miss Priscilla and her mama, Mavis said she felt compelled to kept quiet, even after Edmund Overton showed up. "Mr. Lynch made a visit to Miss Priscilla again after that, and Miss Priscilla seemed real happy. Mr. Lynch was not so happy. Said Miss Priscilla needed to hurry and get Mister Cole back, so he could wrangle Miss Jacy for himself. Wanted to tell her the truth 'bout that sea captain, so he could be her hero."

Cole ran his hand down his face. *So that's what Lynch is up to.* The man's behavior was sadly delusional. *Jacy would never be interested in him, under any circumstances.*

"When Samuel told me 'bout your and Jacy's troubles, I knew I had to tell him what I saw and heard," Mavis whispered.

"She told me Sunday, at the beach," Samuel said. "I hope this helps. Helps you and Miss Jacy."

Cole looked out the window. The driver was doing as instructed; they were clip-clopping through Cape May Point. Angling his head, he peered up at the lighthouse towering over the town. A wide smile crept across his face. "What you just told me will help me and Miss Jacy, I am sure of it, Mavis. I don't how—yet—but I am confident it will. That it will help a great deal."

Mavis gave him a shy smile. "Good. I am mighty glad."

"And don't worry about losing your job with Miss Priscilla," he added. "Because I would like to hire you. Would you be interested in working for me?"

Mavis beamed. She glanced at Samuel. Leaning forward, Samuel reached for Mavis' hand and squeezed it.

"I like that," Mavis said. "I like that a lot."

* * *

COLE HURRIED to White Caps to find Jacy.

The front desk clerk informed him that Jacy had gone out with Lydia, so he wandered out onto the beach, anxious and restless.

Mavis' revelations had unnerved him, and he needed to do something, talk to someone.

He saw Lynch and Overton together by the water. *Perfect.* He had wanted to speak to Jacy before confronting either man, but why fight fate? He was in the mood to take care of business.

After he had bought Samuel and Mavis a picnic lunch at a Cape May Point store, he had told the carriage driver that instead of going to the steamship pier, he wanted to be taken to White Caps. He gave the driver a generous amount of money to take Samuel and Mavis to Poverty Beach. He told the driver to wait for them there, and when they were ready, to take them back to Priscilla's.

Recalling the happy expression on Samuel's face, Cole approached Lynch and Overton from behind. Having the two together would certainly save a lot of time.

Lynch turned around. "Stratton." He greeted him with the enthusiasm of a bored child. "Going for a swim?"

"Do I look like it?" Cole glared at him. "I'm not exactly wearing bathing clothes."

Lynch wore his characteristic smug smile. "You looking for Priscilla?"

"No. Should I be?" Cole wanted to punch the smirk off the lifeguard's face.

"As a matter of fact, she—"

"I'm not looking for Priscilla, Lynch." He was shouting and did not care. "I was looking for Jacy, but the two of you will do."

Overton took a step back. Frowning, he put his hands on his hips. "What do you want with Jacy? Stop bothering her. I agree with Mr. Cape May Hero here—you would be better off setting your sights on another woman. And from what I have seen, Miss Priscilla Day is—"

"Shut your mouth, Overton. I don't want to hear your opinion about Miss Day." Cole's furious gaze pivoted to Lynch. "I am, however, interested to hear what you think of her. Are you friends?"

Lynch opened his mouth, then shut it. "What?"

"You heard me. Are you friends with Priscilla Day? Courting her by any chance?"

Lynch's eyes grew big. "No, I wouldn't say we're friends. And no, I'm not courting her." He snickered. From what I can tell, she wants you, not me."

"*Really?*" Cole let the word linger. "If that's the case, why do you keep calling on her? I happen to know you visited her house several times this summer."

A shadow flickered across Lynch's eyes. "How do you—"

"Never mind. I know that you and Miss Day conspired to find this *fine upstanding gentleman*"—Cole jerked his thumb at Overton—"and bring him to town. *Why?* To destroy my relationship with Jacy. So Priscilla could win me back."

"Huh?" Lynch's jaw dropped. He glanced at Overton.

"What did you hope to gain from this, Lynch?" Cole took a step closer. Lynch stepped back.

Turning back to Overton, Cole said, "Haven't you wondered about that Captain? He's planning to tell Jacy the truth about you. Once I'm out of the way and happily nestled in Priscilla's arms."

"The truth about me?" Overton turned to give Lynch a questioning stare. Lynch shrugged and said nothing.

Cole braced himself. Might one of them turn violent and lash out at him? If so, he was ready. Jacy was worth fighting for—he would do whatever it took to get her back.

Surprisingly, Overton remained undisturbed. "What truth about me? I've told the truth about what happened. Jacy knows, and she loves me."

Cole balled his hands into fists, keeping them at his side to restrain himself from bloodying Overton's face. "Jacy doesn't believe you had amnesia," he said through clenched teeth. "I don't believe you had amnesia. And Lynch certainly knows you didn't."

Cole was guessing, but he knew in his heart that it was true. Overton's story was poppycock, and Lynch helped him come up with it.

A sly smile crept across Overton's face.

Apprehension rushed through Cole's body, followed by fear for Jacy. The man had some kind of power over her, and he was not afraid of using it.

"Stay away from my woman, Stratton!" Overton spit the words out, each one dripping with menace. "Jacy is mine. She loves me. Just ask her why. I dare you."

Overton gave Lynch a look of contempt, as if he was a bug not worth squashing, then spit on the ground and walked away.

CHAPTER FORTY-FOUR

*J*acy twisted her hands in her lap and gave Lydia an apologetic smile. "I'm sorry if you feel I have been ignoring you. I have not meant to be rude...it's not like me...it's just that I have not been myself lately."

Their carriage lurched over a bump in the road. Jacy covered her mouth and let out a strangled cry. She did not feel like shopping but had agreed to go because she had missed her friend. *I should have begged off.*

"Jacy, my dear, don't apologize to me," Lydia said as the driver directed the horses onto Washington Street. She leaned forward and patted Jacy's hand. "Do not for a moment fret about my feelings. I am worried about you. You and Cole."

The driver pulled over and parked the carriage, jumped down from his seat, and poked his head in the open window. "We have arrived."

Jacy, unable to suppress her grief any longer, began to cry.

"Thank you, thank you," Lydia assured the man, who stared at Jacy as if he had never seen a woman in tears.

Jacy turned away, embarrassed by her inability to control her emotions.

"We aren't going to get out just yet," Lydia told the driver, her voice soft and matter-of-fact. "My friend and I are going to sit here and talk. If you wouldn't mind, could you please give us some privacy?"

"Of course, miss." His fingers gripping the edge of the window as if glued on, he didn't move.

"Maybe you can attend to the horses, get them some water, brush them down? I don't know how long we will be." Giving the driver a knowing nod, Lydia scooted over to sit next to Jacy. Draping her arm around her shoulders, she pulled her close.

The driver finally got the message. "Of course, miss," he said, un-prying his fingers and backing away. "Take all the time you need..."

Jacy sniffed loudly. Lifting her head off Lydia's shoulder, she rubbed her eyes, reached into her pocket for a handkerchief, wiped her nose and sniffed again. "Thank you for understanding," she said in a choked voice. "I can't go on pretending everything is okay."

"Of course, everything is not okay, that is clear." Lydia's tone was firm but compassionate. "And I didn't really want to shop, anyway. I only used that as an excuse, so we could have a chance to talk. I can see that you need to, and I am someone you can trust."

Someone she could trust? Jacy sighed and looked out the window at the cheerful women on the busy street who were looking for the latest fashion in a bauble, dress, or hat. And why not? They were living in the best possible place, at the best possible time. Life was a lark for them. She, too, could be as carefree if she had not made such a terrible mistake.

Jacy turned to Lydia. She longed to confide in someone. But what good would come of it? Lydia could not help her. No one could. She was trapped by her past.

"You can trust me," Lydia repeated, with a saintly, patient smile. "Please, dear, please. You have a secret, don't you? One that is tearing you apart...that only Edmund Overton knows? Is that what he is using to control you? Because something is terribly wrong."

Jacy stared at her friend. Lydia had become a dear, dear friend. Poppy would always be her best friend, but she could not tell Poppy what had happened between her and Edmund.

Maybe she could tell Lydia, though.

Her secret was eating away at her, the pain becoming unbearable. She had to tell someone. And Lydia said she could trust her.

"Edmund and I..." Jacy's voice caught in her throat.

"Yes?"

Edmund and I..."

"Yes, Jacy. Take your time. Just tell me."

The words came out in a rush. "We were intimate once." Jacy covered her face with her hands. "I am not a virgin."

Jacy looked up and stared into Lydia's eyes. She had told her. She had told another human being. She swallowed hard. Her heart raced. She waited for Lydia to say something.

Say something. Say anything.

"I see," Lydia said in a whisper.

Jacy put a hand over her mouth. She turned to stare out the window.

The silence between them stretched on.

Jacy willed herself to keep breathing. It was hard. She wanted to die. What *could* Lydia say? Her secret was ruinous. She had just burdened Lydia with it, and Lydia could not help her.

"I think you should tell Cole," Lydia said. "He loves you. He will understand."

Jacy turned and stared at her in disbelief. "*What* did you say?"

Lydia looked deep into her eyes and patted her arm. "Confess to Cole. He loves you. He won't condemn you. I know him well, and I am sure of it. When you love someone, you love them flaws and all. And your flaw, while scandalous, is not all *that* bad..."

"What?"

"Well, it's *bad*. But it's not something so awful it can't be overcome. It's not like you *murdered* someone."

"But I'm stained. Forever stained."

Lydia reached for Jacy's hands and held them between hers. "You are not stained. Unless you believe you are. It happened once, you said?"

Jacy nodded, grim-faced.

"Then it was a mistake—made in the heat of passion. It happened and it's over and it's in the past."

"*Really?*"

"Yes, truly." Kindness, compassion, and understanding flowed from Lydia's eyes. "I don't believe we are defined by who we once were. We can always recreate ourselves. We learn from our mistakes. And if we are good and wise, we go on to become better people. It is the decisions we make in the present that matter. I think you should go to Cole and tell him. It's your decision, but I really think you should."

Jacy's breath caught in her throat. Could Cole really forgive her? If he did, she would be free from Edmund, forever. His power over her would disappear. He could still spread scandalous gossip about her, but with Cole by her side, who would believe him? He would look like a jealous fool. And what would it matter? Cole's love was all that mattered.

She had to take the risk. If Cole rejected her, she would have to accept it, painful as that would be. At least she would be rid of Edmund. She would find a way to live life as an independent woman. If Poppy could do it, so could she.

She had to tell Cole.

"Lydia," Jacy whispered. "Thank you for not condemning me. You're right. I'm really scared, but I do need to tell Cole the truth. I am not being fair to him. I am not being fair to myself. My secret has kept me in a prison of my own making, and I am ready to set myself free."

Lydia nodded, holding Jacy's gaze. "You're making the right decision. It's the courageous thing to do, and I admire you for it."

"Tell him to meet me atop the lighthouse tomorrow morning, at sunrise," Jacy whispered.

"Alone?"

"Yes."

Lydia gave her a bemused smile. "Okay. I will convey the message."

"And please don't breathe a word about this to anyone else. Not even Henry."

"Of course." Lydia nodded. "You can trust me, remember? Your secret is my secret."

* * *

JACY SET out for the lighthouse in complete darkness. Too nervous to sleep, she wanted to talk to Cole, be with Cole, confess to Cole.

Her legs shook as she walked along the shoreline. Mid-route, her knees buckled. Pulling herself together, she began to run.

Gasping when she reached the lighthouse, she caught her breath and dashed up the stairs. She pulled on the door to the observation balcony, stumbled out, and collapsed in a heap.

Struggling to regain her dignity, she sat up and pulled her knees to her chest to calm herself. Finally, she stood and was captivated by the serene sea and vast sky. Both were turning pink. Weather-wise, at least, it would be a glorious day.

Jacy closed her eyes and felt the sea breeze on her face.

Would Cole come?

What if he doesn't?

She heard a noise and turned. The door to the balcony opened. Cole stepped out. He was not wearing a hat, and the salty wind blew his hair off his forehead.

Jacy stared at him.

He went to her and reached for her hands.

She gave them to him.

"Jacy." He gazed into her eyes. "Lydia said…"

Jacy's heartbeat hammered in her ears. The ocean's low roar and the sound of the blood coursing through her veins became one. She squeezed Cole's hands. They were warm. She knew hers must be icy cold. "Thank you," she whispered, "for coming."

"Of course." He looked at her with an expression of confusion mixed with hope. "How could I stay away when she said you wanted to see me? She said it was important."

Jacy pressed her lips together and nodded.

"Does this mean what I think it means? What I fervently want it to mean? That you are ending it with Overton? So you can be with me?"

Jacy swallowed hard. Their eyes locked in a knowing gaze. Jacy squeezed Cole's hands again. "I have decided to end it with Overton, one way or another..."

Cole grinned. "That's wonderful. I am so happy and relieved to hear that." Beaming, he took a step closer and started to pull her toward him. Then he stopped. "Jacy, what's wrong? You look upset. There's more, isn't there?" A look of apprehension came over his face.

"Cole." Jacy closed her eyes and lowered her chin. She dreaded telling him. But she had to do it. "Cole," she said, keeping her head down. "Yes. There is more."

"I'm listening."

She looked up and met his gaze. It was warm, compassionate, loving. Her heart turned over. "I...I love you, Cole," she whispered. "I never stopped loving you. Even when Edmund came back, it didn't change how I felt about you. And I am sorry, oh so sorry..."

"For what, Jacy? You said you needed to give him time. I respected that. I hated it but respected it."

"I'm sorry I didn't tell you the truth."

"What truth?"

"I didn't need to give him time. My feelings for him had already changed by the time Frank brought him back to me. Meeting you, getting to know you, and loving you made me see the truth about him and about myself. He was no good. I was a fool."

"I see." Cole gave Jacy his heart-warming grin. "I am glad I was able to help you heal the wounds Overton inflicted upon you. You helped me walk again, and I helped you in return." Reaching over, he lightly ran his index finger down her cheek.

"Cole." Jacy took a deep breath, let it out slowly, and looked deep into his eyes. "Did you hear me? I didn't need to give Edmund time."

"Okay..."

"Just because I had once accepted his proposal of marriage, didn't mean I couldn't change my mind."

"Of course not."

"He was blackmailing me." Jacy lowered her head and stared at her boots. "And I didn't know what to do."

"Jacy…"

She kept her head down. "He was blackmailing me with our secret."

"Jacy…"

She could not look at him. "We were intimate, Cole. Edmund and I. Just once. The last night we were together. He asked me to marry him and I said, 'yes,' and then…"

"Jacy…"

"I'm not a virgin, Cole. I am a soiled woman. Forever ruined."

"Jacy…"

"You deserve better."

"Jacy, look at me."

Jacy lifted her head and stared at Cole. His expression, to her amazement, was tender. A smile tugging at his lips, he pulled her toward him and kissed her. He stepped back, reached for her hands and grinned. "See?"

"See what?" Her voice was a croak.

"I still love you. Despite what you just told me."

"You do?"

"Yes. Actually, if you must know, I am profoundly relieved."

"*Relieved?*"

"Yes. If the secret you just revealed to me was all that was keeping us apart, I am deliriously happy." Cole pulled her to him again and kissed her with a passion she did not know was possible.

Wrapping her arms around his neck, Jacy pressed her lips to his and returned his passion. Melded as one, they kissed as the waves crashed onto the shore below them and the sun climbed higher in the sky.

Breathless, Jacy leaned back, felt the sun on her face, and gazed into Cole's eyes. "You forgive me?"

He raised an eyebrow. "What's to forgive?"

"You don't care?"

He titled his head. "Care? Of course I care. I care that Overton took advantage of you, the—" he stopped. "What I want to call him is too impolite for your ears. Jacy, you were young. You were naive. He was older and conniving. I care about that. I care that you suffered with your secret." He lightly touched a finger to her lips, which had parted in awe of his understanding. "I care about you, Jacy. I love you."

"Oh, Cole…"

"You need to forgive yourself."

"I do?"

"Yes. You made a mistake. You learned from it. It is in the past. It doesn't matter anymore."

"It doesn't?"

"No. Because you are a beautiful, lovely woman. And I would like to make you my wife."

Jacy gasped. She searched his eyes. "Are you proposing?"

"Isn't it obvious?" Cole's eyes glistened. He took her in his arms and their lips met again. They were warm, and she felt warm all over. He put his head back and grinned. "Well?"

Breathless, she whispered, "Well, what, sir?"

"Will you marry me, Jacy James? Will you be my wife?"

Jacy's heart swelled. She gave Cole a beaming smile. "Yes, I will marry you, you wonderful man. I thought you would never ask."

CHAPTER FORTY-FIVE

*J*acy and Cole held hands all the way back to White Caps. When they reached the hotel, several people were strolling the strand, including Edmund. Hands on his hips, the former sea captain stood still as Jacy and Cole approached.

Jacy refused to hide her happiness. She would not be intimidated. Giving Cole's hand a squeeze, she pulled him in the direction of her former lover, whispering, "Might as well tell him now."

"Might as well," Cole agreed, tucking Jacy's arm in his. "Seems like a fine time."

Jacy felt her happy smile slip as they approached Edmund. His dark scowl deepened when Cole gave him a cheery "hello."

"What are you doing, Jacy?" Edmund narrowed his eyes to slits. "Why are you publicly flaunting a relationship with this man, when I am your—"

"You are nothing to her anymore." Cole said. "Because she is engaged to me. I just asked Jacy to marry me, and she accepted."

Edmund took a step back. For a moment Jacy feared what he might do. His face reddened. His frown turned menacing. Staring at Jacy as if she had lost her mind, he switched his attention to Cole, breathing heavily as he stared at him in stony silence.

"Really?" Edmund turned back to Jacy. "Is what this man just said true?"

"Yes." Jacy lifted her chin. "It is."

"How?" Edmund clamped his mouth shut, then opened it again, inhaling and exhaling with the angry energy of a snorting bull. He shook his head. "How is this possible? I don't understand. Jacy, you are betrothed to me."

"Not anymore." She looked at Cole. He let go of her arm, slipped his hand in hers and squeezed it in a show of support. Despite the gravity of the situation, Jacy felt a warm tingling all over. "I've changed my mind about you, Edmund, and about myself. I am not the woman I was when I accepted your proposal. I was naïve about the ways of the world, and the ways of some men. You took advantage of my youth, my craving for love."

"Did she *tell* you?" Edmund looked at Cole. "Did she tell you the truth about herself?"

"I know the truth about Jacy," Cole said. "She is the most incredible woman I have ever met. I feel fortunate to—"

"Did she *tell* you?" Edmund repeated in a louder voice.

"She did." Cole nodded. "I know what happened the last evening you were together, before your ship disappeared."

"And it's *alright* with you? That she gave herself to me? That she gave me what she was supposed to give her husband on his wedding night?"

"No." Cole lowered his voice to a quiet growl. "What you did, Overton, is not alright—not in my eyes, or society's. What Jacy did, however, is forgivable in my eyes, because I love her and cherish her. And I will for the rest of my life."

'Society's eyes…" Overton chuckled. "I am glad you brought that up. Because I will tell everyone I know the truth about Jacy. It will ruin her reputation, and yours."

"No, you won't," Cole said. His eyes met Jacy's and he gave her a nod. "Because if you tell anyone about the night you and Jacy were together, Jacy will go to the police and tell them she doesn't believe your story about having amnesia —after your so-called shipwreck."

"What?" Edmund stared at Jacy. "You wouldn't do that."

Glancing at Cole, she pursed her lips. "Yes, I would."

"But I really did lose my memory."

"Really?" Cole glared at Edmund. "It sounds farfetched. Fabricated. Fictitious." He turned to Jacy. "Do you believe it, Jacy?"

"No," Jacy whispered. "I do not. I only told the authorities I did because I was afraid Edmund would reveal my secret. I only told them I believed it to give myself time to think."

"You hid out for months, which is suspicious, Overton," Cole said. "What really happened to that ship? That's what—"

"It went down in a storm. I was knocked out. I didn't know who I was…"

"And an elderly woman nursed you back to health." Cole gave Edmund an I-don't-believe-you smile.

"That's right." Edmund's smirk flickered and dissolved.

"You know, Overton, I am as capable of hiring a private investigator as Frank Lynch. And if I were to hire one…just if…I bet he could find your elderly caretaker without too much trouble. And I bet…it's just a hunch…that she wouldn't be quite as old as you claim…and that she might harbor some bitterness toward you for leaving her. Just like you left Jacy. All the sudden," Cole said, snapping his fingers. "Gone."

Edmund stared at Cole, unblinking.

"I'm sure my private investigator could prove you were just hiding out in New York City. Then the authorities would want to take a much closer look at that shipwreck. Whether it may have been your fault. They might even want to arrest you and put you in jail while they investigate."

Edmund blinked and lowered his head. The tide was coming in. Another few inches and their shoes would get wet. Edmund backed away a few steps. Jacy and Cole followed.

Folding his arms across his chest, Edmund looked at Jacy. Fear flickered in his eyes. "It was an accident and it wasn't my fault," he muttered. "I didn't want to be blamed for the loss of the ship and most of its crew members. So, I hid. I'm sorry if that caused you pain."

"You did me a favor in the end," Jacy said.

Overton stared at her.

"So," Cole said. "What shall it be, Overton? Should I find myself a good detective?"

"Not necessary." Edmund frowned. "I won't say another word to anyone about Jacy. I'll leave town. I'll let the police know where they can find me, then go to Philadelphia and track down my friend Higbee. I'll stay with him for a while. When the authorities give me the okay, I'll look for another captain job. Go back out to sea."

Cole nodded. He glanced at Jacy and smiled. "I like that. We were going to invite you to the wedding, Overton. But it looks like you won't be able to make it on last day of August. Oh well."

"The last day of August?" Jacy looked at Cole wide-eyed.

"It will be the official end of the summer season," Cole said. "The perfect day. We can hold the ceremony on the White Caps lawn, and invite all the hotel's guests, and most of the townspeople."

Jacy smiled. "I love that. It doesn't give us much time to plan, but it sounds wonderful." She turned to Edmund. "Goodbye, Edmund. I'm assuming you will leave town today?"

He shrugged. "Yes."

"I'm sure Frank Lynch will miss having you around," she said. "But —oh well to that, too."

* * *

JACY AND COLE continued to hold hands as they entered the dining room for breakfast.

Cole looked for Henry and Lydia. He found them sitting with Poppy and Aunt Helen. Everyone would be excited about their news.

"Jacy."

She and Cole turned.

"Father," she said. "I didn't know you—"

"I took the early train this morning. Missed the *Republic* yesterday and was in a hurry to get here." A grin spread across his face as he looked down at Cole and Jacy's hands and back up at Cole. "Well, I was worried about Jacy. But maybe I don't have to worry after all."

Cole nodded. "As a matter of fact, Mr. James, you are just the man I wanted to see. I have a very important question to ask you."

"Indeed." Tobias James looked across the room and back at Cole with a twinkle in his eye. "Is there any chance you could ask it in the company of my sister and niece? They are waving for us to join them. Waving very eagerly, I might add."

Jacy beamed and waved back.

"I think that's an excellent idea," Cole said. "I believe everyone at the table will want to hear my question."

As Cole helped Jacy to her seat and sat down beside her, he caught Henry's questioning gaze. Lydia whispered something in Henry's ear and they both beamed.

"Tobias," Helen said in a high-pitched squeal. "I did not know you were in town."

"Just got here, and at the perfect time, sister dear."

Jacy twisted her hands in her lap, looking nervous and excited. Cole reached over, gave her hand a reassuring squeeze, and cleared his throat. "I have a question for Mr. James, and he requested that I ask it in front of all of you."

No one moved. They all seemed to be holding their breath, especially Aunt Helen, who pressed a hand to her mouth.

Cole turned to Jacy's father. "Mr. James. I would like to marry your daughter. Do we have your permission?"

Helen squealed.

Poppy giggled.

Henry and Lydia put their heads together and smiled.

Tobias James beamed. "Of course, my son. Of course, I give you permission to marry my daughter." He turned to Jacy. "I can tell by the look on your face that you have already accepted Cole's proposal."

"I have, Father. And Cole and I are gloriously happy."

"As am I." Tobias James' smile faded as a perplexed look came over his face. "I am a curious man by nature, however. And so, I must admit to being slightly confused. What happened with Edmund Overton? I hesitate to ask but feel I must."

Jacy gave her father a satisfied smile. "He's gone. Gone from my life. Thankfully, leaving Cape May. I finally realized the kind of man he was. And came to my senses." She sighed. "Do you want to know more?"

"No, Jacy, please. The only thing that matters to me—and your dear Aunt Helen and cousin, Poppy—is that you *finally* realized the truth about him. And the truth about yourself—that you deserve much better. *And* that he is gone, truly gone from your life and from our family."

Jacy nodded, casting a smile at Cole that caused his heart to flip.

Henry reached over to shake Cole's hand. "Congratulations, Cole. Lydia and I are supremely happy for you and Jacy."

"Thank you," Cole said. He stood. "And now—I have more wonderful news. Jacy and I want to marry on the last day of this month. Which only gives us about two weeks to plan. We will need help."

"And you shall have it," Aunt Helen pushed her chair away from the table and rose to her feet. Giving Jacy a loving smile, she declared, "I am very good at organizing parties, my dear. Just tell me where to begin."

* * *

"Congratulations, Miss Jacy." Samuel flashed her a grin as he stepped onto the White Caps porch, where she and Cole sat holding hands. "Mister Henry just told me. Such happy news."

"Thank you, Samuel." Jacy said, feeling herself blush. "I am still pinching myself. I can scarce believe it is true. Everything is happening so quickly."

"Congratulations, Mister Cole." Samuel saluted his employer.

Cole grinned and saluted back.

Samuel lowered himself into the chair beside Cole. "My Mavis will be happy to hear 'bout it, too, Mister Cole. Specially since you hired her and all. Just think, me and Mavis get to be together in your new house—with Miss Jacy as misses. Will make for a mighty happy household."

"Indeed," Jacy said, beaming.

"Yes, I didn't have a chance to tell you that I've hired Mavis," Cole said.

"I think that's wonderful," Jacy said, looking at Samuel. "I like Mavis a lot."

Cole reached over and took Jacy's hands in his. "When I began to recover, and realized I would live, I contemplated my future. I knew I wanted you in it. I knew, somehow, you would be. So, I told Samuel about my plans to purchase a larger home this fall, and that I would need to expand my staff."

Jacy gazed into his eyes. "Cole…"

"Now, you and I will be able to house-shop together, Jacy. As husband and wife."

"Cole." Jacy swallowed hard. Love for her fiancé flooded her being. Tears welled up in her throat. "This is so wonderful." She glanced at Samuel then back at Cole. "It will be such fun to look for a house together—and we need to be sure it has large rooms for Samuel and Mavis. So they can both live there."

Samuel coughed. "Well, since I was planning to ask my Mavis to marry me…she and me might only need one big room."

"Wonderful." Cole leaned over and shook Samuel's hand. "It's settled then. Jacy and I will look for a house with a large side wing."

"Yes." Jacy smiled. "But, Cole. We need to hurry with our wedding plans. Aunt Helen is anxious to get started with the arrangements."

Cole winked at Samuel and turned back to Jacy. "You're right. Let's get back to the subject at hand, shall we?" His eyes twinkled. "You and I love the morning, Jacy, right?"

"Right…"

"So, let's plan the ceremony for shortly after sunrise."

Jacy laughed. "What a pretty time of day. On the White Caps lawn, overlooking the sea."

"With all of Cape May in attendance—or whoever wants to come." Cole gave a bemused smile. "We'll invite everyone we know, Including, I suppose, Priscilla?"

Samuel shook his head. Miss Priscilla would not be attending, he said, because she was packing to go back to Philadelphia. "When Mister Henry told me the good news, I ran and told my Mavis. Miss Priscilla heard me. Looked like she might faint." He chuckled. "Miss Priscilla told Miss Zinnia she can stay and finish the season, but as for her, she done."

Samuel gave Cole a hopeful look. "So, maybe my Mavis can start working for you today, Mister Cole? If Miss Zinnia don't need her?"

Cole nodded. "Zinnia Day can hire someone else. I will rent a room for Mavis in your boardinghouse, Samuel. We can use her help to prepare for the wedding."

Jacy smiled. Her future was unfolding before her eyes. Any feelings of shame from her past had already faded away.

One thing continued to trouble her, however.

Twisting her hands together, Jacy blurted out, "Cole, I hope my stepmother, stepsisters and stepbrothers will come. My stepmother and I have never been close. Since my step-siblings are much younger than I, we have also never been close. I see where I have been partially at fault, and I want to make amends."

Cole gave Jacy's hand a sympathetic squeeze. "Of course, we'll invite them. And I'm sure they will be happy to come."

"It's part of what I've realized about myself, Cole," Jacy whispered. "Edmund wasn't the only one causing me problems. I needed to grow up."

Cole laughed. Jacy loved the way he laughed. He did not make fun of her. He looked at her with pure love in his eyes.

"I love you, Jacy James," he said. "I love the girl you were, I love the woman you are, and I love the wonderful wife you will become."

CHAPTER FORTY-SIX

*R*ays from the early morning sun lit the White Caps lawn. Jacy beamed as she took in the magical setting. Dew drops blanketing the grass twinkled like thousands of tiny diamonds. She looked up at the sky, where glorious pink and orange clouds dotted the heavens.

Ocean waves broke softly on the sand, just beyond where she and Cole stood side-by-side.

The preacher read from the Bible about love and forgiveness and blessings. Jacy smiled as she listened, grateful for the presence of family and friends. Despite the early hour, hundreds of people had come, including her entire family. Her stepmother sat in the front row, holding baby Eliza in her arms. Next to her, Theo, Tim, Thomas, and Ellie wiggled in their seats.

Frank was the only person invited who had declined to attend. Someone had to guard the beach, he had said.

Poppy, looking lovely in a coral gown that matched the sky, stood next to Jacy as her maid of honor.

Henry, who looked dashing in a light gray suit, stood next to Cole as his best man.

Jacy's beloved father, who had walked her up the aisle, was at her side, ready to give her away.

Aunt Helen sat in the front row, too, next to Lydia, Cole's parents, Samuel and Mavis.

Jacy flashed Aunt Helen a grateful smile. The dear woman had been true to her word. She had planned a grand wedding in a very short time.

Inside the dining room, a scrumptious breakfast buffet awaited the guests. A ten-piece orchestra was poised to play. The party would last for hours.

Jacy glanced down at her white gown, dotted with tiny pearls. Her gaze met Cole's, and her heart leapt with gratitude for the admiration in his eyes. Dressed in a white suit and matching hat, he had never looked more handsome.

Cole's eyes crinkled in the corners as he smiled at her.

Jacy blushed. Her lips trembled as she smiled back.

At the preacher's cue, she promised to love and cherish Cole for the rest of her life. Cole promised to love and cherish her for the rest of his.

"And now, you may kiss the bride," the preacher said.

Cole lifted Jacy's delicate veil and draped it over her shoulders. He removed his hat and handed it to his brother.

Then he kissed her in front of their entire world, and she kissed him back.

* * *

"WHAT A LOVELY IDEA FOR A HONEYMOON," Jacy said. "Sailing off into the sunrise."

"It fits us, does it not?" Cole pulled her into his arms. "Just you and me, out at sea..."

Jacy laughed. "Leave the poetry to Poppy," she said with a saucy grin. "Anyway, it's not just you and me. We have an entire crew sailing this ship. Waiting on our every need."

"And anyway, it's not exactly sunrise," Cole said, playfully running a finger down her cheek. "Since we stayed at the reception a few hours, it's closer to noon."

"Wouldn't have looked right to run off *too* soon," Jacy giggled. "Even though we were longing to steal away."

"And here we are." Cole draped his arm around Jacy and pulled her close. "Isn't it glorious?"

When Cole had told Jacy about a large schooner for hire at the Cape May Yacht Club, which came with a captain and three-man crew for their honeymoon, she had jumped at the idea. The vessel had a wide deck, where they could cuddle and take in the view, as well as a large, private master suite. They had agreed to take the month of September to travel up and down the East Coast, going wherever the wind took them.

As they rounded the southern tip of New Jersey, Jacy snuggled up to Cole. She had insisted they head south first, so they could bid farewell to the places that had brought them together.

Cole had wholeheartedly agreed.

Jacy waved to the stretch of strand linking Cape May and Cape May Point and shouted, "Goodbye, Beacon Beach!"

She waved to the lighthouse standing proud and majestic beyond the dunes.

Gazing up at the beacon as they sailed past, Jacy smiled. How many mornings had she stood at the top searching the sea for answers? Now, out on the sea, embraced by the love of her life, everything was clear.

She loved a wonderful man and that wonderful man loved her.

ACKNOWLEDGMENTS

Special thanks to my fantastic editor, Caren Burmeister—for her encouragement, guidance and expertise throughout the writing of this book.

Thank you to Robin Ludwig Design Inc. for the cover. Robin is an extremely talented artist. The way she captured the essence of this story took my breath away.

ABOUT THE AUTHOR

Maggie FitzRoy is a lifelong fan of love stories and history. She enjoys writing novels that sweep the reader into the past, where love is an adventure. *Beacon Beach* is her second romance novel. Her first, *Mercy's Way*, took place in 1845 on the Oregon Trail. A former journalist and magazine editor, she lives in Ponte Vedra Beach, Florida.

Visit her website: maggiefitzroy.com

Made in the USA
Coppell, TX
22 July 2021